THE GENTLE KINGDOM OF GIACOMO

The Gentle Kingdom of Giacomo BY EVELYN WELLS

It is great work to make things beautiful, and after your work is done, perhaps the thing you have made is too weak to stand alone.

—GIACOMO DANERI

DOUBLEDAY & COMPANY, INC., GARDEN CITY, N.Y.

Library of Congress Catalog Card Number 52–13373

FOR NORMA AZALEA—*one of the lovelier daughters of the California flower people.*

THE GENTLE KINGDOM OF GIACOMO

ONE

IT was three in the afternoon this May Sunday, and a
thousand of Giacomo Daneri's friends were ending dinner
in his longest greenhouse, known as "the Drive." Another thousand, replete with drink and food, were wandering through the
nursery's fifty-four glasshouses that stretched like colored ribbons
over the Colma hillside, holding within their whitewash-flaked
walls more than fifteen compact acres of roses, carnations, gardenias, lilies of the valley, and, most splendid of all, the Daneri
orchids.

The Drive had sheltered Giacomo's pioneer plantings nearly
half a century before. Now the long glass shed held the jungle
odor of ferns and plants, the scents of food rich with herbs, and
of wine and contented humanity.

Bales of fern root had been pushed back against the glass walls
to make way for the table, and broken drainage shard was piled
in the corners behind tall terra cotta pillars that were stacked
flowerpots. Under the glass roof fluttered the paper ribbons of
festival: red, white, and green for an Italy many of the guests
remembered; red, white, and blue for the land all considered
their own.

And all the way down the table, over the heads of the diners,
tubs of rhododendron tossed fistfuls of rose- and cream-colored
blooms.

Ohime mi! What a table!

The table itself was as long as a long city block, and made of many worktables strung together and sheathed with white wrapping paper. And there was not a square foot of it that had not been set with a dish or bottle by the thirty extra waiters brought down from "the city" to assist Cesare, the Lombardian cook who sang grand opera and who had been with Giacomo twenty-five years. Cesare could be seen through the glass, steaming majestically as he basted garlic and anchovy sauces over the meats and fowl in the charcoal pits sunk outside the Drive, pausing between arias to bawl orders to his grinning staff.

Along the table were scattered the broken meats of festa. Hundreds of platters held the remnants of antipasto, salads, black and green olives, young onions, peas, and artichokes fried in batter, *torte* of vegetables and eggs and cheese, and thick-crusted bread. The immense bowls still steamed with cioppino, rich with tomatoes and herbs, and crowded with bass, crabs, and shrimps from San Francisco Bay. Hundreds of steaks and chops and young chickens had been rushed from the charcoal pits outside to the plates of the diners, and there remained ravaged mounds of the pastas—the spaghetti, macaroni, and ravioli in their gold-flecked sauces, and the rice yellow with cheese and saffron and crammed with cockles steamed in their shells. All Italy met in tradition on Giacomo's table. The minestrone had been made by a recipe perfected centuries before in Genoa by Daneri women. The risotto had been tasted first in Lombardy. Then there were hillocks of imported cheeses and pungent Italian cookies and fat round loaves of the cakelike anise-flavored panetone, and many-colored California fruits, and bowls of nuts and raisin bunches, and hundreds of fast-emptying bottles and demijohns of California wines, and whiskies and beer and imported liqueurs, and jars of Queen Anne cherries pickled in spices and brandy.

For this was Giacomo's annual "growers' picnic" that for close to fifty springtimes had climaxed his nursery's growing year.

At the head of his table sat Giacomo Daneri.

Granite and bronze was Giacomo, a giant of a man who spoke and moved slowly. There was about him an almost primordial stillness. His thick frame was trunklike, slanted with long years of labor; his hands like thick roots jerked from soil. Under the ragged brows his eyes were questioning and very kind.

They were questioning his granddaughter, Tosca Levenridge, seated a few places away, a young woman long-boned and splendid, delicate but possessed of power; one who could be both flowerlike and smoldering and whose moods were given to dancing beyond those of ordinary people and to vanishing, nearly always, in laughter.

Tosca was laughing now, a little wildly, and there were wings of red along the beautifully planed cheekbones that were not from Giacomo's wine.

But why not? her grandfather thought staunchly. Surely this is a splendid festa. And it is good for the young to have days such as this to remember.

There had been times, during the bad years all prayed might be ending, when the Daneri Nursery had been unable to celebrate with abundance the completion of the Easter harvest. Times, in fact, when there had been little or no festa—but now, by the kindness of God, it seemed dark times might be lifting and men might dare to hope again, and all through the feasting the talk around the table had held a new brightness: talk of the new President, the New Deal, the new beginning that might shoulder away depression. A flower grower showed his faith in this change by gathering his friends together and pouring out largess as, centuries before, his ancestors had poured a libation on the earth.

Gently, in the silence he kept intact from all others, Giacomo at the head of his teeming table offered up his own thanksgiving.

Grateful, too, that Tosca had been sheltered from the bad years, he thought, watching her tenderly: She has been given everything!

There were few of Giacomo's guests who had not suffered from the shock of '29. For they were the flower people, and the flower industry, a luxury trade, had been among the first to feel the depression. During the troubled years, when the flower growers had not known what to plant or whether to plant at all, Giacomo had let none of his workmen go; he had stubbornly continued to grow orchids and had sunk to the hilt his considerable flower-made fortune into the developing of new beauty in a world giving over to panic.

"Root out the orchids. Grow potatoes," his banker son-in-law, Tosca's father, had advised.

But Giacomo had been stubborn.

"People need potatoes, yes," he had agreed, "but, too, they will always need orchids."

Giacomo had been right. The depression years had seen a steady increase in the demand for flowers. Bread lines appeared in San Francisco streets, homes were lost, and human life, but his guests on this day were the men and women who were bringing the flower industry through to its victorious place as the third-greatest industry in California.

Under this glass roof, set in the hills south of San Francisco, a representative force of that many-faceted city was gathered. Around Giacomo's table were men, with their families, who were leaders in politics and business and who represented positions made and fortunes won, and sometimes lost, in banking, commerce, production, and trade. Scattered among the guests were the police and fire chiefs, legal lights of the Bench and Bar, a friendly and relaxed group of priests, and, remote and gray among them, California's leading banker, founder of "the Bank," as it was known generally, as if there were no other bank in California, and whose early life paralleled the harsh beginning of Giacomo's. And on Giacomo's right sat the mayor, and he, like Giacomo and the bank founder and the majority of Giacomo's guests, was of Italian origin.

Under this glass roof was successful immigrant Italia. Milan, Florence, Turin, Rome—such ancient metropolises had sheltered the ancestors of many of Giacomo's guests. And many, like Giacomo, were from Genoa, a gulf city, not unlike San Francisco, which had ever sent out its sons as traders and adventurers over the seas of the world. Giacomo himself had come from Genoa as a child with his father, a handsome and energetic gold seeker, in the great Italian immigration of the '60s. Much of the Italo-American population in the West dated from that time, for only a handful had come in the greatest gold rush, in '49.

The flower people made up the bulk of Giacomo's guests, and of these the majority were of Italian blood. They represented an industry started in California soon after the gold rush when a young, unknown Italian hawked bunches of violets in San Francisco's muddy streets. "California, Land of Flowers," was one of the West's earliest slogans.

Among them were retail florists from the cities around the bay who on weekday mornings might be seen competing in San Francisco's Flower Market for the choice Daneri blooms. Also there were the sellers of fancy boxes and shipping cartons, of ribbons and strong twine, and all the other paraphernalia that make up the florist's stock in trade. And there were people from the telegraph offices that delivered by wire "flowers around the world."

Many at Giacomo's table had hands like his, gnarled and competent-looking, steeped in soil.

These were the agriculturalists, the horticulturalists, the hybridists, or, as they called themselves, "the growers." They were the growers of seeds, of seedlings, of potted plants, trees, and ornamental shrubs. Some were "outdoor growers," who raised blooms without benefit of glass, such as the Brocks, that large group of related families who for three decades had grown outdoor flowers at Santa Cruz. The Brocks formed a solid blond block at the table, with a place empty. Eric Brock, Giacomo's assistant, belonged there, but Giacomo knew where Eric would be at this time, in the seedling house with a new hybrid about to bloom!

Dozens of Giacomo's rival growers were present, whose nurseries lay in other sections of Colma and in South San Francisco, San Anselmo, San Leandro, and Santa Cruz.

Of the "glasshouse" growers a certain percentage specialized in growing the choicer flowers, while among these perhaps no more than twenty grew orchids. And since every world has social strata of its own, so it is with the flower people, and the orchid growers are the royalists of the industry.

But none of the others grew orchids like those of Daneri!

Many of his guests had begun their lifework as his gardeners. Giacomo was proud of having schooled so many California growers; proud, too, that no man who worked for him had ever willingly left his employ unless he set out to grow flowers of his own.

His present crew of fifty-odd gardeners, with their families, were his co-hosts on this day. Most of them lived at the nursery. They came from stock that had bred close to the soil in England, Holland, Germany, or, the majority, in Italy. Some had been trapped by urban living in a strange country, and he had found and rescued them and brought them to their rightful place on the growing earth. When the time came, he would help them to build and develop their own nurseries and homes; he would take pride in them as rival growers and business rivals, and in the knowledge that he had helped them to independence.

The long glasshouse was laced across with affection for the gray-haired man who sat like a patriarch at his table's head.

There was the imprint of serenity on the faces of the flower people. There was the look of goodness born of hard and interesting labor, healthy living, regular hours. These were people whose heartbeats measured the slow, magical turn of growth, tides, moons, and harvest. Their eyes were filled with peace, but lively with interest. Giacomo bore that expression. The patience of centuries was on his lined face, but under the hooded brows his look was as eager as any child's.

Giacomo's guests were enjoying their festa in a way other people could not know. Ordinary holidays were not for them. Easter, Christmas, Thanksgiving, Big Game Day were periods in time when their strong bodies and serene minds were driven to the breaking point, leaving them too weary to enjoy whatever tag ends of celebration might be left. However, these were hazards of the trade, such as blight or a drop in the market might be, and the flower people could celebrate between holidays, as on this May Sunday, after the Easter rush and before the rush of weddings and graduations began in earnest.

There were no people more content in all California—no, not in all the world—than the flower people.

And it was noticeable that the married couples among them, particularly those of Latin descent, sat together at table by preference, because they were happiest together.

"We are all here," Giacomo called happily down the table to his friend, Adolph Brock. Then he added, "At least those of us who are living."

And it seemed to him that his entire lifetime lay written under the glass roof of the Drive, all the chapters in it human, and all dear to him.

Toward so many he felt the tenderness that comes with special knowledge. The burly Cesare; the banditti-resembling, gentle-hearted Pietro who tended Giacomo's rose houses; Ernesto, the gardenia specialist, who looked like a poet; Stoob, in charge of the lilies; Laddie, the littlest apprentice . . . Giacomo's glance went back uneasily to Stoob, who had grown his first lily pips along the Black Sea and had been Giacomo's lily master for a quarter of a century. In all that time Giacomo had not been able to like Stoob as a grower should his lily master, nor could he care deeply for Ludmilla, Stoob's daughter, who helped her father in the lily-of-the-valley houses and was as pale as the flowers they tended.

They were not like the rest of the flower people, Giacomo found himself thinking with some distress, because he wished to regard them with affection as he did the others. But Stoob was not the kind to inspire affection. Like Giacomo, he was first-generation American, but he had brought over with him from his poverty-ridden section of Western Europe the ugly elements of resentment and suspicion. He was a little man with a fiercely held round head and seemed to tower over anyone he was with, and at the moment it was Ludmilla. He talked to her in a surly monotone, ignoring his neighbors at the table and never ceasing to eat.

Grumbling, even today, thought Giacomo. Poor Stoob.

A dull man, Stoob seemed, with a dull daughter.

Hurriedly Giacomo looked away to his own daughter Marie, who was sitting between her husband, Vincent Levenridge, and their daughter Tosca. Ah, here was a true daughter of the flower people! Marie is herself today, he thought fondly. She is always her truest self when she comes back to the nursery that was her home. No one loves flowers like Maria, he thought, calling her, as he did in his innermost thoughts, by the name she was given at her christening, after her mother, the first Maria. Marie was a name that belonged to the city, to the great house on the hill where, overly dieted, overly careful of manners and speech, Marie's dark eyes were often darkened the more by melancholy. Today she was joyous, almost coquettish in the tightly fitted black suit, eating too much, drinking enough to be gay, as if the well-groomed and somber husband she sat beside lost the power to overshadow and subdue her in this world of flowers.

She is happy because she is home, Giacomo thought again, and wondered, did she try too hard, perhaps, to fit into Vincent's world? Well, it was not a father's business to pry, not even into the life of the only child left to him, and such a good daughter, too, as Marie. He looked hard at Vincent Levenridge, but in reality Vincent sat in the city. His thoughts seldom left the bank he served as one of the many vice-presidents. As Giacomo watched, he saw the banker push his plate aside, then with a gold pencil Vincent was figuring long lists of numerals on the white paper table cover, and his eyes were bleak and cold.

Giacomo sighed. A cold son-in-law and a strange being to have fathered Tosca. But Tosca—his glance warmed as he looked at her again—was like the brilliance of fire in the chill shadow cast by her father.

With the appreciation of the artist-genius Giacomo regarded

her against the spreading background of his flowers. Loveliest of all his creations, Daneri's grandchild. His struggles, his long years of toil had perfected her. The strong and slender body, the careful grooming, the expensive education in the convent across the bay, these Giacomo had given. She was perfect, old Giacomo thought humbly, like one of his own orchids, like the one tucked carelessly under the narrow rim of her halo hat, against the sun-blond hair. She had snatched it that morning in an orchid house over Eric's protests. A fine Cattleya Rex hybrid called "Triumphans." The single gold note of the flower with its slightly purple Negroid flange warmed the clear gold of Tosca's delicately tanned features, the rich dark of her eyes.

"Let her have it," her grandfather had said, and Eric had protested, "You spoil her. You let her have everything."

"But never enough," Giacomo had answered inwardly, smiling with fondness at the young people. Always bickering, Eric and Tosca, as if, in their own eyes, they had not outgrown childhood. Giacomo was continually amused and bewildered by the flare-ups, apparently without reason, between his ordinarily good-natured assistant and a girl who in many ways had the look of a medieval angel.

For despite the gray sports frock from Paris, the Daché halo, and the orchid, there was about Tosca a look of the romantic and antique. In the carved mouth perhaps, or the classic way her head lifted. Her Latin heritage was unmistakable. It covered with warmth and color and depth the fine long bones brought down through the Levenridge line.

She was like one of antiquity's tenderer angels, her grandfather was thinking, when over her wineglass Tosca tossed him a gamin grin and her lovely dark eyes crossed with deliberate insolence—startling him into a low burst of laughter that went unheard in the high-pitched conversation around. Then the grin vanished and the celestial look—the flower-look, he called it—was back, hurt and imperious and wondering why he was laughing, and why at Tosca! And why indeed, Giacomo wondered in turn, marveling at the way her moods could spin and carry him, old as he was, along with her.

In that moment she turned her head from him in mock hauteur, and the clean cheek line, the wildly beautiful gesture were so like Paul that Giacomo Daneri felt an abyss widen and drag in all the happiness of the moment, as if the skies had

16

turned black over the glass roof, and the hollow trumpeting sounding in the sudden emptiness of his heart was the terrifying knowledge that he had no sons.

That knowledge shrank to a core of anguish and took the shape of one who seemed to rise tall and shining at the table's end, glass in hand, calling a gay toast down over laughing, admiring faces. Paul the beloved, Paul who had been his son; but his heart dragged against his ribs at thought of Paul, and, turning sharply to the commissioner's wife, Giacomo asked with kindness, "Is it true as they tell me that you are pleased with the begonia named for you?"

But the hollowed beat stayed within him, a muffled drum to steps forever soundless, and the biblical cry of eternal loneliness, "My sons!" They were gone, Vittorio in the World War, before he knew what life could be . . . Vittorio was a memory marching down Market Street endlessly and forever to the music of brasses and drums, with a khaki uniform that did not fit his awkward young frame, and heartbreaking puttees that kept unwinding as he marched. But the wound that was Paul's memory was open and terrible; whatever one might do, it was there, and over the gay chattering, the rich dining, ran the lonely questioning: "Why did you not wait, Paolino! Can you not see there is enough again for us all? That there was always enough?"

Stoob was still grumbling over his many-times-refilled plate.

"Creem-inal display!" he was complaining, but in such a low voice that only his daughter could hear. "How much is this costing, will you tell me? How many lilies are we devouring at this meal, tell me that!"

Ludmilla showed a rare spark of interest. She seldom interrupted the steady flow of complaining that had been poured into her ears since her mother's death.

"I know," she said. "Eric told me."

"Well, then?" Stoob rapped the barbecued bone he was gnawing on the edge of his glass.

Miserably she wished he would finish his meal; the others were through the dessert. But she answered: "Four thousand, Eric said, on this one meal."

"Four thousand dollars!" Consternation held the meat from Stoob's mouth, then he gobbled, as if the fear of starvation drove him. With a full mouth he launched his jeremiad. "A fortune! I could bring a shipload of bulbs from Holland; I will tell him that.

The old idiot. Festas and orchids! Lilies are never good enough for such a man, oh no, he must buy orchids, and raise orchids, and spend fortunes . . ."

As if the thought were unbearable, the lily master shoved the at last emptied plate away and drew a platter of sweet cookies forward with one hand while he lifted a carafe of white wine over his glass with the other.

"The speeches are beginning," whispered Ludmilla unhappily.

But Stoob continued to mutter and eat, although nearly everyone else had stopped eating and was settling back in his chair to listen.

"You see why I tell you to watch out for yourself?" Stoob continued. "Who else, after I am gone! Do I have to do everything to protect your future? And what future has anyone with that one? You'll see, he is going soft in the brain with his orchids, and Eric will be as crazy as the old man unless someone stops him."

Ludmilla stared into her coffee cup. Ever since she had understood human speech she had listened to the perpetual debate Stoob waged, usually under his breath, arguing the merits of his lily houses over the orchid houses, and his jealous resentment of all flowers save those he tended.

"You have to watch that Eric," said Stoob. Then he sneered, "You can keep an eye on him, can't you? You're a woman, aren't you! Or are you? Hold your head up, sit straight . . . The way you hold yourself, flat in front like a fish . . ."

Still she did not speak, as if her ears were sealed to the familiar taunting, which Stoob continued in the half voice no one else could hear, while he munched cookies and washed them down with wine.

But the mayor of San Francisco stood up to speak.

The mayor was of the flower people, of Italian descent, and a grower of orchids. There was authority in his gesture as he pointed to the ribbons of color stretching out in every direction from the Drive.

"We are surrounded by flowers, my friends," said the mayor. "And among them are orchids, millions of orchid plants representing well over a million dollars. And there are no finer orchids grown in this world—no, not even in England, where their hybridization has been an art for more than a century. Here in this country we have Giacomo Daneri, our oldest grower, our pioneer hybridist, and this man, our respected and beloved host, has to

18

his credit the largest collection of seedlings in North America and the longest list of prize-winning hybrids!

"No man will ever need to write the life of Giacomo Daneri. He has written it himself in the *Book of Orchids*. . . ."

And by their Latin names the mayor began calling the honor roll of the most famous of the Daneri hybrids.

Tosca was listening, leaning against her father's shoulder, her slender body almost poured forward in her intensity. It was not in Tosca to half attend. She listened, as she did all things, with all her intense and vivid nature.

At this very moment, the mayor went on to say, a dozen or more—who could say how many?—orchid hunters were at work in lonely places in the world, stalking other orchid hunters from the Argentine to the Arctic, combing the orchid auctions, questioning natives who might have glimpsed rare blooms in the jungles; and these hunters were hired by Giacomo Daneri to seek endlessly the newly discovered, the never-before-seen specimen, to add to a collection already unequaled in the Western Hemisphere. Why, at this moment, the mayor said, his voice sharpening with interest, he had reason to believe a Daneri hunter was penetrating a certain dangerous pass in upper India in search of a fabulous orchid once sighted there, only to be lost and never found again.

"Talk of the discovery of gold!" said the mayor, whose family had come as gold hunters in the early days. "Why, the story of orchidry is as exciting as any gold rush! And for anything you want to know about orchids, ask that fine citizen and foremost grower, Daneri. . . ."

Shyly, across the littered table, Giacomo's glance touched Tosca's for reassurance. How he loved and dreaded this testimonial time that seemed to put an end to his life. As if he were being praised for work finished.

Finished! When even then his thoughts were humble, straying from all this talk-making to a moss-filled pot in the seedling house where Eric was watching unfold, like a bright moth from its wrappings, an orchid Giacomo had hybridized, with an earnest hope for its beauty, nearly nine years before!

The Warneri Aurea should be open by now! He had hugged the thought to his mind through the long relays of dining.

If only one could be certain of the mutation laws! Giacomo owned the plant mother and father of the hybrid about to bloom.

Even so, one could be certain of nothing, save that on this day there would appear in Giacomo's seedling house an orchid such as had never before bloomed on this earth. His slow pulse quickened at the thought. He had been growing orchids for nearly fifty years, and thirty of these had been spent in hybridization, but he had never been able to overcome this almost sickening expectancy when a plant of his breeding was about to show color and form. Never knowing what might be!

Mendel, the painstaking priest, had tried to pin down the laws of expectancy. Those who did not know Giacomo Daneri well were always astonished to discover how much the seemingly inarticulate old man knew of the genetic laws. But even with Mendel, the great lawgiver of genetics, who knew? Perhaps for a hundred generations a type ran true, and suddenly there appeared the unexpected or the throwback, the birth of the utterly new or the rebirth of a stock unremembered . . . For a moment Giacomo's thoughts were with God. Flowers, animals, mankind, all were capable of this strange burgeoning, this rogue branch thrust out from the unknown.

Thinking this, his look was strained upon Tosca.

How different, from Giacomo, her parents, those about her— from them all!

She had grown bored with the technical listings and settled back with a brooding, almost moody expression. As her grandfather watched, she lifted a small decanter and laced the cup of black coffee before her with brandy. Seeing this, he frowned, for repeal was new and liquor strange to the younger generation, and to one of his temperate nature it seemed on its way to becoming a dangerous innovation to those unused to it.

She stirred the coffee, bending her finely shaped head with the glowing orchid and he saw a look of fleeting loneliness pass over her face.

Who knows, Giacomo pondered once more, the truth of the bloodline? One traces the veins of a leaf or a human hand, but who can follow the imperceptible lines of impulse and desire? Tosca was the product of two worlds. The reticence of that transplanted New Englander, her father, might be responsible for her appealing, almost wistful, appearance. That gentleness did not deceive her grandfather. Another element in her nature he recognized—he had known from babyhood it was there—and that was the flame of the Genoese, those ancient hot-blooded pathfinders

20

who had deserted Italy for other worlds. Like them, if she willed, Tosca would strike out blindly; she would take what she wanted; she would give, if she chose to give, everything.

The hybridist, Giacomo Daneri, was qualified to know how fiercely opposite worlds might be at war in such a girl.

Something was missing for her, he realized, at the festa he had given with her pleasure foremost in his mind. Was it still another world Tosca was missing, one not represented at her grandfather's picnic, one he did not know?

"Blood of the orchid," Giacomo sometimes said to Eric Brock in praise or condemnation of a plant. "Wild blood is in this one," he would say, "throwback to the jungle."

And for Tosca, in secret he feared the wild blood that had leaped like a dark flame across the centuries from ancestors who, like Tosca, like Paul, could not be bound, who had set sail from Genoa to leave their bones in lands unknown, leaving the children they had sired to Italy.

There had been no restless stirrings in his own veins, nor in those of his daughter Marie. Only the need for subsistence or land carried their kind to new horizons. For generations the Daneri had been hard-working and devout; they were a contented breed. In Tosca their strength and determination had been refined and made sensitive to an almost dangerous degree. The flame of the Genoese that had by-passed so many generations blazed in this strong and sensitive young woman, leaving her restless, driven with an almost abnormal need for action, and wild, suddenly, to be gone from this glassed-in place with its stifling atmosphere of humans and flowers.

Ma perchè? Giacomo wondered unhappily. Why does she want to go?

And the mayor, who had finished his speech, lifted his glass of red Napa Valley wine.

"*Salute!*" he called down the long table, his voice clattering against the glass roof. "To Giacomo Daneri, the Orchid King!"

There were shouts of "Daneri!" and "Bravo, Giacomo!" and a thousand glasses were lifted. "Bravo!" Tosca found herself crying, the scarlet wings glowing on her cheeks. In that moment of recognition, as she turned to her grandfather again, their glances touched and the flesh and years fell back and pure love held them. In such moments she felt her love for Giacomo was deeper than for anyone else in the world.

Carmine ebbed into Giacomo's leathery cheeks as he lifted his big body, slanted the more with shyness, and stood up to speak. His ragged brows wrinkled under the heavy gray hair that fell over eyes, deep and anxious, looking down the long table with immeasurable kindness.

He is magnificent! Tosca thought intently, as if in defense of him. Like a sketch I've seen—some drawing of Da Vinci's . . .

Giacomo looked down the receding glass tunnel upon friends acquired in seventy-four years of living. Much as these people meant to him, he could not tell them, not even those closest to his life. Vincent, his son-in-law, Marie, his daughter, Tosca, who more than all the others was Giacomo Daneri's own—his brooding glance sought them separately. Cesare had crowded his enormous bulk in the stained apron into the open doorway to hear, and between Cesare's feet crouched, terrified, the Maltese kitten that at other times was to be seen following Giacomo.

Rooted and voiceless stood Giacomo. Only his hands spoke, the rough, misshapen hands, stained by so many decades of craftsmanship in the earth, that were capable of such delicate artistry. Even as his hands indicated a clumsiness he did not have, so his speech came twisted and without form. In Italian, Giacomo's speech was fluent and almost classical, and the Latin horticultural terms came easily to his lips, but his efforts to express his thoughts capably in English were like those of one who is tone-deaf and tries to sing.

"It is my pleasure to have you. My great pleasure. The finest thing we can have is our friends . . ." Through the stumbling words came the sudden discordant shriek of accordions. The orchestra hired for the dancing was tuning up in the shipping shed.

"What we do is hard work," Giacomo continued earnestly, lifting his voice. "Flower growing looks easy. Visitors come, and they say to us, oh, what a pleasure it is and like a vacation almost to work with flowers!" There was a sympathetic round of laughter and hooting from Giacomo's audience. "But we who grow them know it means up early and late, and the worry, and never knowing what is going to happen. So we growers do not talk too much. What we have to say we say with flowers!"

There, it was over, and on the final note of the familiar trade quotation Giacomo sat down gratefully but without hurry, and let his lined forehead unlock with relief. "For he's a jolly good fellow," Cesare boomed from the doorway, and his voice was joined by a thousand more, and outside the Drive hundreds of other voices took up the chant against the now thundering rendition of a Strauss waltz coming from the shipping shed, until the conductor of the city's symphony orchestra jumped on his chair and with a bread stick for baton tried to beat order into the opposing torrents of sound.

A little ashamed of his own emotion, Giacomo smiled at Tosca, the smile of age that so closely resembles that of childhood, being complete in its moment and unreserved.

"Did anyone mention lilies?" Stoob remarked to his daughter.

His voice was low, but it made itself known through the deafening sounds: the ending notes of the song and the clatter of the guests rising to leave the table and of waiters anxious to clear away and take part in the fun. But Stoob, fending off the waiters, bent his small body over the table as if to hold his section of it against despoilers. He had finished a variety of desserts, including the cookies. He clenched a stalk of celery in his fist and crunched it as he spoke.

"No mention was made of the lily houses, no. And who handles the lily houses for this big-talker, this four-thousand-dollar-dinner giver! And does he thank me for it in public, as a decent man would? Oh no, we must hear about orchids. Orchids! Always for him the glory. Drudgery, always, for a man like me. . . ."

But Ludmilla was not listening. Her thin body had arched with excitement. Her look became secretive, alive.

Eric was making his way through the outgoing crowds toward the head of the table, where Giacomo was sitting.

Tosca noticed Eric. She thought instantly, It's the Aurea! All this time—and he hasn't even bothered to change!

Eric looked warm and wind-driven, as if he carried with him both storm and sun. He was blond and square like all the Brocks, but the Colma sun had darkened his face and narrowed his eyes to slits of living blue. His blond hair, sunburned to an almost alpine lightness, was pushed back damply. He was flushed with eagerness and his long watch in the heated seedling house.

Giacomo rose like a boy under the clap of Eric's hand.

"Hey there, Maestro," Eric said, and the apparently jesting salutation told Giacomo all he wanted to know.

For Eric was like his son. His Absalom. His own were gone, but Eric had come in their place as acolyte to master, leaving his

23

own teeming family and their broad acres of cut flowers that flourished farther down the coast line at Santa Cruz. Adolph Brock had trained this son for the land. But the study of biology, botany, genetics, and Latin at the University of California, and two postgraduate years at agricultural college, had only served to whet Eric's earliest ambition of working with his ideal among hybridists, Giacomo Daneri. He had brought to Daneri's the newer methods in floriculture, horticulture, and soil study, and in turn was learning from Giacomo secrets of the propagation of orchids that are not taught in schools.

"You have not eaten your good dinner," chided Giacomo, because nothing else could be said with so many open ears around them.

"I'll attend to that later," said Eric. He caught up a slice of panetone and munched on it hungrily. "Say, Giacomo, could you step outside for a second? A man wants to speak to you." He winked.

"Oh, run along, you two," said the commissioner's wife good-naturedly. "You aren't fooling anyone. But whatever it is, tell me about it later."

"Whatever it is, it shall be laid at your feet," Giacomo promised with old-world gallantry.

Eric shouldered their way through the slow-moving crowd. Tosca caught up with them before they reached the door.

"Don't think you're leaving me out, "she remarked sotto voce, sliding in between them. Her fingers closed over Eric's bare arm and pinched. "Well, speak! Has it or hasn't it?"

"*Silenzio!*" scolded Giacomo over Eric's pained yelp. His voice lowered. "Eric, it is pretty good, eh?"

"Oh, not up to your standards!" Eric's lack of concern was elaborate. "Hurry up, can't you, before some of these orchid pirates tag along?"

They struggled through the crowded door and into the path outside. The blue kitten had been crouching under the wall of the Drive. Sighting Giacomo, it raced desperately through the undergrowth of feet and after him, its small tail a spikelet of despair. Through the glass Ludmilla watched.

"You would think, with all the money spent on this table, more hot coffee would be provided," the master of the lily houses was complaining in the almost deserted Drive. "Well, we might as

24

well go. There will be refreshments in the shed with the dancing.

"Dancing!" he added spitefully. He looked with contempt down the littered table. "Typical of the waste," he snorted. "Typical of the degeneracy of the capital-eestic system."

Ludmilla had nothing to say. During the long dining she had furtively watched Tosca. She had seen Eric make his way to Giacomo and guessed at the mysterious excitement between them.

Now, through the frosted glass, she watched Tosca leaving with Eric and Giacomo, and her narrow chest shrank with bitterness.

Like conspirators, the three fled joyously from the Drive.

TWO

ONCE they were outside, their lungs expanded, expelling the heavy air of the Drive, and draining in the cold air spiced with the smell of growing things and of the salt winds that race in from the Pacific and over the Colma hills at the southerly tip of San Francisco.

Eric and Tosca adjusted their steps to the slower pace of Giacomo. They walked, these three, with the unison that comes of long and perfect understanding. The kitten skipped ahead, its apprehensions forgotten.

Along the paths between the glasshouses, in contrast to the bright blooms within, Giacomo for his own pleasure had planted the simple Shasta daisy developed by Burbank. The three went casually between the silver flowers, like strollers with no definite end in mind. They stopped at times to chat with groups of guests who were deserting the flower houses and turning toward the shipping shed, where the dance music was now in full swing.

The glasshouses divided at the end of the Drive. And to Giacomo, as always, the land seemed to rush upward from the sea to meet him, and his weathered face lifted against the racing wind, seeing in this burgeoning terrain his kingdom. This was his land, striped north and south to catch the noonday sun with the silvery-gray houses splashed with flowers. It remembered his earliest hopes. It held the bones of his youth.

Pregnant land, this, subirrigated, enriched by centuries. And on the other side of these hills, in land equally rich, lay, in marble-outlined rows, the city's dead. Over this hill, Giacomo never ceased to remember, was the Italian cemetery that held his wife and sons.

(Where Paul lay apart and alone, in unhallowed ground.)

His arm went over Tosca's jauntily held shoulders, as if to hold her safe. Here, on the open land, Giacomo dared remember his sons.

A dynasty he had planned for this Colma land.

Colma was "growing" region, with hills crisscrossed with black and green stripes that were the truck gardens, glossy with vegetables—purple and jade cabbages, fledgling spinach, and frosted artichokes; and set between these were the silvery glass squares of the many flower-growing nurseries, gleaming like shields as they reflected the sun from the sea. Colma had served as garden for San Francisco since gold-rush days, sending vegetables and, almost as early, flowers to the city on the bay.

Daneri's was one of the larger nurseries. It lay in a sheltered fold against the hill, doubly protected by a windbreak of eucalypti set out twenty years before by Giacomo and an outer break of gnarled cypress, bent by the winds against the hillside, which had been planted by Spanish settlers a century before.

The three stood with the hill at their backs, looking toward the westering sun. Before them stretched the swells of green that were the golf links and beyond these the high blue shining wall that was the Pacific. To the south more nurseries and streets and homes lay scattered, but on the north the city of San Francisco swept like a tide over the bay hills, sending tongues of clean, cheap little houses in the direction of Colma. Licking the hills toward Giacomo's stronghold came the white tongues of houses, threatening the suburban openness of the nursery on the hill.

Tosca pointed to a new subdivision rising in skeleton formation against the sky line.

"Really, Giacomo, every time I come here the city seems nearer."

"It won't be long," said Eric. "We'll have to move inland someday, Giacomo."

26

Giacomo shook his head, and his shock of hair moved like a stubborn lion's. How long, he wondered, could he hold his rich land against the Moloch city?

"But not in my day," he said bravely. "While I live, this old earth has its flowers."

"I don't think you like houses," said Tosca. "Unless they're glasshouses. I think everyone would live in gardens if you had your way."

"Not so! I would have houses. Houses for everyone." Giacomo frowned; if only he could express his meaning! "Beautiful houses," he said, and into his voice rushed the stuff of dreams.

Eric shied from emotionalism. "How was the speech? Did you give them a good talk?"

"Magnificent." Giacomo's eyes twinkled. "A *nada* of a *nada*. I said nothing. And the mayor, he said twice as much."

Still he wished Eric might have heard what the mayor had said of him.

"Giacomo made a fine speech," said Tosca loyally.

The glasshouses had emptied. The festa had transferred in full force to the noisy shed. The three walked without interruption through a small and silent city made almost entirely of glass.

Daneri's Nursery was in effect a small-scale commonwealth, with life and customs of its own. As a working unit it was almost complete, having within itself every representative of production, labor, commerce, and trade necessary to its existence, from its community cook to the mechanic whose sole duty it was to attend to the nursery's fleet of bottle-green trucks. In its work patterns and social groupings it reflected the life of a city in miniature. And the grayish-white blocks of narrow glasshouses mounting the hill, row on row, gave an effect not unlike the planed lines of a modern city.

Three homes rose above the glasshouses. Giacomo's was the smallest. His white frame cottage under the eucalyptus-tree wall was flanked on either side by the orchid houses and in the rear by a small orchard. He had built this house on the untilled land purchased nearly half a century before. He lived in it alone now, save for the times Tosca spent a night there in the little white room that had been her mother's.

The other two houses were larger and handsomer and were set in small formal gardens on the south side of the greenhouses. These Giacomo had built for Vittorio and Paul. Neither had been occupied by a Daneri. A dozen of the gardeners who had no families and Cesare, the cook, occupied the house that was to have been Vittorio's. Eric had taken possession of one room in the white house empurpled with bougainvillaea that was still referred to as "Paul's house."

The nursery lay between the two houses and Giacomo's cottage. The electrical plant, machine shop, steam plant, warehouses, potting sheds, shipping sheds, and the icehouse, where the more perishable flowers such as orchids were kept in the interim between their cutting and the start of their trek into the outer world—these, together with the fifty-four glasshouses, roofed a perfectly geared industry.

Below the nursery a green lane ran down the hill to the San Francisco highway. It was lined with hundreds of cars, representing in their differences the cosmopolitan nature of Giacomo's guests, for among them were town cars and imported limousines, roadsters, many cars of cheaper and older make, and not a few small flower trucks that had served to bring families of flower growers to Giacomo's picnic. Tosca's yellow roadster was parked in a tilted position at the entrance, as if she had stopped it headlong at a moment's whim.

On the other side of the lane were several acres that also belonged to Giacomo; and on these stood half a dozen small neat houses in which lived those members of his crew who had families, such as Garibaldi, the chief mechanic, and Pietro with his swarming brood, and Stoob, the lily master, who lived with his daughter Ludmilla in a small house directly across the lane from the shipping shed. Around these houses, for which no rent was paid, Giacomo's gardeners had planted their own small gardens, and nearly all were experimenting with plants and shrubs to be taken with them on the day when they might buy land and start greenhouses on their own.

It was noticeable that no flowers grew around Stoob's house.

Otherwise, wherever one turned at Daneri's, there were flowers. One looked up between the flower-filled glasshouses to the hill, beyond the dark compost heap and the now barren gardens where the Easter lilies had grown before being brought indoors and forced into Easter blooming, and lying against the breast of the hill, like clouds of amethyst smoke, were small forests of heather.

In a narrow strip beside the compost heap a battalion of sunflowers, not yet in bloom, strained to kiss the lowering sun, and these Giacomo planted each year for the birds.

He knew his greatest fault as a grower. Eric and the others pointed it out to him often enough, delighted to find this chink in the hybridist's armor. This was his reluctance to uproot, to destroy. In Giacomo's "own" garden, the kitchen garden beside his house, which contributed vegetables and herbs to help feed his teeming family of gardeners, the rows were kept neatly as strips of paint, but every corner of the garden was riotous with old-time flowers that had no commercial value: heliotrope, marguerites, and tansy, long past their reasonable bloom. He let them run wild against a windbreak of rose mallow and Queen Anne's lace, with their stalks entangled in poppies and lupine.

And if Eric offered to go in and clean out the "weeds," Giacomo shook his head in refusal. It seemed to him there was room enough for all God had intended to make grow. More than most men, Giacomo Daneri loved the vast showy segments of growth that through the seasons splashed color the length and breadth of California, the glowing vegetable farms, the cherry, prune, apple, and pear orchards in full bloom, the purple wash of vineyards, the indigo stain of lupine, the golden strike of the Escholtzia Californica, that nugget-gold poppy California has chosen for its state flower. Color, rampant, dramatic, and passionate—there could never be enough for him. And still he could lower his huge body, as he did now between the glasshouses, halting Eric and Tosca, to study a coral pimpernel growing in a silvery tattoo of filaree. These were weeds, and they claimed his attention, not alone for their minute and exquisite patterns, but because of their incredible potential, the surmise as to what they might become in time if given cultivation and care.

And when they exchanged smiles, he pointed to a Shasta daisy almost as wide as his palm. "You may laugh. But I knew that when it was a little flower, no bigger than a button!"

Their progress through the nursery was slow, but a delight to the three because there was so much for Giacomo to see, all of which he had seen so many times before.

It was plain that Giacomo was dawdling, delaying what would be for them the greatest moment of the day. It might be, too, that he was a little in dread of what might be waiting in the seedling house.

So they went slowly between the lily houses, although there was little there to hold their interest now that the Easter lilies were gone. The long bins of lilies of the valley were swathed in burlap against the sun. The bulb section was Stoob's special domain, and even Giacomo never interfered with the lily houses.

But the other houses were recharging with bloom after the great spring harvesting. The gardenia houses were starred with waxen splashes, as if great candles burned on polished jade altars. In the carnation houses the silvered foliage was splashed with the enameled faces of pink, rose, red, and garnet flowers.

Then they came to the orchid houses, and their steps quickened.

For the adult orchid houses were less like greenhouses than like long transparent cages wherein hung brilliant tropical shapes that seemed more like birds or insects than flowers. The three walked slowly between these houses, looking from side to side, recognizing with pleasure the familiar blooms Daneri had made famous around the world.

The last of the orchid houses was the seedling house. The long glass shed was seemingly barren, and since it held few blooms, it had attracted no visitors this day. There was nothing about this greenhouse to indicate the fact that fortunes had grown and were growing under its glass roof and that the entire story of orchidry was being perpetually retold within its narrow walls.

But the three who had been chattering gaily fell into silence as they entered the first of the glass sections.

The potting shed at the entrance was unheated. Tosca shivered, glancing about with distaste. In this unlovely place Giacomo and Eric worked together hour after hour, potting and repotting the orchids in their various stages of development. On the zinc-lined workbenches lay their tools, the planting sticks and shears, and the sticks used were not the ordinary pointed wooden pegs but were cast according to Giacomo's own design of hollow steel in his machine shop because he had worn out so many of the wooden ones. Orchidry owed many of its innovations to Giacomo; for example, the metal ant traps that protected the orchid tables had been cast in the machine shop to a pattern he had designed.

In the shed were bins of the Osmunda, shredded peat fiber from the Jersey canebrakes, broken shard, and charcoal, all used in orchid planting, and stacks of the orchid pots brought from

England, which were different from ordinary pots, for the clay was hard-burned to discourage fungi.

The only touch of life in the shed was that of the green plants, hanging overhead, of the Odontoglossum, at this time of year dormant, an orchid from the high, cold regions of Ecuador that could not bear the heat of the interior of the greenhouse but throve in the cold air of the shed, where it would bloom around Christmas time.

Tosca was looking at the door of the small room that was Giacomo's laboratory, set between the potting section and the locked incubator section. It was so like Giacomo, she thought, that while the door of the laboratory where he brewed his miracles was kept religiously locked the key to the cubicle that held his most valued secrets hung trustfully beside its door.

"Then I know where it is when I want it," Giacomo was wont to explain.

A tenderness overcame her at sight of that locked door. All her life she could remember Giacomo crowded into that tiny place, his great trunk arched over the microscope, his shaggy head lowered over the tubes of agar, his branched hands lifting with miraculous caution the invisible orchid seeds and the all but invisible threads of green that were his baby orchids.

This was his alchemist's hideaway.

They went with respect past the locked door and into the nursery section.

Here in warm moist air, on wooden tables, were growing thousands upon thousands of Giacomo's infant orchids, planted in "communities," or groups, in pots that ranged in size from containers no larger than Giacomo's thumb to the three-inch-wide pot that held the three-year-old orchids, planted one to a pot by this time, and each pot carefully labeled with its numbered, waterproof tag.

Tosca took little interest in these nurslings that were like tiny green hands, splayed, tuberous, or poniard, according to the species of orchid, stretching up through their cufflets of fiber. Her interest was in the finished product, and she took no pleasure in the banks of unrelieved tender greens. But Giacomo and Eric walked between the tables with the absorption of obstetricians going the rounds of the infants' ward. ("You watch them like babies," Tosca had once gibed, and they had answered together, "They are babies.") In this nursery the glass-born orchids were tended for at least six years with a tenderness and skill shown to few human children. During all those years they would never be left alone or neglected for an hour. Their moisture and air supplies were guarded, fresh air was permitted to flow in upon them cautiously through the glass panes regulated with jointed steel arms, and night and day the endless war against insects and disease was waged over their slowly developing forms.

The baby orchids were of absorbing interest to other growers. The casual flower lover was seldom permitted in this section. But the experts, the orchidists from all over the world who visited the Colma nursery, eyed with longing these nurslings whose value was yet to be proven, and often offered fabulous prices for them, balancing against the chance that they might prove worthless the hope of the Daneri potential that had already added such quotas of beauty to the orchid world.

"You'd get offers today if this house had been left open," Eric commented.

"How can I set a price on them?" argued Giacomo. "In this house are millions of baby plants." He lifted an inch-wide pot containing a year-old seedling. "This may be worthless. It may go to the compost heap in the end. And again it may be beyond price. And so all our children must have their chance to grow up and see what they can be."

He chuckled, looking fondly from Eric to Tosca, as if this were some special joke between them.

Then the amusement was gone and they were quiet, opening the last of the frosted doors and filing into the largest and last of the glass sections, which was known to Giacomo and his gardeners as the seedling shed.

THREE

$\mathcal{G}$IACOMO closed the glass door behind them, and they were in the tropics. The seedling section was massed with orchid plants. These graduates from the nursery were at least seven years old; they stood a foot high in their full-size pots; they were preparing for, or were in, their primary bloom. Splayed against the darkling greens were orchids, and although these were all first blooms and hence small, with here and there a twin, their splashed colors and myriad patterns appeared diffused by the warm, moist tropical air, so that the place seemed flashing with rainbows.

Warmth and mist came from silvered pipes that ran under and over the tables, and, as always the moment he entered an orchid house, Giacomo marked the thermostatic control. "Close to sixty-five," he said softly without even glancing at the indicator at the door.

But Tosca did, to check him. "I don't see how you always know."

He knew, just as he could tell when the moisture supply was nearing the saturation point. His great body seemed to carry within itself the information needed to supply his orchids with the maximum of care. He did not remove his coat, although Eric pulled his shirt more open at the throat and Tosca pushed the narrow bandeau higher on her forehead, loosening the orchid. Looking about her, radiant with pleasure, she pulled the gold orchid from her hair and without looking at it tucked it carelessly into her belt. A moment later she turned and it was crushed against the table's edge.

There were dozens of tables, built with double steel mesh trays. The lower trays held coarse gravel to contain moisture, and the upper levels were thickly set with the Daneri seedlings, their roots tamped down in moss, their strange shapes bursting from the labeled pots. Each plant stood stiffly and proudly, as if conscious of its royal strain, and those with their first blooms seemed to stand proudest of all.

There, weaving their glowing patterns through the misty green, were the light spring shades that had been chosen by Giacomo years before for these, the bridal months: the softly lavender Cattleya hybrids; the pure-white crosses for which Daneri's was famous; a table of late-blooming white-and-pink Phalaenopsis Amabilis from the Philippines with its flower spray trailing and vineline; cool Cymbidiums from Siam; Laeliocattleyas more darkly purple than the pure Cattleya; gleaming white and bronze lady's slippers; Oncidiums with their immense yellow-and brown-spotted lips; and, most marvelous of all, the tribes of purple-and-gold-striped Aurea being urged into earlier bloom, into greater beauty, by Giacomo Daneri.

One table was glowing with the Anthurium Victoriane, the scarlet Anthurium inaptly named for the demurest of queens, and overhead, folded on their barked shields like branched trophies, hung the non-blooming staghorns.

Giacomo moved with ponderous care between the burdened tables. Eric winked at Tosca. Her grandfather was obviously postponing the moment with the Aurea.

"Do hurry," said Tosca. But her voice had absorbed the warm languor of the greenhouse. "No wonder you and Eric are such slowpokes. You spend most of your lives in here below the equator."

But Giacomo would not be hurried. Not a leaf, not a bloom, went unnoticed. He stooped to study carefully the almost animalistic component parts of the plants, the irregular cruciate blooms, the curiously shaped leaves, the swollen, bulblike stalk that had given the orchid its phallic Grecian name a thousand years before Christ. He examined the vigorous exposed roots that drank in life for the orchid from the moist air, and not, as was long believed, from whatever they rooted upon. Visitors who referred to orchids as parasites annoyed Giacomo.

"A little more spread to this one," he observed, pointing to a new Laelia.

Eric crowded into the narrow space with him.

"A little more color would help too."

"Perhaps by crossing this Laelia with that Cattleya—next year, perhaps . . ."

So they were planning, thought Tosca impatiently, and so they were always planning. Ten, twenty years ahead stretched the stuff of the hybridist's dream, always more intricately beautiful and more to be desired.

Giacomo laid two fingers on two pots that were side by side.

"This is in need of water, and this is sodden."

"How do you know?" she demanded.

"How does a father know if his children are hungry?"

"They cry."

Giacomo's blunt fingers could hover over a plant as delicately as insect antennae. Touching a bulblike leaf, he answered, "These cry."

34

Then, sighting a yellowing leaf, he knew that plant was ill and made a mental note to return to it later, and for some reason this brought poignantly to mind his deserted two thousand guests.

"Perhaps we had better go back to our friends," he began. Then he saw the young people were laughing and, straightening his shoulders, he led the way to the last table. It was screened with staghorns and set solidly with plants, as identical as if they had been turned out of the same mold; and while many showed the bruised-appearing buds of orchids, only one plant held erect a single, open, splendid bloom.

Tosca drew her breath in sharply, with an exclamation that was not a word but the pre-speech sound of admiration and wonder, and Giacomo stood huge and silent, like a priest between his acolytes, feasting upon this newest Aurea with vision concentrated as if behind a microscope, hunting any possible flaw, any faint imperfection. No, there was none. It was perfect, finer than he had dreamed, and his look lost its burning intent and gentled before the beauty of the Warneri Aurea.

Tosca spoke finally.

"It's the most perfect. Oh, Giacomo, it is, isn't it—the most beautiful?"

He chuckled in a deprecating way. "The last baby is always the most admired."

It occurred to her that she had never heard Giacomo say of a flower, "This is beautiful!" Were they too much a part of Giacomo to draw spoken praise from him, as if they were extensions of his being? But she knew his creator's pride and she took his hand and stood close to him, as so often she had when from childhood on he had brought her shyly before one of his new miracles. The three stood close, regarding the jewel-like petals of the great orchid, and the warm content of the seedling house seemed to seal them together.

Eric was always practical.

"Say, I'll bet that measures four and a half inches," he said emphatically, and although it was not necessary he took his tape measure from his pocket—he and Giacomo were seldom without the hybridist's steel tape, ivory-handled knife, tweezers, and planting stick, and Giacomo had even been known to carry his to the opera—and he measured the orchid, and yes, it was exactly four and a half inches across.

"Growing an inch a year," he summed up smartly, "this baby

should wind up with a seven-inch spread. What a honey! You've really hit it this time, Giacomo."

And Giacomo, who was as practical as Eric, but never seemed to be, added softly, "See how she holds her head, like a queen!"

Tosca was the romanticist. "And from such little seeds—too small to see—Giacomo, did you guess it would be this beautiful seven years ago?"

"Nine years," corrected Giacomo. "This has been a stubborn Aurea. She has waited nine years to bloom."

Nine years! Why, he had been almost a young man, only in his sixties, and stronger than most men in their thirties. Was it possible nine years had passed since the day he had touched pollen to pistil, with hands steadier than they were today, and started the slow forward movement of the miracle that never seemed less a miracle because it had been duplicated so many thousands of times under his hands? For who ever knew what the result would be, or what new complicated design might be formed by crossing together the jungle-born species?

And still he had been almost certain it would be like this! The three flawless petals, each carved like a jewel lip, were royal purple over sepals lipped with garnet, and the delicate inner flange brush was stroked with an opal's undersea green. The golden lip Giacomo remembered in its father, a magnificent male Cattleya Dowiana Aurea. The deep purple came from its Cattleya Warneri mother. Strength from the mother plant, color from the father, was a horticultural adage Giacomo had come to believe in firmly, although not all orchid growers, he knew, accepted the theory.

How the Warneri Aurea dulled the other younglings putting out their first blooms in the seedling house! Only a tray of savage-looking Cyps stared back, tawny as spotted leopards, and as insolent.

"Nine years ago," said Eric suddenly. "That was the time everybody was busy being millionaires and talking about going around the world." ("Not I," interrupted Giacomo, smiling. "I liked it here.") "Everything was wonderful and everyone was rich; God, what a time it was." And he stopped because he had been about to speak of Paul, for it was difficult to speak of the gay times without mentioning Paul, who had helped make them gay. "Well, I was chugging away at UC and missing all the ex-

36

citement because Dad was wonderful but he wasn't rich. And Tosca was a brat."

"You missed nothing," said Giacomo. "Everything is ahead for you."

"And Tosca is still a brat," added Eric, and his steady look went with meaning to the orchid crushed at her waist.

"I was in boarding school," said Tosca smugly. "I was being nicely brought up."

"It didn't work," said Eric.

They were bickering as usual, but Giacomo was still thinking of the nine years. He would have few more such years. Tosca had been growing tall in middy blouses and blue serge skirts, visiting Giacomo during vacations and considering a snail hunt by flashlight in the dark orchid houses one of the greatest of adventures. At such times she had clutched his hand a little nervously, for the orchid houses could be eerie by night, with the pale shapes of the blooms about, almost like human faces glowing in the dark. Tosca's hand was in his now, but she was so tall and smartly groomed that there were times when her very essence changed and it seemed impossible that she could belong to him.

All this time they had been absorbed by the beauty of the Aurea. In its turn, as if it sensed the judgment being passed upon it, the very flesh of its petal seemed to gleam with the pristine quality of its newness, its unique and special glory. And Giacomo Daneri knew, and his younger companions felt his knowledge, that it was for this unique and special orchid he had been waiting.

So when Tosca asked softly, "What are you naming this one, Giacomo?" she already knew the answer, although the Aurea's tag showed only a numeral.

For every orchid plant was tagged and listed, and if in the seedling house it proved its worth, it was registered under its own name, through the American Orchid Society, with the Royal Society in England. For more than a century every orchid grown in the horticultural world had been entered in the *Book of Orchids,* the official registry which is to the orchid specialists what the stud book of horses is to the equine-loving world.

It was the rule that plants which were the duplicates of other plants must carry the names of their original developers, but the creator of a new orchid had the privilege of giving it the name of his choice. Giacomo and Eric knew each of the million adult

Daneri plants by name. This Aurea was one long planned for and awaited, as Tosca knew, and she had been certain upon first glimpsing the orchid that it would be registered by her grandfather in the *Book of Orchids* as the "Tosca Levenridge."

"I have waited a long time for this one, Tosca *mia*." He drew the pot forward gently with his roughened hand. "It is for you."

She could not speak for a moment. She looked fixedly into the opal throat of the Aurea.

"I've always wanted one," she said at last in a small voice. "The other growers' wives and daughters were always having flowers named for them, and I used to wonder . . ."

"We were waiting," said Giacomo. "For the best one."

Eric was trying not to look too pleased.

"So now you are famous," he said lightly. "As long as plants grow, the name of Tosca Levenridge will stand out in the world." He added unnecessarily, "Like a billboard advertising soap."

"Oh, shut up," said Tosca, swallowing. "Giacomo, how long will this plant keep on blooming? I never want to lose track of it."

How long? The two men shook their heads. The orchid had proven itself and would be removed now to one of the adult orchid houses, where it would continue to grow and flower indefinitely. Who could say how long!

"I do not know," said Giacomo. "But a long time, Tosca."

"When I was in England," said Eric, "I was shown an orchid that has lived in the same pot since 1806. Think of it, nearly one hundred and thirty years! I told you, Giacomo. And it was still blooming."

Giacomo nodded. "And rain-water-fed."

"Yes, fed all that time on rain water. Funny the way the English think orchids need rain water."

"They grow fine orchids in England," said Giacomo.

"And then there is your mother orchid," continued Tosca, for since all three had more or less the same thoughts, it was not necessary to sort them out in sequence the way people must who are not close to one another. "How old is the old one, Giacomo?"

"As old as Giacomo," said Eric.

"Oh, older," said Giacomo.

And they remembered with respect and affection the gnarled and bulbous mother orchid that was the first orchid plant purchased by Giacomo Daneri and that was still flowering in season and had its own place of honor in the worker house.

"I wonder how much that old girl has earned for you," said Eric.

But Giacomo refused to reduce the conversation to monetary terms. Waving his hands in refutation, he answered stubbornly, "She has earned her keep.

"She was old when I bought her," he added, "and that was nearly fifty years ago."

The young people, feasting their eyes on the Aurea, were as conscious as Giacomo of the indomitable purpose and the patience that had gone into those years. They remembered him as they had seen him so many times, as he had been nine years before in selecting the lines for this Aurea, studying every plant in his orchid houses before choosing orchid to mate with orchid after determining the color, durability, and lasting qualities desired, and even the very month, many years away, in which it would best serve his purpose that the new creation should come into bloom.

And once the parents were selected and the breeding done— "I am doing a moth's work," Giacomo explained drolly of the processes of cross-pollination—the long watch began. The starting of the seed formation, the swelling and ridging of the flower pod to maturity, the harvesting of the invisible seeds, the skillful planting of the seeds in the agar solution that was one of Giacomo's many secrets—these tasks nibbled at the edges of the years that were his most priceless possessions.

For nine months, so very human is the orchid, so much closer in appearance to the animal than the vegetable kingdom, the seeds of the Aurea had gathered the forces of growth in its infinitesimal cells. Slowly, irrevocably, the nine years of waiting had gone by, and Giacomo Daneri, the hybridist, could stand humbly before an orchid that had never been duplicated before in this world, and still marvel, after half a century of hybridizing, at this new life shape of his own construction, with its curious welded whorls and bright designs, like heraldic devices. Only the leaves of the Aurea remained unchanged.

Oh, there was never any end to the long waiting, the persistent hoping. In his locked laboratory at this moment, stacked to its ceilings, were hundreds of glass jars and tubes and retorts where millions of his orchid seeds were showing the first verdant shades of life in their nutrient agar.

("Here! Here!" he rebuked the kitten that had made its way to

39

a table and was trying to catch a twin Laelia between its paws. "These are not butterflies, my little friend.")

No, there was no end to the waiting, with the new orchids coming on always and forever, iridescent tides of Orchidaceae pouring splendidly over the years. No end to the watching and tending, the disappointments, the hazards, the minor tragedies and major victories. Always the seed invisible, the new potential, the final exultation of the first blooming, such as this one.

"Patience," Giacomo reminded himself. "*Pazienza.*"

"I never dreamed of having an orchid like this," Tosca was saying. "I don't deserve anything as wonderful. Do I, Eric?"

"Less than anyone I know." Eric tilted the orchid to her. "See, there's a drop of honey on your Aurea! Remember how you used to drive us crazy, licking the honey off the orchids?"

Laughing with him, she bent her head over the orchid, remembering a taste wildly sweet and like no other honey, but she did not touch the lip of the orchid. She felt her senses fall and become lost in the divinest of all floral perfumes, the elusive fragrance of the orchid that rarely makes itself perceptible to humans, and then soon after blooming and for so short a time. Eyes closed, lost to ecstacy, she drank in the scent of worlds both antediluvian and sophisticate, of flowers growing under moss— the savage jungle sweetness that is the breath of the orchid. The sun, lowering at that moment, forced a path through the frosted panes and the heated misty air to burst around her in a series of small rainbows, making Tosca seem for the moment spun of ineffable beauty, with her background of orchids and rainbows and the hybrid held close to her shining head.

Eric, the practical one, stared almost openmouthed for a moment, and without letting himself think too deeply of the matter, he noted that her mouth was as red as the Anthurium beside them, and that over her was the additional dewiness that was youth, radiant with longing, and untried.

But he spoke briskly.

"Say, we'd better be getting back to the picnic. And it might not be a bad idea to tuck this out of sight. A lot of people are wandering around today, and while of course we're all friends . . ."

"Oh yes, we had better hide it," Giacomo agreed, twinkling, for a person who would not touch a penny belonging to another might not be above wiping off a wisp of pollen that was plainly

40

crying out to be taken, and there were six, seven, perhaps nine years wiped away!

Eric stored the light pot in a narrow cart used to collect rubbish. Tosca watched with regret as the bright face of the Aurea vanished. Impulsively she pulled Giacomo's gray head down to hers and kissed the deep-wrinkled cheeks.

"For the honor," she said softly.

Giacomo's speech stumbled, as always when he was angry or happy.

"And not for Eric?" he managed to say. "Eric has taken such good care of your orchid."

"It was no trouble," said Eric carelessly, and gave no sign when she kissed him, but they both knew the moment was beautiful for Giacomo.

"*Floralia merita,*" commented Eric jokingly, for he often spoke Latin to Giacomo to tease Tosca and had even picked up from him a smattering of Genoese, which is not pure Italian but a cadenced and guttural dialect from cosmopolitan Genoa in which the remnant patois of many tongues can be traced.

After they had pushed the cart containing the Aurea out of sight behind the tables, locked the doors of the seedling section and nursling section behind them, and were out of the potting shed and into the open air that seemed colder and saltier than before now that the sun was going down, Giacomo snapped his fingers in remembrance.

"That *gatto!* Always, when I am out, he is in!"

And he had to reopen the doors again and rescue the kitten that had been left behind among the seedling orchids.

Tosca was giggling. She could always remember Giacomo being followed by a kitten that was forever getting locked into greenhouses, and always, with infinite patience, Giacomo remembered.

"*Bella Santa,* now I must get over to the shed!" Giacomo exclaimed, recalling with dismay his duties as host to two thousand. "Eric, change your clothes and hurry over. Tosca will save a dance for you."

"If I'm there," said Tosca.

They went between the orchid houses and circled the gardenia houses, passing the compost heap on their way toward the shipping shed, where the sounds of festa were increasing in volume. The compost consisted of mounds of fertilizer containing the ashes of burned plants and carloads of virgin soil brought down from various untouched sections, such as the Santa Cruz Mountains or Oregon. A rich and acrid odor rose from the dark mounds.

Tosca's nose wrinkled.

"I never can see why the compost has to be next to the gardenia houses," she said with unexpected vehemence. "For everyone to see. And smell!"

Giacomo looked surprised. Eric chuckled.

"Why, in some countries the manure pile stands next to the house. It's a sign of thrift, to say nothing of wealth."

"It's disgusting."

"You may think that. We think it's beautiful, don't we, Giacomo?"

And Eric pointed to a mound as dark as peat that was the nursery's pride. "Know what that is? It's the entire crust of an island from the Sacramento River. Giacomo saw it when he was riding upriver in the boat and went back later and bought the topsoil and shipped it down by scow. That's pure flood-washed delta soil."

Tosca was unimpressed.

"It's still mud, isn't it?"

Giacomo was disturbed by the sudden argument that had sprung up, as arguments usually did, apparently out of the air. To Giacomo, who could spend any amount of time marveling at the way a vein pulsed and narrowed along a leaf's tip under his microscope, or the diversified constellations and universes that could be brought to light in a minute segment of such a vein, the compost heap was alive with excitement. Such creatures as stirred there, such scenes as were played out, might not be altogether pleasant for the squeamish to contemplate, but they held endless fascination for the scientific mind. The entire life concentrate could be observed in a fragment of mold. And since life was important and never to be disturbed, save for purposes of betterment, the compost heap held for Giacomo all the elements of high drama.

Also, was it not the final resting place of all importance? The tides of fruit and flower and vein and bone and leaf and root rose only to recede back to the earth, so was not the compost the end of all glory?

"We are required to give back. We do not always take from the earth." He was fumbling for words, not to chide Tosca but to make her realize the importance of understanding. "In this world there are the men and women who devour all the land can produce and give it nothing, and there are those who feed back to the earth so that it can produce again, and are not these the good citizens?" Knowing the poorness of his words, his poet's longing to say what could never be said, Giacomo asked this with his forehead wrinkled with effort.

"All right, so I'm a devourer," said Tosca. "I still don't like compost."

"You may not like it," said Eric, "but it's in the food you eat and that Paris original you have on and the perfume you're wearing."

"I'll still take mine imported." They had passed the compost, and Tosca was tired of the subject. "Giacomo, you're really an impossible host! Why, we must have been out here half an hour."

"I know, I know." Giacomo was driven between guilt and a pleased awareness. He looked from Eric to Tosca, smiling. "No wheelbarrow needs three wheels. Only, don't be late to the dancing."

And he walked away toward the shipping shed as rapidly as ever he walked, with the kitten bounding ahead.

They both watched him go.

"He thinks we're in love," said Eric.

"He always has," she said.

No sooner had Giacomo disappeared around the gardenia houses than Eric moved rapidly. He seldom forgot details. With one movement he ripped the Cattleya Rex from Tosca's belt, scowled at its crushed petals, and tossed it in the direction of the compost.

"You had your nerve taking that one," he said levelly. "I'd have stopped you if Giacomo hadn't been there. I counted on getting five dollars for that tomorrow at market."

She was complacent.

"I wanted it."

"And that answers everything, doesn't it? Why don't you try growing up!"

Then for the first time that day he saw her serious, and his anger stopped.

"That's just it," she said tensely. "I have."

He studied her narrowly.

"Walk over to Paul's house with me," he said. "I have to change."

They left the phalanx of glasshouses and entered the house Giacomo had built for his younger son, the house Paul had never occupied, preferring the large house in the city. The single room Eric used was neat—a student's room, one might have thought it, with its desk and microscope, and the bookshelves he had built to the ceiling, filled with books on horticulture and magazines relating to the flower trade. His desk, a leather chair and reading lamp, and a studio couch completed his living arrangements. On the wall above the desk were dozens of framed photographs of Brocks, all so much alike that, superimposed one upon the other, the total might well have resulted in one face, and that face, Eric's. Giacomo often remarked that the Brock characteristics were all dominant.

Tosca dropped down on the neatly made couch, and Eric, after starting the water running in the adjoining bath, closed its door and joined her there.

"Okay, so it's happened," he said.

"I said I'd tell you." Her hands were folded over her knees, and he saw them trembling.

"Sure, I know." He was studying her face, her hands. Her face was fair and trained in courtesy, but expression could override it like shadows, like the shadows of an ancient music.

He leaned over and unclasped her hands and held them in his own.

"Okay, let's take this easy. Who is the guy, what's his name, where did you meet him, and how far has it gone?"

"Mark Cantrell." To her, this seemed to answer everything.

"Never heard of him."

"Well, you wouldn't."

"Social?"

She nodded.

"Not enough. I'd have heard of him. I look over the society columns, you know. I like to see who is wearing our orchids."

"Just the same, he is. Or at least he gets around. I really don't know much about him, Eric. I've only known him a few days."

Eric looked relieved. "Well, if it's all right for you, it should be for the rest of us. Meaning Giacomo. And that reminds me, what did you mean by that crack by the compost, that you'd save me a dance if you're there?"

She would not meet his eyes.

"I didn't mean anything."

"Tie that!"

"Well, I had made a sort of date . . ."

"A date—with the festa going on?"

His look was suspicious and hard. He dropped her hands.

"This guy Cantrell—why isn't he here today? We always ask everyone we like to the picnics. Not too social for us, is he? Or—any other reason?"

"Now you're being nasty!" she said furiously. "You don't understand."

"No? Maybe I do. I used to breed spaniels, remember?"

She sprang to her feet and he rose with her.

"I told you I'd tell you when it happened, and it's happened and I've told you. Now I wish I hadn't."

"Oh, run along," he said wearily. "Giacomo will be awfully sunk if you don't get on over to the shed. I don't give a damn what you do, but I do care about Giacomo. He's old, and you're about all he has left."

He stopped, for he had seen the anger give way to a puzzled look.

"Eric," Tosca asked with sudden gentleness, "you're sure you don't care for your own sake?"

"Me! Hell, no."

"I'm glad of that. Sometimes I've thought . . ."

"Well, stop thinking. I'm too busy and I know when to keep hands off. Besides, I couldn't stand a caviar diet. I like plain fare."

He had hurt her.

"I suppose by that you mean Ludmilla."

He said, "What does it matter to you or anyone else what I mean!"

Alone, he sat, sock in hand. Of course he minded. Still, he had told Tosca the truth. It had been hands off in his mind, for she had too much, more than he could give her for many years, no matter how hard he worked. Times had changed in the past few years, and men worked dollar for dollar now, with no fancy dreams of fortunes born overnight. He and Tosca might have been living in different periods of time, for although the material with which he worked was for the luxury trade, still his was bread-and-butter work, and he had so much more to learn about it, because, like Giacomo, Eric could never know enough about orchids. While Tosca already possessed and took for granted things for which many men work all their lives and even then are not always able to give the women they love—the splendid homes, the furs, the cars, the pearls—women who, by the time such things are given them, have as a rule grown old.

The kitten deserted Giacomo before the yawning entrance of the shipping shed, which was crowded with onlookers watching the dancing and listening to the drumlike clatter of hundreds of feet on the cement floor and the clamor of accordions and violins under the corrugated iron roof. The vast shed was strung with colored lights and the inevitable colored ribbons, and in one of the green delivery trucks the orchestra sat and played like madmen, sitting on the floor of the open truck with their legs swinging over the side in time to the loud, fast music. The metal cavern thundered with sound.

From the loft of the warehouse next door came the steady roar of happy treble screaming. *Mickey Mouse* and other juvenile movies were being shown there to the children.

The loudness hurt Giacomo's ears as he made his way into the crowded shed, but it had to be loud to be heard by two thousand people. The cement floor was covered with couples young and old, dancing the newest steps and occasionally, when the music changed, breaking into an Italian folk dance. The older couples danced these with remembered gusto, while the younger couples, especially those of Latin origin, tried to follow the steps with little certainty but much gaiety. Cesare, his chef's hat askew over his immense flaming face, shouted directions as he danced with the wife of a rose grower.

The dance floor brought into sharp focus the friendly spirit—so unique it might be termed the California spirit—that linked the flower people. The festa made one immense family circle of Giacomo's friends. Giacomo smiled to see the little apprentice, Laddie, frowning with concentration as he led the wife of one of the fire chiefs around the dance floor. Dancing, Giacomo felt, was part of the privilege and expression of life, and it was wrong not to take advantage of that privilege when one was Laddie's age.

"I am too old," Giacomo answered, smiling roguishly at the offers to join in the dancing as he made his slow and friendly progress around the great room. "Or the music, maybe, she is too young."

46

And to himself he hoped for a waltz when Tosca came. Had he not—long ago, to be sure—won small silver cups for his waltzing?

He made his way to the walls. Against one side of the shed had been placed the long heavy packing tables upon which, on other days, the flowers were packed for shipment, and on them now were casks of white and red wines, and beer, and crates of soft drinks, flanked by snowy drifts of paper cups. Stoob had taken up his position by a keg of beer and was standing, cup in hand, looking with contempt at the dancers. In the packing shed nearby a bar for stronger drink had been installed, and the shouting and singing coming from the place sounded more loudly each time the music paused. Still, despite the tremendous amount of liquor, Giacomo knew there would be little or no drunkenness at his festa. The flower people in the main stemmed from temperate stock to whom liquor had been for generations a source of relaxation and sociability, not one of stupefaction.

His happiness grew because he saw so many who were happy, and he spent some time gallantly perched on one of the shelves along the wall where the older women had found seats from which to watch the dancing. He found a gay, kind word for each. Among them were so many, black-clad, thick of waist, bright-eyed, who had been young with him. The years! What they do to us! he thought, recognizing in a shrunken black pudding of a great-grandmother the once glamorous Caterina Anducchi, who had been the liveliest beauty of the Italian colony on Telegraph Hill half a century before.

Was she remembering, looking up and smiling the soft-mouthed smile that made her suddenly lovely, a flashing-eyed, black-haired giant whose capacity for work and play had made him a legend in their pre-turn-of-the-century San Francisco? Giacomo remembered how he had worked the days and nights through in those years and still been as zestful for festas and celebrations as any, once the work rush was over.

Ah, that was why he took joy in the festas; they were for the strong and young. Like Eric, like Tosca, and how he wished they would hurry, not to miss any of this fine celebration! The iron shed with its colored lights and ribbons seemed to grow brighter as the skies, seen through the open doors, darkened and blended at last with the sea.

Levenridge and Marie drifted past to the music, and Levenridge moved stiffly but with apparent enjoyment, while Marie seemed as carefree as any girl. Giacomo smiled and waved, but all the time he kept watch on the yawning doorway where at any moment Tosca and Eric would appear.

He saw Laddie pausing by the soft-drink stand after his gallant efforts on the floor, and he went to him and put a gentle hand on the boy's arm.

"Laddie, when you have finished your drink, could you find time to switch on the lights in the glasshouses, perhaps?"

They should glow like festive lanterns on a night like this, he thought, watching the boy dash away proudly on his assignment, and, turning, he saw Ludmilla standing in the shadow of the truck that held the musicians, her pale eyes fixed on him in a curious way.

"You are not dancing, Ludmilla," he asked, for he took particular pains to be kind to her. And when she did not answer, he added gently, "Eric will be here soon. You will dance then."

He was aware that Eric disliked Stoob to an unreasonable degree but, like Giacomo, he was always kind to Stoob's daughter.

"Where is Tosca?" she asked suddenly.

"She is with Eric." He frowned. "Ludmilla, please, would you find them and tell them to hurry? It is not right to have them stay away so long."

She looked at him in a suspicious way and then moved swiftly across the crowded floor and out of the shed.

Dusk had cast a silvery grayness over Colma. The girl made her way between the glasshouses, running lightly as she neared Paul's house. She almost ran into Eric, who was standing near the compost and scowling, as if he had some reason to be annoyed by the heaps of rich refuse. Laddie ran past. "Giacomo told me to light all the houses," he called in an important treble, and the glass phalanx broke into long straight rows of bluish light, revealing in clearer beauty than before the long banks of Daneri flowers. She saw Eric in the brightness, and he looked very handsome, she thought, neatly dressed and combed and in the dark blue suit, then she saw him bend down and scoop up a palmful of dark earth. He sniffed it, slowly and with appreciation. She did not understand the look on his face, but she knew that particular mound, dark, rich, crumbling from centuries in the northern forests, brought down from Oregon to service with new fecundity Giacomo's land; and sympathy for Eric and what he was thinking

48

rose in the girl's thin throat and choked her, so well, so very well, she knew.

She came, soft-footed, to his side.

"You love that, don't you?" she asked gently.

Eric laughed shortly. "Fertilizer?"

"The earth smell. I love it too."

He dropped the earth and sheepishly brushed his hands.

"You can smell the redwood in it," he said.

A plain white handkerchief was in the breast pocket of her plain blue linen dress. She offered it to him.

"Better use this. Tosca won't dance with you if you have dirt on your hands."

"I don't think she will object," he said coldly, but he accepted the handkerchief.

Then he took Ludmilla's arm, not in the familiar way he treated Tosca, but awkwardly, and they turned toward the shipping shed and the music. Eric had known Ludmilla nearly all her life, as he had Tosca, but he was always a little ill at ease with Stoob's daughter. For one thing, the paleness of her skin and hair made her seem dangerously frail, but still her hands were strong and dark, almost like a man's, and she worked with her father among the lilies almost as capably as Stoob. She was rather like one of the lilies, Eric thought—glancing a little furtively as they walked along at her white-gold hair—like a lily of the valley. City-bred, the girl Ludmilla might never have reached maturity. The healthy life of the Colma nursery had given her endurance, and she was far stronger than she seemed.

"I've noticed something," Eric remarked, looking down into Ludmilla's eyes. They were almost startling, for they were a marvelous shade of pale blue, and Eric, in spite of his accurate hybridist's color sense, had only realized at that moment they were of an extraordinary shade of blue that is occasionally, but very rarely, found in the floral world.

"What do you know!" he exclaimed. "Your eyes are the exact shade of wolfsbane."

"I don't think I like that," she began, torn between doubt and the impulse to be pleased, for it was seldom that anyone noticed Ludmilla.

"Well, I like it," Eric said emphatically. "It's a beautiful color, and very rare."

"Then I like it!" said Ludmilla with unexpected emphasis, and smiled, and as with so many who are not given to happiness, hers seemed all the sweeter to Eric because he realized how rarely he had seen Ludmilla smile. A protective impulse came over him, born of pity for this quiet girl and of resentment against Stoob, who had taken advantage of his wife's death to make a drudge and confidante of the daughter left to him.

They were walking more easily now toward the clamor of music and singing and the happy hysteria of children, and she gained enough courage to raise her voice and hold him back a moment.

"Eric, why weren't you at the table?"

"I was in the seedling shed. The first of the new Aurea cross came out today. We've hidden it. Gosh, it's a beauty."

He added thoughtlessly, "He's naming it for Tosca."

The pale eyes narrowed with interest. Ludmilla, too, knew every plant on the place. Had she not been born on Daneri land?

"Can I see it, Eric? Now?"

He was both pleased and resentful, for she was showing more eagerness than Tosca had for an orchid named in her honor; then he was listening to the sound of a car screaming above the other noises as it plunged out of the nursery lane and down the hill toward the highway that led to San Francisco. Only one person they knew drove so wildly.

"Come along," he said between his teeth.

But when they came to the doorway of the clamorous shipping shed and looked about them, Eric shrugged his shoulders and his look was bleak.

"I don't think I'll go in just yet."

Her thin face went taut with hurt.

"You won't dance at all, Eric?"

"Later, maybe."

But she knew he would not be back. And she knew why.

They both had seen that Giacomo Daneri, towering among his two thousand guests, was like a man alone; that the festa he had designed to give happiness to Tosca lay about him in ashes. Eric scowled as he strode away from the shipping shed.

By the sorrow on Giacomo's lined face Eric knew that Tosca, who had been so wild to leave, so driven by that unknown flame —Tosca had gone.

$\mathcal{S}$HE drove as if the incubus of guilt clawed her shoulders. The low car devoured the ocean highway and the sky line and streets of the city, roiling with lights over its darkened hills, and dragged to a screeching stop halfway over the curb before an unlighted white house like an Italian villa, on the crest of the Presidio hill.

The Levenridge mansion might have been built for a de' Medici. Its marble portico and gleaming triple stories looked over half of San Francisco and beyond, to the curved lines of light that were the other bay cities, Sausalito, Berkeley, and Oakland, circling the dark sweep that was San Francisco Bay. Sketched in points of light on the water were smaller patterns that were mercantile and passenger vessels lying alongside the lighted wharves, and other moving patterns were ferryboats plying the black water pathways of the bay.

The two bridges newly spanning the bay thrust four fingers of light through the night. One bridge was incomplete.

The door of the great house was Florentine. Tosca unlocked it and thrust her body's weight against the heavy bronze. It opened and she slipped into an unlighted hall, letting the door fall to of its own weight.

She was alone in the house. For a moment she stood in the dark, sensing about her the great hallway and the rooms empty of life. She was accustomed to that emptiness and to the darkness. By day most of the rooms in this house were shuttered; by night, unlighted.

With a sudden impulsive movement she ran her gloved hand down the row of buttons beside the door. Branched chandeliers sprang into life for three stories above her, revealing the rose and white shell of the drawing room on her left and the shining beauty of the marble staircase curving down through the immense heart of the house. The staircase had graced a ducal palace in western Italy, where Giacomo's father had served as gardener.

Giacomo had brought it in sections to this country and this house, that Tosca might walk down it as a hostess, as a bride. And still her first formal appearance had been made in one of the large hotels, and any entertaining by Tosca or her parents took place in restaurants or hotels or one of the clubs Vincent Levenridge still belonged to, in spite of their reduced standards of living.

To do him justice, Tosca's father had not wanted such a conspicuous home. Marie had been disturbed by the offer of such a costly gift. They had yielded to Giacomo's insistence for the sake of the growing Tosca and for Paul, who had made his home with them when in San Francisco. So the house was built in the boom years, when so many others were building palatial edifices, some of which would never be occupied. And because it had been built of profits made from Daneri flowers, the Levenridge mansion was referred to by their neighbors on the Presidio hill as "the house built of orchids."

The crash of '29 left Tosca's father aware of the futility of trying to maintain such a house on his diminished salary and savings, both of which showed symptoms of vanishing completely. He had tried repeatedly to sell the house on the hill. But it had become overnight a "white elephant," along with thousands of other houses in the stricken city, that no one could afford to maintain, and certainly not to buy. Giacomo was having his own struggle trying to keep the nursery solvent. Levenridge completed plans to have the by this time hopelessly mortgaged house wrecked and the marble interior sold, with the intention that a corporation should build an apartment house on the land if times ever became better. Giacomo learned of Vincent's plan and paid a visit to his old friend, the president of the bank.

It was common knowledge on the hill that the family of the haughty and reserved Vincent Levenridge continued to occupy their villa-like home through the courtesy of the bank, owing to the influence of Giacomo. There was no disgrace involved. Too many other San Franciscans were occupying homes they could not afford and could not sell, and were fighting in the privacy of these homes to conserve food, lights, clothing, and the appearance of human dignity in this shocking new struggle to survive.

No blame was laid on poverty since '29. Men and women had seen their life savings wiped away through no fault of their own. Stronger forces than thrift and moderation and faith in one's own capacity for survival had brought them to failure, and in so swift a space in time.

Even without servants and with many of the rooms shut away —the rooms Paul had occupied on the third floor, with their commanding view of the Golden Gate, were never opened—the house was too heavy a burden for a man like Levenridge who was trying to find his way back along with the majority of the nation's population.

The house Tosca had entered was less a home than a vast, empty shell of a building, beautiful and chaste, as a museum of particular beauty might be when the doors are closed to visitors and the rooms with all their lovely objects are unseen.

Vincent and Marie lived in as little of the house as was possible, and as economically as they could.

Only Tosca continued to run free and untroubled through the house built of orchids. She was not often home. She had many interests. She had her own generous allowance, settled on her by Giacomo, and the car he had given her. All might have seemed as before in the great house, only Paul was gone.

This Tosca remembered, flicking on the rows of branching lights as if in a frenzy to have the cavernous place come alight and alive.

The clatter of her spike heels drummed against emptiness as she ran up the stairs.

Tosca's room, outlined with many windows, looked down over the darkly forested mass that was the Presidio to the dark incurve of hills divided by the Golden Gate. Its walls were a deep Mediterranean blue with white scrolls outlining mirrors, windows, and doors. The furniture had been brought from France; it was of a simplified modern design painted an eggshell white.

The same frantic haste that had brought Tosca from Giacomo's festa drove her from bath to dressing table, from wardrobe to the mirrored dressing room, completing her dressing for the evening in an incredibly short time. Rather one might call it a form of undressing, for when she paused at last before the glass pages of the mirror, dashing French perfume on her finger tips and running it through the sleek hair brushed close to her head, she saw herself in tawny satin and tulle of the warm shade called nude, which showed every subtle line and under which, any observer would have sworn, not another scrap of material was worn. This was untrue, and she turned anxiously, surveying herself in tripli-

53

cate for any slight fold that might reveal the presence of the bra made of a hair breadth of the same satin, and the brief scanties made of a scrap of the same and a handful of blond lace. The dress rose deceitfully high at the throat, but the rear view registered apparent nudity, for the back of the dress was cut to the waistline. Shoulders and arms were bare; bare, too, were the tanned, well-powdered legs, and her bare feet were thrust into slender satin slippers made of the same satin as the dress.

Frowning, she decided the shade of the satin was pleasing to her sun-warmed skin, and almost frantically she considered she looked well. She threw a light cape made of gold sequins over her shoulders and at the same feverish tempo ran down the stairs, forgetting as she always did her parents' admonishments to please turn out the wasteful lights; she left the house ablaze.

Again she drove as if her need for flight raced ahead of the car, down slanted streets and along the curved roads of the park to the highway, where a white rib of sand curved palely along the darkness that was the sea. For the second time that day she swung southward, with screaming tires, into the ocean drive and dragged the car to a stop several miles below before a low-roofed, rambling building lying concealed and dark in a grove of cypress. The building was apparently closed, but streaks of light stabbed the drawn blinds; and the presence of dark shapes that were parked cars under the trees and the clamor of music and high-pitched voices within betrayed the progress of a large party going on inside the building.

Evidently a buzzer had signaled her flying entry through the gate, for the spurt of a flashlight revealed a uniformed attendant at her door. Tosca yielded the car to him, and she who had been in such panic haste to come to this place mounted the low flight of unlighted steps as if heavy weights dragged at the naked knees under the satin sheath. She had heard this could happen but not that it could happen to one who had been trained to walk with proud assurance. She stood before the dark door unable to lift her hand to hunt the bell, but the door opened and a waiter ushered her hurriedly inside.

"Mr. Cantrell's table." She could not raise her voice.

She found herself in a dark-beamed echoing bell of a place, smoke-filled, and lighted only by sparks of light cast by lamps concealed by the beams. A small orchestra drummed in one corner, tables were set in horseshoe formation around a dance floor and facing a mirrored bar, and several hundred women and men in evening clothes were dancing or drinking or dining or milling about the room, all, without exception, talking or shouting or singing, and at the top of their lungs.

A major-domo came forward.

"Good evening, Miss Levenridge."

He knew her, but where? she wondered. At the St. Francis perhaps, or one of the private clubs, for she had never before been in this place.

"The young lady is asking for a Mr. Cantrell's table," murmured the waiter, and, recognizing a situation outside his range of authority, he slipped away.

"But there are no private tables, Miss Levenridge. Mr. and Mrs. Ballinger are entertaining. We are closed to the public tonight."

The major-domo added without expression, "You may have made a mistake."

Dignity mattered, regardless of how the blood sent waves of humiliation through a body held stiffly erect.

"This is Bird's Nest?" she asked.

"Bird's Nest, yes. For the night, private . . ."

But Mark's arms were about her and Mark's laughing face close to her own, and at sight and sound of him the stiffness melted, the major-domo vanished, and this place and party were where she belonged and where she had longed to be. All that was newly recognized, all that was woman within her seemed to turn tremulous, to cave in and grow weak, and this weakness and all else she was knowing and feeling and thinking then were Mark's. She belonged to him as completely as if chains held her ankles and wrists to his own, as if the clothes he wore clothed her and his laughter came from her. Mark, flinging his arm carelessly about her waist, caught her to his personality, his mood, leaving no word or impulse left that was her own.

"Oh, Mark, you darling fool!" was all she could say. "I asked for your table. I thought this was your party."

"Mine! Where would I get money for a ruckus like this? It's wonderful; everybody's floating." Then, in complete refutation, "God, I'm glad you came. Things were getting so damn dull."

He was steering her across the floor between the noisy dancers, and his hands clasping her bare arms under the sequin cape were unbearably caressing.

"Imagine things going dull with you around," she gibed back over her shoulder, for the dread and the tension were gone, the incubus fallen, because Mark was close to her, because he held her, as it were, between his hands.

"There are two—let's grab them!" He wheeled her about to two bar stools a couple were deserting in favor of the dance floor. "You need liquid nourishment. The rest of us are way ahead."

Mark was well ahead, she could see. His eyes were hollowed, emphasizing the lean dramatic cast of a face that had seemed, since her first glimpse of him, to have a light on it always. The bony structure of his face was chiseled in so pure an outline, it was almost beautiful, but it avoided too great perfection by the laughing-faun look Mark nearly always wore. She had seen him so few times but felt she knew him better than anyone else could, and she had never seen him, and could not imagine him, without that air of splendid gaiety.

"The Ballingers!" she exclaimed, stopping against Mark before the bar.

"Who?"

"Our hosts. Hadn't we better . . ."

"Oh, those! Never mind them, they're around someplace." And he slid her masterfully onto the high stool and took his own place, and they were crushed together instantly by the drinkers who crowded around them four-deep, and there were voices calling, "Mark! Mark darling," and, "Sit over here, old boy . . ."

But he smiled and turned his back to them all, so that instantly she was sealed in with Mark in a small secret place he had made.

It was the first time she had sat at a bar. Bars for women were new and had come in with legal drinking, and she felt awkward and out of place on the cushioned stool and would have been ill at ease with Mark's noisy friends had Mark not been there. But he could bring grace out of absurdity, and when he said, "You're so far behind the rest of us, I'll order doubles and string along with you," his order seemed to bring the entire situation into balance. It seemed natural to be sitting with Mark, each with a glass at either hand, and to feel alone with him in spite of the men with their black ties askew and eyes staring and the women falling against them and screaming, "Mark, dance with me—you promised!" But he shook his head to their offers, gaily, without turning their way. And she knew that in his mind, as in hers, they were complete in their solitude.

56

She knew this, because she knew Mark as she knew herself. And still she had told Eric the truth, Mark was virtually a stranger. She had met him for the first time at Chuck Alison's party the week before and in that first moment had felt she had known him always.

"Here's someone you should meet, Tosca," Chuck had shouted in his breezy way. "You're too formal and Mark's crazy . . ."

And when they had stood facing each other with plates of cold cuts in their hands, "Are you really crazy?" she had asked, drawn by his careless good looks, the droll and sensitive smile, and the answer had been pat, as if rehearsed, "Crazy for you—from now on." And it had been that way from that moment.

They had met in the half world of drink and smoke and music that lies between reality and dreaming. Now, as then, to be close to Mark, to watch the flash of lights over mirror and glasses and glossy heads, to listen to the drumming of dance steps and orchestra and the sound of his voice speaking, this sense of illusion and languor, out of all the experiences that had gone before, this only was real.

"I'm sorry I'm so late," she said, speaking loudly, for one had to. "The traffic was awful along the highway."

"You're not late. You're just in time."

And his hand slid down her bare shoulder in an apparently careless gesture, but palm spoke to satin skin like a radioed call, and she could only wonder, weak with longing, why the slightest touch of his hand brought such weakness, and what if he should kiss her here, in this crowded place?

And she sat under the light, careless weight of his hand as if it held her powerless.

This she had yearned for since womanhood began. She was matured and fully woman, and he was the first man to bring that fact to realization. Of all the men she had danced with, flirted with, half loved, kissed, he was the first to win the recognition of her womanhood. And, yielding to him, she knew even then that these were curious times and strange conditions under which to come alive.

"Hi, chum," he said gently, and again the signal was secret and electric and said everything.

"Hi," she answered, lost to Mark and the moment now, being close to him and the world lost.

The world would not stay lost. Never had she been pressed

about by such a broken kaleidoscope of color and sound, certainly not at the League affairs, or the St. Francis or Palace, or any of the places she had known. Warm bodies, the women's half clad, pressed to theirs, faces as friendly as puppies and somehow familiar, came closer, and the loud cries of welcome kept on. "You got here, Tosca. We thought you couldn't make it." "Tosca's grandpappy was giving a barn dance down on the farm," Mark explained. "But she made it! Didn't you?" And his eyes slanted their special message over the glass. "I made it!" she echoed, and tried to keep the words from shaking with happiness. It seemed a proud matter that Mark and his friends knew that coming to this party had been a difficult achievement, but no obligation or sense of love or duty could have kept her away.

The tables were being cleared of one course and set for another. "Are you hungry?" Mark asked, but she shook her head. It was obvious he was not interested in food, and she could not have touched a bite after Giacomo's festa. For the time it was enough to be with Mark, surrounded by friends, for these were all Mark's friends who kept falling against them and interrupting.

"You'll have to catch up," Mark scolded. "You're gallons behind."

He pressed the cold rim of the glass between her lips; it was an act of tenderness. The drink was sharp with gin and tore her throat, unlike the mellow wines and brandies of Giacomo's festa. Almost instantly its effect struck like a blow behind the eyes, leaving her vision uncertain and her lips seemingly thickened. She felt confused and a little numb.

"Let yourself go," he was saying gently. "I'm here."

She was mute with love. She bent her head over the glass, and he watched the broken colors of the spinning lights break like small colored wings on the highlights of her smooth hair.

"What have you been doing all day without me?" he asked softly. "How was the barn dance?"

"It wasn't a—— Don't be silly. It's a picnic for the flower growers my grandfather gives every year."

"Well, my mother mixes around with roses. Why wasn't I invited?"

"You're not a professional grower. This was just for the trade." Then, quickly, "Oh, that's not true! Lots of people come who don't have anything to do with flowers."

"Then why . . ."

"I didn't think you'd have fun there," she said lamely.

"I have fun anywhere."

"Without me?" It was a daring thing to ask.

"You were without me. Wasn't the picnic fun?"

"It was wonderful," she said. It wasn't wonderful, she thought. It was awful, wondering all the time where Mark was, and knowing that wherever he might be, whomever he was with, he was having a wonderful time.

He had an elusive way of studying her, lids narrowed, so that she could never be certain whether his eyes were gray or brown; and his voice was low-pitched and resonant, so that it could be heard under the screams around them and draw any secret from her.

"Why didn't you want me there, Tosca?"

But she had to cling to this small fragment of pride a little longer.

"I came here, didn't I?" And she smiled impudently, or tried to smile.

"You're still not answering." Then, as she pressed the glass's rim between her teeth to avoid speaking, he chuckled softly. "All right, tell me when you're ready. I shan't press you." He signaled the bartender cheerfully. "I never ask anyone to do what they don't want to do," he added lazily, and the idea seemed to amuse him in some secret way.

But she was filled with gratefulness and yearning because he had not pried her secret from her at the very moment he must have known she was ready to yield.

She could not bear to tell anyone, Mark least of all, why she had not asked him to the festa. She had always accepted without question what had been given her. But Mark Cantrell was her first discovery, and finding him was the first independent act of her life. And because he was her primary venture into reality, she wanted to keep the exquisite secret that was Mark to herself until the situation was exact and she could bring him before Giacomo with all the information necessary to such a moment. She could not submit Mark to that questioning kindness until she was sure.

For the first time she dreaded that searching look of Giacomo's —his microscope look, she called it.

Since she could not say to Mark, "You are certain you want me?" she could not explain to him why he had not been invited to the picnic at Colma.

And it was this she had not been able to tell Giacomo. She had not been able to face him, after the talk with Eric, and explain that she was leaving the festa, and why. She could not bear to think of having hurt him, and, remembering this, the wildly lost look that Giacomo had seen and feared at his table in the Drive crossed her clear young face.

Mark noticed. He was watching her over the glasses that had been filled again, as if her face were a book that delighted and amused.

"Little wild wahine," he whispered tenderly.

"What's a wahine?" She spoke with care now, separating her words.

"A woman. In Hawaiian."

Thoughts spun jealousy.

"You liked Hawaii, didn't you?"

"You would love Hawaii," he countered. "You and I could have fun in Hawaii."

She loved the way his slender fingers strummed the bar in hula rhythm, and rhythm was in the graceful bones of his hands and his moving shoulders, and even his feet on the rail below shuffled with melody. He was all music, she thought; he was everything the moment could hold, and he let it flow through his bones. And when he said, "C'mon, let's dance," his reckless and restless mood swept her joyously to the floor. The room had darkened; the broken colored light spokes wheeled from the rafters over the slow-moving and suddenly silent dancers, moving ever more slowly to the slow-paced drumming of a beguine. A sensuous awareness was in the room, in the rhythm of the bodies and the music, in the colored light flakes moving over the gleaming backs of the women.

"You're tight!" said Mark, his look drinking her in, and he chuckled low and deep to the music.

"I know," she whispered, radiant with him. "I like me that way."

"I like you that way too. Let's stay this way forever . . ."

". . . ever and ever . . ."

This was solemn and beautiful, with the others gone and reality with them, and it seemed in logical sequence that they should now be two at a table where one fluttering candlebeam took them in and held them.

In this small oasis of light glasses appeared, brimming with the strong white drinks, and over them Mark's face was blurred and beautiful, and a memory burst into the mood, and she heard her own voice breaking through the music.

"Mark, what were you doing in Hawaii?"

He grinned lazily over his glass.

"What is this—confessional?"

"I've told you everything. Or almost. And you never told me what you were doing in Hawaii."

"I just happened to be there." For a moment the look of amusement left his face and he looked almost tired. "I was on my way around the world, and Mother put a stop to my travels. Rather, the crash did. The folks were just about wiped out, and she wanted me home."

"She?"

"Mother, of course." He chuckled with sudden amusement. "But I stayed on and rode out the depression on a surfboard."

"You worked there?"

"I was a beach boy."

"A beach boy!" She recalled with shock the giggling confidences of schoolmates who had visited the Islands. "You mean you were a gigolo?"

"Hey, that's not a nice word! A beach boy isn't a gigolo. At least he doesn't have to be one unless he wants to. He's just a fellow who likes to swim and lie out on the sand."

"But how did you live?"

"Oh, there were still some rich women left in the world, even in '29."

He was teasing now, and she stared at him doubtfully.

"But you liked it there," she said.

He nodded, and she tried to keep the ache from her voice.

"What if you hadn't come back? If we'd never met?"

His hand went over hers in sensuous understanding.

"You would have met someone else."

"And you?"

His answer was to lift her hand and kiss it in an amused and gentle fashion, and the gesture was in recognition of the way every part of her body seemed to cry out, begging for reassurance.

This evasion on Mark's part had baffled and drawn her from the beginning, so well did she know what had given birth to it and how powerful a weapon it could be to such as they. The hair-breadth discrepancies in understanding only served to make their

61

sense of belonging more complete. This recognition between them had been apparent from the beginning, and it had been no surprise to learn their lives had paralleled in many ways.

Like Tosca, Mark had reached maturity with the concept of the times: everyone, or almost everyone, they knew had everything that could possibly be wanted in a material way. Mark's early-Californian family had made their money in the silver rush of the 1860s, and, like Tosca's family, his mother still lived in the old-fashioned towered mansion at Atherton she could not afford to maintain properly, set in gardens neglected, as so many estate grounds were because there were no gardeners now to keep them in order. Mark hated the place and shared an apartment on Sutter Street with several other men who were also sons of once-wealthy families, living on small allowances. Like Tosca, he was a victim of the depression, of the revoking of a security that was to last forever, and she loved him because, having so little left, he had managed to wrest happiness out of this fall from luxury to penury and was capable of such splendid excitement and appreciation for all that remained. This she reverenced because she had shared the tragedy of Paul, who had given up forever; and if this splendid capacity for staying alive included of necessity the evasion of all responsibility, this, too, she could understand. For had she not learned—like Mark and all this faunlike crew—the futility of responsibility? So she was thinking: If Mark had been a beach boy, a gigolo even (and I know he was not), I would understand why he needed to be these things; I would forgive Mark as he will always be forgiven.

The decision left her inexpressibly happy, so that she lifted her head and looked about into the spinning, spark-whirling darkness, and recognizing in the moving shadows the last of the courageous, the fighters against regret and death and madness that had overtaken those who looked back to what had been or might have been, for the first time she knew with passionate loyalty that these were her people and she belonged with Mark and with them. The human maze was right for this place and this night and this year, after all that had gone before and must be forgotten. The women, stripped as Tosca was stripped, bare of arms and throats and backs, were expressing the trend of nudity and the contact time between changes too tremendous to be recognized. This was no time to be burdened with regret for what had happened or might happen; it was no time to be burdened with many things, among them, excess clothing. And the women, chameleons of trend, revealed the universal need to lay bare all that remained, as if to say, "So much has been taken—take all. See us as we are." So in this curious time of melding between the lost time and the new, one heard of formal dinners in the city and down the peninsula, where unclad men and women were served by discreet maids and butlers with a mad and proper dignity. And there were communities in the Sierra and the Coast Range where nudists vacationed in an ecstasy of exposure that resembled a new and curious religion.

She knew, looking at Mark and beyond him to the dancers, that to understand one had to be one with this city and this year. This was the younger San Francisco crowd, society and pseudo, that was fast becoming known as the drinking crowd now that prohibition was over. Some had lost everything, and others had nothing to lose. During the long drought, while they were growing up, they had learned to knock on speak-easy doors, to call bootleggers by their first names, to carry cards or murmur, "Joe sent me." But now liquor could be served openly, the first real liquor many of them had tasted, and they were not certain how it could be made part of their lives again or how they should behave. Many of them showed an almost hysterical need to drink too much, and too rapidly, as if to make up for the lost time. But all had this in common—they would try anything once. And the dominant talk was of drinks and the mixing of drinks and the proper glassware to be used, and a feud started at the bar, dividing the choice between stemmed glasses or thin for champagne. Someone shouted, "Ice in champagne? You're crazy!" And, "The Prince of Wales puts ice in his," a woman countered shrilly, for after the long following of the liquor that had run underground, it seemed there was little knowledge left concerning such things, or in the measured intake that makes for sobriety.

The guests of Giacomo had not drunk with such desperation, as if their happiness depended on their drinking.

And Tosca, watching the dancers with her hand in Mark's, wondered if her close association with Giacomo had made her more thoughtful than these who were of her own generation, and many of them older.

Under Giacomo's glass roofs had been the hard-working and responsible. Under these dancing lights were the innocent and elfin children of a many-faceted city struggling to recover from economic tragedy, and replacing sanity with foibles and madness because sanity had failed them. Here was the end of wisdom, and the terrifying need tore her to remain with them, she and Mark with them always.

They had wrung this wisdom out of violation and despair. The shock of depression had struck San Francisco with particular violence because it had been from its beginnings a city given over to nonsense, gaiety, a zest for poetry and music and laughter; it had been a city of many richnesses, material and aesthetic and spiritual, and its appetite for these things had made it feel the shock of deprivation most keenly; the depression had come as treason to an unsuspecting breed who had thought they owned the earth.

They had learned one lesson, these innocents: that anything can happen.

And now, open and aboveboard and on every hand, was the means for the refutation of reality. Winking from the glittering shelves of new bars were the means and the end, carrying with them no risk of raid or blindness or even death, such as the bootleg brews had held. The mirrored bars were the doorways to forgetfulness, and until stronger objectives came along, they must serve.

And this, she knew, was wisdom. For the time. For the year.

Oh, what did they know of her, Giacomo and her father and mother and even Eric, who, being nearer her own age, might be expected to understand! Untroubled and carefree they thought her, shielded like a butterfly whose wings have been kept iridescent through the storm. What could they know of the anxieties that had torn her and the way her young faith had broken under the weight of their grief? They thought they had kept sorrow hidden from Tosca, their darling, but she had felt it in their voices and read it on their unmoving lips. Giacomo, the serene and stout of heart, had she not heard his voice break at mention of Paul? She had watched her father growing grayer and colder over the endless lines of figures that outlined the shape of his shattered world. She had seen her mother's eyes darken with continual grieving. They thought her too well protected, too heart-free, to know. But she had known, she had cared, and Mark was the solution of this dark and lonely questioning. Mark, studying her through candlelight, was proof of lightness and laughter, that a small bright nucleus of candlelight could hold them together in the heart of Mark's wonderful, noisy, joyous world.

There was almost a mysterious exaltation in being with Mark and the others. They were the understanding. These were the wise.

She did not like Roscoe, however. She had not known she did not like him and in fact could not recall having seen him before. But she knew he lived in the apartment with Mark and she distrusted him for this and for the way his piggy-pink features thrust through the candlelight between them and spread and pinkened in a threatening way.

"Hey, what's wrong with you two? You oughta mix. You're crabbing the whole works. Why don'cha mix?"

"Good old Roscoe," Mark said lazily. "Tosca, Roscoe is my best friend."

My enemy, thought Tosca, noting with unexpected clarity the pointed pink features.

"It's no fun with you hiding out." Roscoe ignored Tosca. "You're crabbing the whole works, Mark."

"Better mix," Mark agreed amiably, and caught her suddenly onto the dance floor so that they came together in a split second of timing in the music. "We'll mix, all right," and he spun her to another couple and caught a black-tulle-clad girl in exchange, and Tosca was dancing with a stranger and Mark was gone from her and, black and white and graceful, he had become the center and motif of a game that was taking place on the dance floor, involving a frantic mixing and exchange of partners and dance steps to the staccato beating of "Shuffle Off to Buffalo." She was spun from partner to partner and then she was dancing with Roscoe, who was holding her with her face clipped to his porcine jaw. "Too tight?" he grunted, and "Too tight!" he hiccuped. "Mustn't hold Mark's girl too tight." She hated Roscoe by this time, but his words were beautiful and she saw Mark spinning a hundred dancers in the whirlpool of hilarious nonsense he had created, and she did not mind because now she had it on the authority of Mark's best friend that she was Mark's girl.

It was all wonderful then, with Mark as the center, Mark dancing the hula with a garland of napkins caught in his cummerbund, Mark coming back to her a dozen times as if they were about to leave, and "Now," her heart hammered, to be leaving and alone with him, but his friends surrounded them and swept them different ways, and the mad nonsense rose to a high thin note of ecstasy too keen for some to bear. Men slumped in chairs, asleep, women staggered to dressing rooms and stayed there, conversations clotted around the bar and were repeated like broken records over and over. A woman of dowager aspect sat perilously on a bar stool and groped deeply in her black-lace-draped bosom. "Somebody copped my hankie," she kept repeating peevishly. Couples fell back into shadows, locked in silence. Mark was back; his hands and the look of love, of gay deep understanding, came out to her, but again they were broken apart and surrounded by friends who stretched out in drunken parading to the chant of "The Old Gray Mare." She pushed to the head of one column and Mark to the other, and they marched through the lightening cypress grove and over the damp gray highway and onto the lapping, wet-lipped rim of the Pacific. The first signals of morning flashed far above them and far away, from the windows of the Cliff House, and, "Look," someone screamed, "it's morning," and someone else remembered, "Say, it's Monday. I better get started to the office," and Mark made a speech, standing on a spile driven in the sand, demanding that the government put an end to all offices and work of every kind—Mark with the last of the moon on his face, primordial and beautiful, she thought him, a creature of another time and world, as if the tips of a faun's horns showed in the wind-ruffled hair.

"Santa Cruz?" someone was saying, and someone else, "Yes, Santa Cruz for waffles," and why, when so many other cars were leaving the cypress grove, did there have to be so many people in her car, with Mark driving, with cars racing before and after, down the curved highway? "To Santa Cruz!" Roscoe was bellowing, his porcine head thrust between theirs as he lurched from his place on the folded top. "Santa Cruz for Merry England!" "I'm going to tell him what I want for Christmas," shrilled the girl in black tulle. "Who?" "Santa Cruz . . ."

They were driving too fast, too fast, but she was close to Mark and her brain screamed with a long note of excited music and it did not matter, and then they met the trucks—and what if they died together, and wasn't it all part of the exaltation and the glory?—the bottle-green burdened trucks speeding up the highway from Colma.

"Dodge!" yelled Roscoe, and the roadster shot between the trucks, and "Mark, please," she was screaming, but strangely thrilled by the expression of high, mad joy on his face, and over her screaming came closer and louder the shrilling of a siren and she saw clearly the motorcycle and the unsmiling, impersonal face under pushed-up goggles and the weary "See here, why don't you folks go home?"

Then she was alone with Mark and they were driving quite sedately over Twin Peaks. "Might as well go home," Mark had said gaily. "Always another night coming." She had been grateful, and on the crest of the pointed hill, caught for a moment between the city and the sky, she looked down over the wakening city surrounded on three sides by water, and the beauty of the city swept her with sadness.

"Mark, those were my grandfather's trucks," she said in a small voice.

"You're crying," he said softly, and he did not look at her, nor did he ask why.

And she could not explain the grief she had felt when she recognized Giacomo's trucks in the dawn, hurrying into San Francisco with the tons of his newly cut flowers. Seeing them, she had remembered Giacomo, the patience and love of Giacomo and the grief she had given, and sorrow had poured over her like an attack of illness.

Mark did not question her, and his silence revealed his understanding. He was sober, and his clear-cut profile—or did she imagine it?—seemed like a tragic mask for a moment against the clearing sky before the car tilted over the steep grade and down into the city.

The silence held communion, and they did not speak again until he drew the car up before the Levenridge home.

The lights had been turned off in the silent house, and the hall was lighted by a small alabaster lamp. They stood close, reluctant to separate, and he put his hands under her arms and held her as if she were precious material. The look of seriousness and longing, studying her face, her mouth, was too much for her to bear. But he did not kiss her until she stood bewildered and tense between his hands, trapped by his withdrawal and his obvious desire.

Still he waited, and she sought some word to release them.

"The Ballingers!" she said, startled.

"Who?"

"Our hosts. Mark, we didn't even say good night to them!"

"How could we?" He chuckled. "I don't even know who they are."

"You mean . . ." She could not speak for a moment. "You mean you gate-crashed that party and invited me?"

"Don't be so uffish, sweet. The explanation is perfectly simple. We like parties, Roscoe and I and our crowd, and parties like us. We can't afford to give them any more, so we go along and give everyone else a good time. Who cares how many come to affairs like that! And you have to admit we helped bring the old Bird's Nest to life."

"And you asked me!" she continued, barely able to control her voice. But she had to admit it would have been merely a dull drinking party without Mark and his coterie.

When he did not answer, but took her close to him, she felt her understanding deepen and melt into slowly mounting desire. Still he held her, and she felt the last of her anger going under the warm pressure of his hands.

"I think——" she began helplessly.

"You think too much," he answered softly. "You weren't made for thinking."

Her eyes flickered under his.

"What am I made for?" she dared ask, and he answered more softly, "To be loved. Just for that."

He kissed her with deliberate slowness, almost with reluctance, and then drew his mouth and hands away. The smile was back on his face; it was beautiful with love and the tenderest understanding, but she saw it with the sense of being stirred and dissatisfied and bereft of him.

"I'll phone," he said.

"Tomorrow?" she tried to ask lightly.

"Can I help myself?" he countered a little bitterly. And then, with the familiar gaiety, "Around five."

She told him good night and saw the heavy door swing back, shutting away the faunlike grace of a man who seemed like a boy, the light that was always on his face, and the tormenting, tender smile. His kiss was still warm on her mouth. Weak with longing, she knew this was not enough.

$\mathcal{I}$N the villa-like house on the hill Tosca woke, oppressed by a dream of Paul. He was real to her still, the merry, adored young uncle who in this house had taught her to dance while he hummed or broke into song to their dancing. He held for Tosca, as he had for so many others, the glamour and passionate excitement of the boom years that had died with the suddenness of a quenched flame when stocks went down.

In her dream they were dancing, she in her first formal, the rose pleated chiffon floating about them as they moved over the drawing-room floor, Paul alive as only he had been able to be alive, and Tosca herself half woman and half child. Then Paul, singing to their steps, smiling down into her eyes with the gay teasing look she remembered, stumbled and fell, and she—laughing—looked down and saw him as she had seen him that last time, without the mark on the temple showing as he lay with the splendid dark head pressed into crumpled white satin and with Giacomo's orchids covering him with lavender and white wings; without the mark of the bullet showing at all. That first scar on a girl's memory—would it never heal? That had been '29, when so many were ruined, and Paul, whose fortune had been piling overhand, on paper, lost two and a half millions within the space of three hours one August morning. In her dream Tosca struggled with closed eyes against the headline:

"Playboy Paul Daneri Suicide!"

Then the note he had left, the one they did not know she had read, leafing her way through the sympathy messages on her mother's desk after the funeral, hunting the crumbs of words tossed after his memory. Paul's handwriting was beautifully strong and bold, in the blackest of inks. "Sorry I can't face it . . . die rather than be trapped in poverty and not able to live my way . . ."

At the time, brushing tears from her schoolgirl serge, hiding the letter again under the telegrams and letters, Tosca had been passionately certain she alone understood. Giacomo and her parents had never been able to understand Paul's violent end. There had been enough left, surely, even for a young man reared like a princeling! But Paul had been too proud to face mediocrity. His life had been eased from the start by his father, the Orchid King.

The five years since his death had not lessened Tosca's defense of him. It was a covenant she shared with Paul. It had given over secret areas of her heart to desolation and left her at times driven by the need to escape, to hide, from the dangers of loss—death—dissolution—all the evils she had faced when Paul left her to find her way without his sure and merry guidance into the darkness of the adult world.

This they had never known, Giacomo and the others. They had forgotten a schoolgirl's adoration for a young uncle who had epitomized for them all the wonder of the new and gloriously rich in those spendthrift and glamorous years. They thought she had forgotten the house blazing with lights and excitement, the wonderful gay people Paul gathered about him, the six Lincolns in the garage, the yacht and the speedboat on the bay, the quiet-voiced servants. Her mother had been serene and lovely in those days and Vincent calmly dignified, and Giacomo came often from the nursery to look in on the great friendly household with warm, enveloping tenderness. And the soul and nucleus of the great house and of them all had been Paul.

And the song Paul had been singing while they danced, when he fell—— Why, when the dream was over, could she never remember that song?

Taffeta comforter over her head, long limbs clenched, Tosca was sobbing.

"Tosca, dear one, you are crying!" Marie Levenridge swept the covers aside and held her daughter to her heart. In her rose wool robe, against the dark blue wall, Marie looked like a church statue.

"Tell me . . ." She was hovering and inarticulate as a mother bird. There were times when the wings smothered.

"Nothing, it is nothing at all!" Every defense in Tosca was fully awake. "I'm glad you woke me. It's time I was up."

She struggled against her mother's arms, and her look of panic changed to one wide-eyed and remote. There were things one could not tell. So she pushed the soft arms back, avoiding the stricken look of a woman who feels her love rebuffed.

70

"I'll bring you some breakfast," Marie said finally. "Hot coffee will make you feel better. You stay out so late."

There was reproach in her tone, and to avoid it Tosca looked drearily at the blue enameled French clock by her bed. Nearly eight o'clock . . . She had had three—or was it four?—hours' sleep. So short a time since Mark had kissed her and promised to phone. She had these to hold to through the long day to follow, and she wished desolately she had not dreamed, had not wakened, and could sleep through the hours until he called.

"I don't want you to bring up my breakfast," she said crossly. "Just because we can't afford help is no reason for you dragging trays upstairs."

"Now you are talking like your father," said Marie, sure of her ground. "If I like doing such things, what harm is there in my doing them?"

And she stretched her strong body that had been constructed to hold more flesh that she permitted to be there, because Vincent Levenridge liked her better that way.

"And I don't see why you can't go to sleep nights and not stay awake wondering why I don't come in!" Her mother had no way of knowing that Tosca's peevish words were a smoke screen thrown up to defend the memory of Paul from any criticism that might remain in the hearts of those he had left—even Marie's.

Marie, to hide her hurt, leaned over and picked up the dressing gown that had fallen to the floor and drew it over her daughter's shoulders. She asked quietly, "You were with Mr. Cantrell again?"

Tosca nodded. Marie's broad, soft features grew a little older. She had met Mark once, when Tosca brought him home for a cocktail before dinner. "I do not know him!" Marie had protested when Tosca, trying to seem unconcerned, had asked her opinion. Although she did not know Mark Cantrell or the world he lived in, there was something almost psychic in her distrust of him.

"I'll be down the minute I shower," Tosca promised, trying not to say in words, Leave me alone, go away, and she dragged the blue silk robe after her slapping high-heeled mules across the deep rugs and into the tiled bath. What a household, she thought, dropping the robe and chiffon nightdress and jerking a shower cap over the sun-tossed hair. Sometimes you had to hide in a shower to get away from those who wanted to hold you.

They had never been able to do that. Her mother had been

too unworldly, her father too preoccupied, to follow Tosca's dancing feet. Only Paul would have understood the Tosca and the Mark Cantrell who had been the first to return reality to her since Paul's death.

She turned the shower on full and spoke his name into it softly. Mark Cantrell.

The name stung her to wakefulness. The water rushed over golden shoulders and loins, and her strong tall body arched to meet the smiting cold. She turned it on fuller, colder, and lifted her face, with eyes closed, to the rush of the shower.

"Mark!" she whispered, and stretched her arms in icy ecstasy, and her flesh shrank with the cold and the memory of the exquisite provocative touch of Mark's hands.

A plump hand sparked with diamonds reached through the wet curtains and patted Tosca's shoulder. Instinctively she pulled back from the touch, as if Mark's hands were upon her still, separating her from those who had loved her before he came.

"Tosca!" her mother was calling. "Nonno wants you on the telephone. Something is wrong."

Giacomo was seldom vehement. Tosca, patting herself with an enveloping towel as she listened to her grandfather's message, found herself smiling at his intensity. She had feared the call might have something to do with her leaving his festa. His excitement cost him the clarity of his English, and some of his words were in the Italian she had never troubled to learn, although she could understand the gist of such speech.

"Tosca, the Aurea—she is *scomparire!*"

"Disappeared? How can it——"

"*Ma senti!* Let me tell you! The first cutting crew must have taken it with the first shipment. Tosca, it is not depollinized. If someone sees it——"

"Has it gone to market?"

"No, to Matraia's."

"Oh, that's worse." She had a clear and disturbing vision of the newest Daneri hybrid on display in Matraia's flower shop with its tiny sack of valuable pollen available to any sharp-eyed observer. And Matraia's would be thronged at this time of the morning with flower growers from the outlying nurseries.

"Can't Eric go?" she asked.

"Eric has gone to the airport. Please, Tosca——"

"I'll hurry, Giacomo." She was ashamed of the slight hesitation. "Don't worry about your hybrid."

She selected a small vial from the collection of perfumes on her dressing table, shook it free of scent, and washed it clean. She slipped this and a pair of tweezers into her purse and cast a critical glance through the wide windows. The bay looked coldly blue, so after writhing skillfully into a dark jersey dress she topped it with a light tweed coat.

"Breakfast!" Marie pushed open the door. She was beaming over a tray set with blue-and-yellow majolica. "See, was this such an effort? What did Nonno want?

"Why," she added in surprise, lowering the tray, "you're dressed!"

"Giacomo wants me," said Tosca, and seeing her mother's disappointment, she stopped halfway through the door to kiss her. Impulsively she kissed her again, remorseful of the morning's mood. "I'm sorry, Mama, but he's in trouble over the new hybrid —tell you later. I'll have breakfast at the nursery with him."

Marie said no more. Whatever was for the nursery was right. It was the ground that steadied all their steps. The wish to go with Tosca showed in her dark eyes, for the nursery was home to her as this great empty house could never be. She had grown to womanhood on the Colma land and left it to marry the energetic young Vincent Levenridge, then an accountant in the bank he know served as vice-president. She had realized without caring either way that his steady advancement in the bank had been due at least in part to the solid credit standing of his father-in-law. Vincent's successful dealings in the stock market, their sudden dizzying rise to wealth, and the equally swift descent to pinched standards of living had meant very little to the daughter of Giacomo Daneri.

Money that was not measured by its full quota of work could never impress a woman brought up on the land.

She had tried to fit herself to the luxury patterns set by the boom times. She knew Vincent had need of such things for the sake of his pride and his career. They were façade, and the edifice of wealth had vanished, but the façade must still be held between Marie and all she wished for most.

So when Tosca had gone she sank down on the peach satin chaise by the windows and her body went slack. *Ohime mi!* she thought wearily in the Genoese she never spoke aloud, and in that moment, despite the years of massage and careful grooming and the perpetual fight against the healthy flesh that strove to cover more comfortably her sturdy body structure, Marie looked all of her fifty years.

She had seen banks fall and stocks crash and men perish. The nursery remained. To every day of Giacomo's life he had given the full total of his strength, and all he had earned, frozen into the assets that were his orchids, was still Giacomo's own.

Nothing could change Marie's sense of permanency while Giacomo's orchids stood behind them all like a wall both colorful and strong.

But his daughter, born Maria Daneri, had no adequate work for her hands.

They lay in the lap of her woolen robe, large hands studded with several diamonds that never ceased to trouble her with their value. She did not care for jewels. They were part of the façade, and she wore them because they seemed safer on her hands than in the safe built into the wall behind the antique iron scrollwork of their bed in the largest of all the bedrooms. The broad gold wedding ring she had worn for nearly thirty years stood solidly against their platinum-bound magnificence, but she did not mind this difference.

Her hands ached for action; her body yearned for work the results of which could bring satisfaction. There was little to do in the immense house where so many rooms were kept shut. Her mind went to the upper floor where all was left as in Paul's life-time—the oil paintings, the bibelots, the treasures brought from his restless traveling around the world. Paul, who had so loved beauty . . . As she thought of him—and who among them did not think always of Paul, whose death still lay heavily upon them?—she heard Tosca's car back from the front of the house, where she had left it instead of putting it where it belonged in the garage, and, turning on protesting tires, tear recklessly down the steep hill.

"She drives too fast," worried Marie. "Tosca does everything so wildly."

And she looked stolid and defeated, sitting there, although she was neither of these things, for she was sharing the same deep fear Giacomo had felt for Tosca since he had found her, a small starry-eyed girl, walking the glass roof of the Drive under the lash

74

of Ludmilla's whispered dare, and he had known then, as Marie knew, she was like Paul.

And Marie wondered with anguish, as she had so often, was it because they had grown up unburdened, their lives eased and enchanted by the boundless love of Giacomo? Marie had been older than Paul, who had never known what she remembered—the earlier years of Giacomo's struggles to own and then develop the land. She had not forgotten the building of the first glasshouses, the putting dollar after dollar away against the mortgage, and the buying of the orchid plants, one by one in the beginning. Built into her being were the calculation and the building and the need for saving—not from the niggardly passion for saving, but because a judicious putting aside in no matter how small a degree was the sane and decent way to achieve dignity. But by the time Paul grew up Giacomo had been able to send him to an Eastern university, and later Paul had traveled and bought race horses and the yacht and at the time of his death had been negotiating the purchase of a plane. Paul had seemed more of Tosca's generation, the third of the Daneri in California.

Many of the third-generation Italo-Americans were like Tosca, slim and poised and at ease with modern living. But none of them, Marie knew, shared Tosca's capacity for splendid excitement. In that, again, was the resemblance to Paul.

Why? Marie wondered, and pushed her fingertips to her temples. "Don't frown!" the masseuse had warned. She felt contempt for the modern fear, not of growing old but of looking old. But Vincent was driven by this need for eternal youth. He explained that a youthful appearance was a necessity in a competitive world, and she was willing to help him battle the years. Her mother had not known that fear. Bottle-shaped with child-bearing, as Marie remembered her, Maria Daneri had remained beautiful in the eyes of her children and her husband Giacomo until her death.

Marie carried the tray down the marble stairs and into the kitchen, which since the depression had become the most used of all the rooms in the house built of orchids.

The kitchen held no interest for her. It was fashioned of steel and white enamel and was as impersonal as an operating room. In Marie's mind, hidden from Vincent, was a small colorful kitchen she had never seen but had always wanted. It was small and low-ceilinged, with a massive iron stove and a small fireplace that always held a blaze that was reflected in the copper pans of many sizes hanging on the walls. From the dark beams hung bunches of marjoram and thyme and rosemary from Giacomo's garden, and on either side of the door—Marie smiled to herself at the picture—were clusters of dry red peppers and pumpkin-colored ears of corn, and the door was always open to fields where stalks and leaves stretched high in their passion to touch the sun.

And the food cooked in this kitchen was not for Marie and Vincent Levenridge, that handsome middle-aged couple who looked so much younger than their years and who dieted so carefully to achieve this desirable end.

With an impatient gesture she set the tray on the shining sink and left it there. A cleaning woman came in several hours each afternoon.

"No matter how poor we are," Vincent had told his wife, "I will not have you doing housework."

Nor would he believe her when she protested she wanted to do her own work. Instead, he had been proud of what he considered her courage in never complaining of the change in their living conditions. He could not believe she preferred the straitened way. The house had overridden her natural impulses for home-making. She had never been able to select a piece of furniture of her own, or hang a picture or mirror on the walls. Every room in the house had been perfected by the famous woman decorator hired by Giacomo, and any changes Marie might make would only interfere with the completed décor. In her own dressing room she hung family portraits and an extra Madonna or two on the walls with a feeling that was almost guilt.

There was one small room she considered her own.

In this, the tiny conservatory built out from the kitchen, she spent a contented half hour working with a dibble around the roots of potted plants brought from Daneri's. She dug with enjoyment, for the craving for earth was in her, but the feeling of guilt remained.

"You can at least wear gloves," Vincent often told her.

But she wanted the comfort of earth on her hands.

If only we had a little house, she was thinking. Alone in this empty shell of magnificence, she was oppressed with the feeling of homelessness. A little house would have room for a shrine.

So many of the old-fashioned Italian families had niches in their homes that held blue and gold statues of the Madonna.

How incongruous one would be in these well-appointed rooms!

Marie was not without humor. This house is too big for comfort, she thought. In a little place one would have room to pray.

The burden of the house fell away from her a little later as, hatted and furred, she trudged down the Presidio hill. She would have enjoyed carrying a basket. There was nothing so sensible as a basket for shopping. But to carry a basket would have been almost as unforgivable as to have enjoyed the comfort of wearing a shawl. Mrs. Vincent Levenridge could, however, indulge in the whim of doing her own ordering, an innocuous fancy tolerated by her more conventional neighbors.

In the shopping district at the base of the hill Marie elbowed the happily less fortunate over bins of vegetables, pinched the cheeks of fruits, and argued merrily in Italian with the butcher over the cutting of beef against the fiber. The various departments of the big market were operated by Italians. The cheese vendor told Marie with gusto of his latest-born and the vegetable man spoke at length of his wife's operation. Tears came into Marie's beautiful eyes as they spoke of such things. And with others she joked in Genoese.

For an hour, buying and bargaining, she was a charming and dynamic woman and exquisitely alive.

Then, leaving the market, she looked aimlessly about the busy street. "Take the car!" she could hear Vincent scolding. "Why do I keep the extra car, so that you can walk over the hills like a peddler?" But she had never cared for driving and there had been no chauffeur for five years.

Marie inspected her nails. They showed the results of her work in the conservatory. The feeling of guilt returned as she boarded a streetcar for the shopping section.

Downtown she would have her nails done. She would glance, without appearing to, at the left hand of her manicurist. The girl had a child in a sanatorium. If the wedding ring was not there, that meant the child was worse and the ring had been temporarily banished in favor of medicine. Then Marie would leave too large a tip from her small allowance. And she could listen, pity, advise. In such matters, spreading her love over the troubles of the world, she was not unlike Giacomo.

There were duty calls that could be made to please Vincent.

It was not easy to find ways to fill the hours until Tosca or Vincent came home.

And if neither came? That happened often now. Vincent was held late at the bank, and Tosca's hours were unpredictable since she had met Mark Cantrell.

The cable car lurched to the cry, "Look out for the curve!" and Marie folded her arms to her breast in a protective gesture. Her eyes darkened and shadowed her broad, gentle features with the look of incipient melancholia, because she did not want to go back into the great empty house on the hill, because she was lonely always for children, for the other children Vincent had not wanted since his ambitions demanded a free and unburdened way, and because so little was seen of Tosca now that she had met this man Cantrell. Marie tried to use reason, to argue, as she sat dignified and proud-appearing in the lurching car, that surely it was wicked and unfair to draw back from a young man one scarcely knew; and as for his idleness and not working, that was not to be held against him, not in these times, when so many young and older men had no work. And then she remembered the trains, and the tears pushed heavy and hot against her lids and would not go away. She could see again the blurred and terrible trains pulling slowly across the California landscape with the thousands of hungry-looking young men riding the boxcars and the roofs of the cars because they had no homes and no families to help them any more and there was no work anywhere that would enable them to build homes and have families of their own. No, one could not condemn any member of the legion of the young, not in such years as these. Judgment must be reserved against the young, because they had been betrayed.

Her tears stayed unshed for them all, darkening her eyes, and her thoughts and her unshed tears followed Tosca, who had driven away so wildly on the errand for Giacomo.

SIX

The hegira of the flowers had begun in the night. All through the early hours and into the morning they came pouring into San Francisco, fleeing from the Napa and Santa

78

Clara and Salinas valleys, the saline cove that was Santa Cruz, the wooded county of Marin, the rounded hills of San Leandro, and the warm belts of Colma and Daly City. Hurtling over rails and highway came the flowers, by truck and train, to converge in fragrant avalanche in San Francisco.

There they divided into colorful streams, some going to the Flower Market and the flower shops of the bay cities, and a small remainder to the flower stands that made gay patches on the gray streets. And much of that bright avalanche was destined for the markets of the continent and paused only briefly in the city before being rushed on by rail or water or air.

Streaming along with the flowers, through the night and into the morning, came the vegetables and fruits in their seasons. Giacomo often likened the beauty of a truckload of freshly washed golden carrots to a display of his own pointed talisman roses. He took pleasure in seeing his truckloads of blooms join forces on the highway with the trucks and an occasional wagon loaded with vegetables and drawn by plodding horses who knew the route so well into San Francisco and down Mission Street that their drivers sat hunched in sleep over the reins as they rode. And to him the bright mosaic made by purple cabbage and ruby beets from Colma, the spiked and silvery artichokes from Half Moon Bay, and mounds of jade-green lettuce from the silt-washed banks of the Pajaro in the Salinas Valley were as beautiful as the enameled jewel work of ancient artisans.

He liked watching the truckloads of shining Watsonville apples streaming between the hills and bay, and the globes of amethyst that were prunes from the Santa Clara Valley, and other jewel mounds that were grapes, deep purple and palest green, and the apricots with the color and fragrance and flavor that are theirs alone.

Tosca, spending the night in Giacomo's house, had often wakened in the dawn to hear the rumble of trucks along the highway and looked through her window to watch the procession of fruits and vegetables going by, as beautiful, in their way, as were the flowers.

Only the flowers had to be handled more rapidly and with far greater care.

In the pre-dawn hours, while others slept, the flower people were hardest at work, for the beginning of their day was actually

79

its climax, and the perishable goods they handled must be set out swiftly in the unending race against time.

Because Tosca knew so well the haste and the tenderness that were the driving forces behind the avalanche of beauty, she had been shocked into full recognition of the futility of their own maniac race when she and Mark and their friends had met Giacomo's trucks speeding up the highway.

She had thought then of Giacomo and that darkened hour when he set out with the first cutting squad through the electrically lighted glasshouses, and the careful choosing and cutting and carrying of the baskets of fresh bright blooms to the shipping shed, and the sorting and stripping and packing there, always against time. Giacomo would be working with the first crew, and Eric too, and Ludmilla would be working silently and swiftly, helping everyone who might have need of her adept hands. But most of all she would try to be with Eric.

There was upon them all the look of absorption and goodness as Tosca remembered them in the hours of their hardest labor, and the contrast between their pre-dawn hours and the night at Bird's Nest had been brought sharply home when her own car filled with drunken and screaming revelers had met the bottle-green flower-burdened trucks in the dawn.

She was still suffering from the guilt of that meeting when she brought her car into the crowded street in front of Matraia's.

The entire block before the flower shop was crowded with honking trucks and cars that belonged to growers who were struggling to deliver their loads of flowers. Among them several of the Daneri trucks stood out like green beetles, and there was a scattering of the sky-blue Matraia trucks that were trying to return to the shop with loads of flowers from the Flower Market. The clamor of voices and horns was deafening as the vehicles jockeyed and fought for position. The traffic police stationed at either end of the block were trying to bring the crowded street to order. All other traffic had been diverted from the apparently hopeless blockade. Tosca was accustomed to the struggle—it was an ordinary scene to her—and she followed a Matraia truck into the melee in time to see Pietro leave the shop, having delivered his roses, and make his way to a Daneri truck. She screamed and blew her horn at him and he saw her and with a wave of his hand pulled away, leaving a clear space by the curb for her car.

She stepped from the car into what was apparently an orchard in full bloom, for full-sized flowering fruit trees had been set on the curb by Matraia's men, and their trunks were fixed in plats of gala daffodils. The policeman stationed before the flower-filled windows was doing his best to keep the sidewalk free of pedestrian traffic and permit the flowers to go through, but to San Franciscans the flower business was the dearest of all trades, and crowds gathered every morning to watch the trucks disgorge bundles of wood fern still dripping dew from the mountain redwood forests, boxes of hothouse greens, and trays of flowers so choice that they had not been taken to the public Flower Market but were brought directly to Matraia's by their growers.

The shop was not yet open to the public. Matraia, in a black work smock, was standing in the doorway bargaining with a viola grower. Men and boys from the nurseries hurried past him with their fragrant burdens, delivered them to members of his staff, and rushed out again. Tosca followed them through the door, nodding seriously to Matraia as she passed.

Already in Matraia's the florist crew had been at work for hours.

The tiled floor was slippery with spilled water and wet fronds and leaves stripped from ferns and roses. The more experienced florists were hard at work lining the shop with patterns of bloom. They worked with great speed and without wasted effort. Working in groups, but without verbal consultation, as if they read one another's minds, they were arranging flowers in bowls and vases and placing them on white iron and glass tables against mirrored walls that quadrupled their beauty, reflecting them on every side of the mirrored store. In their movements was the rhythm of craftsmanship. They followed laws of arrangement imperceptible to the untrained eye. The selection of vase for flower, the formation of cones and triangles, circles, squares, and high points of color were traditional and in many cases had been taught from family to family, from father to son. Nearly all these men were of Italian ancestry.

So swiftly did they work, not a petal was bruised.

At intervals an iconoclast of color would defy all the known laws and attempt the improbable. He would combine, perhaps, gladioli and African daisies, flowers that usually defy combination. He would assemble them, weld them with highlights of yellow or white or blue. Then he would stand back in triumph and the entire crew would stop work and admire. Such moments of admiration from one's fellow craftsman were like the awarding of a gold medal. Then the growers, hurrying through the shop to the workroom with their trays of flowers, would also stop to praise.

Tosca, walking swiftly over the slippery floor, spoke to everyone but did not slow her steps. Among the flower bearers were several of the orchid growers, and one of these, while looking over the Matraia tables, would not be surprised to find a splendid new orchid and might glance into its jeweled depths and see the pollen there.

The hands of the florists did not slacken as they greeted Tosca. Their memories were still gay from Giacomo's picnic the day before. Their faces held affection for her because she was the granddaughter of Giacomo and they had known her always. The personnel of the flower world did not change very much. A florist was born a florist and remained a florist. A grower was always a grower.

So they chaffed her as if she was still the child they remembered.

"Hey, what happened to you, Tosca! I wanted to dance with you. Why did you walk out on the picnic?"

"I had an important engagement." She smiled her meaning. There was no use trying to fool these men who knew her so well.

And she walked among them swiftly, under almond trees that dropped spring petals on her head; but her eyes were trained to beauty, and she missed not a flower in all that mirrored place. Every fragrance born of spring, every color mixed by nature, was in Matraia's. Here was the ending place of the hegira of the flowers. She recognized them, as if they were friends' faces, seeing behind each flower the generations of human effort, physical and mental, and the hunger for greater beauty that had helped perfect them. Those pure gigantic gardenias she had seen grown by Ernesto, who had charge of Giacomo's gardenia houses. The hybrid tea roses were Pietro's specialty, and the hyacinths—pink and white and yellow and Holland blue—and the tulips, ranging in color scale from palest heliotrope to metallic bronze, had been gathered in the Daneri houses under the jealous eye of Stoob. From no other nursery had come such marvelous shadings, such thrilling sweetness.

But the embankments of larkspur spired with cobalt and azure and salmon, and the delphinium sweeping in sea-colored masses from foamlike white through fifty shades of blue to the darkest marine, ah, those could only be of the special Brock strain developed under the masterly care of August Brock, Eric's father. The Brocks of Santa Cruz were the West's greatest specialists of tuberous begonias and delphinium.

Tosca recognized other nurseries by their fragile representatives. She walked between tribes of golden-trumpeted narcissi, kitten-faced pansies, gold-spotted and tigered calceolaria, anemones in all their springtime shadings of shell pink to purple, deep-toned azalea, many-tinted cineraria, pastel columbine, and lilac, pink, white, and lavender, and sentimentally sweet; all these appeared swiftly to Tosca as the personalities who had tended them. Because of Giacomo's training she could glance at these flowers and recognize them as individuals as surely as Matraia could glance at a flower and tell to the hour when it had been cut from the plant.

She passed tables that held vases of orchid sprays and, without seeming to look, knew that the orchid she hunted was not there.

She went into the workroom in the rear of the flower shop.

The barnlike room was humming like a busy factory. Dozens of other members of Matraia's crew were working at metal-topped tables, with rapid movements stripping the flowers of their leaves and stems and weaving them into designs. Six were working at a funeral pall, like workers at an old-fashioned quilting bee, using only spray and Cattleya orchids. "How many in that one?" she called, and when they told her five hundred orchids, she knew this explained the early demand for orchids that had caught up Giacomo's newest hybrid. A group of younger men were weaving creamy ropes of gardenias to outline the aisles at a fashionable wedding. A squat, dark-visaged worker was holding up and studying a bride's bouquet he had fashioned of butterfly orchids and showers of lilies of the valley, and beside him a boy who looked like a young priest was carefully putting together tiny old-fashioned blossoms to accompany a gift to a newborn babe. Others were shaping centerpieces for banquet tables, baskets for bon voyage, sprays and bouquets for congratulation or condolence or memoriam. Ephemeral tokens, these, for all emotional crises, for the wedded and the dead and the loving and the living and the ill and the triumphant and the newly born.

For more than forty years, in Matraia's workroom, the story of a city's living and dying, its travels and returnings, remorses and

83

romances, despairings and high adventurings, had been written with flowers; and of that story, not a petal was left in evidence. Only the memory of beauty remained.

She had walked the length of the workroom, noting every flower set out on the tables or in buckets along the green-strewn floor, and now she knew where the Aurea would be found. The refrigeration room yawned whitely as she opened its door. Shivering, she paced the icy floor. The enameled shelves were stacked with open trays and boxes that held the costliest and more perishable blooms. In the Daneri trays lay Giacomo's largest and most perfect gardenias, their fragrance stilled in the cold air, and dozens of orchids bedded in cotton nests; and among these, glowing like a jewel, was the Tosca.

It had of course come directly to Matraia's. Its unusual beauty would mark it for the shop that held prior claim to Giacomo's finest orchids. Tosca lifted the hybrid carefully by the stem that was encased in a glass water-filled tube, and for an anxious moment studied the opal-green and garnet depths. The tiny sack was there.

Knowing it safe, she lost herself in its beauty. The severed Aurea seemed far lovelier in her hand than it had in the seedling house.

"You're not taking that back, are you, Tosca?" Matraia had come into the cold room without her knowing. "I've a favorite customer picked out for that one."

"Just depollinizing." Tosca flashed him an extravagant smile. Matraia was one of her favorite friends, and she was happy because she had reached the orchid in time. She opened her purse and took out the vial and tweezers, and while Matraia watched she snipped the white vellum sack from its sea-green casing as Giacomo had taught her. For a moment a million potential Warneri Aurea were gripped between the metal points of the tweezers. Then she dropped the pollen into the little flask. "There, that's safe."

Matraia grimaced with understanding. "That happens, that happens," he said, nodding. It was not an unusual event for a grower to enter his shop in haste to recover pollen overlooked in a fine orchid.

In another century Matraia might have been a Cellini. His darkly clever, pointed features locked with concentration as he rearranged the orchid delicately on its cotton bed. He worked with flowers as a jeweler would with gems, with an artistry that had made his shop world-famed. Once, as an immigrant boy, he had peddled violets along this very street.

"Giacomo has really stretched himself on this one," he said, appraising the magnificent hybrid through narrowed lids as a jeweler might a fine emerald. "But Giacomo always does whatever he does better than anyone. What a party he gave us yesterday, Tosca! My boys are all walking in their sleep this morning.

"Say, Tosca, what's the name of this orchid?"

"The Tosca Levenridge!" Tosca's eyes danced. She felt carefree and triumphant now that the pollen was safe in her handbag. "Aren't I lucky, Matraia, to have an orchid named for me?"

His somber, incurious eyes surveyed her. Matraia seldom smiled, he seldom looked at anyone fully, and when he did his concentration was startling. His loves were few and deep; they included his wife, his children, his shop, and the grower, Giacomo Daneri, who long ago had given a frightened little Venetian his first flat of violets. Something in the burning intensity of the child Matraia had drawn the attention of Giacomo, who in those days was tending his own flower stall in the old flower market, then on California Street. "You want to work, eh? Take these and see what you can do with them."

In that moment the house of Matraia began.

That had been more than forty years ago. Matraia was a lad of nine. When he was seventeen Giacomo had lent him enough money to rent and stock a shop little bigger than a stall which was in time to become the famed Matraia's. Since then much had happened, and of great importance to Matraia was the fact that Giacomo Daneri had grown old.

The thought was insupportable to Matraia.

And this girl, he was thinking, studying Tosca without appearing to look her way . . . Matraia felt he knew where she was heading. There was little that went on in San Francisco the florist did not know. Through Matraia's poured the secrets of the city. The stories of its loves and tragedies and intrigues were in the sales slips checked over by Matraia. The faithfulness or infidelities of its citizens were told to him by the flowers they ordered.

Birth, death, romance. Love, intrigue, bribery. It seemed little could happen in San Francisco that could not be said with flowers.

These were San Francisco's secrets, not Matraia's. He kept them as inviolate as a doctor keeps the confidences of his patients. And so, watching Tosca while seeming to admire the hybrid, Matraia struggled against the ironbound training of his forty business years. He did not have the right to tell this girl who was the darling of his friend Giacomo how much he had learned, of her friendship with Mark Cantrell and of Mark himself.

The man was no more than a name to him, to be signed at the end of intimate messages ordered over a telephone by a drawled and sleepy voice, to be sent with lavishly ordered flowers. By the nature of the flowers ordered and their recipients, he knew the man.

Matraia, his pointed features locked over Giacomo's newest orchid, fought with his conscience. The integrity of a lifetime kept him silent.

"Yes, you are very lucky, Tosca," he said at last. "Maybe a little hard luck might be good for you. There is such a thing as being too lucky."

For a moment Tosca thought starkly, There was Paul!

Matraia walked with her to the street door. He was relieved because he had not spoken, and seemed to relax a little.

"Tosca, is it true that Brock has a new break?" he asked with a curiosity rare to him. "Everyone at market was talking about it. Have you heard anything?"

"Wouldn't he have told us about it at the picnic?"

"Did Giacomo mention your orchid?"

Tosca smiled. "I'll ask Eric, Matraia. If there is one, I'll let you know."

In the car, because the morning was a cold one, she removed the vial of pollen from her purse and slipped it between her breasts.

Colma looked different, almost like a foreign village, in the morning sunlight. The misted air gave the hills an aspect of unreality, as if they were brushed against the sky, and from the furrowed fields a warm mist rose in clouds to meet the sun.

The air was heavy with the indescribable piercing fragrance of growth, the acrid scent of fertilizer, and the saline sharpness from the nearby Pacific. But as Tosca stopped her car in the nursery lane these were overcome by a woodland odor like that of moss and wet violets under moss, and out of the shipping shed were

86

hurrying the men of the second cutting crew, carrying flats of tiny plants nodding with purple viola out to the half dozen trucks that were already back from the first market delivery. The predawn rush was the greatest of the day at Daneri's, but deliveries would be leaving the nursery at intervals during the day and even into the night, for the city shops must be constantly replenished, unexpected orders filled, flower stalls restocked, and consignments hurried to train or boat or airplane. Tosca sat in her car to enjoy the passing of the viola, empurpled as a papal procession, and after them came furry African violets in their small pots, and finally, recognizable only by their bridal scent, for the boxes were covered, there was carried past a shipment of lilies of the valley.

Where there were valley lilies, Tosca knew, Stoob would not be far away.

But it was Ludmilla and not Stoob who appeared in the wake of the lilies.

Ludmilla came hurrying across the damp spring grass. She seemed a delicate figure in her printed yellow house dress save for her hands, which were thrust into workmen's gloves. She carried a clasp knife in one hand, and her thin features were strained.

Taking her place before the shipping shed, between the flower processional and Tosca, she was like a person standing guard.

SEVEN

$\mathcal{I}$T annoyed Tosca, stepping out of her car before the shipping shed with the sense of conquest upon her, to find Ludmilla blocking her way.

"Did you get it?" Ludmilla demanded almost in a whisper.

"Certainly," answered Tosca a bit coldly, annoyed the more to learn that Ludmilla knew of the accident that had befallen her orchid. Sometimes it was difficult to remember that Stoob's daughter had been born at Daneri's and that its daily affairs were her entire existence. Ludmilla seldom went to the city, even for an afternoon's shopping. She had never spent a night away from the nursery.

And still Tosca found herself wondering how Ludmilla had known.

Ludmilla closed her clasp knife and dropped it into the pocket of her dress. She put out a gloved hand.

"I'll store it in the lab for you since you're in such a rush."

"I'm in no hurry at all."

Tosca tried to speak serenely, but for a ridiculous moment it seemed that the precious dab of pollen was being tugged between them, and it became a matter of importance that Tosca and not Ludmilla deliver the pollen to Giacomo. Not even to herself would Tosca admit that its rescue had been reparation on her part, and she had no intention of facing Giacomo without it.

For the first time in her life she dreaded meeting her grandfather.

Several of the trucks roared off down the hill.

"Where is everybody?" she asked.

"Eric has gone to the airport." Ludmilla was purposely misunderstanding. "We had a big orchid special from Matraia's." Tosca nodded, for she had seen the orchids there. "And then we had to get out seven hundred gardenias for a special shipment to Philadelphia. Some big wedding going on down there."

"Where's Giacomo?" Ludmilla knew she was not interested in Eric. Besides, this was always the time Eric was out with the second fleet of trucks, racing between the shipping sheds at Redwood City and the Flower Market and the airport to check off shipments, so that no one could ever say where Eric might be. And in this comparatively peaceful interim between the first and second shipments, Giacomo as a rule made his morning rounds of the glass houses, starting with the gardenias and carnations, peering into the glassed-in dominions of the lily houses he seldom entered unless Stoob needed his help there, moving on for a more complete survey of the orchid houses, and coming out into the open for a pleased survey of the heather plots against the hill.

So she was surprised when Ludmilla said vaguely, "Giacomo? I think he drove down to Santa Cruz. Eric's father phoned that he has a new salmon gladiolus that will really hold its color."

"Then it's true!" Tosca was pleased to know Brock actually had the rumored break, and her voice quickened with the excitement that would be shared by the network of the flower world from

West to East before the day ended. "I think Giacomo would walk a hundred miles to see a new break!"

But the pleasure she felt in the news, and the relief at not having to face Giacomo so soon after her desertion of the festa, was overshadowed by a sense of having been this time deserted by Giacomo. It was a new experience and too painful to bear.

There was also a definite impression that she was being urged away from the nursery by Ludmilla. How long, she wondered, had this feeling of crowding existed between Ludmilla and herself?

With all her faults, she was forthright, and with Tosca, to wonder was to voice her wonder. She stopped in the entrance of the shed and faced Stoob's daughter.

"See here, you aren't mad for any reason, are you?"

As she spoke she recognized the question as being both childish and familiar. It was one she had asked Ludmilla many times when as small girls they had played together about the nursery. Tosca, who had given way to every emotion as it came, had never been able to understand the quiet girl whose moods ran deep below the surface, to rise like bursting lava at unexpected times and places.

The pale eyes shifted under her accusing stare.

"Why should I be?"

"I don't know why. I never know. Is it something I did—yesterday, maybe? Anything I've said? Or because I left without saying good-by to anybody?"

And she realized for the first time the enormity of the hurt she had done, not to Ludmilla, but to Giacomo.

"There's nothing wrong and you're being ridiculous," snapped Ludmilla, and walked stiffly into the shipping shed.

You are in love with Eric, thought Tosca, and it may have something to do with that. Or are you angry because I have had an orchid named for me? Surely if anyone deserves to have a flower named in her honor it is Ludmilla, who has worked with flowers since she was a child and never had freedom or fun the way other girls do. I shall speak to Giacomo about a flower for Ludmilla when I see him again. And there was no sensible reason to be annoyed because Ludmilla had learned of the loss of the orchid's pollen. Tosca wiped the matter from her mind and blithely followed Ludmilla's thin figure into the shipping shed.

The vast metal cavern had resumed its everyday utilitarian appearance. About thirty men and boys were hard at work around the sorting tables that had been replaced in the center of the cement floor. The paper streamers and strings of colored lights had been removed, but their bright primary colors were not missed, for the shed was made brilliant and fragrant by the tons of flowers heaped along the tables and the wall shelves where the old women had sat the night before to watch the dancing. There were mounds of carnations of every known shading, richly tinted roses, drifts of smoky pink and purple heather, and snowbanks of magnificent gardenias against their glossy leaves. And everywhere between the flower drifts were the familiar materials of the nurseryman's trade: the bundles of old newspapers, rolls of heavy wrapping paper, waxed paper, and tissue, the shears, spools of wire, boxes of clips and rubber bands, spools of cord and twine and hanks of flax for tying, and the stacks of cartons and trays and cases stamped with a name known around the world: "Daneri's."

The orchids were packed in their own special section at the back of the building, nearest the icehouse, and Tosca, looking through the glass door, could see that the mesh ledges were almost naked of the wooden orchid flats. The orchids were given the swiftest and most skillful handling, and the first morning's cuttings were either stored, awaiting rush orders, or had been sent on their way by Eric.

The workers were standing at the tables on wooden drainboards and many wore rubber boots, for the cement floor was partly under water and thickly littered with sodden plant trimmings that would be swept up with great care and burned to prevent any possible spread of disease.

"This is the second crew," observed Ludmilla, knowing that Tosca knew this quite as well as she.

The nurserymen were working with the same easy measured rapidity that had marked the work of the florists in Matraia's. Not a moment, not a movement, was wasted. They worked against time, and still they were at peace with time.

For she noted again, picking her way with Ludmilla between the tables across the littered floor, the look of calmness that was on all these faces. The Giacomo look, she thought it. There was no undue tension in the rapid movements of the packing crew as they gripped the long stalks of the roses, graded each flower according to the length of the stalk and the shape, color, and size

90

of the rose, and set it carefully in the silver-colored tubs reserved for roses. There they were lifted out again to be packed, and in all the process of sorting, grading, counting, and packing, never a petal was bruised. The place was a factory in effect, but this was not factory labor. The man who packed a rose in wet moss and damp paper was not handling a mere rose. It was a personality, one that he knew as well as his own. He had helped create that personality, he had guarded that small life, he had watched the slow growth and the unfolding of exquisite beauty. He had waged his share of the unending fight against pests and disease that this perfect blossom should lie for a moment, glowing with life, between his hands.

So in preparing this rose—or lily or viola or orchid—for its flight into the world beyond Daneri's, he was completing its destiny and a small share of his own. Therefore, the work in the shipping shed held the component elements of love and pridefulness, and the faces of the workmen revealed the satisfaction given by work well done and their faith in the value of their labor, which is awarded only to the fortunate.

And apart from the content they felt in their work was the faith they held in Giacomo.

On the shipping-shed wall, beside the blackboard where messages and orders were scrawled, was the time clock that checked off the work hours of Giacomo's crew members, every one of whom was a member of the Floriculturalist's Union. The clock regulated their working hours, but it did not change their attitude toward Giacomo. He was more than boss to these men. He was their Padrone—that word difficult to define and often abused, holding as it does the medieval connotation between patron and father, and the new regulations and checking of hours and pay for overtime made little difference, because Giacomo had never known what it was not to be generous and fair, and so he still remained to them their Padrone.

Tosca, calling out morning greetings and pausing to admire an unusual basket or sheaf of flowers, realized again, as she had in the flower shop, how smoothly and unobtrusively the years pass among people whose lives are lived with flowers. The flowers changed with the seasons, and some might change, always for the better, under the coercion of the hybridists, yet the people who raised and sold them changed but little. She had known nearly every person in this shed as long as she could remember.

Here again she was loved less because she was Tosca than because she was the granddaughter of Giacomo, but for the first time she sensed in the welcoming a restraint that was alien to these men who spoke so frankly on all subjects that came to mind and were not given to curbing their sometimes boisterous humor because she was there. And it could not be the aftermath of the festa that left their voices muted and almost like those of strangers.

"Hi, Tosca," and "Mornin', Tosca," they said, but not one asked what had become of her the night before or why she had not been in this shed to dance with him. By this omission—for they were blunt men and not accustomed to hiding their thoughts —she knew again how deeply she had hurt Giacomo. She knew Ludmilla was aware what she was feeling, and she turned from her pale accusation and the unvoiced dignified hurt of Giacomo's crew and walked over to the wall shelf, where Laddie was working, his young face intent over heaps of split carnations.

"Somebody forgot to lower the heat in the excitement last night," he explained shyly. "And a whole houseful burst."

His hands did not stop in their work of fastening the broken calyx of the burst carnations with tiny metal clips. The piles of repaired carnations were fresh and fragrant and apparently perfect, and would go out in the ten o'clock shipment as "seconds" suitable for funeral pieces for the "cemetery trade."

She stood marveling at the way his sturdy hands darted among the bright carnations. Laddie had the "green hand," as had so many of the Daneri workers. It seemed almost an inherited gift, for Laddie's father and grandfather had worked in turn for Giacomo, and many of the younger workers seemed to have had handed down to them the talent for making plants thrive and for handling flowers with a touch marvelously light.

Ludmilla has that gift, thought Tosca. She looked down at her own smartly gloved hands and wondered why she had never shared Giacomo's urge, and her mother's, to work with flowers.

She had helped Giacomo around the nursery, to be sure, ever since she had been able to follow him through the glasshouses. He had praised and encouraged whatever she attempted. But it was always halfheartedly done, and she preferred seeing the flowers in perfect bloom and ready for her pleasure. There had always been flowers for Tosca.

Ludmilla came up to them.

"Your feet are getting soaked, Tosca," she said crossly. "Let's get out of here."

Her stout brogues led the way out of the shipping shed and between the clumps of daisies flanking the glasshouses and into the seedling house.

Not until they were in the cold potting shed did she turn and look uneasily at Tosca.

And Tosca, meeting the searching wolfsbane look, found herself bracing in a mood of inexplicable stubbornness. She was as conscious as Ludmilla of the locked laboratory door with Giacomo's key hanging beside it in open view. But she did not look at the key. She looked at Ludmilla and waited for the girl to speak.

The wait became awkward. Twice Ludmilla seemed about to speak, but as she so often did, she did not come out with whatever she wished to say. And still Tosca made no move toward the key and the door.

Giacomo did not permit many people to enter his laboratory. Even Eric seldom entered it without him. The vial of pollen was safe where Tosca had hidden it, and it would remain there, no matter how plainly Ludmilla was showing her interest in seeing it in the laboratory or in seeing the laboratory with Tosca, whichever it might be.

"Let's see if any more of the hybrids are out," Tosca suggested instead in a bright voice, and now it was she who led past the locked door and through the nursery into the seedling section.

The familiar warmth and fragrance did not serve to soften her thoughts toward Ludmilla.

Then she stood shocked and disappointed before the table of Aurea plants. Several more of the buds had opened during the night, but the orchids were inferior blooms—their lips were small and unshapely and the petals narrow, with some of the fleshly pristine quality that had given the first Aurea its breath-taking loveliness. So far the orchid whose pollen lay against her flesh was the only sensational bloom.

"Not very good, are they?" Ludmilla was saying, but Tosca did not answer because she knew now she would never give the little flask to anyone except Giacomo.

I'll wait here all day if I have to, she decided, thankful that Mark was not to call before five, and feeling the lost and familiar longing she always knew when she thought of him. Her head was pounding, too, in a fashion new to her, and she thought, I never drank gin before last night and I shall never touch it again. And standing beside Ludmilla, with the orchid plants rising around them, she lifted her aching eyes and renewed them upon beauty, for dozens of other young orchids were in bloom today that had not been before, and it was wonderful to see the old patterns unfold in new splendor. But as she looked and exclaimed, she was redramatizing the incident of her orchid.

Reconstructing the routine of Daneri's was a simple matter. Tosca had spent so much time as Giacomo's companion that she knew every minute of the nursery's program as well as she knew every square foot of its land.

. The early crew was always at work before dawn, with Giacomo or Eric overseeing the cutting of the roses, carnations, and other of the commoner flowers.

Seven was the crux of the morning. At that hour the cutting crews entered the glasshouses and with the utmost care began the process of gleaning the choicest flowers. Eric and Giacomo opened the orchid houses then, and under their watchful eyes the most skillful cutters began the almost reverent cutting of the orchids. It was then that a tight-lipped Stoob, pudgy with importance, led his own crew into the "valley" houses and with his own hands rolled back the burlap covers from the bins, and bursts of divinest fragrance filled the air as he exposed to view the yellow-green shoots and starry sprays of his guarded lilies.

The orchid had gone out with the first shipment, Giacomo had said. It could not have been cut in the seedling house with Giacomo or Eric watching.

Therefore, the Aurea hybrid had been taken before seven.

How had it happened? Tosca wondered. Eric had hidden the plant in the compost cart. She and Giacomo had watched Eric place it there, and no one else knew. The cart was still in its place by the glass wall, piled with trimmings, and who would think of looking there for a valuable orchid?

And she found she was staring hard at Ludmilla.

"You knew about the orchid, didn't you?" she said.

For a moment—whether moved by indignation or anger, she could not tell—Ludmilla's thin features resembled the puffed countenance of Stoob when he was angry.

"Who tells me anything around here, may I ask!" Ludmilla countered pettishly. "I'm not important."

And she stalked over to the tray of mottled Cypripedium and thrust her gloved fingers between their upthrust leaves. Angry as she seemed, she touched the leaves with exquisite care, bending over to study the roots, the branching leaves, and the rare infrequent young orchids.

She is furious with me because of yesterday, Tosca decided, and this has nothing to do with the Aurea. A person whose life centered around the nursery as Ludmilla's did would never have tossed Giacomo's newest creation into a haphazard shipment. She felt rising in her the tragic need to apologize and explain, to anyone, even Ludmilla, why she had left the festa. But how could she explain to Ludmilla, or to Giacomo or anyone, the smooth head of Mark Cantrell over a table in candlelight, and the strangling rush of blood around a newly awakened heart?

What apology, Tosca wondered despairingly, for life?

For Mark meant that to her. Let them all know. There was no help for it now, no fighting against it. It was no longer Tosca's life. There was not an hour or a moment now that did not belong to Mark.

Even in this warm and languid place her flesh grew chill as she remembered him.

She sighed deeply, brokenly.

Ludmilla bent with interest over a mottled orchid. She took her clasp knife from her pocket and jerked it open.

"Look at this," she said.

Only an expert could have noticed the almost imperceptible flaw in the tawny flange of the Cyp.

With strong and careful hands Ludmilla amputated the slipper-shaped orchid at the base of its stem. For a moment she held it out to Tosca, and the smile on her pale mouth was contemptuous.

"Looks perfect, doesn't it? But what good is it! A space taker."

She tossed the Cyp into the cart.

Space taker, thought Tosca. She had heard Giacomo use the term. The space taker was the inferior growth, a plant, or its blossom, that took up valuable space and the care and warmth and air and water that were needed by its betters. The space takers were the misshapen from birth or the flawed by insects or disease or by water drops that can blur the color of the petals. She had often watched Giacomo burn on the compost heap the wastrel orchid seedlings that had not come up to his standards.

She had watched him tending the cremation of inferior orchids and had not been able to subdue her pity at the loss of the beautifully fashioned organisms whose faults would have passed unnoticed by less critical eyes than Giacomo's.

And she thought: There are people, too, who are wastrel, but there are no compost heaps for those who take the space and bounty of the earth for granted and give nothing in return. Her mind went back to the night before and to Mark and his friends and the party and Bird's Nest and the race down the peninsula, and she found she was staring with repugnance at the apparently perfect Cyp lying on the rubbish in the cart.

"Does Eric know you do that?" she asked sharply.

"Eric taught me," retorted Ludmilla with obvious complacency, and again Tosca had the feeling that she was being pushed from familiar ground.

A softness circled her ankles, and the kitten mewed under the orchids. Giacomo loomed in the glass doorway. His great bulk was crowded into overalls and his gray hair was shaggy as a lion's mane. He saw Tosca, and his wrinkled face broke into tiny lights, all bright with love for her.

"You brought it, Tosca *mia?*"

His expression was saintlike in its tenderness. If she had wounded him, she knew herself forgiven.

And she went to him joyously.

"I thought you had gone to Santa Cruz!"

"Why should I go to Santa Cruz, with you coming, Tosca-nina!"

"Ludmilla said——" But it did not matter what Ludmilla had said.

"Come, we put it away safe," said Giacomo. "Then you are in time for lunch. A good lunch, from yesterday. Coming, Ludmilla?"

But Ludmilla had her back to them and apparently did not hear.

After they left the seedling section Ludmilla kept on with her hunt through the orchid trays. Knife in hand, she moved among the Cyps. As she bent to peer through the crowded plants for flaws, insects, or the first traces of disease, the delicate precision of her movements was that of the hunter stalking its prey.

EIGHT

HERE was only one chair in Giacomo's laboratory.
The hybridist did not encourage visitors in his place of miracles.

Tosca perched on it. "Hide your eyes!" And when he obeyed, covering his eyes with his great paws to humor her, she whisked the tiny bottle from its hiding place.

"There!"

"*Dio mio!*" He felt the warmth of the flask. "I did not intend you to be a hen. No matter, we will take care of that."

There are men who grow handsomer with age, she thought, watching with appreciation as he moved about the small space, each slow movement forming a complete statuesque pose, relaxed and yet commanding. With painstaking care he pasted the name and number of the Aurea hybrid on the vial that held the pollen and stored it in the refrigerator which, lined with glass shelves containing agar-filled bottles and jars, formed one wall of the laboratory.

This was the womb of the nursery. Here were conceived in secrecy the souls of his unborn orchids.

In this room, with its door closed, Giacomo seemed most complete; fully in command of himself and his world.

It was a small world, sealed in with the metal filing cabinets containing the records of his orchids, and, under glass, the cups and bowls and medals—gold, silver, and bronze—and the prize-winning ribbons; his worktable and microscope, a bookshelf holding books solely about orchids, the refrigerator, and, marching to the ceiling, the metal shelves with the hundreds of labeled glass retorts, their narrow mouths stopped with cotton, holding in their slender shapes the seeds of his orchids in the clear agar jelly that was Giacomo's secret solution.

In the retorts where the pearl-tinted agar showed clear the seeds had been newly sown.

In other retorts the seed formation was commencing, like shadows, in a pale brownish crust on the diminishing agar. These were plants, thousands of them to a plat no larger than a thumbnail, too small for the clearest eyes to see. They would lie the months through, consuming the agar, and only when the crust turned to a sensitive green, like mildew, and then to a fine-chopped-parsley semblance, could one distinguish the minute plants of the orchids.

Giacomo studied a shelf of jars where the green had thickened like moss and the agar was nearly gone. Looking more closely, he could detect the first spatulate formation of leaves, no larger than fingernail clippings, and knew that in another month the last of the agar would vanish and only a minute mass of miniature roots and leaves remain. Then, for the first time since their conception, so susceptible is the orchid seedling to germs, he would remove the cotton stoppers from the retorts, and the fetal plants would for the first time be permitted to taste moisture and air, both warmed to a temperature of seventy degrees.

He pointed out the developing plants to Tosca.

"Pretty soon we will have a planting day. You will help, maybe, Tosca, for luck?"

"Maybe," she said without interest, and he recognized the evasion in her words and, smiling, took her slender hand with the ultra-long fashionable nails. "Must they be so long? *Ma perchè?*"

"Everyone's wearing them long." She folded the nails against her palm. Long and dark as blood, she might have added, for all her feminine friends in the city were clawed and tinted to a strange degree this season. But it was Giacomo and not Tosca who wondered if the fad was not symbolic of the times, a throwback to some defense need or to the implication of non-working luxury. Chinese fingernails, the young people called them, and some of the girls wore them gilded in the manner of oriental nobility.

Again, since this was a page he could not read, Giacomo turned from it gently, leaving Tosca with the certainty that if she did not help with the planting of the new orchids Ludmilla would, for the square stubby hands of Ludmilla were almost as deft as Giacomo's. It was a fact that Giacomo was not without his foibles, and he liked a woman's hand in the orchid planting. There were certain orchidists who permitted only women to do this work, just as Eric's father, Adolph Brock, hired only women to gather the seeds of his marvelous delphinium. Yes, many growers believed, almost to the point of superstition, in the efficacy of feminine hands. So Ludmilla would certainly be among the selected skillful few—Eric and Laddie and several others—who would gather in the seedling house when the incubator babies were ready to leave their glass cribs, and all would be striving to emulate the deftness of Giacomo as he lifted the minute green fragments on the pointed stick and set them, thirty or forty plants together, in the miniature pots and tamped the bits of fiber around the veinlike roots, while pots, plants, and fiber were swallowed from view in his immense hands.

"Now!" he would say at the task's end, standing back to survey a kindergarten of the fairy transplantings in their thumb-sized pots, and it was apparent that only then did he consider his orchid babies fairly launched.

But Tosca had other interests, and to change the subject she twirled on the revolving chair to face the microscope and remarked idly:

"You haven't thanked me."

"Thanked you?"

"For getting up early and saving your dab of dust."

Giacomo's smile was kind because she knew better.

"A million Tosca Aureas may be in that dab of dust. And if they all lived, *cau Segnu!* What a jungle this world would be."

Tosca adjusted the lens over the slab of glass. She bent her head over it. There was nothing to be seen.

"Well, why don't they? You plant them. Nothing can get to them to hurt them. Why don't they all grow?"

"Ma perchè!" echoed Giacomo thoughtfully. Why indeed.

Her idle question went deeper than she knew. He towered over her like a puzzled giant, at a loss for words. Making pollen survive was one of the master tricks of orchidry, and he had been one of the first growers in America to accomplish the miracle. In this small crowded place, lined from ceiling to floor with agar flasks, Giacomo had brought into being the Daneri orchid houses, seed by seed, plant by plant, year by year.

His unending patience, his inflexible will had forced them into life.

And as he remembered these years and the glory that had come to life under his hands and spread around the earth, and how, during this time, so much else he would have given his life to preserve had been brushed from the face of that world, his eyes glazed with anguish over the bright bent head of Tosca waiting idly the answer to a question idly asked. She had pushed her hand below the lens and was studying the veins of her palm. Plainly, she was not interested, and he felt himself alone as he was so often, locked in with the unanswerable questioning that is the ultimate loneliness. As if hunting a clue, his look went around the crowded place that was his sanctuary, walled in by glass and nurtured in agar; that held, actually, only room enough for Giacomo and his microscope, his tweezers and scissors and test tubes and his infinite, almost terrifying, patience.

So many questions had been answered in this room. In orchidry, for example, the explanation was simple enough. Patience was the true parent of the orchid. Armed first with the necessary genius for color detection, without which a hybridist could no more breed orchids than a tone-deaf person could learn to play the harp, one studied first the parental flowers, selecting them carefully by their size, color, shapeliness, resistance to disease, and by the months in which they were to bloom. There were, now and always, in what were known as the breeding sections of the orchid houses, certain fine flowers detectable by their slit lips, whose pollen had been brought together by the careful hands of Giacomo. Hybridized, the flower died, the seed pod in the stem swelled and ridged slowly. When the pod split, the seeds were ready for his gathering and their planting in the tubes of agar.

"My goodness!" Tosca exclaimed, staring at her magnified palm. "My life line looks like Market Street on Saturday afternoon!"

To bring the seeds to planthood, ah, that was the triumph. Giacomo had been among the first in America to attempt the fascinating venture. England had been hybridizing—creating man-made orchids from species brought from the tropics—for more than half a century before Giacomo Daneri, alone and without known precedent to guide him, had begun his experiments in this laboratory. His first hybrid had taken him eight years. Since then they had poured out in a steady iridescent stream from his seedling shed, by the hundreds of thousands.

And the answer to the whole problem had been the simple agar solution! The early growers had not known about that. For years they had grown orchid seeds by the substratum method of keeping them damp as they lay on canvas. Only a few would sprout, so the first orchid growers had found it more practical to bring their plants ready-grown from the tropics.

Then Giacomo and a few others of the craft had stepped ahead of nature. Looking back, Giacomo could contemplate with awe the temerity of that younger Giacomo whose broad shoulders had stooped so painstakingly over microscope and agar.

A dab of pollen, Tosca had said. Into that smear of dust had gone not only his own irreclaimable years, but a million prior years of Orchidaceae. Every seed contained a summary of all that had gone before in the jungle-born story. And as always, surveying the rows of stoppered tubes, Giacomo felt his dreams widen and color to take in the world and the ages.

In that moment, surveying the worlds within worlds, the aeons on aeons trapped in the slender tubes, he looked the conqueror. His was the right to choose, to dream and bring into being. There were more than four hundred genera of orchids, and probably twelve thousand species, and as for the hybrids, he who was responsible for so many would not even hazard a guess as to their number. There was no rude awakening, no ending, to the long bright dream of the hybridist. And to himself, in limpid Italian, Giacomo spoke clearly the words he longed to speak aloud but which were too difficult to translate even to the person one loved most: You see, Tosca *mia*, this is the beauty of the long task of trying to capture the magical, that in the growing of orchids a man need never weep because there are no more worlds to conquer!

The longest life was not long enough.

A hybridist could begin growing orchids as a young man and still not hope to see more than five generations of his slow-growing beauties come to maturity during his lifetime. Patience was the mother of orchidry, time was the father.

Ah, for time, he thought! And he was not afraid of dying, as are so many who grow old, perhaps because the living fabric with which he worked gave him a sense of continuity and deathlessness. Leaving his work would not put that work to an end as long as Eric, and others like Eric, remained to carry on with seed and retort in Giacomo's world. In this world there remained in perpetuity such immortal matters as flowers and children. And he found he was staring down at the bright head bent over his microscope.

"And so it goes on," he said aloud.

And sighed, so gently Tosca did not hear.

Ah, to live on, he was thinking. To see the now invisible

orchids swell to full beauty in the glasshouses of Daneri. To see Tosca complete in her blooming. He could never understand the old who weary of living. I could ask for seven more years, he calculated humbly, for seven would permit him to glimpse many of the primary blooms of these now invisible in their gelatinous cradles, and for Tosca, one longed to be sure what the years might bring. And why not seven more? argued Giacomo, remembering his father, who when well into his eighties had kissed his three grandchildren good-by in the little white cottage behind the glasshouses and returned to Italy, to die while sleeping in the sun in a garden of his own making. To live on—seven, fourteen, any number of years—he would take his chance with age and weakness, only to see how well he had guessed, how ably he had planned.

Tosca swung about in the chair and looked up at him.

He has forgotten I am here, she thought a little wistfully. He had been standing so long, lost in his own thoughts. She took his hand to call him back to her. "I asked you a question, Nonno."

"Eh?" He came back to her across the years. There had been something she wanted to know. It was not often the young found need to question the old.

Then he was trembling with anxiety to tell her all he had longed to say. From the bookshelf he took down a volume and began riffling through the brilliantly colored pages. She knew it was one of his treasures, a signed copy of Sander's *Reichenbachia*. One after another he pointed out the pictures of the most admirable orchids, and his fingers trembled in his eagerness.

"Observe these, Tosca *mia*. You know how we figure? With orchids everything must be planned. The new orchid must have a place ready for it, and it must be ready for that place, and in the right time. And because they are not born that way, we make them so.

"You know that. Always you have heard me saying that.

"You know the months people most want orchids! In the opera months. In the months when they marry. In June the girl graduates or she marries and she wants the white orchid. In the fall comes the opera and she will wear gold or purple orchids. But Nature does not consider our times for marrying and attending theaters. Nature has a strong white Cattleya and she brings it to bloom in February, and what good is that to us?

"So the sellers of flowers say to us who are the growers of flowers: What good is a white orchid in February?

"So we make our plans. There is, let us say, a Laelia that blooms in June. It looks like a Cattleya. It will cross with the Cattleya. And we study them both, selecting which shall be the mother and which the father, and then we wait and perhaps after many years we have the strong white orchid that will bloom in June in time for the bride!"

"Yours!" she said with pride in her voice and her eyes, for as he spoke she saw the Giacomo Daneri who was the recognized master of the orchids that in their turn were the masterpieces of all the floral miracles. His intuition that had kept him abreast and even ahead of the flower fashions was almost mystic, for he seemed to see ahead of the trade demands, sometimes by as much as a decade. Ten years before, for example, there had been no market for white orchids. Then Giacomo developed his sensational wide-lipped snowy Cattleya Daneri and hundreds of the plants had burst into bloom on the crest of an unexpected nation-wide demand for white orchids.

But what she sensed and could not see was the real secret of Giacomo, which was the gentle and infinite patience and the imagination that enabled him to vision unborn compositions of color and shape; this is the genius of the hybridist.

For it was genius. His hands were soiled with moss and earth, but in their touch was divinity.

Now he was looking at her almost timidly. In the strong overhead light his eyes, once so flashingly black, were almost gray. He was a gray giant towering above her, but helpless, caught in the desire to speak and yet trapped by lack of words and by the years that lay between them. There was so much he longed to explain.

What was it? Tosca wondered.

In his heart he could say it, in strong and certain Italian, even in Latin. But this child of his heart could not understand such speech.

Because he had all her attention, his words stumbled. Tosca was listening, absorbed, and it was not often she listened. He talked so seldom, this Giacomo, and in her wild young heart she revered him.

He began uncertainly. "Not so many are strong, my Tosca."

Then he waited, thinking his way through the labyrinth of thoughts to all he wanted to say.

The strong species brought from the jungle survived almost incredible hardship. They went through drought or famine, they were uprooted and transported, they traveled far and were given rough treatment by the heedless, and they survived. But their children bred in civilization lacked their fortitude. Hybridization could weaken the orchid. Some became sterile, for reasons only a careful study of genetics could explain. You bred to ever-greater beauty, thought Giacomo, despairing of making his meaning known, and to increasing weakness. The seed pods of his hybrids —the ones with the slotted lips—were bursting with seeds, but the seeds became weaker and fewer as his work of improvement went on, until few of the seeds were capable of reproduction.

"They are so helpless, these beautiful ones," Giacomo explained uncertainly. "In the jungle they grow—sometimes, I think, for pleasure in their own beauty. But when they come to us we make them work for us, and we change them around and make them what we want them to be. So all the year round now, because of our selecting and crossing, we have the right orchids blooming just when we want them to bloom."

You studied them so carefully, he thought broodingly. It was a stud plant of the main female tail lines that produced the main male tail lines. He had come to be certain of that. Working from that premise, an orchid grower could almost be certain what to expect. Each single chromosome, as with humans, carried the entire characteristic of the plant to be. If only one could see ahead!

"Sometimes we are wrong," he said. "We select the parents we hope will make the new orchids we want. And something happens! *Ma perchè?* I do not know why. But seven years ago I crossed two beautiful dark flowers and all this time I have waited for dark orchids in April, and after all my care, what is it we have in the seedling house? Nearly all of them little white orchids no one would want. After all my care!"

"As you say, *ma perchè?*" Tosca asked amiably.

Giacomo shrugged his great shoulders. He had no idea why. Somewhere in one of the dark masterpieces had lurked the ruinous sub-dominant characteristics of unremembered white ancestors.

"They were no good. They were space takers."

"The compost," said Tosca suddenly. She was thinking of

Ludmilla flinging out the beautiful marred Cyp. And for some reason she felt again as she had with Mark when they met Giacomo's flower trucks on the highway.

"Eh, the end of them." Giacomo sighed. This was not at all what he had hoped to tell Tosca. It was so different with this new restraint between them since the festa and her leaving without a word to him. He remembered when she had told him everything, pouring out confidences with a child's lack of reticence.

"People are not seeds," he plodded on. "One is given one thing and grows, and another is given the same thing and it grows, if one is a seed. Or a bulb, perhaps. But with people"—by the note of pain in his voice she knew his thoughts were with Paul—"one never knows in what shape they will grow. Two are given the same food and the same parents and the same house and a good education, and one will become a fine man in the land and perhaps another . . ." And he lost trace of his thoughts in pain and accusation, with the old question gnawing his mind, what harm had he done to Paul, what blame was his?

She sensed his grief, and it made her restive and unhappy, and the noon hour was surely here and never had she known Giacomo to talk so long. While it was evident this was a matter of tremendous importance he was trying to tell her, what it was she could not guess, nor was she interested in trying to find out, the way she felt now. Her head was being stabbed through at the temples in a curiously painful fashion.

"Do you know I haven't had breakfast?" She slid down from the revolving stool. "Aren't you going in to lunch, Giacomo?"

Seeing her restlessness, he became desperate.

"I selected." He plodded on through his attempt to make her understand. "I bought the finest. Strength from the mother plant —that I have believed and followed. Six years ago—do you remember?—I sent Eric to England to get the finest stud plants he could find. Ten thousand dollars for an offshoot! That was the St. Gothard he bought that made Stoob so angry. That was a great deal to pay for a parent, no? But worth it! Even the little ones of that parent are worth seventy-five dollars now in the little pots, and some are worth five hundred dollars. But I will not sell them. They are worth more to me. I know what they are worth because I know all about them. They have proved they are good."

Tosca flared. "What right has Stoob to be angry? Why does he have so much to say about what you and Eric do?"

But Giacomo continued his argument. "I was building," he went on slowly, puzzling for words into which he could pour his meaning. "I was building the best I knew. It is like the building of a business. Or a family. You put the best you can find into the blood of the orchid. That is how at last you have something like your Aurea hybrid, Tosca. Something that will be living long after I am not living, and it will still be beautiful. . . .

"After so much trouble and working—something strong and beautiful comes. But what if it is no good after all? Like the white Gigas—so beautiful, but sterile. They cannot reproduce themselves. So after all their growing, what use are they? The family ends. The work is wasted."

Trouble was in his words, and his lined face was pleading.

"It is great work to make things beautiful, and after your work is done, perhaps the thing you have made is too weak to stand alone! Tosca, *figlia mia,* one must be so careful!"

She kept her face down. She was beginning to understand.

"What are you trying to tell me? Everyone wants something of me—something different. You, Mother, Father—everyone. I can't please everyone; I can't even please myself. What do you want with me, Giacomo?"

Proud and helpless, the answer came: "To see you married. With *bambini.*"

"And why?"

"I do not know why. God says——"

"Let's forget God for the moment, Giacomo. Why should I marry and live stupidly like everyone else?" And as she spoke she knew she was quoting something Mark had said in some moment of levity.

"Well, now"—he scowled in uncertainty—"it is true I do not know why." And he found it impossible to describe to her the power of the dark strong wall stretching back through the centuries of which she was the newest and most glorious part, and the struggle to speak in her tongue as fervently as he felt in his own left him helpless.

Then his face warmed with love. "Without you, *cara,* where should I be now, and what will you be without grandchildren when you are old?"

"That's different." She was sure of herself again. "You lived for us, Grandfather. You never want anything for yourself. That awful old car, and I have to make you buy new shirts."

"But I have everything," he said cheerfully. "I have more than enough."

"No, Giacomo. The pity is you have only one of me. You should have dozens of grandchildren."

"In Italy that might have happened," he agreed. And added thoughtfully, "We would have been very poor."

"And very happy," said Tosca a little bitterly. "Why is it, when people are able to give children all the advantages, they have fewer children?"

Giacomo shook his head. "You see, I do not know. But truly, should it not be the other way?"

"You are a geneticist. You should know."

"I grow old, and the thing I say most is I do not know. I do not know why it almost seems a law of the land that the finest and most beautiful is the first to wither and die, and the species that are colorless and without interest and even without use seem to live on forever." The familiar pain was in his voice once more, grieving her in a way he could not know, and he put out his hands to her pleadingly. "Tosca, when one is young one makes this mistake about life—we think it is short and soon over. But that is not true! It lasts forever."

She had turned to the door as if to escape from him. His words were accusation. Now she knew his meaning, and she wanted to go away from him, anywhere, in her need to be free. But she turned again to face him, with her back to the door.

"What do you know?" Her cry was defiant. "What have you —Father, Mother, Eric—all of you, against Mark? What do you know against him?"

Giacomo spread his worn hands. "I? I know nothing. Never before have I so much as heard his name."

And the sadness in his voice was for the way she turned from and against him, Tosca, so closely loved, who had been a spoon-slip-shaped bundle fitting into one's arms, and then child, girl, and woman, and now, in her place, a strange woman.

"Then why are you talking to me like this?"

"Something is wrong," he said slowly. "You did not bring him to the festa. You do not want him here. Is he someone I must not know? Are you ashamed of the nursery, Tosca, or of your Nonno?"

"Of you?" she laughed hysterically. "Darling Giacomo!"

In relief she came back to him and put her hand to his gray

locks and brushed them back to kiss the lined forehead. His look searched hers, and his face was tired and old.

"Then it is of this Mark you are ashamed?"

"Why, no!" Her eyes flared wide. There was a look in them close to fear, and she laughed a little wildly. "Oh, Giacomo, how can I expect you to understand! It's just—be patient with me. You know you are always telling me—*pazienza!*"

He held her arms like a babe that must be protected. "Tosca! Always before we have talked. Little one, tell me!"

The closeness of the small laboratory seemed to close her throat. "Wait, until I know myself," she whispered. She broke from his hands and wrenched open the door. "Come along, we're being silly and I'm starving."

But his words struck after her.

"Then it is wrong!"

NINE

*M*EALS at Giacomo's table were conducted in an atmosphere of vaudeville. The crew ate in relays, twenty at a time. Their overalls were dirt-stained, but this was "clean dirt," as Giacomo often said, and hands and faces were scrubbed clean. Many had been at work since dawn, and others longer than that. They ate tremendously, and Cesare, enormous in his white apron, urged more food upon them and sang snatches of Verdi as he moved ponderously between the table and his immense gas range.

For hours he had been serving the noon meal. Dinner was eaten at noon at Daneri's, and Giacomo liked to have everyone who worked for him share in this important event. This had been his custom since Daneri's began. Even the men who made their homes on his land dined with Giacomo, and Tosca, taking her place beside him in the long shedlike kitchen that ran the length of Giacomo's cottage, was not surprised to see Pietro there, and Stoob, whose house was only across the lane, sitting between Ludmilla and Laddie. The wives and daughters of the other workmen would be in their homes across the lane at this time, but Ludmilla hated cooking and housework and preferred the work in the greenhouses. Many times Giacomo had offered to put her on the pay roll, but the usually avaricious Stoob had always refused, for reasons he would not explain.

Ludmilla sat rather sullenly with her pale head bent over a bowl of steaming minestrone. She did not look up or speak.

Tosca looked about for Eric, but he was not at the table. She made up her mind to wait until he returned from the airport.

The kitchen reeked with the odors of rich foods left over from the festa of the day before, but its heat was allayed by the sweet coolness rising from Giacomo's newly watered herb garden under the open windows. Tosca looked at the heavy platters of food with faint revulsion and poured a cup of coffee from the gallon graniteware pot being pushed around the table.

After twenty-five years with the nursery Cesare felt it his duty to take liberties.

"*Mangiare!* Eat!" he bellowed musically over Tosca's head. "*Bella Santa,* you are scrawny like a little pigeon. Why do I cook, that people like you should resemble the famine?"

With the gesture of an outraged Othello he thrust back the plate of ravioli she had pushed away.

"Eat!" Giacomo urged her. "The ravioli is always better on the second day."

But the others stayed silent for a moment, which was an unusual event at mealtime at Daneri's, and only Stoob looked furtively over his food to study her face in a way she did not like.

Then they were talking again, singly or together as the mood moved them, and Cesare continued to urge on her the delicacies left from the day before, but she refused and drank another cup of the thick black coffee and ate a handful of the fresh cherries which, with cheese, were the dessert. And she thought, listening to the loud cheerful talk around the table, that Giacomo's kitchen was like a private club, with the best of food and good feeling and fellowship, and it was understandably rumored that the agricultural inspectors, when traveling around the country among the nurseries, on the lookout for thrips, white flies, or any of the other pests that were the enemies of the floral profession, planned their visits so that the noon hour brought them to Daneri's Nursery.

The restful sensation of being in another country and another age—the almost medieval atmosphere of Daneri's—came out most strongly at mealtimes. At this main meal, with the heaviest part of the day behind them, the men could relax for an hour or more, as they chose. Giacomo sat like a patriarch at his oilcloth-covered board, listening to the talk of his crews—his indoor growers and field workers and office staff. Their talk was of flowers and plants, of personal jests new and remembered, of work done or work to be done. Now, while the loaves of Italian bread were broken, the bottles of red wine passed, was the time for resting and eating and adjusting differences and recounting the gossip of the flower-growing world. It was a healthy and, to these people, an absorbing world. The news of it came to this table, brought out of the greenhouses by the workmen, and back from the flower market and the flower shops by the driving crews. The nurserymen were engrossed by the reports of what was being grown at other nurseries, what flowers had been brought into the city and by what growers, what prices were being quoted for roses and all other flowers at market, what prices might hold or fall, what crops were threatened, and any incidents for better or worse that might have befallen any of the flower people. All gossip was recounted, to a chorus of commiseration or amusement. A San Leandro rose grower had overslept and arrived late to market with his flowers that morning—an accident that would make him the butt of jests for many years.

Politics, finance, social questions were passed over lightly at Giacomo's table. The men's talk might edge upon competitive or personal jealousies, but its commonest theme was that of growth and of the urge for beauty—for ever-greater beauty.

The main talk was of flowers, and it developed that the conversation, before Tosca and Giacomo came, had centered around the report being discussed in and around the flower circles that morning, wherever flower people met.

"Padrone," Pietro was the first to ask, "is it true that Brock's new break is a salmon?"

Now Giacomo was the last to assert that a break was true until he was sure, and even Stoob stopped munching to hear what he might say.

So Giacomo finished his soup before he spoke.

"This I will say—it may be so," he commented at last. "Adolph Brock telephoned me this morning, and he is like Eric in that he does not say a thing is so until it is so." Here Stoob opened his mouth as if to speak, but instead pulled it down to a sneer. "When his great break came—the Brock delphinium—did he say one word to any of us until he was sure? And yet he had waited for it twenty years!"

There was reverence in his words. The faces of the crew reflected that reverence. A break was the miracle—the revolutionary change a grower accomplished in a flower that, if proved permanent, would mark this flower as his own. A true break was an event to impress the entire world of flower people.

But a salmon gladiolus that would not change! Such a probability had been discussed and dreamed about for many years. Those at Giacomo's table, with one exception perhaps, wanted to believe in Adolph Brock's good fortune.

"It must be hothouse," stated Pietro, and all agreed such a wonder of a flower could have been grown only under glass.

Then Stoob put in with his fluted treble:

"Impossible! You will see, the color will not hold."

During the twenty years he had eaten at Giacomo's noisy and cheerful table he had not acquired a single Latin mannerism. Even now he did not raise his voice as the others did, and still they listened.

"No giant glad remains true to salmon," he stated positively. "Why that is, I do not know, but I've grown and watched gladioli ever since I came to America and I've never seen a salmon hold its color through the second season. And anyway, salmon is an unlucky color in flowers. Don't forget, you have those salmon-tinted orchids, Giacomo, and nobody wants them!"

"They will sell. Give them time," said Giacomo good-naturedly. "Five years ago I couldn't sell a white orchid, either——" But his argument was lost in the men's laughter, for Stoob's resentment against the orchids was one of the standing jokes of the nursery. And when Giacomo tried to speak again Cesare's voice was loudest.

"You never lift your head above the little lilies," Cesare jeered over Stoob. "Sometimes I think you get to look like a lily. So white! More pasta, old man, so you bloom more!"

He thumped the long wooden salad bowl on the table before Tosca. "Meex!" he shouted sternly, drowning out Stoob's sputter. "Time you do some work, Tosca. What you do all day in that beeg house in San Francisco, eh? Eat and sleep?"

"Tosca has done good work this morning," Giacomo began

loyally, and approbation ran in a warm circle around the table, for all knew of the pollen that had gone to Matraia's. She looked up, laughing, into the enormous face of Cesare. "See, some of us are born to be loafers," she teased, and instantly knew she was quoting Mark, and even imitating his amused way of teasing. But Stoob and Ludmilla did not laugh with the others.

Cesare glowered critically while Tosca lifted the wooden spoons and lightly turned the fresh leaves of endive and lettuce and romaine through the wine vinegar and olive oil spiced with herbs from Giacomo's garden. There was satisfaction to be gained in coating dark leaves and pale and not bruising a leaf. Even Cesare was pleased.

"*Artista!*" he pronounced. "I tell you, I know if a person has the *artista* appreciation by the way they meex salad."

Laddie's face was innocent. "Then you must be a great artist, Cesare."

Cesare thumped his white cap with a magnificent gesture. "I contain the soul of Caruso! Leesten! I make orchestra."

And with his wooden ladle he drew a clatter of sound from the pans and kettles strung above the range while bellowing the opening strains of *"Donna è mobile."* Pietro and Garibaldi joined in; the others hummed or waved their laden forks in appreciation. All the Daneri workmen knew opera. There was scarcely one who did not attend the opera at least once every season, not only to hear again the familiar music, but to observe with a personal pride the beautifully gowned women wearing flowers they had grown.

Stoob showed his disgust. Ludmilla did not look up. They were so very cheerful and so very noisy, thought Tosca. They were making her head ache. And what had they to be so happy about? Mark . . . She knew how Mark would be amused by them, and the emptied sense of loneliness followed her thought of him. If he were there, with his faun's laughter and his never-to-be-limited appreciation for the amusement of others . . . He would be at home here, at Giacomo's table, she thought, but in a curious defensive way, and she lifted her eyes to find Giacomo watching her with the patience that was so close to sadness.

"To cook is to make music," declaimed Cesare from his stove as the burst of singing ended.

"I don't see much sense to it," said Tosca, perhaps because she was weary of the sight of so much food vanishing so relentlessly, particularly in the vicinity of Stoob. "You work all morning on a dish, and it's gobbled up in five minutes."

"And have you not enjoyed it?" demanded Cesare. "For that matter, how long does a flower last? Men like your Nonno work for years on one flower and it fades in a night, and me, I am working for one day to make some thing all can enjoy. A dish of risotto with saffron and mushrooms—is that not beautful like a bed of marigolds?"

"And better eating," said Giacomo, helping himself to more salad.

"When I make a salad," said Cesare, contentedly watching his performance, "I do not make a salad. I make a flower garden."

And as passionately as if she were arguing with Mark in their behalf, Tosca found herself in agreement with Cesare's nonsense, because there was sound reason in what he was saying, and he and these others who worked with Giacomo Daneri were artists and her friends. By other standards, perhaps, they might be considered illiterate laborers. Not to her. She listened with respect to all they had to say, and even in this time of relaxation their talk was eager and was about their work, and when they would push their chairs back and roll the checked napkins in the wooden rings marked with their names, they would return in eagerness to that work, disappearing, with content in their bodies and thoughts, into the glass-bound forests of azalea and fern, roses, gardenias, orchids, and valley lilies.

Pietro stood up to leave. "My rose houses are showing more color. June is not far away." And four members of the rose crew left the table with him.

"The Number Three House, she is resting," he told Giacomo. "Write it on the blackboard, please, not to water her." He winked at Tosca. "Like the brood mare, she sleeps."

There was a clump of rubber boots dropped on the porch, and Ernesto stamped into the kitchen.

"On the radio, in the shipping shed," he announced dramatically, "we hear it about Chancellor Hitler. He is perhaps going into Austria!"

There was a slight flurry of comment, but only Stoob showed active interest in the news.

"You will see," he said portentously, "he will take Europe!"

"He should be stopped," said Cesare, tapping his chopping board with his cleaver and eying Stoob as if he wished his neck were under the blade. "Stopped in his tracks, and his neck wrung."

One could not be certain whether Cesare meant Stoob or the German chancellor.

"When have the small been able to see greatness?" Stoob rolled his bulging eyes toward his daughter, who did not look up, and Giacomo, who could be capable of great stubbornness, frowned and spoke with a sternness rare to him. "It may be as you say. But I cannot believe good can come from men who make people they do not like drink castor oil."

And because his thoughts were older and worked more slowly than those of the others, his mind returned to the salmon gladiolus.

"Eric's father is a good grower," he argued, as if the subject had never been dropped. "Eric's father is not a fool. And if he tells me he has a good gladiolus, then it is good."

Stoob glared over his pasta. He seemed angry about more than one matter now, and when he spoke his attitude was that of a superior.

"Well, you'll see, Giacomo. Next season it will start to streak and then it will go back to variegated, like all the salmons. Like that pink delphinium he got us all excited about. It went back—last year!"

"Maybe this time the color will hold," said Tosca unexpectedly.

She was not interested in Stoob's argument. She only wanted to support Giacomo. She noted how quickly Ludmilla showed interest, turning her narrow pale eyes on her for the first time, so that Tosca went on, speaking to Ludmilla:

"Eric's father has a way with glads. Maybe this time he has it!"

"Maybe!" echoed Giacomo, and his eyes were bright under their wrinkled lids.

The word gripped the men around the table, so that even Pietro, who had been standing in the open door, came back and took his place at the table again, and his crew members returned to listen and give their opinions too. For work could wait a few minutes or even another hour, and talk was important, and of all speech no word was more important than the one word, "maybe." It was the sounding note of their profession. Maybe—the color will hold true, the shape remain good, the sturdiness bred into this season's flower survive through other generations. The word gave thrill and vibrancy and the gambling urge to their daily labors. It rescued them from monotony. A flower burgeoned under glass, a bud unfolded in a valley, something different and never seen before spread slowly open, petal by petal, and over-night the entire flower profession knew and quickened.

In the hush of waiting that followed that word Tosca spoke softly, and her face shone. "I remember the excitement," she said, "over the Brock Field of Blue."

How well she remembered! She could remember Stoob, who had scoffed and refused to believe that the giant cobalt and azure delphinium was a true break. She could remember the hot young voice of Eric discussing it with Giacomo over her twelve-year-old head.

"You won't believe it until you see it, Giacomo! Dad really has it this time. It's worth walking to Santa Cruz to see. A blue sunburst—there's no other word for it!"

And Giacomo's voice, a little apprehensive:

"So? Now maybe you will want to go back and grow del-phinium instead of orchids?"

And she had shared Giacomo's happiness, hearing Eric's scorn-ful laughter. Grow other flowers, when one could grow orchids? Not Eric! And not Giacomo Daneri!

"Consider the lilies!" Stoob rebuked them often. "That is in the Bible."

The others laughed at Stoob. Bulb flowers were profitable and fairly safe and had their place in the world. But the talk at Giacomo's table was of more dramatic blooms.

There were times when, as now, the conversation became rain-bow talk that dripped color. Tosca sat spellbound, forgetful of time, and the others forgot. These men loved the excitement of bright words. Hands and eyes helped them speak as they talked again, as they had so many times before, of the great hunts and discoveries that made the story of floriculture a series of thrilling dramas. For behind every flower was a legend, an adventure, a miracle or a tragedy, and a life longer than Giacomo's would not be long enough to absorb the full story of the flowers.

For years, at every grower's table in the world, the drama had been told and retold of the Golden Gleam, the nasturtium that would have been lost forever had not its last seed been found on a dead plant near a revolution-demolished farmhouse in Mexico. No hunter stalking in the wake of legendary pirates had ever discovered greater treasure.

Part of the endless hunt for the breaks was the endless effort to bring about the still unaccomplished, and a grower could spend his life attempting to develop a yellow sweet pea, a snapdragon that could resist rust, a blue rose.

"A blue rose!" echoed Tosca, and all felt with her that such a thing must someday be. By such dreams the faces around the table were set glowing, each with dreams of its own, and Giacomo's eyes were very bright as he listened to each tale and nodded in agreement, saying, "Someday—perhaps. *Pazienza!*"

For were there not miracles without number that had once been considered equally impossible dreams? The drowsy California poppy, once given to wrapping itself in sleep at all hours, had been made to change color and size and to stay awake! Canterbury bells, which once had bloomed only after their second season, now burst into flower in six months. Tremendous changes had been wrought within the past few years in the African daisy, the sweet pea, larkspur, aster, petunia, zinnia, and a hundred others. The marriage of the French marigold to the African marigold had made horticultural history. A zinnia rescued from the blades of mowers had lived to change completely the zinnia pattern. The petunia, with its incomplete reproductive system, had been pollinized and forced to capitulate to many changes.

In Daneri's, as in fields and greenhouses all over the world, the patient struggle of the beauty makers was never-ending, changing and fixing shape and color and strength through the generations, selecting and crossing and discarding in the eternal hunt for the break—the latest, newest flower that would come closest to perfection.

The stories they knew, these men! And Tosca, lost in fascination, chanced to glance at the tiny diamond-framed watch Giacomo had given her upon her graduation from the convent and saw that the midday was flying and Eric was very late. Giacomo, she knew, had forgiven her for slipping away from the festa. But if, as Ludmilla's sullenness hinted, Eric was still displeased with her, Tosca wanted to make her peace with him. Eric was part of the life surrounding Giacomo, and that life was still part of Tosca. She did not want to leave the nursery again, leaving Eric angry.

She wished he were there, for the flower talk led naturally to orchids, and of all the stories, the most thrilling were the tales of orchidry. Eric, she knew, could never hear enough of these stories.

Oh, the stories they had heard, of hunger and death and incredible adventure endured in the search for orchids! Men had tracked their fellows and fought them to the death for orchids. The stories they told—of the man in India who found the fabulous Cypripedium, and while carrying it home was mauled to death by a bear and the orchid lost, so that other men would lose fortunes, and their lives, hunting it in vain. They told again of the marvelous white orchid of India that came riding into a jungle village on a load of wood and was seen by many, but never glimpsed again despite all the expeditions that have hunted it. And they recalled the legend of the blue orchid in South America that is more desirable than any jewel and has been seen only by savages.

Such tales had been old when Giacomo was young, and they still were new. The lost orchids had bloomed and were still blooming in their secret hiding places while men braved hardship and pestilence in the hope of finding them again. Fabulous were the prices paid, the lives sacrificed, for such treasure. And Tosca, watching Giacomo, saw that the stories that had fired his youth could fire him still.

Then Laddie, who had been listening with his lips parted, ventured to put forth in his high voice a question that had troubled him. Was it true plants could feel? There was a diversity of opinion as to whether they could or not, and because all turned to him, Giacomo spoke carefully.

"Plants do not feel?" countered Giacomo. "The pitcher plant that snaps at the fly, can you say its nervous system is different?" With the great fingers of his hand he caught up a chicken bone. "See? I cannot feel I am so different from the cannibal plant!"

And Pietro, who was a tease, chuckled. "Why, Laddie? The carnations—did they cry this morning when you pinned them together?"

"What a pity so many burst," Tosca said without thinking.

Then she saw Stoob pause with his cup in hand and knew it was an idle comment that should not have been made. Like most rude people, Stoob was acutely sensitive where his own feelings were concerned, and it was instantly apparent to Tosca and the others that Stoob regarded her remark as criticism, aimed directly at Stoob. In a moment the joyous camaraderie around Giacomo's table was blasted and an ugly tension held them all.

"Am I being accused, then?" began Stoob. "Of carelessness, perhaps?"

His voice was high with affront, and this was inexplicable because it was no more his duty than any other man's to keep an eye on the steam pressure. Every person on the place, from Giacomo to Laddie, was supposed to watch the heat that was the lifeblood of the flowers.

"Nothing but trouble with the heating system," put in Garibaldi a little uneasily, because the pleasant happiness that had held them together was no longer in the kitchen, and he spoke like a man voicing an opinion no one else could be expected to share. "We really should put in a new boiler, Giacomo. Eric thinks so too."

But Giacomo, seeing Stoob's round head jerk with resentment, said placidly, "The boiler will last a little longer. And who knows? I may not last as long."

And he smiled so broadly, even Stoob seemed about to smile with him but thought better of it. Instead, he drew his lips down.

"Oh yes, we must save," he agreed bitterly. "In the important matters, we must not spend. But when it comes to foolishness, that is another matter!"

Now he had everyone's attention.

"You mean something, perhaps?" Giacomo asked quietly.

Stoob, taking a deep breath, said the words that had been bursting within him since the preceding day. "Four thousand dollars!" he said, biting down on the painful words. "In times like these!"

"So I thought." Giacomo spoke with sadness. "It is the festa that troubles you. Stoob, in all my life, in every year of my life, I have heard men say, 'In times like these!' Always, they say times are bad, and times are never as bad as this time, they say. And if the years are good they worry because they are too good to last, they say. Now perhaps such a day as yesterday is extravagant, but may it not"—here he paused, unable to explain the ancient urge for the libation poured out—"may it not be that if we have the faith to indulge in such matters it will be repaid? Was it not a good festa and a good way to share what we have with our friends?"

He would not say, not to Stoob, And how much longer have I in which to meet my friends over my own table? But that, too, was in his thoughts.

"Besides," he said instead, making a joke of his inner feelings, "our older friends are going, and when can we bring them together at our table if not now?"

"Old folks!" said Stoob in a tone that indicated this, too, was a sore point with him and that generations beyond his own survived to keep him from his desirable goal. "What are they for? To clutter the earth!"

"Well," said Giacomo, and he was not smiling now, "it is time I go and clutter the earth around the heather so we can make more money."

No one had paid any attention to Cesare. He was looking at Stoob from his place of command by the range, and the cleaver was still in his hand.

"There is nothing wrong with your face that could not be improved by busting it wide open," he remarked now to Stoob with great interest.

Stoob speared a roll with his fork, crushed it between his hands, and sopped the gravy from his plate. Ludmilla took a forkful of food, but her hand was trembling.

"You see," Stoob boasted, "I waste nothing."

"And sometimes that does not help," said Giacomo quietly, because he could not help being hurt by Stoob's criticism of the festa, and he could not help remembering, as everyone in the kitchen was remembering—with the possible exception of the lily master himself—how Stoob had come to the shipping-shed entrance to beg for work thirty years before, a young immigrant who had tried to start a lily house of his own in the new land and had been left without a bulb or a dollar. From the first Stoob had shown genius with the lilies, having learned their breeding and care on the Black Sea, where his family had grown lily pips for generations. His talent for bulbs had grown with the years, and with it had grown the Daneri lily houses.

Three times Stoob had traveled as the Daneri representative to Europe, to strengthen the respect of the growers of valley lilies and tulips there and to guarantee their finest bulbs and fastest service for the nursery at Colma. After one visit Stoob brought back a flaxen-haired, unhappy-looking bride who had never learned to speak English and seldom was seen outside the small cottage Giacomo put at their disposal across the lane, and who died, leaving Ludmilla.

Stoob had always worked as if driven, careful against waste, and never considering the hours.

And perhaps because Stoob was also remembering much he would have preferred to forget, the little man seemed to swell with arrogance and his cheeks puffed as he sopped up the last of the gravy.

"Four thousand dollars!" he repeated contemptuously. "For food like this."

"Why do you not choke on it?" suggested Cesare, for the annual festa was his responsibility, for which he planned and worked weeks in advance.

But Giacomo answered without rancor. "Was it not worth it? Did we not have a fine festa yesterday?"

And his look was on Tosca, pleading. But Stoob had not listened.

"A fortune," he said bitterly. "A man could set up a lily house with that money. Such a way to do business."

"Business!" shouted Cesare before anyone else could answer. His face was a flaming disk. "What business had you that was so important when the Padrone took you in and you made his business your business?"

Ludmilla's head went lower over her plate and she went on eating, plainly without knowing what she ate.

"A typical victim," commented Stoob, staring up at the towering Cesare with his cold, contemptuous eyes. The color withdrew from his cheeks and he was again pale with the mushroom pallor that was his most curious characteristic. His lip curled back. "I pity you, typical slave product of the capital-eestic system."

With a large and deliberate gesture Cesare drew his honing steel from the rack and proceeded to whet the cleaver blade over Stoob's arrogantly held head.

"You and your capital-eestic seestom," Cesare shouted. "Better for you I carve that seestom out of your seestom——"

"Please, Cesare," said Giacomo, as if he were speaking to children, for both men were approaching hysteria.

"Very soon," bellowed Cesare, ignoring Giacomo and whetting his blade, "Daneri's will be without a lily man. If I go to San Quentin for twenty—two hundred—one thousand years!—I swear this."

"But not until our bulbs are in, please," countered Giacomo, attempting to flatter Stoob and placate Cesare with the same words. "Stoob is the best bulb man in——"

"I am a bulb man and not a woman," interrupted Stoob. "I do not cook for a living."

"Cook?" shrieked Cesare. "I am chef! *Artisto!* You section of pig's gut——"

But half the men around the table were on their feet to divert Cesare's wrath and his blade from Stoob, and Giacomo, realizing that these storms were born of drama on Cesare's part because he loved to nettle the excitable lily master, merely shook his head in the direction of the melee and remarked gently, "Cesare, someday you go too far."

"That *pappagallo!*" muttered Cesare, subsiding, "Someday I will wring his neck, parrot that he is."

And he slung the cleaver down into the chopping block so that the kitchen shivered at the blow, and in another minute, bringing fresh coffee to the table, he was humming a delicious peasant love song. Again Cesare was master and content in his kitchen, where the men around the table were again eating and talking as if no tornado had been averted there. Only Ludmilla and Stoob were silent, and the girl's thin cheeks were as pale as her father's.

Again the talk was of flowers.

Eric stopped the bottle-green truck outside the shipping shed and sprang down onto the spongy turf. The roar of the planes was still in his ears. He had been at work since four on the sweet-smelling snowy cargo he had just sent on its way; directing the first cutting crew in the gardenia houses, overseeing their packing, and finally watching from the airfield as the planes moved over the bay and toward the mountains, rushing eastward the Daneri gardenias. He had felt slightly Napoleonic, and a little foolish that he was still young enough to have such thoughts, as he saw the flowers flying through the skies. And he was estimating, twenty thousand gardenia bushes grew in the Daneri houses —a million and a half of the pure-white blooms every year. There were other growers who owned four times as many plants, all yielding flowers for America.

Now, as he hurried over the gravel walks between the daisies and toward Giacomo's house, he was thinking that because of this morning's shipment the glossy-leaved bushes in the gardenia houses were left stripped and nearly flowerless. He had plans of his own, and gloatingly he looked forward to a day when the last of those shining bushes would be gone, and he envisioned all the glasshouses he was hastening between as filled to bursting with priceless Daneri orchids. Greater than the Sander's houses, more fabulous than the houses of Rothschild, Eric dreamed them! Like Giacomo, Eric could never believe that a grower who had worked with orchids could ever again give full sympathy to the lesser flowers. And he wished Stoob would realize this and stop talking his damned endless nonsense about lilies!

The gardenia shipment had been a large task well done, and Eric was hungry and tired and glad to be home. And also he had seen Tosca's car in the lane. But it was none of these things that lengthened his stride as he passed the herb garden.

The sight of Giacomo's kitten washing its small face on the kitchen steps reassured him. Eric had important news, and the kitten was never far from Giacomo. So he came bursting into the kitchen, his light hair wind-blown and his dark face ruddy with wind and sun. Seeing Tosca beside Giacomo, a look of hesitancy on her usually impudent face, he stopped and placed his hand over his heart and bowed low.

"Your Excellency!" he murmured, but his eyes were suddenly cold and unamused.

Then he spoke rapidly to Giacomo.

"Guess what I heard at the airfield!"

"We know!" Giacomo answered happily. "Your papa telephoned and says he has a true salmon glad to show us, and when can we go down to Santa Cruz."

He cleared a place for Eric beside him.

"I'd like to go right away," said Eric, and he seemed greatly pleased. But he did not comment further on the gladiolus, and only Stoob was moved to pronounce darkly, "You will see—the color will not hold."

"I'll get your soup for you," said Ludmilla. It was the first time she had spoken. Her thin face burned as she walked to the stove and dipped into the steaming kettle of thick minestrone. She found an unbroken loaf for Eric and poured his coffee while the others watched.

Eric looked embarrassed, but he smiled at Ludmilla and his teeth flashed white in his dark face.

"Say, thanks for the attention," he said. "It's nice to see a girl who thinks of someone except herself."

He has not forgiven me for leaving the festa, thought Tosca.

And she glanced at her watch again, remembering Mark and how long the hours must be until five, when he would telephone, and it was then Stoob made another of the spiteful remarks he seemed unable to control.

"I am surprised," he said to Eric, "that you would consider going to Santa Cruz to see anything so common as gladioli."

"I have nothing against glads," said Eric, spooning his soup.

And he spoke lightly, in a way that seemed to infuriate Stoob far more than Cesare's thundering diatribes, and Tosca noticed that when Stoob and Eric spoke together the words were quiet, man to man, measure for measure, and this was far more sinister than any shouted anger.

"If it weren't for the other flowers on this place, there wouldn't be any orchids. Never forget that," said Stoob.

Eric's good-humored smile was gone.

"If I had wanted to grow cut flowers, Stoob, I would have stayed on at Santa Cruz."

"Why didn't you?"

"Eat! Eat!" urged Cesare. He took up Eric's empty soup plate and set a dish of steaming ravioli in its place. Food was his answer to all problems, and he took no interest in an argument not of his own making. But his head inclined toward Stoob as if not to miss anything the lily master might have to say.

Giacomo was turning his shaggy head in a pleading way between Eric and Stoob.

"Orchids are good, Stoob. We make good money on orchids."

Stoob did not hide his contempt. "There is too much waste to orchids. Seven years, and what have you! Perhaps a good one, perhaps a dud. But a bulb—look at it, and it is as good as a lily already. Put it in the ground, and what it will be it will be. No tricks. No disappointments. And there is exactitude for you."

He pronounced the long word with triumph.

"An exact science," he stated flatly. "We have that in the lily houses, while in the orchid houses—trial and error and waste."

It was not often Giacomo became angry. He was angry and weary of Stoob, but still he hesitated, for it was a harsh thing to point out to another man that much of the ample life given him came from the orchids he professed to despise. And he hesitated mainly because he had come to pity Stoob, who was not a creator, who carried on only what others had created, and who lived a poor, mean sort of life despite the fragrant lily harvests. There were lives one could pour into and never fill to the brim, as Giacomo's had been filled, even when he had been very little and very poor. And he remembered the happiness of having been a young man, setting out in the dark morning hours with a lunch in his pocket put up by Maria, to work all day in the greenhouse in San Leandro for one dollar a day. He recalled the pleasure of working among the roses, and then the orchids had burst upon him and changed his world, and he had been ready to sacrifice the savings of years for a single plant, and out of that had come the greenhouses crowded with the proud, beautiful breedings that might have come from his very heart.

But while he hunted words in which to reprove Stoob and defend the orchids, Eric took up the argument in a calm and reasonable way.

"May I point out to you," Eric remarked across the table to Stoob, "that three sprays of your precious valley are equivalent to the price of an ordinary orchid in the present market, and I can't see where you get the idea that the orchid has any edge on the lily as a luxury flower. Frankly, I think you're cracking wide open on the subject of lilies."

Stoob was sibilant.

"They earn! The orchid is always taking time, money, care."

"Oh, so the lilies take care of themselves! That's news to me. Hear that, Giacomo? You don't need anyone to tend lilies, so you've been wasting Stoob's salary all these years."

"Oh, patience, please, a little more *pazienza*," said Giacomo uneasily, forgetting all he had intended to say. "Eric, enjoy your good ravioli." And he tried to believe he imagined the word "Leftovers!" Stoob released under his breath.

Tosca was thinking she had never heard such nonsense. Still, it went on and on at the nursery, and how Giacomo put up with it she could not see. Why, was still another question. She thought back a few years, when Eric had worked with Giacomo during college vacations. Eric had never answered Stoob in those days but only scowled at the lily master as Giacomo hunched his great shoulders under the steady torrent of criticism and complaint. But now that Eric was Giacomo's right hand he had taken a defensive attitude toward Giacomo, and she could see that Stoob's peevishness was being intercepted and resented by Eric before it could reach the more placid Giacomo. In effect, Eric was standing between the grower and the lily master, and she could see at last how Giacomo had been disturbed by the attacks against which he had never tried to defend himself.

Even now Stoob directed one last word to Giacomo.

"You know that the bulbs and outside flowers support Daneri's," he said pettishly. "And all I make——"

"The warehouse is jammed with your goddamn bulbs," interrupted Eric. "You spend a fortune every year on new lily pips and hyacinth bulbs. So why not stick to your lily houses and let us run the orchids?"

"And all I make," Stoob continued, ignoring Eric and speaking only to Giacomo, "all I make on the bulbs you put into orchids. What of those plants Eric brought from New Jersey?— twelve dollars apiece—nearly four thousand dollars for a new hybrid. And you sent him to Europe, and what did he buy! One bulb—one single orchid bulb—for ten thousand dollars!"

The St. Gothard, Tosca remembered, watching Eric. But this was such nonsense, Eric was no longer annoyed. He grinned at Stoob.

"So that's what has kept you in such an uproar! I thought you'd forgotten that deal. Listen, I've bought orchid plants for as low as twenty-five cents for Giacomo, and I've paid thousands for others, but I've never brought in a greater bargain than the St. Gothard. That 'one bulb,' as you call it, was a prize winner and has proved its value as a breed. And while we're on the subject, those Cyps from New Jersey you mention have already paid back the cost of their two new greenhouses and their own cost too. You're crazy, Stoob, if you think anyone can have too many orchids."

"So, I am crazy." Stoob's pallor had changed until his skin was almost lavender. Ludmilla had shrunk away as if driven back by the fury of his thoughts. But he could find no argument to answer Eric, so he only muttered, "We shall see what we shall see!" an ominous threat with which Stoob invariably closed any argument he had lost.

And Eric, feeling himself the victor, turned to Giacomo and said with enthusiasm: "Well, how about getting started for Santa Cruz?"

There was an answering rush of eagerness in Giacomo's voice. But he thought it best to temper his enthusiasm.

"Today, so soon after the festa? I had planned to chop peat today, Eric."

"That's Laddie's job, isn't it, Laddie? Come on, Giacomo. We'll see the folks and the new glad."

He stood up and twirled the chair about with a flip of his hand.

"Let's go, Giacomo," he coaxed.

But Giacomo had turned to Tosca.

"You will come?" he asked, so humbly that her conscience hurt, remembering the festa and the way she had left it the evening before. And she knew at once she would go with him, to give any small happiness her being along would hold for Giacomo. It was so seldom he took a holiday.

"But I must be back early," she said worriedly. "I have to be home by five."

"We'll get you back," said Eric, but he spoke coldly and his eyes were challenging.

"Fine," said Giacomo happily. "We go in my car."

"That heap! I wouldn't be caught dead in it. We take my roadster," said Tosca.

"On one condition," said Eric. "I drive!"

"Nobody ever wants to drive with me," Tosca complained, but since the purpose of the trip to Santa Cruz was to give pleasure to Giacomo, and since whenever he drove with Tosca he clung to the car seat as if riding for his life, she yielded without argument.

Another crew came in from the gardenia houses, where they had been watering the stripped plants, and Giacomo led the exodus from the table to make way for the hungry newcomers. Tosca, following, tried to ignore the cold anger in Eric's eyes as he held the door open for her and the sullen contempt on Stoob's face as he watched them go.

TEN

THE flower people indulged in pilgrimages.

Many times in the small white room in Giacomo's cottage that had been her mother's Tosca had brushed her hair and touched her lips in preparation for revisiting scenes that were

126

bright in Giacomo's memory and kept fresh by revisiting year after year.

In the past he had made longer pilgrimages. He had attended the English orchid shows for many consecutive years and visited the leading orchid houses of two continents. In England, Belgium, and Holland—making it a point to be in Holland at tulip time—he had studied with absorption the growth in the greatest orchid houses, including those of Rothschild and Sander, and found none he considered finer than his own.

There were simpler pleasures nearer home. Nearly all the California flower people were given to visiting, following a floral tracery along the West Coast from Seattle to San Diego. Sometimes they crossed the Canadian or Mexican border to enjoy the work of the horticulturists in these places. They traveled to see what developments and advances were being made in the flowers and to observe and compare as well as to admire. Giacomo made several trips a year through the nursery network, and when Tosca had been younger, he chose the times when she could go with him without interrupting her schooling.

Each spring for many years he had driven down to Lompoc, in the southern part of California, to feast his fading vision on four hundred or more acres of vari-tinted scented butterflies that were sweet peas, or a hill painted blue with moonflowers. On these great California farms that grew half the flower seeds of the world, fields of flowers, like rippling flags, striped the southern hills with red and indigo, sky blue, scarlet, and gold.

Such beauty was stamped irrevocably in a man's memory; still it was a glorious experience to see such things again and keep their colors fresh in mind.

Sometimes, in the wake of the spring rains, Giacomo had been known to drive deeper into the south, not overlooking any of the great orchid houses of Southern California on his way, and penetrate the rolling arid areas of the Mojave to observe the desert lilies, the sharp candle-flame-tipped ocotillo, the sand verbena and yellow poppies and creamy, spiky yucca that tinted the desert with exquisite aquatint springtime colors. But he took no interest in the growing fad for cactus gardens. In fact, he loved best the plants and trees that flowered.

Later, almost every spring, he drove with Eric or Tosca up the Redwood Highway into Oregon to see the rose-tinted fields of wild azalea, and on, to visit the bulb fields, piercingly ruby and white, and the rainbow-tinted iris fields of Washington and Oregon. Returning homeward, he did not miss the collection of rare native plants at Ukiah. Then, following the familiar track of his pilgrimage, he turned toward Lake Tahoe, where the wild dogwood was nearly as large and fragrant as magnolia, and the Ceanothus, or wild lilac, drifted like blue incense over the mountains. In the higher Sierra he searched the late snowdrifts banked along the highways for the dazzling ice plants, those queerly lovely growths, pineapple-shaped and crystalline, glowing with magenta and orange, pink, purple, and scarlet.

He had visited the azalea gardens of Florida and the Carolinas and the famed camellia gardens of the South.

But now it was a rare pilgrimage that could carry Giacomo far from Colma, and Tosca had noticed his increasing reluctance to leave the nursery for any period of time. But he tried not to miss the floral events. The Rose Festival at Portland, the Parade of the Roses in Pasadena on New Year's Day, the Blossom Festival, held when a million prune trees covered a gigantic tableland with sweet bouquets in the Santa Clara Valley, only a short drive from Colma, the Chrysanthemum Show at nearby San Mateo which celebrated the annual harvesting of a four- or five-million-dollar crop of "mums," and, all over California, the Orchid Society meetings, the rose growers' associations, the gardenia groups, and the many flower shows—all these brightened the year and took time from a man's life. But Giacomo Daneri had learned that life consisted principally of time and that it was wise to spend it doing what one liked best to do.

If only I could be calm like Giacomo and content in little ways, Tosca was thinking, brushing her hair before the narrow mirror until it took on the sheen of buffed copper. But she knew she could never be, not even if she lived to be Giacomo's age. Still there was something in the atmosphere of the nursery that was quieting; this little room, she thought, holds the nucleus of peace.

The girlhood of Marie Levenridge, touchingly simple and innocent, remained in the room. The walls held the fragrance of lavender stalks gathered in Giacomo's garden by Tosca's mother when she had been younger than Tosca now. The white scarves on the bird's-eye maple bureau were of her embroidering, and the spread covering the sleigh bed had been crocheted by Tosca's grandmother, the first Maria.

Over it massive gold framed a bright chromo of the Madonna. This and a valise that held clothing and two large bags containing lamb's wool for bedding had been all the worldly goods brought from Italy to California by the immigrant bride of Giacomo. The bed's deep mattress was made of this virgin wool. The imprint of Maria was still over Giacomo's home, and he spoke of her always as if she lived. Tosca could remember a small and tidy little person whose serenity and dignity matched Giacomo's. She had often noticed that Giacomo held special affection for many of the men on the place, such as Cesare and Pietro, because they had known the soft-spoken and quiet-faced Maria.

Her head ached under the brush, and she went to the window and stood between the parted lace curtains, drinking the sweet cleanliness of the morning air sweeping over the glass roofs from the sea. The scent of sea and swelling fields, the medicinal smell of eucalyptus leaves smoldering on the compost filled her lungs and limbs with a freshening sense of renewal. She looked down to the gray glass squares of the roofs and saw that the sun brought the many colors of the flowers to the glass surface as if reflected on mirrors. One glass rectangle was blazing with roses, and beyond it stretched the velvet gardenias, while a house of Stoob's tulips was a block of blazing gold.

And she thought, Mark would love this because Mark loves beauty. At this hour—provided, as he had explained, he rose in time—he would be at the auction rooms on Sutter Street awaiting the appearance of a Chinese screen he had set his heart upon owning. She pictured the way he would manage to appear at ease and even lolling in the uncomfortable chair, not growing tense over the bidding, as another might, but calling out his bids in a lazy fashion, as if it made no difference whether the screen was to be his or another's. And the look of amused tolerance would be on his face, as if Mark were surprised at finding himself there.

He would not be alone, she knew. Roscoe or another of his satellites would be along to share even this small adventure.

This gift for amusement and his passion for sharing a gift were the qualities that charmed her most, while they baffled. Remembering, she felt her body slacken and grow weak with longing. Why had she permitted herself to be challenged—for Eric's displeasure had challenged her—into this untimely jaunt to Santa Cruz? Mark might phone—even now—one of his unexpected moods might send him in search of her. She would go, she knew, the weakness overcoming her again, as if her steps carried her against her will into the lounge or hotel bar where he might be waiting. She would go, she who ever before had been the proud one, waited upon, deferred to, adored. She who had always led was now the one who followed. Her hands clutched the coarse lace curtains, and she bowed her head between them, lost and emptied with longing, resenting and accepting the weakness that gave him such power over her and had taken from her the audacity and pride and assurance she had known before.

But Giacomo was to be considered, and when she rejoined Giacomo and Eric there was no trace of the cataclysm that had left her, for a few moments, with the feeling that she could not, dared not, go so far from San Francisco that afternoon.

But she questioned Eric again in the car.

"You're not forgetting we must be back by five?"

He made a monosyllabic reply, and it was plain that he was still angry with her. To hide this from Giacomo he spoke of Stoob.

But Giacomo answered with patience. They were rolling down the ocean highway in the direction of Santa Cruz, and Giacomo was determined to let nothing spoil the day.

"It is only Stoob's manner," he answered serenely. "Poor Stoob, he cannot help himself."

"I don't see why you had to pick him out," Eric grumbled. "There are always plenty of lily men."

"But none who needed work as Stoob needed it then. Stoob has known what it is to be hungry and afraid in a strange country."

"So have you, Giacomo," Eric pointed out, speaking over Tosca's head, and he spoke his name with a gentleness many used when they spoke to Giacomo, as if the syllables contained special sounds indicative of respect and affection.

"Did I ever tell you," Giacomo said to them both, knowing that he had, and many times, "how the earthquake came just as I finished building the first houses and there was not a pane left whole in the nursery? The mortgage looked bigger than the skies to me then, and who knew if any insurance would be paid! It seemed like a judgment upon me for setting my plans so high. But my Maria had her prayers and the insurance was paid and the plants did not die, and so we built the greenhouses again.

And so what had seemed like the end of the world was not the end, and we found out it was the beginning."

"You were brave," said Tosca gently.

"Brave? No. I was afraid to be afraid."

"None of which explains Stoob," persisted Eric. "He was in trouble and he crawled. Now you've given him everything and he struts. I don't see why——"

He stopped abruptly and gave all his scowling attention to the road.

Giacomo finished the sentence. "I should tell him to go?"

"There are plenty of good lily men."

"Where would Stoob go, Eric? Even a number-one lily man like Stoob would find it hard to get a new place these days."

"You mean," Eric corrected him, "that no other grower would take in a man who couldn't get along with you."

"I agree with Eric," said Tosca, but neither man listened to her.

Giacomo spoke with rare sternness. "There is Ludmilla, Eric. This is her home. No, I cannot send them away. If Ludmilla can bear with him, maybe he is not too bad."

"She deserves better, poor kid," said Eric.

"I wonder what she would be like," put in Tosca with sudden interest, "with a different father."

"That's easy," said Eric. "She would be different."

For some reason they thought this deliciously witty. The tension relaxed between Eric and Tosca to a small but noticeable degree.

"Dress Ludmilla up, take her around a little," said Eric, "and she'd be a beauty."

"Stoob spends so little on her," said Giacomo. "It is a pity she has so little."

"It's a shame," said Eric. "If he were my father, I'd poison the old goat." Then, as Giacomo showed his disapproval, "Why not? I take a practical view of things. We poison pests, don't we? Well, Stoob is a pest. I wake up every morning feeling wonderful and come in to breakfast, and my God, there's Stoob. Wherever I go—Stoob."

"Try to get on with Stoob," said Giacomo.

Eric took his eyes from the highway to stare at him in frank wonder. There was a note of defeat in Giacomo's request. Eric had seen the way the scene in the kitchen had put a slowness into Giacomo's step and speech. His eyes met Tosca's for confirmation. She, too, had seen what Stoob's ill will could mean to Giacomo.

"Oh, sure," agreed Eric, relenting. "I won't talk to him any more than I have to. I just wish he'd keep that white mug of his in the lily bins and out of the orchid houses."

Giacomo knew what Eric was thinking. He would have liked to see any man tell him how to run his business when he was hotheaded and Eric's age. What was wrong with the years that they made cowards of the strong? Life, which puts so high a price on many things, puts the highest valuation on peace. He had to keep that about him.

He could not expect Eric, or even Tosca, to understand.

He leaned back to lift his eyes to the cathedral spires of the redwoods. They were riding the crest of the mountain sky line, dark on every side with forests; the air was heavy with the fragrance of California's centuries. The look of peace came back to his face, and a sense of reverence filled him. He glanced shyly at Tosca and beyond her to Eric and saw that they shared with him the communion of the forests.

Then he looked again at Eric. The stubborn mouth was quirked with some inner mirth. It was a look Giacomo knew.

"Eric," he said sternly, "you know something."

Tosca studied Eric.

"He's up to something," she agreed. "Make him tell, Giacomo."

Eric's muscular body rocked with laughter.

"Oh, I'll tell all right," he told them, laughing so that he had difficulty straightening the wheel on a mountain curve. "I just wanted to get as far away from Stoob as I could before letting you know."

Tosca and Giacomo demanded together that he tell them.

"Well, at the airport this morning," said Eric, drawing the news out to torment them, "I heard about Dad's break. I told you that. But I didn't hear about it from one of Dad's drivers. It was one of De Paoli's men who told me about the glad."

Tosca felt Giacomo's big frame charge with interest at the mention of De Paoli. She thought quickly and remembered De Paoli owned orchid houses in Santa Cruz.

"He was sending out a shipment of orchids," Eric went on, pronouncing his words with emphasis to allow Giacomo his full measure of anticipation, "and he told me"—again Eric paused—"that De Paoli is closing his orchid houses."

"Close them?" Giacomo stumbled over the words, for who could imagine closing orchid houses?

"From now on De Paoli isn't going to raise anything except cut flowers—like Dad's delphinium and sweet peas and such."

And then, as Giacomo seemed unable to comment, Eric wound up dramatically, "The auction starts tomorrow. And we might—since it's you, Giacomo—we might get an advance peek at the plants today!"

"You plotster!" marveled Tosca. "To think you've known this all morning and didn't tell."

"I wasn't going to spill it before Stoob," answered Eric. His annoyance with her was melting before the pleasure she and Giacomo showed in the news. "So I thought, if we went today, we could see Dad's break and maybe take a peek at the orchids."

"It will not hurt to look at them," agreed Giacomo happily. "Not to buy, of course. *Ohime mi,* what Stoob would say!"

"What Stoob doesn't know won't hurt him," said Eric, and they rode on, happy because Stoob was being outwitted and need never know.

Then between the spires of the trees the Pacific rose like a towering wall of blue, and they fell silent as the car raced down the falling green planes of the hills and into the seaside city of Santa Cruz. They drove southward past the cliffs that jutted into the shining expanse that was the sea, and Tosca, sniffing in ecstasy, cried, "Oh, Eric, I can smell your farms!"

Eric turned the car between the sandy hillocks and drove slowly into the mile-long ribbons of color that were the Brock flower farms.

"Ah, this is beautiful," she said softly, and the men's faces reflected her pleasure, for on this sandy expanse below Santa Cruz more than two thousand varieties of flowers were grown by the Brock families to supply cut flowers and seeds to the markets. Stretching in every direction, like silk swatches rippling the low sandy hills, were field flowers brought from Mexico, Asia, Europe, and the two Americas, and with them the demurer California flowers, all being forced into more glorious bloom. The pastel fields were stock, the sheets of fiery gold were zinnias and marigolds, dazzling coppery-yellow sheets were nasturtiums, and, like blinding sunlight on the sea, the wide fields pinnacled with cobalt, azure, amethyst, and indigo and threaded with salmon were Brock's fabulous delphinium, the Field of Blue.

They rode between the flowers like people drunk with beauty, and Eric exclaimed huskily: "Will you see what Dad's up to—he's stuck hundreds of beehives in the marigold beds. The lazy old buzzard—putting bees to work crossing his marigolds!"

"That is easier than pollinizing with a little brush, flower by flower, the way most people do," scolded Giacomo.

"Women's work," said Eric, grinning.

They drove with crawling pace for a mile and more between the butterfly fields that were sweet peas, now at the height of their fragrant blooming, and they exclaimed their admiration over the always more beautiful strips of these bonnet-like blooms in the colors and shapes perfected by Adolph Brock. Giacomo, studying the large and beautifully shaped and unbelievably fragrant blooms, remembered how small and unattractive a flower the sweet pea once had been, and how miraculously it had developed since it had left Sicily nearly two hundred and fifty years before.

A magician in orchidry could appreciate the miracles Adolph Brock had brought about by using the commonest of field flowers.

Eric, letting the car roll slowly through the blossom metropolis, was searching the bright squares for his father.

"He'll probably be at the trial farm," he said, referring to the wind-swept shallow, set well back from the sea, where his father's house stood.

But it was Adolph Brock who sighted them, for only his head showed where he stood up to his square shoulders in a sea-wash of azure delphinium, and he shouted loudly and waved his broad straw hat to attract their attention.

He made his way toward them through the spiky bloom. He was a short and powerful man with a face as open and washed by emotions as the sea itself. His tow hair stood up in damp spikes through the broken hat, and he wore overalls and his hands were stained blue and green from his work in the delphinium. But there was about him an air of authority, knowledge, ownership, difficult to define, and when he met his friend Giacomo with outstretched hands it was a royal welcome and one knew two chieftains, men of worth and dignity, met again. As for Eric and his father, Tosca realized anew the shock it was to see the two together, for in the way they spoke, smiled, used their bodies and hands, they were men in duplicate. Brock was deeply tanned, but his square face was unlined, and his eyes were as fiercely blue, as capable of warmth and of almost terrible coldness as Eric's.

"Come in! Come in!" he was shouting, his sound teeth warming his tanned features like a shaft of light. "My old lady'll skin my rump if you don't look at the new glad right away."

"We heard you had a new buttercup or some fool thing." Eric joined his father, and the two pounded one another on the shoulders with such violence it seemed that any moment a fist fight might break out between them. They were like two companions long parted, and yet they had spent the previous day together at Giacomo's.

"Everyone in the city is talking about your break, Adolph," said Giacomo.

"Tosca insisted on seeing it," explained Eric. "Giacomo and I just tagged along."

"She shall see it," said Brock proudly. He walked along with his arm over Eric's shoulder. "And everyone should talk. Wait till you see. But first we get the old lady so she can see your faces. . . ."

They were walking toward the farmhouse, which was hidden from the highway since it lay in a convexity of flowering fields from which the flowering farms of Brock's other children spread out like banners. The house had begun as a cabin with two rooms and had been added onto and built up by a series of ells and lean-tos as Brock's family grew, so that this unique growth of a house was not only a building of careless architectural charm, but the record of a family and its growing.

Two seed warehouses, as large as office buildings, towered behind the spraddled farmhouse, and between these, like crystal links, were the two glasshouses which were the only hothouses on the Brock farms.

As they neared the cluster of buildings Brock put his fists to his mouth. "Leni!" he bawled in a voice that could be heard far out to sea.

His wife came running from the farmhouse, looking at that distance like a girl in her starched gingham dress and with her short red hair flying. She was a little coppery woman, charged with vitality, and Eric's arms swallowed her in a bear hug that revealed the humorous adoration which all her family showed to Leni Brock. "The old lady," Brock called her, a term that on his lips became one of almost romantic tenderness. Brock himself, since his earliest thirties, had been known to the trade as "Old Man Brock," perhaps because his qualities as a master grower, his sense of leadership, and his energies were unflagging. He treated his wife, as did Eric and all her sons, in half-reverent, half-teasing fashion and as if she were of thistledown stuff that might blow away at a breath. But she was not a frail woman, only small-boned, light of weight, and active as a bird, and always busy with work, either in her home or, when her husband permitted, helping at the lighter tasks among the flowers.

"You scamp, put me down," she ordered her son smartly. "I want to speak to Tosca. Dear child, why didn't you let me know? Why didn't you come to lunch?" She began accusing them all in turn, including her grinning husband, then she said breathlessly, "I must phone the children, they'll all want to see you."

"Wait!" Adolph captured her in gossamer flight. "They want to see the salmon first."

"Oh, of course!" And suddenly pink-cheeked and shy, she linked her arms into those of her two sturdy men and marched them between the warehouses and into the nearest of the glass-houses.

And here, as always, Giacomo became the paramount figure, for he seemed to expand and absorb the world under glass as if it were his realm only, and all waited for his pronouncements, Leni Brock most anxiously of all. Now he led, walking between tables rampant with strange and marvelous colors, where flowers, less sturdy than their brethren blooming in the outside fields, had been coaxed under glass into giant bloom. He moved in silent appreciation through the areas of tuberous begonia, pausing at times to lift with gentle fingers the heavy heads of waxen pink or salmon or white blooms. Then, at the farther end of the hot-house, they came to the gladioli, and he stood silent.

Here, impaled in their green blades, the giant gladioli had been forced into unprecedented beauty, until each bloom, observed singly, was as beautiful, Giacomo was thinking, as one of his orchids. He studied them reverently and knew Brock had every right to be proud, for in this group were colors as variant and splendid as any Giacomo had seen, and among them one brave little group of green spears held aloft—he looked more closely—yes, they were tipped with flame-like salmon blooms.

Ai, it was here, the long-hoped-for and talked-about permanently salmon glad, for surely a grower who could bring this miracle about had every reason to hope the shade would remain true.

Since the others were waiting for his pronouncement, he made it with enthusiasm, although the words came slowly.

"Yes, this is truly a fixed salmon. This must be a true break, Adolph."

And Brock and his wife stood hand in hand, regarding the salmon with renewed admiration because they knew no better words could ever be spoken of their brave new flower.

"Now I must telephone the children," said Mrs. Brock, and like a ginghamed wraith she was gone with a last shy look flung back at her husband, and Tosca, following slowly through the glasshouse, noticed furry green arms, tendriling the roof, from which dark ruddy globes were hanging.

"What wonderful tomatoes," she exclaimed, "and so early."

"Dad's hobby," explained Eric. "He grows them under glass all year for Mother."

"My old lady likes tomatoes," explained the elder Brock, and his voice was gruff. With new perception she thought, Eric's father and mother are in love in a romantic way despite all the children and grandchildren, and the longing weakness for Mark swept her again at the realization that such tenderness could last.

Giacomo was continuing his march around the greenhouse, appreciating in every fiber the master plantings of his friend Brock. He stooped to see the way a bed of baby begonia was splitting the dark earth bed with translucent baby fingers; was any thrill equal to this? he wondered, and remembered far back to lifting a shred of pink blanket from the face of a newborn child.

This was the perpetual miracle, the earth riven and thrown back to reveal the thrusting green. Whether it was weed or valued flower that would not be denied, it was the eternal birth, the incessant springtime. This was the knowledge that kept him serene in faith despite all that might happen. He saw Tosca coming toward him with her young face drained and troubled by some anxiety he did not know, and he laid his knotted finger against the knifed earth.

"See, Tosca *mia!*" he said roguishly, but with underlying sincerity. "This is what wisdom is: knowing how and when to grow."

The elder Brock tore at the damp collar opened at his thick throat.

"I don't see how you and Giacomo stand working in these places all day," he complained to his son. "I'd never have a sheet of glass on the farms if I had my way."

"You can't raise a glad like this one without glass," Eric reminded him. He was still admiring the salmon.

"I know that. But I can't breathe in here. If it weren't for your mother——"

And Brock ended on the thwarted note of a man who is born to work under open sky.

Father and son chuckled as if at some special joke. It was a favorite charge of Brock's that his wife had captured a contented outdoor grower and pinioned him under glass. Like all his jests, this held a small degree of truth. Leni Brock had taught botany in a San Francisco high school before her marriage. The seed farms were a source of beauty and delight to her, and it was she who had persuaded Adolph to build the two glasshouses on the trial farm and turned his interest to the gladioli that after so many trials had resulted in the salmon.

It was from her that Eric had learned the first principles of botany, which was originally taught as the science of healing. Healing it remained, thought Tosca, walking with the others to the farmhouse, for one could not fail to be impressed by the sense of fulfillment and content that seemed to hover over people like Eric's father and mother, and Giacomo and Eric, and so many others who made their living from flowers.

Eric's mother, it seemed, could never have enough of them around her. Miles of blooms could be seen from every clean and shining window of the farmhouse, and within, the simply furnished rooms were lined with house plants that were her special care.

And Giacomo, smiling as if recognizing old friends, said, "Even here!"

Leni Brock suppressed what might have been considered a giggle from anyone but a grandmother, no matter how girlish and gay. "Isn't it ridiculous?" she admitted shyly. "But when I was a little girl in the city we lived in boardinghouses, and there was one place where the landlady put flowers on the table. I used to look at them instead of eating and my mother would scold."

"Maria too," said Giacomo. "My daughter Marie, I mean. Never enough flowers."

She looked across the room to Tosca. "And Tosca?" she asked. The birdlike voice was strained. Her question asked many questions, but Giacomo could only shake his head and shrug his enormous shoulders, for who could tell about Tosca now? So he answered, "Flowers, yes, to wear," and passed the matter off as a joke.

But the mother's eyes remained on Tosca, who was in heated conversation with Eric over some matter or other, and it was plain that she could see no humor in any subject that might concern her son.

By this time other Brocks were arriving from the seed warehouses and the outlying flower farms Brock had settled upon his sons and sons-in-law as his family branched and formed other family groups, and their families came in crowded cars that raced between the flower lanes to the farmhouse to bring the tribal divisions together.

What an immense family, thought Tosca as the farmhouse filled with Brocks, for as sons, daughters, nephews, and cousins married they brought their mates to the Brock farms, and in time the in-laws took on the strong characteristics of the dominant Brocks. They were people charged with vitality that came from the sun. When abroad they presented a solid front of almost stodgy dignity, but when they came together under the farmhouse roof there was a great deal of chasing and teasing and cries for help going on. There were a bewildering number of Lenis and Adolphs and Erics of all ages and sizes, because a good name was considered worth using many times over in the Brock clan. And throughout the noise and laughter Adolph Brock sat smoking his pipe in silence, for although when out of doors he spoke and acted with sound and vigor, here, within his own walls, he was content to lapse into mute admiration of his small and bustling wife, and wherever she went, his eyes followed her.

If there was a man on earth to be envied, it was this man, Giacomo was thinking. There were many growers in California like Adolph Brock, heading family nurseries where many-branching generations worked and were sufficient unto themselves. Such a living, Giacomo could not help remembering with sorrow, he had planned for his Colma land.

He had been struggling to recover from the shock of Paul's death when Eric came to him. Eric's passion for orchidry and his scientific curiosity that in Giacomo's mind bore such a strong resemblance to faith had helped him retain his courage.

"You do not mind his coming here?" Giacomo had questioned Adolph Brock, and Old Man Brock had thrown his square shoulders and laughed uproariously. "Miss him? With all the mouths I have to feed, Giacomo?"

And while Brock might have been disappointed in Eric's desertion of the seed farms, he was well able to spare one son to Giacomo. He had fathered six other men, and his daughters had brought extra sons to work with him in the flower fields. Between the two nurseries, the one under glass at Colma and the other on the open earth at Santa Cruz, was the strong bond of friendship that was Eric. His father was proud of having a son working with the hybridist Daneri. But even more than Brock, Giacomo knew, Eric's mother understood her son's devotion to the alien orchids.

"And how goes everything at Daneri's?" Brock called to him over the tow heads of the lapful of grandchildren he was holding, as if he had not been a guest at the nursery only the day before.

"Well enough." A shadow crossed Giacomo's face, and Eric explained, "It would be if Stoob weren't shooting off his face as usual."

Brock made no comment, but his expression stated plainly he would not have such a man as Stoob around.

"He has nothing to complain about, either," Eric went on heedlessly. "He's getting three times the wages I'm getting."

"Oh, so now you are being underpaid!" said his father with a twinkle.

Giacomo and the Brocks laughed knowingly at this, for while it was true that Eric was still receiving only the good wage Giacomo would pay to any skilled nurseryman, it was well understood that a day would come when Giacomo would turn over to his assistant a share in the orchid houses. In his own secret plans Giacomo had regarded this gift as a sort of dowry, for he had permitted the hope to grow for years that Tosca and Eric would care for one another. But the festa had made it plain that this was an unlikely dream. He tried to hide the sad conviction that had ruined the festa for him, but he would not permit it to ruin this day with the Brocks. As for Eric, it might be better to give him his share in the houses very soon, despite Stoob's certain wrath, for who knew what might happen, although the matter was provided for in his will! And while this way of conducting business might be considered by ordinary men to be unorthodox and unbusinesslike, still it was Giacomo's way and had made him a rich man, and many others had arrived at affluence because of him.

He tried not to admit to himself that the reason he hesitated in taking this step was because he dreaded the wrath of Stoob, and that Stoob had become a millstone hung about his neck that could not be dropped because of pity for the girl Ludmilla.

What reason for Stoob? he wondered. Stoob came from the same section of Europe that had given birth to the progenitors of Adolph Brock, but the difference between the two men was that which is between open kindness and closed suspicion. And he wondered if it might be that the Brock richness of spirit was based upon the sense of security that comes to those who have for generations tended their own land, who owned and were not owned by the land. The Brocks, now, were proud people, and every plant in their fields, every plank in their homes had been placed there by their proud labors. And Giacomo, relaxing, drinking in the sprawling noisy comfort of the simply furnished room given life and color by the potted flowers, admiring the gay and healthy faces, the pretty, competent Brock women bustling about with trays of strong sweet coffee and slices of apple cake, thought again that he had known no finer people; he could have no better friends.

"You must stay to dinner," the women were urging from all directions before the last crumb vanished, and the Brock wives began exclaiming among themselves over which dishes were to be cooked in their individual homes and brought back to the farmhouse, for dinner at the Brocks' was a tribal picnic to which all divisions might contribute.

But Eric made his voice heard above the hubbub.

"We can't stay. Tosca has a date."

Tosca faced the sudden silence and the not unfriendly curiosity of the Brock clan, all so alike, from Adolph to the smallest babe in arms, that it might have been one directed stare from one pair of eyes.

"Besides," Giacomo put in hurriedly, to help her, "there is De Paoli."

Brock gave the familiar impatient jerk to his collar that told he had stayed too long within walls. He went out and Eric followed him, and they were back in a few minutes with armfuls of the pale pink sweet peas known as the Leni. These they piled into Tosca's lap, and the sweet fragrance flooded the crowded room.

"Coals to Newcastle," said Eric gaily. "Dad insisted, Tosca. I told him it's been rumored we grow flowers at Daneri's."

"Not the Leni," said his mother placidly, for the sweet peas had been named for her. "And besides, no one can have too many flowers."

Nobody answered this because there was no answer; everyone present knew it to be true.

"Especially orchids," Eric added, to tease his father.

But his father waggled a flower-stained hand at his son.

"Whose bread you eat, his praises you sing. You can't work for Giacomo Daneri and not like orchids. He and orchids are made of the same stuff—cut his finger, he bleeds pollen."

This struck the clan as being exceedingly humorous. Flower people find so much to laugh about, thought Tosca, wondering again what Mark would make of their humor. The talk among flower people was of people and flowers, and both were sources of endless merriment. But amusement as Mark saw it belonged to nighttime and the city.

Adolph Brock said, as if the matter had been mentioned, "Giacomo, the De Paoli orchids are good. He just lacks the touch for orchids. Not that I know anything about orchids!" he finished boastfully, and winked at his wife.

"*Ohime mi!*" exclaimed Giacomo, more to himself than to the others, as if a matter had been brought to mind he had thought it best not to remember.

"They are beautiful plants," Leni Brock said in her childlike determined voice. "It's a shame he's selling them. I'm going to the auction tomorrow. I've never seen an orchid auction."

There was a chorus of interest in the clan as others laid plans to attend the auction, and the question of who was to stay on the farms the next morning, that some might attend, became the source of one of those excitable arguments that livened everyday living among the Brocks.

But Eric stopped the discussion with a brisk warning to Giacomo.

"Maybe we'd better run over and see the orchids now, Giacomo, since we won't have time tomorrow."

And his steady look sought and held Tosca's. At once she knew her help was needed, and without a moment's hesitation she went over to Eric's side.

"I'd like to see the De Paoli orchids," she said positively, knowing this would fell the last of Giacomo's objections.

It was plain to everyone in the room that he longed to see the orchids. Only Eric and Tosca knew why he was reluctant to go. With a sense of mischief they combined their forces to make Giacomo do what he longed to do.

"You see, Tosca wants to see them," Eric said triumphantly to Giacomo.

"*Andiamo!* Then we go," agreed Giacomo happily, and added hastily, "Not to buy, of course! But it will not hurt to look at them."

The Brocks flocked about them in blond droves as they clambered into the roadster. Eric's mother stood on tiptoe to pull Giacomo's shaggy head down to her own and kiss his deep-grooved cheek.

"Good-by, dear Giacomo. And remember, no more orchids."

"Oh no," he agreed, twinkling. "But perhaps one small plant, Leni. Maybe two."

They drove away through the fragrant lanes to a chorus of good-bys waved by that strong and happy tribe that was the Brocks, who stood calling and waving to the last, and behind them the Brock fields streamed their glorious floral banners against the strong bright blue that was the sea.

ELEVEN

*L*ATE afternoon found them returning over the Santa Cruz Mountains. They rode in silence. Eric had his own thoughts and they were large with plans, and Tosca had fallen asleep with her head on Giacomo's shoulder. As for Giacomo, he was reliving and savoring again the fullness of their day, as is the way with the old.

He had not intended to buy the Laeliocattleyas.

He recalled this now a little apprehensively, even while tasting again the surprise and pleasure of his act. It was always beautiful to learn that life continued to offer surprises. He recalled that he had entered De Paoli's greenhouses determined to buy nothing, save perhaps, as he had hinted to Eric's mother, a pot or two of the exquisite Laeliocattleya which De Paoli had purchased in Belgium a few years before.

This stock, Giacomo had remembered, was from Sander's.

But De Paoli lacked the hand for orchids. He was of urban origin, his formative years had been spent as a city tradesman, and the painstaking precision necessary to the grower of orchids was not in him. For ten years he had been trying to build up marketable orchids and he had failed. He had bought the strongest and finest plants and been unable to bring them to bear. Even Sander's plants, brought with such care and cost from Europe, had yielded only a few scraggly blooms.

Standing small and anxious beside them in the Cattleya house, De Paoli had explained that he was closing the orchid houses to devote all his time to the hardier outdoor flowers, such as the marigolds and sweet peas and delphinium and asters that grew in such profitable abundance on the Brock farms only a mile or so away.

"I tell you what I will do," he said worriedly in Italian to Giacomo. "The other two houses of orchids I will put up at auction tomorrow, but these Laeliocattleyas, I tell you truly, Giacomo, I cannot bear to see fall into other hands. Rather I will give them now, *immediato*, to you."

Temptation rode over Eric and Giacomo in glorious waves. Tosca saw the look that passed between them. She saw Eric's lips frame the ecstatic comment, "Sander!" In all the orchid world there was no more magic name.

And she saw Giacomo trying to be unconcerned and calm and casting long looks over the tables to evaluate the gold mine that lay about them in dormant green. More than a thousand plants!

He fingered a poniard leaf, the base of which was swollen as if by a gland, and looked again at Eric, almost guiltily.

"I have seldom seen better plants," he murmured, and between them, without being spoken, was the conviction that together they could make these recalcitrant hybrids bloom.

So often fine plants were snapped up at the orchid auctions by ignorant collectors who could not appreciate them or bring them to their best blooming. And Giacomo found himself thinking

144

how terrible it would be if his own beloved seedlings were to be sold and scattered at auction.

Many times he had envisioned this not impossible tragedy. He had tried not to imagine such things. That was before Eric came —before Eric, who had been left to care? If Paul had lived, or Vittorio! But in his heart Giacomo knew that neither of his sons would have cherished the orchids. Paul had fallen too easily into city ways, and Vittorio, marching down Market Street toward his death in his new khaki uniform, to the stepping of drums, had been too young and eager for the monotony of nursery routine. Later, perhaps, had he lived, Giacomo thought with a sigh, Vittorio might have returned to work with him in the greenhouses at Colma.

De Paoli was watching him.

"For three thousand dollars you may have this house of orchids because you are Giacomo Daneri," he said simply.

The color crept under Giacomo's folded cheeks. He had forgotten that a heart could beat so fast.

"Eric, what you think?"

But he knew what Eric was thinking. Eric stood laughing, his arms folded in defiance.

"Oh no, you don't, Giacomo! I'm not going to be responsible!"

"Coward!" sang Tosca, delighted with the game they were playing.

But Giacomo knew Eric's heart was beating as fast as his own at the challenge of the orchids, and he knew that Eric, shaking his head and laughing, was praying Giacomo would take the orchids. Eric's tanned forehead was beaded. Excitement, thought Giacomo, and also, De Paoli kept his houses too hot. At least seventy degrees, and for Laeliocattleyas! It was cruel to keep the plants in such heat.

And how, he pondered, could they fall into better hands?

He turned ponderously to De Paoli.

"Your price is not fair," he argued in Genoese. "I know what these orchids cost you in Belgium. Six thousand will I give you. They are worth that, and more."

Eric understood. He clapped Giacomo's broad shoulder with a whoop of victory.

"*Digu ninte!* You'll never be sorry, Giacomo." He added, looking about the hothouse with a wicked glint in his eyes, "A carload of orchids! Stoob will be wild!"

"We take the orchids, then," Giacomo pronounced impressively to the pleased De Paoli. The mention of Stoob recalled the ugly scene in the kitchen at noon, and it rankled in his thoughts like a thorn. Now the decision to purchase the Laeliocattleyas seemed even more tremendous.

Once he would not have hesitated. He knew the plants were sound and that Eric would find the time to care for them. Eric liked to have work piling up before him when that work had to do with orchids. But ever in Giacomo's ears of late was Stoob's querulous and persistent argument, urging him away from the splendid expensive orchids and back to the simpler flowers.

Stoob will not like this at all, worried Giacomo. He shifted Tosca's head on his shoulder carefully, not to wake her. His face wrinkled with anxiety. I have had troubles before this, he was thinking. Within a few weeks I shall be seventy-five, and it is time that I stopped having troubles.

Stoob will be very angry, he thought.

No one, not even Eric, guessed how deeply he had come to dread Stoob's disapproval. The thought of that high voice fluted in angry protest marred the victory of his purchase.

He lifted his eyes to the heavily scented and towering redwoods and was comforted. Eric was idling the car down the shadowy mountain highway. Like Giacomo, he had been savoring in silence the fullness of the hours spent in the De Paoli orchid houses and on the flower farms with his own people.

He had never regretted his decision to leave the family nursery. It was good to go back, but it was better to be returning to the orchid houses at Colma.

"I've been thinking," Eric said suddenly, softly, not to waken Tosca. "We can build a new house for the De Paoli plants——"

"Oh, indeed, we must build a new house," agreed Giacomo, interrupting with enthusiasm.

"We can move the compost farther back and start work on the new house tomorrow, before the June rush begins. Transplant the heather, too, farther up the hillside—it won't hurt it to be moved at this time of year. Gosh, wish we could get some of that new glass that lets in the actinic rays. Expensive as hell, but worth it."

"Someday all the growers will be using it," Giacomo stated with conviction. "We see, Eric, how much it costs."

The closeness of their thoughts was a form of communion, and as they drove between the great trees that were fountains of darkness in the gathering dusk of late afternoon, their understanding took in Tosca, crumpled between them in sleep.

"Dad takes solid comfort in his sweet peas and delphinium," remarked Eric. "I can't see how a grower can work up an interest in any other flower after knowing orchids."

"Almost that is true," agreed Giacomo.

He sniffed the wet sweet fragrance of the forest they were driving through, and his trained eyes hunted through the shadowy earth, recognizing wild flora. The scents of wild growth were tantalizingly familiar.

"And yet," he said, "to think they are everywhere. Even here orchids are all around us in the forest."

"Common as weeds," agreed Eric cheerfully. "Funny, isn't it? People think of orchids as rare, and the woods are stuffed with wild species. But they aren't any good until they meet up with fellows like us. We spruce them up and introduce them to society."

"Only there is no such thing as a pure species," rebuked Giacomo. "Even in the jungle, they cross. The bees see to that."

"I know about the bees," said Eric, and they both smiled, knowing how much trouble a bee could make and why one had to take such pains to see the doors of glasshouses were kept tightly closed, and not alone to keep the heat inside, no indeed, for oh the havoc a fluttering insect could wreak in a houseful of flowers!

They were silent again, savoring the fragrance of the jungle-like forests that were older than California, and Eric was thinking that he could never learn enough from Giacomo, so endlessly patient and willing to give freely the full measure of his half century of patience and perseverance. He tried to fight down his resentment against the sleeping and innocent Tosca, for after all, was it not the very kindness of Giacomo, so valued by Eric and many others who knew Giacomo, that had developed her loveliness—as well as her carelessness and her selfish unconcern for others?

Crumpled as a kitten, she lay between them, innocent in sleep, and despite the anger that had stayed firm since yesterday, poor girl, Eric found himself thinking, Who knows what she's going through? And a line came back from an English course, from

Swinburne, wasn't it? "A maid is but a fool!" God save us from virgins, Eric thought piously; they cause most of the trouble in the world, and he turned his thoughts briskly from Tosca and back to the orchids.

Orchids were indeed everywhere, Giacomo was thinking, riding along in bemused contemplation and turning the bright illustrated pages of his mind to pictures of the wild orchids that must hide in these darkling mounds of primeval forest. The lady's-slipper, calypso, bird's-nest, and tree orchids, the eyebrow with its curious labia that can be mistaken for an insect—even by real insects—these and more than a hundred other shy beauties might be hiding in secret places in these woods. These were the wild tribes with their thousands of species that were ever being sought by the expanding commerce of orchidry everywhere in the Americas, the European and Asiatic continents, in almost impenetrable valleys, morasses, jungles, and mountain ranges. Even in the arid desert lands and the tundras of the Arctic, the pursuit of the orchids went on. Starring the secret places of the world, struggling to retain their status as primitives, they were the poor hunted brethren of the orchid world.

The wild orchids—tormented tribes and clans being driven back even farther into their ferny hiding places, like certain birds and beasts that have vanished, like the lost primitive races—why, thinking of them, did his thoughts turn to the sleeping Tosca?

His arm went taut on her shoulders, and she stirred and moaned so that he spoke softly to rescue her from what was evidently an evil dream. Her eyes flew wide and fear was in them, then, orientated, they went to the clock and she cried out:

"Four-thirty! Oh, Giacomo—Eric—we'll never get back in time."

"Eric was driving slowly not to waken you," Giacomo protested with concern, for he had forgotten her urgency about returning to the nursery at an early hour. "Never mind, Tosca *mia*, we go fast now."

But she slumped back between them in utter dejection, not looking at Eric, and Eric kept his eyes on the road and pressed his foot on the accelerator without a word of apology. Appealing to Eric, both knew, would be no better than appealing to a rock.

Mark said five o'clock, Tosca thought wretchedly. Maybe he will not phone exactly at five, he is always late. This time, she prayed fervently, please make him very late.

But it was after five before Eric drove the car up to Giacomo's door.

"Eric, I have been thinking," Giacomo said as he climbed stiffly from the car, "perhaps it will be better if you say nothing to Stoob but let me tell him first about the Laeliocattleya."

And he stooped slowly to gather up the kitten, which had come out to meet them.

Tosca went around the car to Eric's side.

"I suppose you're pleased with yourself," she said bitterly.

"Not particularly."

"You did it on purpose." Her lips quivered. "You've ruined everything by making me late."

He was not a tall man, but he looked down on her from an immeasurable height.

"I hear you nearly got yourself killed this morning," he remarked conversationally.

She was silenced. This, then, accounted for the constraint the crew had shown. Pietro must have recognized her car as it hurtled between the Daneri trucks. She asked in a small voice: "Does Giacomo know?"

"Do you think any one of us would tell him? You should know by this time how much we think of the old boy."

"Meaning that I don't." But Eric was off whistling toward Paul's house to wash up before dinner, and she ran past Giacomo, avoiding his surprised expression, and up the cottage steps into the dim little hall off the kitchen where the telephone was set against the wall. Standing on her toes, for Giacomo was tall and had adjusted the telephone to his own height, she called the number of her home. She had to speak loudly to be heard over the clamor going on in the kitchen.

Giacomo was approaching the steps, carrying the kitten, and his progress was slow. He was at peace because he was home and because this had been a happy day. Such a day was like new growth, and it could heal over the disappointments of a yesterday that had not turned out to be all one had planned.

The kitten sang its pleasure at having him home, and he held it with affectionate gentleness, aware of the small fine bones articulated like delicate watchwork, the silken coat a-quiver with song, the small sheathed paws' acceptance of his attentions, and, beyond all these, the millions of feline years that had gone into the making of one small and perfect cat. It was as delicately fashioned as Tosca, as gay in body and sensitive to hurt as are all creatures designed to dance in the sun. It was as unthinkable that harm should come to this small creature as that Tosca could suffer hurt.

It occurred to Giacomo that life was largely made up of goodness, and despite much that had happened, it had been kind to him. In return he could do no better than to show appreciation where it was due.

"And you," he praised the kitten in Italian, "you are a good boy-cat."

The kitten nudged his chin with a tiny face made interesting by baby whisker antennae and delicate Maltese smudgings.

"Has anyone told you, my little friend," Giacomo continued jocularly, "that you have a face remarkably like that of a pansy?"

The kitten sang loudly and turned against his arm.

"I see that we understand one another," said Giacomo, and they went up the porch steps together.

The kitchen was swarming with the nursery people, and the greetings were deafening because they were led by the affectionate bellowings of Cesare. They subsided, and he could hear the clear impatient voice of Tosca calling her house number in the hall.

This was the end of the day for Giacomo's crews, and some were dallying over their suppers and others, married men from the cottages across the lane, had dropped in, some with their wives, for a last general review of the day and a glass of wine before turning in for the night. Daneri's kept early hours. Ludmilla and Stoob were in the same places they had occupied at the noon meal, so that to all appearances they might not have stirred from their seats since then.

Giacomo's own chair was waiting, and he dropped into it and released the kitten. It immediately curled between his shoes and fell asleep.

The kitchen was filled with good smells, and Giacomo found he was hungry.

"We have *radicchi!*" Cesare announced proudly, gesturing to a steaming kettle of pungent greens threaded with delicate white roots. "Laddie found the green mustard on the hill this afternoon. Always after a big festa we must eat the greens."

And he made this last statement in a scolding voice, as if they were children.

Giacomo accepted a plate of the stewed verdure, a link of roasted Italian sausage, and a helping of new potatoes coated with parsley. The last rich remnants of the festa were stored away in Cesare's massive icebox, to reappear as tidbits at the next day's noon meal. Supper was a bountiful meal but much simpler than the one eaten at noonday. Still the bread was stacked like small logs on the table, the coffee came from Cesare's stove in gallons, and the wine glowed red in the thick glasses clutched in hands that had worked day long among the flowers.

"Mama?" Tosca's voice could be heard sharply questioning in the hall. "Have any messages—— Yes, I'm still at the nursery—— Oh, of course he's all right—— No, we went to Santa—— Please, Mama, let me talk! Has a call come for me?"

To cover the unwonted sharpness of her tone Giacomo stumbled into his account of the trip to Santa Cruz, for everyone present was waiting to hear about the Brock break. The gardeners and their wives drank in the most minute details concerning the salmon gladioli and had many curious questions of their own to ask, but his descriptive powers seemed to wither before the steady disbelieving stare of Stoob.

Now it was surely time to tell about the visit to De Paoli and the new orchids, and if only Eric would come to help him with this. Instead, he heard Tosca's impatient cry:

"And you didn't even ask? Then how will I know—— Mama, I don't care if Louise phoned; she only wants to talk about the club meeting. Oh, Mama, why didn't you ask where I could phone him—where he'll be!"

To cover the naked grief of her appeal Giacomo spoke with unnecessary loudness. "So then we went over to De Paoli's and he is selling his orchids tomorrow and, well, we have bought all his Laeliocattleyas—all of them!"

"A carload of them!" came the gleeful corroboration of Eric from the doorway. "Fifteen hundred. We counted them."

He came into the kitchen and settled into a place at the table. With a satisfied air he heard the storm of excitement that rose over the purchase of the new and wonderful orchids. All the faces showed pleasure in the news, save one.

Ohime mi, thought Giacomo, at my age a man should have left uncertainty behind. One should be able to face the disapproval of any other man without qualm. But Stoob was no ordinary man.

And Giacomo found himself avoiding Stoob's accusing glare like a guilty schoolboy.

"A carload of orchids?" Stoob echoed with such sibilance that the kitten woke and raced from Giacomo's feet to the warm sanctuary under the stove.

"A whole carload," Eric repeated with satisfaction. He turned to Ludmilla. "You'll like them, anyway," he said cheerfully.

Tosca's voice was beseeching. "You're sure, Mama, you're certain he didn't say he'd call back?" It was as if she were being stripped of pride before them all and no longer cared who might listen; and again, in an attempt to shield Tosca, Giacomo spoke too loudly and earnestly to Stoob, because he could see the ugliness swelling Stoob's pallid face and knew that another of the too frequent emotional storms was about to break.

"Perhaps we should have waited to talk things over," he admitted, because his was not a quarrelsome nature and he longed for peace. "But they are such fine plants and De Paoli wished us to have them and Eric and I saw no need of waiting."

It was characteristic of the lily master that he become bolder before any sign he interpreted as weakness. At Giacomo's apologetic words his puffy body seemed to swell with importance.

"So Eric could not wait!" He was almost insanely angry. "Men of experience used to have some say in Daneri's. Now a field grower's son is running the nursery. Maybe it's time some of us older ones got out so he can run it into the ground."

"That might be best all around," Eric cut in before Giacomo could speak, and he fell upon the plate of food Cesare handed him after holding it a moment over Stoob's head as if considering the impulse to garnish the albino-pale crown with boiling greens. "The orchids are coming, anyway, Stoob, and you can't stop them."

"And where are we putting all these orchids, Mr. Know-it-all? We have no more room."

Stoob was gobbling food as he always did when excited.

"I've got that all figured out. There's plenty of space for a new house next to Number Fourteen."

"The compost is there. All that space up to the eucalyptus we could be using for cut flowers. I planned to plant the new Easter bulbs there this fall, but no, when do you consider anything except orchids!"

Eric heard Tosca's voice, pleading, and he knew this was hurting Giacomo and that Stoob was hurting Giacomo, and between them he was driven to answer Stoob angrily.

"There's nothing else worth considering around here."

"Please, Stoob and Eric." In the white kitchen light Giacomo's cheeks were gray with exhaustion. Suddenly he knew he was old, torn between Tosca and her wild grieving and by what was becoming a struggle for power between his assistant and his lily master. "Eric sees only the orchids, Stoob, because he knows orchids."

"And the rest of us know nothing," said Stoob. He looked around the circle of faces as if trying to summon recruits to his side. "Men who have worked for you all their lives are stupid. I am stupid. And so Eric says I must go."

"I did not say you should go," shouted Eric. "Don't make a liar out of me. . . ."

"In that you are right. It is time. It is time," and on a high note of hysteria Stoob stamped out of the kitchen and down the steps.

The kitchen burst into a hubbub of shocked argument in which the voices of the wives were loudest and most indignant. Everyone talked about Stoob as if Ludmilla were not his daughter or were not present, which in fact she did not appear to be, but sat pale and still with her eyes on her plate.

"No, nobody is quarreling," Tosca was heard to say dully to her mother over the phone. "They're all talking over some new orchids—I'll tell you about them later. . . . Yes, I'll be home. . . . No, don't keep dinner. . . . I won't drive too fast. There's nothing to hurry for—now."

She hung up the receiver and laid her flaming cheek against the cold metal box on the wall. The rising indignation in the kitchen was hateful to her, the anger of Stoob hateful, and Eric's insolence, and Giacomo's voice sorrowful in its attempt at appeasement. The wild, grieving longing to escape to Mark shook her until the tears came, for Mark would accept no moods except gay ones and knew how to elude and toss aside trouble; he would not acknowledge trouble, and this ability seemed dearer to her at this moment than ever before. Mark would not care, as she was caring, that she had not been home to receive his call. And it was his capacity for not caring too much that she both feared and reverenced, for it seemed the way to escape lay in this and in

153

Mark. She could not face Giacomo and the others. Blind with grief, jealousy, longing, she fumbled her way up the narrow stairs.

In the kitchen nearly everyone had left for their rooms or the cottages across the way. Eric and Ludmilla and Giacomo sat on at the table with Cesare, who was eating his own supper and grumbling about Stoob.

"Such a nice girl." He pointed his burdened fork at Ludmilla as if she could neither see nor hear. "To have a papa like that."

"Ludmilla's okay." Eric spoke kindly, and the three men saw the white downcast face warm with feeling and were pleased, for everyone at Daneri's suspected Ludmilla's stillness was a blind pulled down on Stoob's incessant scenes.

"Commend me, Padrone, that I did not pour hot *radicchi* on that *stupido*."

"I commend you, Cesare." Giacomo rose. "I go talk to your papa, Ludmilla. I fix everything so we will all be happy again."

But it was Eric's kindness, he noticed, not his, that had planted the first seeds of coquetry in the wolfsbane eyes.

The kitten wove between his steps as he made his way through the daisy-gleaming paths. The night was very dark, but the Drive was lighted with the bluish lights because several of the men were readying a few last plants in there for morning shipment, and its lights set the nursery glowing like rows of opalescent tubes against the hill. Still he turned the lights in the glasshouses on and off as he worked his way through them, noting the temperature and humidity in each, keeping an eye out for moths or other insects that might have made their way in, and always making his way in the direction of his final objective, the orchid houses. He trudged through the blocks of gardenias and carnations and roses, all of which seemed to be waiting his evening benediction, and this was the most pleasurable task of his day to Giacomo—but tonight it gave little pleasure.

For he was certain that somewhere along the glass-bound way Stoob would be lying in wait for him. Stoob did not give up easily.

Stoob's rages were usually violent and short, resulting in a root jerked out or a pane kicked through. This time his anger had been slower and more to be dreaded. Stoob never forgot anything. After the scene with Eric, Giacomo knew that Stoob would not forgive the buying of the Laeliocattleyas.

The lily houses were dark. He did not enter them.

While this was his final official inspection of the day, it would by no means be his last one. Giacomo was given to waking frequently during the night, and what more sensible thing for a man who cannot sleep but to don a warm robe and shuffle through the houses to see that all is well with the orchids?

Stoob was also given to nocturnal inspections. He set his alarm at various hours, and at any time of night he or Ludmilla might be seen scurrying through the lily houses for one more survey of their special charges.

The smell of the compost was jungle-strong in the night.

Giacomo plodded through the shipping shed. He paused at the blackboard by the door to see if any messages had been left for him. "I am going to town with the first crew," Laddie had written in his careful hand. Giacomo smiled, knowing how precious one's day off could be when one was Laddie's age. The sorting tables had been scrubbed and dried and the cartons stacked in readiness for the pre-dawn packing. A swift glance into the refrigerator room revealed trays of choice flowers laid out on the shelves.

A frowning inspection of the boiler plant was less satisfactory. He examined the gauges and decided matters here were as well as could be expected. The ugly throbbing mechanism was the aorta that kept Daneri's alive. It was the life stream of his orchids. Eric was right, they did need a new boiler.

But not now, with this new expense of the De Paoli orchids to be shouldered, and Giacomo squared his shoulders and marched on, proud to be able to carry so much and at such an age as his. Now if one could take a young life on old shoulders and carry it through the torrents to safety! What a blessed privilege had been granted St. Christopher.

This brought to mind a small detail that was apt to be overlooked by the most conscientious of mechanics, and when he entered the warehouse he opened the doors of each of the great green trucks standing there to see if the Christopher medals pinned over each windshield had been well polished. Satisfied, he took the freight elevator to the loft.

He could have walked this expanse of floor in the dark and been able to avoid touching the vats of costly fungicide and insecticide, some of it costing as much as three hundred dollars a barrel, the stacks of bamboo stakes, the rolls of cheesecloth, the immense spools of flax and cord, the stacks of packing cases, and, taking the most space, the twelve-foot trays heaped with the bulbs that were Stoob's special care.

Every effort is worthy of honor, and Giacomo, walking between the piled trays, gave credit to Stoob, whose pale eyes could recognize a good bulb crop when he saw one. All these bulbs of tulips, hyacinths, daffodils, narcissi, and crocuses drying on the warehouse floor had been shipped over from Holland, trip after trip, by Stoob.

Thousands of gladioli corms found shelter in the loft each winter, waiting the master hand of Stoob to draw beauty from their colorless folds. Also, in the past winter, Stoob had sent to the Orient for thousands of Easter-lily bulbs, and now, with so many troubles pending in the world, who knew when such bulbs would again be available! Stoob had tended these with special care, setting them in rows behind the compost heap and bringing them into the greenhouses in late fall to be forced into magnificent Easter blooming. Our next should be the greatest of all Easters, thought Giacomo, forgetting that Easter was barely over, and for this there was no avoiding the fact that one must thank Stoob.

Aye, Stoob was valuable. One could not part easily with such a man.

But of late, so touchy, so overbearing.

A cat came blinking and mewing from behind a forest of barrels. It was the kitten's mother, and the two met with curiosity and little more; when Giacomo left, it was he the kitten followed. And entering the cool dim lanes of the nursery again, he saw the blue overhead lights were on in the Number Six lily house.

Yes, it would be best to placate Stoob.

After some hesitation he pushed open the glass door.

In the bluish light Stoob looked whiter and surlier than before. A small and ugly gnome he seemed in the unlovely setting of the lily bins shrouded like graves in their coarse burlap. Not a patch of color or green relieved the drabness of the lily of the valley house.

"Busy, and so late, Stoob?" asked Giacomo.

"When am I not busy?" And Stoob glared across the shrouded bins as if at an intruder.

But Giacomo stood his ground. A little wholesome flattery had been known to smooth the ruffled feelings of the lily master. He lifted a burlap cover and looked down into a bed of small starry

156

lily of the valley. A wave of sweetness rose; how incredibly fragrant they were, for all their smallness! The yellow leaves were like folded endive and the small lilies were streaked with delicate green.

"*Mio*, they are perfect, Stoob. No one in California has better valley this season."

"It's all in the way bulbs are dried," muttered Stoob. "But I need more room in the warehouse."

He was partly mollified but still surly, plainly determined that Giacomo should admit himself wrong in the matter of the new orchids. This Giacomo was equally determined not to do, but if he could rewin Stoob by some kindness all might again be serene at Daneri's. And Stoob had plenty of room in the warehouse; Giacomo remembered the trays he had seen a few moments before.

But he plodded from bin to bin to admire the lilies, not only the grown ones in their blooming, but the baby sprouts and those that were mere pips healed into bins of warm wet gravel, where they were being watched through the hours by Stoob until they sprouted, greened, and burgeoned. These Giacomo poked with knowing fingers.

"What healthy pips," he said with admiration. "You made a fine choice here, Stoob."

Stoob's bristling manner relaxed, for he was touched as no man could help but be by the kindly praise of Giacomo. Giacomo had recalled to Stoob one of his many triumphs. At the time of the big tulip boom and the bull market that had cornered all Holland —for people will gamble, and even with flowers—Stoob had managed to set sail for America just before the market soared, with his contracts for low-priced bulbs tucked safely in his pocket. Also before the last war scare Stoob had visited Germany and succeeded in bringing out one hundred and fifty thousand valley-lily pips.

Yes, it had paid Giacomo many times over to send Stoob on the trips to Europe.

"I do my best." Stoob's voice was still aggrieved. But his air of importance was coming back, and one could see his rotund form inflate.

"Why shouldn't I get sore when I see Eric Brock running things with a high hand? Why isn't he growing with his father at Santa Cruz?"

His words buzzed in Giacomo's ears, and he shook his head to be rid of them. Giacomo was too old to quarrel. Argument wearied him more than the hardest of physical labors. During his half century as a grower he had known many personal and business cares, but none had been caused by his family of workmen. Many of the other growers had been disturbed of late by labor problems and union troubles, but none of this had as yet touched Daneri's.

"Stoob, please, no more against Eric."

"Then he is right, and you want me to go."

"And don't speak of leaving. Where would the lilies be without you?"

At once he realized the words were gone beyond reclamation. He had not intended to go so far. But Stoob, whose plump body had collapsed in dejection, swelled again with the updrawing movement of power.

"That is so!" Stoob's voice fluted with satisfaction. Craftiness kept triumph in check. "But since it is so, it is all the more unfair that I was not consulted in the matter of the Laeliocattleyas. A carload of orchids, when I could use another house for the German pips!"

He glared at the shrouded squares under the blue lights.

"Gratitude!" he snorted. "That is a word for dictionaries. It is not to be found in the flower business."

For a moment Giacomo was shocked out of speech. Why, Stoob must have a small fortune, and all earned since coming to Daneri's. A lily master's salary was exceptional, and nearly all could be put away since Stoob and his daughter had their living from Giacomo. And Stoob, to Giacomo's knowledge, had never put so much as a dollar into the stocks that had brought ruin to so many of Giacomo's friends. Then there were the bonuses distributed at Christmas and Easter time, the amounts of which Giacomo kept secret; only a few weeks ago the Easter check he had presented to Stoob had represented an average salary for a year in these troubled times. He recalled how Stoob had muttered his thanks almost resentfully, as if the amount should have been more.

Since he had done all he could to make Stoob happy, it must be some act of omission that had put Stoob in this resentful mood. And because he wished to be fair and to understand, he asked with renewed gentleness, "What is it you want then, Stoob?"

Stoob peered into the bin before him and into the corners of the valley house and everywhere except at Giacomo before he answered: "The lily houses. After all these years I've earned the right to them."

Now this was a moment no man could dream might happen, at least not a man such as Giacomo, who had put Daneri's together plant by plant, pane by pane, through a half century of perpetual toil.

His throat was dry when he answered. "But I have had no partners. This has always been a family business, Stoob."

"Family?" Stoob's mouth puffed with disdain. "What family! Your girl Tosca—do you think she wants my lilies?"

Now this was between them and there would never be any use pretending it was not there. Stoob had said what he had been bursting to say and the words could never be unspoken. As for Giacomo, he had no answer ready, only a trembling, "We will wait, Stoob, we will talk of this later," for how can one rebuff another human by saying, "No, Stoob, never while I live!" But he left the lily house with shoulders more sloping than usual, and any pleasure that might have been left in the new orchids was gone.

Daneri and Brock. Giacomo had pictured those words painted someday over the entrance to the shipping shed. Such a move would be impossible while Stoob was against Eric. But *Daneri and Stoob*—never!

The kitten pranced with rocking-horse movements around Giacomo's slow step as he made his way to the first of the "worker" orchid houses. He did not turn on the lights. Enough light came through the frosted panes from the Drive, and besides, he knew every leaf in this house by touch. Tropical night sealed him in, quieting the troubled heartbeat, and his vision adjusted slowly to the dimness where moon-proud orchids glowed. In the moist and swooning air the phantom flower faces seemed to hang suspended, ephemeral and unreal, as notes of music pitched so high as to be beyond human hearing. But they were not unreal to Giacomo, they were his own, and as he walked between them the slow deep happiness that was his life's essence flowed back through his tired frame. His very bones seemed to grow stronger, and he walked a little more lightly between the dark tables, touching the plants as he passed as if he touched the fingertips of children. Most of the plants were dormant, their spring bloom over, and the summer yet to begin, but buds wrapped in cool freshness passed lightly under Giacomo's hand, and each was a promise of beauty made to Giacomo Daneri.

This was home-coming and sanctuary, this return to the smell of greenhouse and jungle, to green blade and white root and sealed bud. Here was the renewal of the pledge of burgeoning.

One plant seemed to stir with recognition as he went to it sure-footedly in the dark.

Larger, darker, more bulbous-leaved than any of the others, it stood on a table alone. It was not fresh and young to his touch as the others were. But it towered over the other worker plants like a queen regent. This was his plant mother. It was his primary Cattleya, the first orchid ever owned by Giacomo Daneri. He had bought it with money earned pruning roses in the gardens of the wealthy on Nob Hill, and even then it had been old. It had come with him to Colma.

Hoary, unbeautiful, gnarled with years, it had mothered his miracles.

The lights flashed blue overhead, and Eric made his way between the orchids.

"I thought I'd find you here. See Stoob?"

But he could not tell Eric of Stoob. And he knew, seeing Eric, that Stoob did not matter, nor the orchids; it was only Tosca and the life before her that mattered to Giacomo.

"Tosca?" he asked instead.

"She's leaving. I'm seeing her home."

It was like Eric, Giacomo thought, Eric who was so displeased with Tosca and who would have to be up and at work again by four, and still he would take his own car and follow Tosca to the city so that she need not drive alone. Also it was like Tosca that she would take the roughly proffered gallantry for granted.

"Won't she stay here tonight?"

"She's in a stew, as you know. Don't we all know! And she's been crying."

There was nothing more to be said about Tosca. Giacomo continued to look at his mother plant, and Eric looked at it too.

"Great old girl, isn't she?" he said, peering carefully for

vestiges of buds in the gnarled mass. "We can always count on her."

"Yes, we can count on her, "said Giacomo ponderously. "Out of one pod from her—I have told you so often—out of one single pod came eight thousand perfect plants, and with them my first two orchid houses were filled, and so at last I was a grower of orchids. So I can truly say that Daneri's came from a single pod from this old mother Cattleya, and still she blooms!"

Eric eyed the Cattleya with respect.

"Remember the year, Giacomo, that we counted two hundred and forty blooms on the old girl? Remember?"

For a moment both were quiet, remembering. Then Eric turned away.

"Well, I'd better get Tosca home. It will be a big day tomorrow getting ready for the new orchids."

"Yes, a big day," agreed Giacomo, but without happiness.

Then his voice rose in pain and he caught Eric's arm to hold him back.

"Eric, who is he?"

For a moment Eric seemed reluctant to answer.

"No one we know," he said finally. "Cantrell. Mark Cantrell."

"You know something about him?" begged Giacomo.

"Not a damn thing. Just that he's Tosca's choice and she's old enough to know what she wants. That should make everything all right."

Giacomo remembered his own shy but persistent wooing.

"It is not right." Giacomo shook his head in violent denial. "Since yesterday I have been sure. When she wants so much to go to him, to hear from him, and he is not there and she does not know—what sort of man is it that can be wringing her heart and not caring? Why should it be that way with Tosca?"

"I haven't any idea." Eric was trying to get away. "We'd better get started. Tosca told me to say good-by——"

"Eric!"

It was not easy for Giacomo to share trouble. The broad shoulders had carried many burdens, his and all others. Now he held Eric.

"You can talk to her, Eric!"

"Me? Talk to Tosca?" Eric's dark skin flooded with red. "When has anyone been able to talk to Tosca? Besides, she's in love with the guy."

"It is not a good love. She is not happy."

"You expect everyone to be happy."

What does Giacomo expect? Eric wondered. He gave them all too much. Paul died wanting a plane. Tosca had everything she wanted before she knew what she wanted. Vittorio—well, he hadn't known Vittorio—but what would Vittorio have had left to work for if he had lived? How can we blame Tosca, any more than we blamed Paul, for riding high and wild?

But he thought this without emotion. Eric had made it a rule to waste no emotions on matters concerning Giacomo's granddaughter. And when he made decisions, he abode by them.

But for the first time Giacomo was pleading, and always before it was Giacomo who gave of his time and goodness and experience. And the loyalty and affection Eric felt for the orchid master were wrung by Giacomo's cry.

"Eric, for me?"

"For God's sake, Giacomo!" Eric was wretched. "I'd do anything I could, but I'd just be sticking my neck out. Besides, he's what Tosca wants and he may be what she needs, and how do you know it's not right?"

"I know!" said Giacomo.

Eric shrugged away responsiblity. "What can I do?"

"You can talk to her. You are nearer her age and you talk the way she does and you have been to college and know what to say. You can find out what is wrong and talk and she will listen."

What girl would not listen, he was saying in effect, to the wind-swept strength and cleanliness of Eric Brock?

Eric groaned. "Well, okay. But I'll be sticking my neck out. Trying to pull Tosca out of the fire like a burned chestnut!"

"When?" pressed Giacomo.

"How do I know? She's in no mood to listen now, and I can't count on her to make dates any more, at least not and keep them."

"The Flower Show! Always she has gone to the Spring Show with me. That is one appointment she will not break, Eric. And I will stay home at the last minute, Eric, and you can take her and talk to her there."

"But for you to miss the Flower Show——" began Eric, for this was unthinkable. The Spring Flower Show was the highest point of Giacomo's year.

But Giacomo waved the protest by.

"I will see it later. I will say I am too busy to go." The transparency of the fib showed in Giacomo's face. How can a man say no, groaned Eric inwardly, to a look like that?

"Okay," he agreed again reluctantly. "But it will be like asking a person with a high fever to cool down."

"She will listen to you because you are young and she knows you can understand," Giacomo answered, and he sighed, because it was not often he met with situations that made him feel helplessly old.

Still, he felt better when Eric had hurried out and he and the orchid mother were alone again.

Through the darkened mass of leaves he seemed to see the smiling features of the first Maria. So she had looked when he bought the Cattleya and she had given him that secret and tender smile of complete understanding. That smile, so long folded under earth, so long forgotten by every other living being except Giacomo Daneri! Maria had crossed half the world in "steerage" to be with him, worked at his side over their first plats of outdoor flowers in the tremendous venture that was to be Daneri's, borne without outcry his children in the small house that was now forever lonely. They had shared their heritage, coming as they did from the same marine city in Italy—their faith and dreams, their trust in one another.

She had had courage, his Maria. Tosca had it, and more. Where was it leading her?

Giacomo's gnarled hand moved gently over a hundred poniard buds.

"Sleep well, little old one," he said softly. "There will be much work for you in a few months."

The kitten raced ahead beneath the orchid tables to the door.

TWELVE

*M*ARK telephoned the next day at noon.

He spoke blithely, for how could he know how far he had permitted her world to crash the night before?

163

"How about getting in a few rounds of golf before the links get too crowded?"

"We can do that." She spoke on a spiral of happiness because she had slept, drugged with emotional and physical exhaustion, and her courage was back and she could match her gaiety with his.

"Then how about picking me up in my place? Ten minutes?"

They compromised on a half hour, and even then she dawdled over her dressing, taking time to admire the pinkish drifts of the Brock sweet peas against the deep blue walls and that blue against the multiple blues and gray of the bay. There was merit in meeting someone who was always late, for there was no need to hurry. Still, it was only little more than past the half hour when she brought her roadster to the curb before the narrow old-fashioned Sutter Street house, built before the fire, that served as a club for Mark and his friends. She honked the horn and waited. Five minutes or more passed before the door opened and Mark trotted down the high steps carrying his golf bag. Only five sticks were in the bag, and this was typical, she thought with amusement, of the irresponsible attitude Mark took toward golf and all sports. Then the sense of amusement and intimacy died as the door reopened and Roscoe dragged a burdened bag down the steps.

"You might wait for a guy," he complained, crowding into the seat with them, and then leaned over to give her a porcine leer. "Surprise, Tosca!"

She had not known how unfriendly a smile could be.

"I didn't know that you played." She spoke to Roscoe from the shelter of Mark's arm, intimate across her shoulders, and tried to cover her real meaning: "I didn't expect you, damn you."

But Roscoe chatted on without apology, talking for the three of them most of the time, and so amusingly that she could understand why Mark liked having him around. He had a fund of scandalous anecdotes, mostly about people he and Mark seemed to know very well and she not at all. But she could not rid herself of the hurt suspicion that he was along as some sort of guard for Mark, and could it be that Mark wanted it that way? And the half-dread, half-jealous resentment she had felt toward Roscoe at Bird's Nest came back and made itself apparent despite her efforts to hold her own in the badinage tossed to and fro in the car.

164

Whatever this curious emotion might be, she was certain Roscoe shared it with her. His lids crinkled with laughter, but the snake's tongue of suspicion flickered through.

"Look!" said Mark. He was wearing a tweed sports jacket with a large checked design and a metal device in the front. He ran the tab up and down. "Tricky, huh? It's called a zipper."

Anything tricky and new, she thought, would be Mark's. That was the way she liked him to be.

Roscoe's jocular antagonism showed plainly when they signed at the clubhouse desk. A couple were about to start out, to be followed by a threesome, while a foursome had been signed to follow that. It was only logical, Mark pointed out to an indignant Roscoe, that he and Tosca should join the twosome and Roscoe follow with the trio.

"Why should I play by myself?" Roscoe protested, and when Mark explained that Roscoe, far from being alone, would be playing with three of the best players on the course—one was the season's runner-up for the National—Roscoe was still surly. She could hear them arguing at the desk.

"If we wait for another spot we may be stuck out here all day," Mark was saying.

"But we were going to play together."

"You'll be right after us. Anyway, you asked to come along."

Pleasure warmed her at Mark's words. Roscoe, then, was the intruder.

She could afford to be pleasant to him, knowing this.

They started out over Lincoln sward made greener by the gray backdrop of dull silver that was the sky and the antique mirror surface that was the bay. They carried their bags because Mark claimed he could not afford a caddy, so she had to refuse one too. He was quick to notice that her bag was heavier than his and insisted upon carrying it as well as his own; a gallantry she found winning no matter how much it slowed their game.

The other couple were a serious married pair who played a mediocre but dogged game. Golf courses were their hobby. "We've shot them all," they said, "from Scotland to the Pacific." Every hole and hazard in the rolling greens reminded them of some other hole or hazard on some other course. They teed off in reverent silence and after the first hole walked ahead in plain disapproval. Tosca did not miss them, and to Mark the earnest pair might have been invisible. He took the game as he did all else, lightly but with natural skill. He was strong-wristed, relaxed, with the sense of timing that cannot be acquired, and it was plain from the first long low beautiful drive that golf was Mark's game. And Tosca, watching in admiration, was thinking: If only he were serious, if he would play with only half the determination of that stodgy man and wife ahead, what a player Mark could be!

She played a careful and consistent game, but she had worked for years to achieve that consistency, and with the best of teachers. But her own shots steadily worsened before Mark's lazy and brilliant trying. It was maddening, the way he made no effort at all, but dropped the long smooth shots just where he wished them to go. After he played the fifth and sixth in par she tossed her putter down in despair.

"I just don't see how you do it! You must play all the time."

"Hardly ever. Golf gets you up too early."

"But you could be a champion!" she cried, meaning it with all her heart, but the faun's look startled her with its intensity and Mark said quickly, "Good lord, what for!"

She walked on with him over the spongy turf, deciding that Mark had made a point in his own favor—why indeed, since he was happier this way?

But her well-meant praise had annoyed him, and for the first time he sliced into the rough. She helped him hunt the lost ball under the trees. The other couple played on ahead up the hill.

And Mark, stabbing the underbrush with his driver, looked surly.

"So you think I should make something of myself too!"

He spoke angrily, and the remark might have been a quotation, and one of unpleasant meaning.

She was caught off guard. Mark had never spoken in that tone before, almost in the voice of someone else. He rushed on without waiting for her answer:

"You want me to go to work."

"Why——" she stammered. She tried to gather words, but there were none, for it was true that she had wondered, no matter how hard she had tried not to, about Mark's idleness.

"Work," he said. "The death march of the civilized—eight hours a day, six days a week, fifty-two weeks a year, and no break in the rhythm. Not my beat, Tosca!"

166

"But if you like what you do——" They stood helplessly apart under the trees, the lost ball forgotten, the game, so far as they knew or cared, ended. "Someone like Giacomo—or Eric—sometimes they work day and night in the busy season, and they just seem—well, as if they were delighted by the extra work. They're tired, but——"

"Slave psychology." His head was beautiful, she thought, tossed back like a stallion's trying to break free of the rein. "They like it. I don't. I can't stand being goose-stepped. Why should I take work from some downtrodden brute who likes it and needs it, when I have enough to get by?"

And she sensed again he was not arguing with her, but with someone she did not know.

"Enough to get by?" she repeated. And stopped. She dared not ask what she longed to know: if other responsibility should be assumed, would Mark have enough—care enough—then?

As if he knew the trend her heart followed, he explained. And he seemed both serious and mocking, so that she still did not know.

"I'm not that kind, Tosca darling. I detest women carrying paper bags and men carrying seed catalogues——"

"I like seed catalogues," she interrupted frantically. "I'm in one, or a book rather—Giacomo's named an orchid after me."

"And I don't like regular hours and regular meals." No hostess ever waited for Mark, and one of his gayest traits was the way he could burst in late on a dinner with the most wonderful explanations, so that no one ever minded, and the dinner became a party once Mark was there.

"I don't like regular meals either," she said. "I like trays all over the house at odd hours——"

"You say you do." The oblique glance evaded. "Maybe you think you do. But you'll change. All women do. All women are two women, the one you know first and—— Oh, I know you! You'll drive me out mornings with a whip. No breakfast. You'll want the house to yourself, you'll say, and all morning you'll talk on the phone to your women friends and complain about me, and you'll meet them afternoons to talk about me, and you'll eat candy all day and get fat and I'll be slaving away in town and you won't get my dinner because you had a club meeting that afternoon with the sweetest little sandwiches and the stores were closed and what's wrong with salmon, it has vitamins, hasn't it? That's what you'll give me—canned cold salmon on a lettuce leaf."

Badinage or sincerity, which? Under the torrent of nonsense she held her head high.

"In that case, I'll have to learn to cook," she said, feeling brave and abandoned by answering him. "And I hate meetings—all kinds. Not that there's anything wrong with salmon."

And she saw the taunting evasive look had gone and a white hunger had taken its place and was devouring her.

"You're fun!" he whispered. "So damn much fun."

They walked out of the woods to the greens again as if they neither cared nor knew where they were. The couple they had been playing with had disappeared over the hill.

"Fore!" came a shout from the rear.

The foursome had come up behind them. Roscoe had teed up and was waving his driver at them.

"Ignore him." Mark was mischievous again. "Roscoe's having a case of ants. Everyone's too serious except us, Tosca."

But she heard every angry word shouted on the wind. "Why don't you let us play through?"

She spoke uneasily.

"We're holding up their game. Why not let them go through? I hate having people pressing at our heels." And she followed Mark up the hill with nervous steps.

He swung along without hurry. "Let them press. It's a free world." Amused, he added, "It's a free links, isn't it?"

"Fore!" came the angry cry again, and with it the bullet-like whistle of the ball. Her waist shrank in at the sound.

Mark dropped flat on his back and lay graceful in death between the two golf bags, with a grin on his face.

"Mark, you fool, get up!" She was trembling, but she could not help laughing.

"How can I? I've been assassinated." But he scrambled to his feet and thumbed his fist at Roscoe, who was standing with his mouth foolishly agape at the tee, his club frozen at his shoulder. "You dope, what are you trying to do, kill us?" he shouted to Roscoe.

Not us, she thought. Not Mark!

The ball lay ahead on the fairway, only a few yards away. The man of their foursome reappeared on the hill above and glared down at them.

"What's all the shouting about?" he called. "Why don't you play?"

Mark took a new ball from his bag and made a deliberate and successful shot to the crest. Tosca followed, taking three shots to his one. Her wrists felt weak.

"Roscoe has the damnedest temper," Mark remarked as they walked leisurely down the other side. "Fellow with a temper like that should never play golf."

He spoke as if Roscoe's drive had been a piece of buffoonery.

They played without looking back, and the foursome did not press again. Mark's easy, careless mood was back and his game was a delight to her. When they curved back to the clubhouse and he said exuberantly, "How about it—willing to make it eighteen?" she agreed as gaily, "You bet I can!"

She was happy, and she knew it was because for the first time they had really been alone together. Always before they had been rushing to meet others or had been with others. How beautiful had been those last minutes under the trees, with Mark tender and jesting and all hers. No wonder everyone loved being with Mark, the perfect companion; no wonder Roscoe tagged in his wake with resentment and envy. And on a wave of happiness she swept with Mark through the clubhouse door, both of them flushed and laughing, and at the same moment they saw Roscoe slumped over a table in the coffee shop.

"You two certainly took your time." But he spoke accusingly to Tosca.

Mark held up two fingers to the waitress, indicating coffee, and pulled out a chair for Tosca.

"How did you get in ahead of us?"

"Walked in. That bunch of stiff-necks I was with——" Roscoe stopped, and Tosca wondered, had there been trouble over the shot she could not forget, that Mark had not troubled to remember? "Hey, how about a drink instead of this, Mark? I know a nice little bar only a block from here."

She was remembering the stinging sound of the ball.

"We're going around again," said Mark, but without the enthusiasm he had shown a minute before.

"Aw, it's just in the next block. You can be back here in ten minutes."

It was not a block. It was two miles, out on the ocean highway. Tosca drove where Roscoe directed, and there they were on the beach again. "We might be enchanted," she told them, "always coming back to the beach."

But no feeling of enchantment went with her into the dark little bar, for the concept of such a place was still alien and even repellent to her. And Mark, sensing this, pressed her to his side as they took their seats in an uncomfortable booth, and his smile was reassuring. For his own part, he was instantly relaxed and at home.

"This is better." But Roscoe was still scowling. He clutched his cocktail glass as if it were a weapon. "I've had enough fresh air to last a year. What started you on this golf bug all of a sudden?"

"Tosca," explained Mark blandly. "She spins energy and I have to think up ways to keep her occupied."

"These energetic women," commented Roscoe, rolling his eyes upward in mock despair, but the clown's gesture did not cancel the mockery in his tone. He tilted the glass, and a green olive slid between his full lips. "Better take out insurance, Mark," he mumbled. "These energetic gals sneak up on a guy."

She kept her eyes on her glass. She could not trust Mark's look. She knew how amusedly tender it would be, and she could not bear his kindness. But when he answered Roscoe it was with the tolerance with which one treats a spiteful child.

"We're onto you, Ros. You've been married and divorced so often your sentiments have soured."

Roscoe was looking about the small dark place. The bartender, glumly polishing bottles, was the only other person in the bar.

"What a dump," snapped Roscoe, forgetting he had brought them there. "Let's mush on. Let's find somebody we know. Let's locate Kelly."

"Too early for Kelly," said Mark, glancing idly at his wrist. "It's only three o'clock. Why do watches take their time up to five and then start whizzing?"

"Let's mush," repeated Roscoe impatiently.

There were waits at her home and their club for brief changes, and then they were in a dim deep-cushioned booth in the smoky hotel lounge where Mark spent most of his afternoons. From this place he had telephoned her after their first meeting, and she had gone to meet him there like a woman driven. The place was reminiscent of that strange and heady reluctance and Mark's welcome. In this dimly lighted rendezvous he seemed in full command, of himself and all who gathered there at cocktail time.

"A corner table," Mark requested, and "We won't need such a large table," she said, and "We will," Mark answered. A small orchestra started tuning up near them and without apparent change swung into dissonance as vague and difficult to place as the faces in the low-ceilinged smoky room. And now it was Roscoe who took charge of their affairs and bustled from table to table, greeting couples and groups and bringing them back to be introduced to Mark, and each time introducing Tosca as if she were someone newly met and not too well known. As he babbled and glistened, ineptly reflected in Mark's warmth and friendliness, his porcine features became ever more pointed, as if he were driving headfirst toward some secret goal.

"Locate Kelly," he muttered at intervals, as if the phrase had become a rallying cry, and once, returning to the table peevishly, "Nobody here knows where Kelly is."

" 'Has anybody here seen——' " Tosca started to sing, but he interrupted:

"Order another fizz for me, Mark, and I'll phone around."

She drank her second rickey, each time holding her breath because she could not become reconciled to the flavor of gin, but it was the medicinal torch that lighted the rapidly filling lounge and made it a place of much glamour and many friendships, so that even the figure of Roscoe seemed for some reason oddly appealing. He was crouched in the telephone booth near the bar, his face growing pinker and his eyes more staring as he telephoned numbers from the small book in his hand, hung up with lips moving in impotent rage, and tried again.

"Why all this anxiety about Kelly?" she wanted to know, but the room seemed to converge and rush in upon them; welcoming, high voices were all around them, and this was always the way when one was with Mark.

How did he manage, she marveled, watching the way he spun women and men into the warm vortex of his charm, to wear always that look of the man who leads the band or heads the parade? Where other men were dull and flat-surfaced, so to speak, he sparkled all over with surfaces, so that each person who knew Mark laid claim to a different side of his nature and seemed to know and hold the whole of the man. Wherever he might be, no matter at what hour of the night or day, a party was in progress. Mark could say, Let's have a drink, or a cup of coffee, and it was no casual invitation—it was the passport to celebration.

She was content to sit back, nursing her admiration like a secret that keeps one warm, loving the full Priapic mouth and the face cut like a coin against the murky depths of the lounge, almost too perfect, too beautiful, she thought with passionate tenderness. The apparently unconscious way Mark accepted his good looks was one of the best of his traits; he seemed to regard his appearance as normal, exactly as he expected those who flocked about him to be good-looking and youthful, she had noticed. Even Roscoe, she realized, despite her deep dislike of the man, had a certain amount of rollicking charm. Mark did not choose his companions for their wealth or social position but for their appearance and capacity to be gay. Any gathering he entered would at once be winnowed of these special ones, and they would join with Mark, singly or by groups or pairs, and become temporary members of his nebulous hierarchy.

A dozen were crowded around their table by the time Roscoe came back.

"I can't locate Kelly," he complained. He drank the fizz and pushed the glass away. "Anything I hate is a flat drink."

"Kelly?" asked Tosca.

"You remember." Mark turned to her fondly. "Black and white at Bird's Nest."

Ah yes. The spinning creature in black chiffon, wound up for perpetual flight.

"I remember Miss Kelly."

"Not Miss Kelly, darling. Her name's Kelly Green. It really is."

"Kelly likes you," Roscoe said to Mark, but the porcine look snuffled over Tosca's naked face. "Kelly's big league. Not like some dames you take out once and the next time they ask for six bridesmaids."

A ring of laughter went around the table for Roscoe, who was smiling at Tosca in his crinkle-lidded, friendliest way. But for her there was no one else, only a terrible space in time and Roscoe, with Tosca helpless before the full-lipped inquisition smile that hid only partially the pincers and spiked wheel and white-hot iron.

Then Mark leaned his careless body between them, blotting

Roscoe away, and his warm, intuitive look came between her and the clown's mask that hid the face of the inquisitor.

"You'll meet Kelly and you'll like her. You'll see her Monday." And Mark said, to Tosca and all others around the table who might know Kelly, "Kelly's tossing a swim picnic at her place down the peninsula Monday."

"I'm not asked." She had not intended to sound so prim.

"I'm asking you," said Mark sweetly. "You can pick me up—and Ros here—and we'll all go down together."

In this confused and wonderful moment which even threat and inquisition could not mar, a vague remembrance rose and took the place of promised happiness. Monday was a date to be remembered, and why?

"The Flower Show," she said, much as Giacomo had spoken the same words to Eric the evening before. "It's the opening of the Flower Show. I always go with Giacomo."

"This once, don't go," and this sounded wittier than it had any right to sound, because of Mark's whimsical smile.

"I can't disappoint Giacomo. Anyone else—I would. But he looks forward all year to the Flower Show."

She was hoping Mark would make some protest. But he had begun piling matches on the mouth of an empty milk bottle someone had ordered, and seemed too occupied to answer. Instead, it was Roscoe who was regarding her fixedly. It was plain that he knew all there was to know about Giacomo. He was the sort, she thought resentfully, who liked knowing everything about everybody and stored away such rag-tail scraps of information—to what end? Surely Mark knew the malice behind that full-lipped smile and the hard calculation in the amusement-slitted eyes.

"I'm going to like your grandfather," Mark said, squinting at the match he was balancing on his splintery pyramid. Roscoe, not to be outdistanced, had sent for a bottle and matches and was starting his own game. He was piling matches with an almost maniac intensity.

"When do I meet the old boy?" Mark added, still intent on his match.

Giacomo will not like you—not at first, Tosca said to Mark inwardly, and Roscoe he'd hate at sight. So she only said to Mark, under the chatter that was going around the table like the whirring of a wheel, "Wait until I know you better."

173

"Oho!" Still he did not look up. "The old-fashioned kind, huh? My hand and all that?"

Roscoe looked up over his matches. His glance was like a blow. She shrank from it, and Mark, sensing her dismay, took one hand from his game and lifted her hand from the table, and still without glancing at her he put it against his lips.

The skin of her hand glazed at his touch. The open avowal made her wholly Mark's and set her as co-regent in his dreamlike, shadowy world. She sank back against the cushions, and her free hand held the thin cold glass like a scepter. Letting go, without words, without question, she let herself drop with Mark into the friendly familiar unreality, animated by faces one knew and did not know, lighted by the rocket-light bursts of talk and laughter and the marvelous clinging dissonance that was music.

In this secret drifting universe one bit of realization came to her. This had been Paul's world! In such places as this, and among such people, he had found this same happiness and the dreaming. Here, still, was the gay lost soul of Paul. This enchanted universe where light sparks wheeled and the whimpering nerves of music netted the darkness—this held enough for Mark, as it had for Paul. Paul had lived through days and nights in this joyous unreality and refused to live when the mists cleared and the music stopped.

This was madness. Her fingernails stabbed her palm around the glass. Lives had been thrown away in exchange for a few hours of dreaming. But when the dream ended, where was the clean earth of reality? Or did one stumble onto garbage-littered sidewalks in the dawn and feel the pavement crack beneath one's lost, awakened feet?

She spoke so only Mark could hear.

"Mark, let's go away. I want to get out of here."

Deliberately he tilted her haunted face to his.

"Why, you're all mixed up!" He spoke with such knowing tenderness that her eyes brimmed. "I like you mixed—all sugar and sweetness and spice and perfume."

"Take me away from here. Mark, I can't stand this place—it's choking me."

And she knew how Eric's father had felt in the glasshouses and whenever he stayed too long between four walls and pulled at the collar of his shirt and bolted out of doors.

"Darling!" The lazy amusement was gone. Mark held her

close and she felt the strong beat of his heart; its slow, strong rhythm seemed to calm her own frantic veins. "I know what it is, darling. In between the second and third, sometimes, it gets you. One more and you'll be in the clear."

"I don't want one more. I want to get away."

She saw that Roscoe had dropped his matches and was staring and that others noticed, and she did not care.

"Well, for goodness' sake," croaked Roscoe. "M'gawd, just a pair of lovey doves molting in public. Why don't you two build a nest?"

"Maybe we will," said Mark, not taking his eyes from her face.

"Well, don't nail him down Monday," Roscoe said unpleasantly to Tosca. "Give the poor sap a little more rope. We need him at Kelly's on Monday."

"I'm no jailer," she mocked, and tried to speak impudently, as Roscoe had spoken, and from the security of Mark's arms she read the porcine features like a pornographic page. Roscoe clung to Mark because he drew the attention of women who would never notice Roscoe unless Mark were with him, and she knew that to retain his share in this reflected desirability Roscoe was ready to offer all the bribes a man like Mark would find difficult to resist—invitations to gay parties, temptations for the too willing flesh, girls who could be depended upon not to demand too much—girls like Kelly Green!

Is it possible, Tosca wondered, that I who have never felt the need to be jealous of another woman should be pitted in rivalry against this buffoon!

I have to keep my head, she thought. He's more dangerous than any woman could be. Kelly Green doesn't trouble me with her spun chiffon and hair like a black lacquer cap and mascara-beaded lashes. How well, now, Tosca could picture every detail of a girl she had scarcely noticed! The image was disconcerting, but it could be brushed away. Tosca was too positive about her own advantages as a woman to feel any sense of anxiety where another woman was concerned, even a girl like Kelly Green.

But to have Roscoe as rival, ah—this called for tactics she did not know.

She rallied her courage and spoke serenely.

"I've changed my mind, Mark. I'll have another drink."

"Good girl!" he said softly, and the stars and music came back and the world of illusion was theirs again.

The waiter brought crackers and Monterey cheese with the new round. "No Camembert?" demanded Mark, and when the waiter said no, no Camembert because of the strikes, the crowding circle around the table agreed it was an outrage, and Roscoe, knocking his matches down peevishly, said it was a damned outrage and they all ought to be shot, without explaining who "they" were.

He slumped back against the cushions. Plainly, he felt cut away from the world of spinning illusions that held Tosca and Mark dreamy-eyed.

"God, I'm bored," he said grumpily. "I wish something terrible would happen."

"No Camembert," repeated one of the men. "Damn outrage."

"Damn outrage," agreed Roscoe. "No Camembert. No fun. Damn strikes ruin everything."

Like an echo, Tosca remembered her father's voice at breakfast telling her mother that the damned strikes were ruining the nation. Anger seemed to be shaking in the air.

"Trouble with San Francisco," someone quoted, "too many bridges!"

Everyone except Roscoe laughed at the familiar quip involving the bridges under construction and the water-front leader of that name. Roscoe took the subject as a personal attack, as he did all matters not to his liking.

And suddenly his face was swollen with excitement.

"Hey, why don't we start a lynching party? Right here. Get a bunch together and hang those guys on the water front!"

Only Mark advised good-naturedly: "Pipe down. Don't get your brains in an uproar."

"They're ruining business," Roscoe insisted, but he took Mark's advice and quieted.

The wild, even ridiculous talk had in it a frightening sound. Even Giacomo and Eric and the others at Daneri's, whose lives were apparently remote from the activities of the city, had showed their anxiety over the mounting tension. Would it be '29 again, Tosca wondered, and the dark confusing collapse of all that had mattered, that had taken Paul's life? Her fingers tightened in Mark's hand. He felt her fear; he was laughing, at Roscoe first and now at her, and at the sound of his understanding chuckle her panic melted. This was bravery, she thought— the ability to throw up a wall of laughter against terror.

176

And with this, the wild pride she felt for Mark grew to an iron assurance that was her own. She turned deliberately, possessively, to Mark.

"Wasn't there some talk about dinner?" she murmured, by the very softness of her words unmanning Roscoe and cutting him away, and Mark's response to her impudence was all she had willed it to be. He was on his feet in a moment, pulling her after him with a friendly offhand "S'long, Roscoe lad, see you at the club." They left him gaping in the circle of dim-faced friendly strangers he had gathered around Mark and hurried hand in hand out of the lounge.

She walked tall and proud beside Mark because their departure was on the wings of victory.

The triumph sustained them through dinner at Fisherman's Wharf, for Mark was aware that it was her victory and was both proud and amused. For his own part, he emptied his pockets on the checked cloth—there were two silver dollars and a scattering of smaller coins.

"My worldly goods," he told the amused waiter. "Get us the best dinner you can out of that and save enough for your tip."

Then, having renounced all responsibility, he was free to turn over to Tosca all the delight and tenderness that were Mark Cantrell.

No, there could be no tenderer companion. She was aware of the riches of each moment with him, of having checked bibs tied around their necks by the same gleeful waiter, of devouring huge bowls of cioppino with the thick sauce red with tomatoes, green with herbs, and succulent with fish brought to the wharf by the gay little brightly colored boats, tossing at rest now on the bay lapping under the window by their table. They ate their dinner, and it was a good dinner, because the waiter was glad that they were happy and young and obviously in love, and because of some curious winning quality in Mark that was always negotiable, even with waiters. And the waiter, who was of Neapolitan heritage, questioning the dark laughing eyes of Tosca and finding the answer without asking, sang Neapolitan folk songs whenever he approached their table.

And Mark's finances, the waiter insisted, allowed for a small bottle of red Chianti, and they sat on long after dinner had ended, dreaming over the dark water streaked red and green by the water-front lanterns, and speaking low intimate words that could never be spoken to or by other people, or not speaking at all. And the waiter, seeing them quiet, did not come back again. Only when he passed on his errands he hummed a Neapolitan love song, not looking, only intending they should hear.

In the silence the wild excitement of the afternoon and the first gay mood of the dinner fell back and far away, and love was a shy and lonely experience. Only the fact that they both shared this sadness made it bearable.

Why, she wondered, when they were so joyous with others and so sure of their love, did this almost tragic loneliness overcome them now they were alone together, despite the fact that was the way they most longed to be? And to defeat this hunger that was loneliness Tosca drank her share of the light red wine and spoke carelessly, a little foolishly.

"Poor Roscoe," she said, though she hadn't intended speaking of him, "what do you suppose he did about the check?"

"Oh, someone always picks up a check. That is one of the proven facts that helps make life bearable."

"Has he really been married?"

"Three times. It just doesn't take."

She did not ask why. The lonely mood was broken and, with it, the enchantment. She looked down on the water lapping the piles under the restaurant, and in the jewel-light streaks on the water garbage was floating—scraps of grapefruit and lettuce leaves and the damaged carcass of a fish. She looked at Mark and saw that for him, too, the illusion was gone.

The waiter said good night to them and his wise face wrinkled with dismay. What had happened, he knew no better than Mark and Tosca, walking without words up the hill to the parked car, because there were no words for this sudden lonely silence. Mark took the wheel and they drove aimlessly over the night-covered hills of the city. She sat close to him, racked by the unreasonable savage pain that came only when they left the crowded places where people swarmed together.

"Marriage," Mark said, speaking at last as the car idled down Market Street through the night traffic. "Doesn't the very thought of it make you retch?"

She shook her head, but he did not notice. He was staring ahead at the car tracks running like platinum wires to the dark shape of the Ferry Building, where the street stopped.

"It's the life sentence," he said. "From then on, as a person, you're ended."

She asked timidly, "But your father and mother—aren't they happy?"

"How do they know! It's habitual with them, like drugs. They've been married so long they've forgotten they're people. A fine thing, knowing you were hatched out of a habit."

She collapsed in relief. "I never can tell when you're serious."

"I'm always serious, Tosca. I'm the most serious person you know. You think I kid a lot, but that's not true. No matter what it is, I mean it."

"You told me not to think," she reminded him.

"You see! And I was being serious. If I stopped to think things over I'd cut my throat. Or everyone else's. The world is being run by a handful of sadists, and do they think of us? They do not! The only way we can get even and stay out of their reach is not to think of them."

"Perhaps you wouldn't feel that way," she began slowly, "if you had something to keep you busy."

"Ah, there you are!" The sensitive lips flexed. "It always comes back to that. Millions are out of work, and you think I should get a job."

"It's not that I think you should. It's only——"

"Now let me tell you what you're thinking, darling." He was not looking at her, but the car spun faster along the tracks. "You think I'd be happier if I worked. That's something all women believe. They aren't happy until they get their men on the treadmill —churning out electric refrigerators and diamonds and mortgage payments and milk bottles and new cars and all the rest of the impedimenta you pile on our heads until we can't stand on our feet any more. You are all like that."

And he was still smiling, looking straight ahead and not at her.

"But I wouldn't be happy," he pointed out.

She asked him, low and strained: "Why don't you tell me?"

"Tell you?"

"That you love me."

"I don't want anything enough to lie for it."

If I make no answer, she thought, I will be glad later. She did not speak or cry out. He felt her anguish, and his hand dropped from the wheel and held hers comfortingly.

"I can't understand you," she whispered.

He looked at her, and the look whipped her blood.

"Darling. Tosca darling. Try to understand this, that none of this is very important. You'll know that later. Believe me, because I know."

"But what do you want?"

"All I want," he said tiredly, "is to go to hell in my own quaint and beautiful fashion."

The crowded bar, she thought, the dim world, the half-world where there was no reality. She clung to his hand.

"Take me with you," she begged.

He wheeled the car toward the curb, taking his hand away, and she felt his withdrawal and, beyond that, his understanding of her bewilderment, and his own evasion of emotion. Then his quick smile was for a woman news vendor clutching her morning papers at the curb.

"You'll have to trust me, Gerd. I'm penniless," Mark said gaily, smiling, as if nothing had happened, at the woman on the curb.

She was a poor tired old creature, toothless and no longer woman, and one could imagine the dehumanizing processes life had perpetrated against her huddled frame. But before Mark's jocular smile she straightened and the woman-look came back to her lined face. Even to this ravaged remnant of femininity, Tosca marveled, Mark is the charming and tender lover. Why he, who was a tease and torment to women, should be able to evade the need to consummate his love, Tosca was not wise enough to know. But he could take his hands and his lips from her, he could exchange a tender kiss for her need of him and leave her again bewildered and bereft at her door.

In the great darkened house Marie Levenridge lay in a queen's bed in the room where her husband slept and knew again that surging fear around the heart that is doom to sleep. This was the night watch for Tosca that went on forever, with ears and heart straining for the turn of the key in the bronze door. So she had waited nights through for Paul, until the final night. The years had gone slowly since that night, but they had not silenced the doorbell's shrilling and the tread of police, heavy as death, on the marble floor. In the emptiness, while Vincent slept, she lay staring out into the dark that held the inevitable doom.

The telephone shrieked in the hall.

Barefooted on the marble, she reached the phone. After a moment of listening she was able to write down the message. The telegram was for Vincent Levenridge, and she repeated it as she wrote:

"Please advise as to my Anaconda holdings stop letter follows stop signed Mallory."

She propped the message against the phone and put her head on the marquetry table in collapse.

Then the blessed door opened in the hall below, and she heard the soft, unhappy words of Tosca in good night, and her high heels, like castanets, on the stairs. At the sight of her mother she stopped headlong.

And her mother, seeing Tosca, beholding in her the temporary lifting of the curtain of doom, burst into tears. Once she wept, it seemed she could not stop.

Tosca held her and read the written message over the jerking shoulders.

"Mama, you see, the message isn't even for you. You see how you imagine things?"

But her mother clung to her, moaning, "I was afraid."

"You'll just have to see Dr. McFee. He'll give you something. They have something new that will keep you from being so miserable."

"No, it's all right. I'll sleep now."

Now that I'm home, thought Tosca helplessly, you will sleep. She felt the unbearable grief of the great house close over her head again, drowning her right to joyous youth, and she wanted to scream out for Mark, who had left her with a farewell kiss at the door. She wanted to cry out her demands for happiness. She was young. She had the right.

A tall gray figure, like a robed priest, advanced down the hall. It was Vincent. His steel-cut hair was not rumpled, and even now, roused from heavy sleep, he was poised and neat. He put out his hand, and Marie went to him, quieted.

"Now you see how she worries when you are out late," he told his daughter.

But he spoke like one from a great distance.

"It's only twelve," she said resentfully.

"Yes, only twelve," said Marie, her broken face trying to smile. "It's early, dear. Tosca is home early."

Tosca kissed the soft wet cheeks. She turned to her father for his good-night kiss and noticed she was nearly as tall as he.

"You see, I'm not your little girl any more. You should never worry about me."

And she wondered, entering the blue bedroom with the sense of having escaped from them, why she seemed doomed to bring anxiety to those who loved her. Giacomo, Mother, Father, she thought, they all seem to hover over me as if a fiend were about to pounce on me at any minute. And their fears for her and the sadness the great house remembered followed her into the blue-walled room, while on the floor above Paul's rooms were silent, empty of all but the dusty, lovely bibelots he had collected in life as expressions of his own gay and beautiful soul.

She thought of him as she lay sleepless in the carved white bed. With Paul there had always been new horizons and more to be wanted. The new car every year, the gadgets and jewels, the newest, the finest, the costliest—all were his. In New York and London, did tailors still keep measurements of Paul's handsome frame? Did weavers in Ireland and Scotland remember his passion for good tweeds, and that little shirtmaker in London's Strand—did he remember Paul? The pipe had to be Dunhill, the studs from Cartier, the ties Sulka or Charvet. She could hear his gay warning in her ears: "You get what you pay for in this world, honey. And don't ever let your uncle Paul hear of your selling Tosca short!"

This had been the popular slogan back there. Don't sell America short. Never let yourself go cheaply, he had warned her. And when you decide to give yourself, baby, give like a queen!

And because such serious talks with Paul had been rare indeed, they had been most remembered.

And Mark, like Paul, followed the beautiful and ever-to-be-desired. She stretched her long clean body and knew herself to be beautiful and desired. The sense of power vied with the helplessness she knew with Mark; why did he whip her senses to the point of madness and then go?

This time he had said nothing of seeing her again. She had longed to beg him, "Phone me, promise!" But she had not; she was glad, at least, for that.

She lay tormented, reviewing every word and expression of their day. Had she said too much, gone too far, gained or lost? She did not know. She did not know how to be sure. And what threads of comment or action might she have left that the subtle Roscoe could use as loops to net her? For she knew she had

Roscoe to fear, and she dared not underrate the power of one man to influence another. She shrank with anguish over words Roscoe had not heard, knowing well what he would make of them.

Mark, at her door, had spoken like a man held by the throat. "Why must you have me—own me?"

She did not know why. She only knew it was so. Of all that had taken place between them, she knew only this, that no matter what happened now she must belong to Mark Cantrell. The will to possess—to be possessed—was all she knew.

Now the tears came, and she hid her face in her arms, biting the tender flesh in her effort to drive back the tears.

THIRTEEN

*I*T had always been Giacomo who waited in the entrance for Tosca on the opening day of the Spring Flower Show. This morning she found Eric there.

"Giacomo had to go back to the nursery," he explained, taking her through the doors that were not yet opened to the public. "We got here early to help with the displays, and one of the retailers from Los Angeles telephoned he wanted to see the orchid houses. Giacomo will join us later, around noon, he said."

This was a long explanation for Eric, and she wondered about it through her disappointment. The Spring Show was one of Giacomo's greatest pleasures, and they had not missed an opening together since she was small.

But Eric had rushed her through the entrance. "What do you want to see first? Ours?"

She stood looking up and around the enormous flower-filled auditorium. Wherever she looked there were enchanted scenes and glimpses and vistas of gardens and grottoed groves and blooming orchards and ferny woodlands, of lawns set with fountains and tiny streams and statuary, and everywhere, everywhere, everywhere—the flowers. Against the walls magnificent newly cut redwood trees rose ceiling-high. A forty-foot waterfall played down one grottoed wall. And mounting the forested walls and cresting the gardens, the flowers were massed in fragrant bloom as if all California's gardens had been crowded together here under a single roof. She stood staring, and her eyes widened and darkened with pleasure until they were midnight pools.

"No, not the orchids," she said finally. "Orchids are for dessert. Let's save them for the last and start with the borders."

And from that moment she led through the assemblage of flowers with rapturous cries of "Oh! Oh! Oh!" while Eric followed more quietly, but no less interested, for in this arena where the Western growers had entered their choicest in competition the flowers wore faces and hands for Eric and Tosca—the flowers were the flower people.

And being with Eric was almost as satisfying as being with Giacomo, because he too knew every plant and its history, origin, name, and its grower.

"We mustn't miss Dad's delphinium—— Look, Tosca, there's Ito's new bronze iris! Gosh, what a beauty, and just in time for the summer trade."

There were very few people in the building. These were growers who were giving the last anxious touches to their displays before the opening of the doors that would bring thousands of flower lovers milling into the Colosseum. The two young people might have been alone in a world that held only fragrance and beauty.

Here before their eyes were the tournament of roses, the fragrant armies of hyacinth, the battalions of apricot viola, tulips, rhododendron, ranuncula, anemone, bouvardia, cyclamen, iris, stock, all at their best and most beautiful, in their dewy opening, their most perfect hour. They wandered between embankments colored and scented by the floral tribes and families that were the very fragrance and the shape of springtime. Their eyes became dazzled by beauty. Their senses reeled under it.

When Tosca said breathlessly, "It's the most colorful of all the shows," Eric answered as feelingly, "Every season we say that."

"Because it's true."

Yes, it was always true.

Every year there was change to be admired, praised, wondered over. The Spring Show told the flower people what their fellows were growing. Eric lingered over an empurpled bed of Cineraria —Rolandi's—and a skillful job of selection over the preceding year's bloom. Eric's critical color sense, which could retain in memory the slightest difference in shades, appraised a bed of cerulean blue. If only one could get that color in an orchid! Perhaps by hybridizing a Vanda Caerulea!

Tosca interrupted with a rapturous cry:

"Over there, Eric! Your father's delphinium! I'd recognize the Field anywhere in the world. And oh, there is Stoob's valley! Eric, those pansies—whose are they? I don't know them."

"Tavish grows them. Over in San Leandro."

There were pansy beds bordered with blue lobelia that were gay as Chinese embroideries, while other beds, combined with English border plants, were as demure as vicarage gardens. Tosca knelt to cradle a wide-petaled blue pansy against her palm.

"Eric, this reminds me of someone. I know! Ludmilla!"

Eric looked closely at the flower. "Not the same shade at all. Blue wolfsbane—the alpine flower. That's the shade of Ludmilla's eyes."

He spoke with diffidence, and Tosca stood up, losing interest in the pansy. The image of Ludmilla had projected itself between them.

They walked on between drifts of white velvet gardenias, deciding that the largest and whitest came from Daneri's, and through yellow and white drifts of calla lilies, and the many-shaded blues of larkspur, and golden banks of calendula.

And Eric, adjusting his longer steps to Tosca's, was hearing the voice of Giacomo: "Talk to her; you are young and can talk to her, Eric." But he found it difficult to talk to Tosca, who walked tall and entranced at his side in this paradise of gardens.

As for Tosca, her thoughts reached through beauty to Mark, and the longing to share this loveliness with him was almost anguish. Anything she might see in her lifetime, she decided, that contained in it the elements of beauty or of wonder would be a little less if they could not be shared with Mark. But she walked with Eric through the flower beds and into the groves of flowering shrubs, which gave way to golden clouds of acacia and rosy fruit trees in full bloom. The trees in their turn grew taller, closer, less profuse in color, until they entered the depths of a man-made forest. A few other men and women wandered there in silence, like spellbound people. Here tree ferns grew tall over their heads, and above spread tropical trees, and over all these stretched the primeval arms of the redwoods. There was a quiet

185

here deeper than the quiet in the great hall, and the human touch seemed so necessary in the forest silence that Tosca took Eric's hand; and in their hands the pulses leaped and quickened as the two entered the mossy fern-ringed heart of the small forest where through branch and fern flashed the strange brilliant shapes of the orchids.

"Like old friends," murmured Tosca, fighting tears, because so many of these were Giacomo's. "Like meeting old friends in the jungle—Livingstone and Stanley." She babbled, through the need to speak pressing her heart, for wherever one looked they were there, hanging their jeweled heads from the twisted branches, dangling crosses of purple and gold over small secret mossy pools, tossing bright-colored flares among the ferns and velvet mosses, or poised like flames or splendid tropical insects or birds arrested in flight in their primeval world.

Then, crowning the jeweled scene, she saw the group of her own Aurea Tosca Levenridge orchids, and it was like meeting in the jungle solitude her own soul. Their pots were concealed in moss, their purple and garnet blooms held like the heads of queens.

"Five more!" she counted, breathless. "Eric, you didn't tell me! Five more have bloomed and they're perfect and I didn't even know you had entered them."

"We wanted to surprise you." Eric looked proud and happy. "And I've more news for you—it's already ribboned by the judges! You'll see your silver cup under glass before the day is over."

And he pointed to a fern cluster that almost concealed the glass box waiting there for the orchid trophy.

Then they stood bemused, hand in hand, like the others who were watching the orchids. Tosca's thoughts brimmed, and she knew if she spoke she would cry. Because only in the flower shows did one see Giacomo's orchids to greatest advantage. One might hunt his orchid houses through to behold so many orchids and then see them scattered, one by one. Here they were massed in the full concentrate of his genius. Here was his deep yellow cross from the Aurea, his beautiful white spray, the Coelogyne Cristata, that once had bloomed only at Christmas but which had been persuaded through his sorcery to bloom for the bridal months of summer. Here were his spraying Cypripedium insigne, the giant spikes of Odontoglossum, the scarlet orchids beloved by Tosca, the delicate green of the shy and exquisite lady's-slippers.

Her eyes filled, for behind the glory of the orchids she could see the gray, slanted shape of Giacomo touching their pollen sacs with his branch-like hands, healing their seeds into agar, cherishing them into life with his tremendous tenderness. Here was the blooming of his long patience. Here was the fabric of his years. The tears were hot against her lids for Giacomo, for her pride in his gentleness and forbearance, and for her knowledge that because of her he was sore at heart.

"He should be here. With us, now," she said brokenly.

"He'll be here soon."

Now was the time, Eric knew. Now, while she was made vulnerable by this onslaught of beauty, was the time to speak.

He looked about uneasily. There was more privacy here, in this patch of tangled jungle, than could be found elsewhere in the building.

"That Aurea is tilted," he said critically. "Let's see about fixing it."

He led her over the mossy incline and between the fern trees to the trunk of a fallen redwood. The Aurea was set in its green branches like a giant butterfly.

"It isn't complete without Giacomo," she said. "Not that I'm not enjoying your distinguished company, Mr. Brock!" She made a face at him behind the sheltering screen of the orchids.

Eric took his knife from his pocket. Using it as a pestle, he proceeded to tamp the pot more deeply under the moss, being careful not to touch the flowers. Now was the time and the place, surely, and how could one find a better place or time? Now, while Tosca wore this gentled, dreaming look in the surrounding of orchids.

And he stood tongue-tied, hacking away at the plant.

"You'll wear that out!" Laughing, she drew his hands from the Aurea. "What's the matter with you? You're usually such a clam."

"You mean I don't talk enough?"

"No, of course you talk. But you're so calm and so certain where you are going and what you are doing."

Then she sighed, and the broken sigh was so like Giacomo's it drew speech from Eric.

"It doesn't always help—being sure. You seem sure enough now of what you want. But are you? Tosca, this Cantrell, is he right for you?"

She was looking at him in a startled way.

"Giacomo asked me that," she said slowly. "Why? Why do you all ask about him as if he were——"

"Wrong for you, Tosca?"

Without speaking, she shook her head, and he noticed the deep shadows under her eyes and the driven look he had seen for the first time on the day of Giacomo's festa. He opened the bladed tool and carefully pruned a bit of tree foliage that was obstructing the spread of the orchid. He kept his eyes on the work.

"You've changed. You're nervous and touchy and—you just aren't Tosca any more. What is he doing to you, Tosca? What sort of a man is he that he can do this to you?"

And because she trusted Eric, the truth.

"I don't know."

He would have preferred dropping the topic then and there. But Giacomo had to be remembered.

"Talk gets around," he said awkwardly. "You can't stop it when everyone knows everybody, the way we do in San Francisco. And Cantrell's pretty well known, you know."

And then, reluctantly, "Women like him."

She looked at him angrily. "Are you trying to say he's a lady killer and that men don't like him? That's not true. Everyone loves Mark."

"There's something wrong with a man everyone loves," answered Eric, trying to speak without rancor, and not quite certain what emotion motivated his words.

There was no doubt in Tosca's mind. Her clear skin flushed.

"I suppose it's natural for men to be jealous of a handsome man," she began bitterly, and was stopped by the obvious fact that Eric was looking very handsome indeed, sunburned and wind-blown, to be sure, but with his tanned blondness enhanced by the neat dark blue business suit. In fact, she thought, looking at him with new judgment, he was probably better-looking than Mark, although in a less beautiful way. But looks—what had they to do with love! It was the strange understanding Mark had of her that held her. She could not struggle against a net woven of intuition and the gay and tender knowledge of her needs as a woman. Such things could hold where brain and biceps failed.

"Since you've brought up this subject," she said coldly, "let's talk it through. Obviously you've been dragged into this by Giacomo. I know you better than to think you would start any such campaign on your own, Eric. So you've talked me over and there are things you want to know. What are they?"

"I don't want to know anything that isn't my business. But he —we thought there might be something we could talk over. It might help," he added lamely.

Damn Giacomo, he was thinking. This is what I get into, trying to help him. Tosca was frowning with suspicion between the orchid blooms.

"Sometimes it's a good idea," he blundered on, "to try summing up everything there is and try to balance the books. What has he to offer and what are you——" Then, seeing her frown deepening, he added hastily, "That is, if you're thinking of marrying the guy."

"It's not a business deal," she said coldly.

"Oh, isn't it! That's where you're wrong. That's how people let themselves get messed up. Because, believe me, marriage is a deal, and it is business. It's partnership, and if it isn't a fair one it isn't likely to last. And there's no reason why these things can't be worked out scientifically. After all, it's based on the most important force in the world. Why let it run wild?"

"You're talking like a hybridist."

"Maybe I am. And maybe that's not a bad attitude to take. Let's look at it in human terms. Take my father and mother. Did you know their marriage was arranged?"

"Arranged?" She was surprised and interested. "Why, they're the most loving couple I've ever known."

"They worked for it," he said grimly. "Their families were old-world and had a lot of old-fashioned ideas that had crossed the Atlantic with them. One of my dad's uncles heard about my mother and said, Aha, that sounds like the right girl for Adolph! He finagled a meeting with her, and then he managed to bring the two together."

"Was it love at first sight?"

"Of course not. Naturally they were both furious."

"But I don't know a happier pair."

"It worked for them," said Eric. "Training, background, ideas, economic factors, all those were worked out in advance. All the young folks had to do was fall in love. That was the old way, and it produced big happy loyal families. Sometimes I think those old folks had some sound ideas."

Mark wouldn't like it that way, she thought. Being poor. Starting out together. But I'd be willing; I'd work for him.

And Eric, skillfully adjusting the pots between the branches so that the orchids showed to greater advantage through the fern trees, looked up in time to see the look of fleeting loneliness cross her face again that tore his heart, as it had at the heart of Giacomo. One of the Aurea blooms swung breast-high, facing her, purple and gold. He stood up, brushing the moss from his hands.

"Tosca, sweet, your biggest handicap is the fact that you've never acquired the taste for dirt. You'd be surprised to learn how working in earth helps straighten out your thinking."

"Is that why you're so sure of yourself?" she asked resentfully. And then, suddenly and softly, "I did have a garden once! My own garden, where the compost is now. I planted bulbs Giacomo gave me and dug them up every few hours to see how they grew, and of course they didn't."

"And you couldn't wait. Impatient. You always were."

"I found out I didn't have to grow them. There were always so many flowers . . ." Her voice trailed away. "Anyway, I may surprise you someday and come out and help you pot the orchids."

"Someone has said," he remarked, eying her curiously, "that we dream like gods and behave like apes."

"Well, nobody can accuse you of being an ape. You're too careful."

It was a pity, Eric thought angrily, that they couldn't talk without falling into argument. He tried to bring the mood back to the channel Giacomo wanted.

"Tosca, why hasn't Giacomo met him?"

Then he was startled by the shadows under the dark eyes and the hurt lost look that was so old, so new to Tosca.

"You can't understand. Mark and Giacomo live in different worlds."

"But that's crazy——"

"When I'm ready—when they are ready, I'll know."

Something apart from himself stood watching her then, grieving and fearing for her the way Giacomo feared and grieved for Tosca. It had nothing to do with the way he ordinarily felt for Tosca; it was alien to the open healthy nature of Eric. He had caught a glimpse of an emotional world he did not know, nor could he understand the black and stagnant lava flow that spread around volcanic outbursts of desire.

And because he did not understand and knew no way to defend her, anger rose hot in Eric. The warm wet air of the fern grove was suddenly stifling, and his hand went to his collar in the familiar gesture.

"Do you have to make a fool of yourself? Is he worth it? Is anyone worth it? The way you talked over the phone the other night, with Giacomo and the others listening—where's your pride, girl? What's the tragedy about? Can't you marry him? That is"— viciously—"if you're sure Giacomo can afford him! Or sleep with him? Anything—only get it over!"

"It's not that simple!" And she parted the ferns blindly to escape.

"Wait!" He held her. The ferns fell back and the great bruised lips of the Aurea swung between them. "Tosca, can't anyone beat any sense into your head? Something's wrong with Cantrell. There must be. You aren't experienced enough to figure it out."

Only to know what I want, she thought, sick with hunger for the tall and graceful Mark, the gentle hunger of lips, the persuasion of slender hands. Only to be held by Mark, and even if it could not last, to belong to him. To be possessed and lost, and beyond that—nothing.

"I love him, Eric. You have no idea how much."

"Haven't I!" The look on his face was brutal. "I could go crazy too, but I won't. I know the difference between love and mania. Yours won't last. It can't last. Mine will."

Her look was pitiful. "I didn't know, Eric. I've been afraid——"

"Well, now you know. And there's nothing to be afraid of. I'm not letting it throw me."

There was finality, even contempt, in his voice and in his coldly narrowed eyes. She stood with her fair head held back against the lustrous pattern of the orchids. Bred in beauty, he thought her, with her womanhood designed to entrap and allure. In all this glory spread about them, this living procreative pattern, she seemed the loveliest part. And something in Eric that was deep and defensively male hated Tosca in that moment.

And because of his anger, against her and against the Mark Cantrell he had never met, and most of all against himself, he flung her aside with a violent gesture and caught at the Aurea that swung between them like a brilliantly colored bird.

"Look, it's all here!" His knife was still in his hand, and in his anger and his need to hurt and his secret need of her he slashed the orchid through. The halved jewel-like organs lay between the beautiful lips, curiously human.

"It's all here!" he repeated, probing in the opal throat with the point of the blade. "Pollen sac, labellum, ovary, stamen, and pistil, that's what this great thing we call romance is in the beginning and that's what it is in the end. Here is the truth for you, Tosca, right here on my blade. The rest is for idiots."

If it were Ludmilla, he was thinking, she would not be looking at him with the wide-eyed wounded look as Tosca was looking now. Ludmilla knew life in its blunter terms. She had been reared among people whose lives were dedicated to the art of propagation and whose minds were trained to accept, beyond the fragrance, the colors, the satin petals—the primordial thrust.

He repeated wearily: "For idiots."

"I am one," she said.

He forgot the need to hurt her. He forgot caution. He forgot all the plans he had made because Tosca, with her vulnerable beauty, with her look of being there for the taking, was ruin to his plans.

"So am I, Tosca. But I could help you get over him."

Now it's all ruined, she thought dully. Everything we had left, that I could depend on, is gone. I had a friend named Eric. . . .

She was crying.

"Does Giacomo know, Eric?"

"He has always known."

I never wanted to know, she thought. Eric, who remembers the day I was four and threw up at Giacomo's picnic. Her lips felt as if they had been numbed by Novocain. They had always quarreled, argued, parted in anger, and met in amicable forgetfulness. This was irrevocable. She had hurt him as he never had been hurt, and before her all his ambitions and manhood were beaten down.

She felt wretchedly guilty. She said again, "I didn't know."

Now he had broken before her and never again would he feel so sure of himself, and the work he wanted to do could not seem so important. He dropped the slashed Aurea and ground it under the moss with his heel.

"Let's get out of here," he said shortly.

He parted the fern trees, and they left the jungle for the pathways beyond the moss. Hundreds of spectators had entered the Colosseum since they entered the orchid grove. The doors had opened. The scent of flowers had grown stronger in the great domed building.

"There's Giacomo," he said.

Giacomo was moving along with the other spectators, walking slowly and looking at every flower. A look of peaceful enjoyment that was almost holy was on his face.

Eric felt he could not meet that look.

"I'm going," said Eric. "He'll see you through the rest of the show." How different, he thought bitterly, from all Giacomo had planned!

"Eric!" She clung to his hand.

"Don't talk about it. Don't think about it again."

"But Giacomo——"

"Tell him I had work to do."

She did not try to hold him. Nothing could help, she knew. The three-ply comradeship shared with Giacomo and Eric was torn apart by this new and unhappy knowledge, and she knew it could never be the same again.

FOURTEEN

*S*TRIKES! Strikes! Strikes!" grumbled Stoob. He was reading his newspaper, sitting with his back to the windows of the small living room in the cottage across the lane. "Student strikes, milk strikes, coal strikes, lettuce strikes—now this talk of a general strike."

He turned the page noisily.

"The capital-eestic system," he snorted.

Behind the plain curtains Ludmilla watched the first truckload of De Paoli orchids being carried into the Drive. Eric stood in the truck, handing trays of the potted plants down to waiting members of the orchid crew. They were working very fast; the plants had to be hurried into the glasshouses so that their blood might be warmed after their trip across the mountains.

"Eric is looking very pleased," she remarked. "You would think they were Eric's orchids."

"I will not look," said Stoob promptly. But the words held a barb to be caught and considered. He dropped the newspaper and began nursing his long pipe, staring glumly into the cold mouth of the iron stove that rested, European-fashion, in the exact center of the cheerless little parlor. He had assured Ludmilla that he would not cross the lane to his lily houses, although it was nearly noon, until the new orchids were out of sight in their designated houses. He had not even been to the window.

"Let him think that," he said sourly. "The time may come when he does not sing so high."

A curious smile her father could not see crossed Ludmilla's pale lips. Father and daughter were in virtual barricade in this bare little room that did not contain one feminine touch. The curtains were coarse and clean, the floors waxed and without rugs, the walls naked of pictures or mirrors, the scant furnishings tasteless. Like Ludmilla, the room was without adornment. Unlike the girl, it had no natural beauty to redeem this barrenness.

Her strong, restive hands pleated the curtain's hem. She did not like being housebound. But they had retired to the cottage after breakfast in Giacomo's kitchen, where Stoob had been at great pains to express what he thought of the business of making room for new orchids now, at the very start of the great June rush. He had made these opinions known while stoking away great quantities of Cesare's good breakfast, as if he were preparing for a state of siege.

It was plain to Ludmilla that the siege was on. Only no one protested their position. In the lily houses the bins of lilies of the valley, at the peak of bloom in readiness for the bridal bouquets of a continent, waited the attention of the lily master and his daughter. The crew were there, to be sure, but Stoob would not admit they could carry on without him.

"Let the old man stew," he remarked sulkily over his pipe. "It will teach him a lesson."

Giacomo did not appear to be annoyed by, or even aware of, the lily master's absence. Ludmilla saw him standing beside the truck and reaching up to receive one of the light pots from Eric's hands. She saw his examination of the plant's nodding blooms, and her sharp eyes recognized the orchid.

194

"Laeliocattleya-Ishtar," she said aloud.

"So?" Stoob swerved to examine the thin figure of the girl against the window. He saw the slender body shrink, and was pleased. It was a good thing to hold a daughter's fear. A motherless girl had to recognize authority, and what other way could this be taught? He had been wise in refusing Giacomo's many offers to pay Ludmilla a salary. Independence was too dangerous a blade to put in the hands of the young.

"Who taught you such things?" he said in his quiet treble that held the threat of menace.

He saw the strong fingers pleat the coarse mesh with nervous strokes. She did not turn.

"Eric taught me. Papa, you do not like him?"

Her courage kept the pipe from his mouth and his mouth open. But she kept her pale smooth head to the light, and what thoughts went on in it he did not know.

"If he kept his place," he said finally, "then I might like him."

The strong brown fingers locked over the mesh.

"But his place is with Giacomo. Always with Giacomo."

Stoob set his pipe deliberately on the cold stove.

"Look at me," he said. There was crafty excitement in his tone. The girl turned slowly; it was as if father and daughter studied one another with new vision. Whatever he had planned to say was forgotten when he looked at her, seeing a girl plain and without allurement, and with her pale, plain features set in a stubborn fear.

"You!" His voice fluted with what appeared to be sudden hatred. "Are you against me too, with the orchids? Why have I done without all these years? For you! Do you think I did not know the things you wanted? Was it for pleasure I denied you the dresses in high school and the bicycle you wanted? You did not have these things, and why?"

Because you are stingy and mean, she wanted to say, as she had so often in her thoughts against him. She had felt demeaned by his scrimping. Did they not live on Giacomo's land, eat at his table, save his good wages? But the white blood of Stoob seemed to be rising in a passion of hatred, and she stared at him fascinated, realizing that this time, as perhaps in other times, this flood of anger was not against her.

"To get in!" The hissed words were triumphant in their venom. "I have demanded my rights. I have the money for buying my way in. Giacomo cannot refuse me the lily houses. And then I will have more! More—if everything does not get sunk in orchidry. Eric has the old man bewitched. But Eric will not last. I have not worked these thirty years to let a field grower cross the Santa Cruz Mountains and take over Daneri's. No!"

Her white fear held a strange element now; was it admiration?

"What do you plan to do?" she whispered, as if they were conspirators.

"The years are on my side," Stoob said grandly. "Do not forget that Giacomo Daneri is soon to be seventy-five. And I am not yet sixty. Between sixty and seventy-five there is a lifetime—for a man who has made his plans."

He saw blue flame in the wolfsbane eyes and gloated. Then he saw it die. He saw the fear come back, as he had seen it often, under the heaviness of his hand.

"But Eric! What will happen to Eric?"

But he did not seem to be angry. Instead he smiled craftily.

"Eric is a good workman. He can always find work in other orchid houses. Or he can go back to his father on the seed farms, where he belongs. One thing I know, he will not be tending orchids here, because there will be no orchids."

His pale eyes blinked with triumph. He picked up his pipe and sucked at the long stem, studying Ludmilla through the billowing smoke.

"You see," he said carefully, "there is only one way Eric Brock can lay claim to an inch of Daneri's land if I have my say."

The open questioning of her look seemed to amuse him.

"No, not through Giacomo." He shook his head, smiling. "I will see to that. I will demand my rights—after thirty years! No, he has only one way, and do not think he has not worked for it! I have had eyes! You are blind to him, but I have watched the way he has looked at Tosca all these years!"

One of the moods of inexplicable anger was on him now, and his thin voice rose to a treble of fury as he stood up, facing the shrinking girl.

"You have been blind. You are always blind! You do not use your head—everything that is done for you I must do. If I had not watched and planned, where would you be, helpless one? Here is a fortune spread out for you, ready for you to take it, and you have not had the brains to see. What will become of us when Giacomo dies, if we do not take steps now? Who else wants

Daneri's? Levenridge cares only for his bank, the sons are dead, the granddaughter is a——"

He spat out a word so vicious the girl cried out in protest.

"Oh, you do not like facts, do you? Do you think I lie? Did the men not meet her with him that morning on the highway when their car was almost crushed between our trucks? We hear of her —here and there and always with him—this drunken waster—— What else can we think her, since we are not deaf and blind like Giacomo? And like Eric?"

"Eric knows! Eric is unhappy."

"Eric is unhappy?" The father paused. In his ever-plotting mind plans were reshuffled and made again. "You are sure Eric is discontented here?"

"I wouldn't say that——"

He pressed her, breathing like a hunter at the scent of blood. And she could see the new plans whirl in his pale and prominent eyes.

"That is the answer!" He was indomitable in his certainty. "Now I know the way! Don't forget we are poor. We must use all we have to go up. Anything!"

He paused, studying the thin and shrinking girl.

"A woman!" sneered Stoob. Something close to envy made him paler than before. "You are a woman, and a woman can do more in one hour than a man who works and sacrifices and saves all his lifetime. In one hour a woman can win fortune—a big place in the world. Yes, it can be done!"

And he studied her, avid, triumphant.

"If I were a woman——" he said; then, lashing at her, "Look at you—the way you stand! Lift your chin so you look like a woman. No wonder he never sees you! Yes, if you tried, if you would only try! You do not know what you can do. What any woman can do to any man."

She was face to face with him now, as if his excitement fed her with the knowledge of a power she had never known she possessed.

"But how——"

"Let yourself know how! He is a man, he is a young bull, and he is not pleased with Tosca. What other women have done, you can do. Get Eric, and I will do the rest. The old man. The lily houses. And after the lilies, the orchids."

"You don't want the orchids."

"No! I will get rid of them. Only, do what you can do."

For the first time father and daughter understood one another. For the first time in their lives they were equals.

"You said—anything?"

"Anything!" Stoob repeated. "Always before, you have hung onto me and pulled me down. Now is your chance to repay me and take us both to the top."

For a fleeting moment her fear returned.

"But what if he does not want to marry me?"

"He will." Every syllable sang with contempt. "Eric is honorable."

And Stoob puffed at his pipe in his excitement until the small ugly room clouded with fumes.

"Oh, a fine thing," he said excitedly, "if Giacomo could turn against him; if he could be turned from Giacomo and toward you."

She went back to the window. The truck was gone from the lane, and Giacomo and Eric and the others had disappeared into the Drive with the orchids. After a moment she turned and walked quickly down the narrow hall to her own room. When she returned her pale lips had turned to a coral red.

"You are going out?" he asked in surprise.

"I am going to help Eric with the new orchids." She spoke calmly.

He knew then she would never be afraid of him again.

Eric was the first to notice the change in Ludmilla.

"Lipstick!" He grinned at her over the trays of new orchids. "Very becoming. Let's have more of that!"

Giacomo looked up with his kindly smile.

She gave them a fleeting, secretive glance and took up her position against the wall of the Drive. She took her knife from her pocket and opened the blade, waiting until the time when she could offer help.

The long glass shed was crowded with plants and men. The fifteen hundred plants of the Laeliocattleya were packed in their trays on the workbenches and shelves. Eric and Giacomo were working rapidly over the trays, sorting the potted plants, few of which showed blooms. The other men, Laddie among them, carried the sorted plants into the orchid houses. Some of the smaller plants went into the seedling house, and the larger ones were to be given temporary quarters in the adult orchid houses. But Eric and Giacomo put the plants that had grown too large for their pots up on the potting shelves, to be repotted as soon as the work of sorting was over. The kitten was dancing along the edge of one of the shelves, showing the liveliest interest in the new plants and the work being done.

After the crew had left with the last of the potted orchids and only Giacomo and Eric were left at the shelves, the kitten continued its circling dance among the strange pots, pausing to sniff curiously at the new plants. And when Eric and Giacomo went to the shelves to start the work of repotting, it caught mischievously at Giacomo's busy hands.

He lifted the kitten between his strong hands and set it farther back on the shelf.

"Be a good boy and do not bother us now," he said absently, and the kitten obediently curled its tail about its feet and began washing its face. Its innocent absorption in the task touched Giacomo.

"There now, I did not mean to speak harshly, *gatto*," he advised the little creature gently. "Sometimes I forget your mother is occupied in the bulb loft and does not have time to teach you——"

Then he paused, dumfounded, remembering Ludmilla, who had also been left motherless and who never in all her life had been spoken to as kindly by her father as Giacomo was speaking now to a half-grown Maltese cat.

But she gave him an oddly assured look as she came forward and took her place between the two men and immediately fell with them into their swift and certain rhythm, carefully removing the orchids from their confining pots, dividing the plants that were too large, clipping away with the precision of surgeons, and the "back" bulbs that would be other plants within a few years. Their deft hands snipped leaves that looked poor or marred. Their trained eyes scanned leaves and roots for any hint of pest or disease or decay. The curious white roots were washed in a nicotine solution. Every Daneri man took pride in the fact that this nursery was rated the freest from pests in California.

Ludmilla's movements were fluid and her brown hands incredibly strong as she reset the cleansed plants into new pots filled with moss and shard and tamped the harsh fiber around the roots with her planting stick. At other times she seemed awkward and unsure; but in this place, and with such work, she was deft and graceful in her movements.

They did not speak at first. They worked in rhythm, and each was aware of the work the others did and approved all that was done. They were working easily and still against time, because June was not a month to brook interruptions, with all the weddings and graduation and engagement festivities being celebrated everywhere with flowers.

Ludmilla, half smiling, thought of her father. Stoob would be driving the crews in the lily houses, sputtering to make up for lost time, now that the orchids were put away.

Pietro came in. Between his big hands, knotted and scarred from a lifetime spent working among the roses, he carried a potted orchid.

"Laddie asked me to bring this to you," he said. "It was sent by mistake along with the Laeliocattleya."

It was a lady's-slipper with a trio of unblemished green-and-copper buds.

Giacomo put out his hand.

"These will be nice for Tosca," he said with a pleased smile.

"Why for Tosca?" Ludmilla could not resist asking, then she remembered. "Oh yes, the tables for the League. She always decorates one, doesn't she?"

"Yes, and with orchids," Eric said a little sourly.

He had been moody since the Flower Show. But Giacomo had not questioned him.

He carefully set the green orchids on a fiber bed on the ledge before them. The kitten paused a moment to look, then went on with its face-washing.

They worked on, rapidly and carefully. Giacomo planted like a young man, so that the others had difficulty keeping pace with him. The orchids had turned out to be even better than he had thought them when he made up his mind to own them that day at Santa Cruz. There was a look of peace upon him as he worked that Eric and Ludmilla did not share. Tosca and her demands had interrupted the even rhythm of their work.

Eric, because he had shrunk in his own esteem since the day of the Flower Show—where had his pride been that day, to speak so to Tosca!—was glumly reviewing his sense of relief when the days had gone by and Tosca had not appeared at the nursery. Giacomo had gone once to the city to dine in the Levenridge house on the Presidio hill, but Tosca had not driven back with her grandfather to spend the night at the nursery, as she had so often. Giacomo had not discussed the family dinner, but Eric had gathered without asking that he still had not met the man Cantrell.

As for Ludmilla, she had her own thoughts, and they kept a strange smile neither of her companions had seen before playing over her newly reddened lips.

And Giacomo, because he was pleased with the new orchids, broke the rhythmic silence by speaking of the orchids.

"Even in worse times than these," he said happily, gesturing to the newly potted Laeliocattleyas, "these would be a bargain. We are lucky indeed to have them, what with the quarantine laws closing down on orchids and many of the South American countries passing laws so that the orchid hunters cannot hunt in those countries any more."

"The strikes aren't helping any, either," put in Eric.

"Ah, the strikes," said Giacomo. "And the talk in Europe—the Reds there and the Nazis there and the Fascisti spreading . . . Such ugly troubles, always, in Europe."

For a moment he remembered the silvered olive groves of a far-off hillside, and then, with a rush of loyalty to the heart, his own lush flower-ribboned land that was safe under his feet. "I am glad that we are here," he said quickly, and then, to Ludmilla and Eric, "No matter what troubles happen, be glad you are here."

"But the laws"—Ludmilla went back to the subject that interested her most—"why do they make those laws to keep us away from the South American orchids?"

"To prevent their extinction, naturally." Eric bent his head to scrutinize a suspiciously dark spot on a leaf. "A hundred years ago there were only a few orchid plants in the United States, and not many more in England. Now we have entire jungles of orchids in our country; the orchid world has moved north to us. So the other places want to keep the wild orchids that are left."

"I saw them once, wild," said Giacomo. He stopped, steel planting stick in hand, and smiled at the glass wall as if at a pleasing vision. "Once in Guatemala, when I was on my way to Europe, I saw them—colonies of them under the great trees. Like little beasts and bees and frogs, they seemed, and all freckled with seed pearls from the jungle mist. One gave the vanilla——"

"Vanilla?" interrupted Ludmilla.

Eric nudged her. "Don't you remember vanilla comes from orchids? The Aztecs used it to flavor their chocolate long before the Spanish came."

"What else did you see, Giacomo?" Her interest surprised them. In fact, when had Ludmilla been so animated before?

"Little else." Giacomo spoke regretfully. "I was hurrying as always—to the European market and back again. When a man is building he hurries. Now I wish there had been more time in which to see."

"I would like to see the wild orchids." Ludmilla's thin face burned and she was looking at Eric as if goading him into sharing her interest. "If I were a man, I would go. Giacomo, do you know many of the orchid hunters? Is it true you hire hundreds of them?"

"*Bella Santa,* the enlargement of talk," marveled Giacomo. "Hundreds is a very large number. Let us say there are hunters in many places. One who now is in Australia, *ohime mi!* The troubles he has lived through, and I with him! Do you not remember the last tray of seedlings he sent me, Eric? Puny as weeds! My attorney is writing him a letter, yes, a strong letter, for sending such plants all the way from Australia."

"You should cut off his salary," said Eric. "That would teach him."

"He must like the work," said Ludmilla carefully.

"*Ai,* to be sure! Hunting orchids is his living and his excitement, and that is true of all the hunters of orchids."

"And where is the best hunting now?"

They had stopped their work and were giving all their attention to the subject.

"In Venezuela and Brazil." Giacomo pronounced the names of these countries with care, because it was true that he had never given up hope of someday seeing them. "The finest orchids are in these places, and the hunting still goes on. . . . And after the orchids are found there are still ways of getting them here. Yes, there are ways. . . ."

"It's dangerous work?" Ludmilla's pale blue eyes were wide on Eric's face, and she could see the restive interest growing there.

"It is only for a man who is very brave," answered Giacomo.

"He must not be afraid of danger and of the fever. He must be able to resist loneliness. He must know Spanish."

"*Yo hablo Español.*" It was Eric speaking. "I had three years of it in high school. It comes back to one, they say."

Giacomo showed his pleasure that Eric was interested. Eric had been so morose since the Flower Show.

"If I were a man——" began Ludmilla slowly. Her eyes were still on Eric, but she spoke to Giacomo. "Didn't you want to go with the orchid hunters when you were young, Giacomo?"

Giacomo sensed that Eric, too, was waiting for his answer. He spoke with sudden heaviness. "I wanted to go to Brazil," he said, and his voice was throaty with an old temptation.

"If I could begin again——" Giacomo started to say once more, and Eric, looking at him quickly, felt with him the heartbreak of the never accomplished. What value was there to all a man had done if there was so much left he might have been able to do? "Yes," said Giacomo heavily, "if I could be young again, knowing what I have learned since I was young—I would create such orchids——"

"And you would hunt orchids?" cried Ludmilla.

"I would hunt orchids," Giacomo agreed. "It is good for a man to know what adventure is before he grows old."

A smile of satisfaction played over the reddened lips. Ludmilla had accomplished her purpose. When Eric dropped his planting stick and said it was time to start on the second shipment, she did not mind.

Only Giacomo called to him as he was leaving:

"Eric, the green orchids for Tosca!"

The orchids for Tosca were before Ludmilla. The kitten, beside them, had finished washing his face and was innocently cleaning a small paw. The mention of Tosca drove Ludmilla's strong hand forward in a gesture of rage. Her brown fingers closed around the graceful spray, strangling the green orchids. With an abrupt turn of her hand she knocked the kitten against the flowers.

"Look, the kitten," she cried harshly. "He's ruined the flowers."

"I told you, Giacomo." Eric came back to the shelf. "That cat's getting too big to be allowed in the houses!"

"But he has been a good cat." Giacomo, protesting, picked up the kitten and held it close. He could see it was frightened; why, he did not know. But he did not like to see fear anywhere, and looking about in distress, he sought the pale eyes of Ludmilla that had always held the lurking shadow of fear. But there was nothing in their blue depths now but a strange defiance.

"The kitten has never made trouble before," he insisted to Eric, and Eric left without another word, leaving the bruised orchids.

After a moment Giacomo followed Eric to the door. Regretfully he set the kitten outside. His step was heavy as he returned to the potting shelf.

"Ludmilla, I will finish these. Run along, it is lunch time. And your fingers must be aching."

He spoke sorrowfully, because this was the first dissonance between Eric and Giacomo, and the girl Ludmilla had observed it all. He could not care for her, much as he pitied her, try as he might. Still the kindness he showed her grew in proportion to his growing dislike of Stoob, which was Giacomo's way.

After she had gone he worked alone in the potting shed. Thoughtfully he wiped a smear from a pot's rim. Only a few days before, it had been an orchid.

In one's lifetime, he thought, a man should do all that is most pleasing to him, if it is in his power. And he tried not to think of the unwonted eagerness in Eric's voice as he spoke in Spanish when they talked of the hunting of orchids.

He had the curious feeling that somehow he had been led through such chatter into some unrecognizable indiscretion.

"Who asked such things of me?" Giacomo found himself wondering aloud, although not even the kitten was there to listen as he patiently drove the steel probe around the white roots of the orchids. "How happened it that I had so much to say about nothing at all?"

FIFTEEN

Tosca arranged masses of coxcomb in a gold porcelain bowl on a table splendidly set with a cream dinner service edged with gold and maroon. The cloth was of cream-tinted damask. The heavy red velvet folds of the flower made a magnificent arch, but it refused to hold its place in the bowl. A stalk snapped.

"Damn!" Tosca breathed impatiently. Why did she not have the touch like Giacomo? Practice, he always told her, and patience. *Sciniu pazienza!*

Around her on the department store's mezzanine other tables were being arranged by other members of the League. Every season the store loaned space, silver, crystal, china, and linen to the table display, and the late summer flower arrangements were made by the League members.

Strike threats were ominous, but the show would be held.

Nearly all the other girls had completed their decorations. Camellias and roses and bouvardia were in unique array. Only Tosca struggled on forlornly with her unwieldy choice.

Vivian Heron looked over a blue and white table she was decorating with indigo flames of the Brock delphinium.

"What, no orchids, Tosca? Girls, I didn't know Tosca knew there was any other flower! And no Eric Brock, either!"

"Hm!" said the O'Brien twins in musical chorus, and their blue black-fringed eyes danced over the Waterford glass vase of green-and-white orchids they were arranging on a table set with pellucid white and green Belleek dishes. "No Eric?"

"No Eric," said Tosca shortly.

She was annoyed with them, and with herself most of all. What had possessed her, at the last moment, to change from her usual choice of Giacomo's orchids to the coxcomb grown by Zavotti over in Contra Costa? The willful desire to be different this time and astonish her fellow members might have had some part in the last-minute change. But most of all, she knew, it had been made in defiance of Eric.

In other years Eric had asked in advance her choice of orchids, brought them to the store, and helped with their arrangement. He was always pounced on by the rest of the girls, and there was a great deal of joyous rivalry as he assisted them in turn with their flowers.

But she had not seen Eric since the afternoon of the Flower Show. She had waited until yesterday and then telephoned the nursery. He was pretty busy, he said vaguely, and his voice was any stranger's voice. He supposed she'd want orchids. Well, they'd be down by the first shipment, Pietro would leave them at Matraia's. Matraia would see they reached the store in time. Any particular selection? he had added.

Anything would do, she had answered as coldly, and ten minutes later, having bitten her index nail down half its brightly painted length, she telephoned Matraia's and asked for the bulky coxcomb.

She had been too proud to bring the matter to the attention of Giacomo. Did not Eric always attend to such matters for Tosca? Giacomo was happy that this was so, and she would not spoil that happiness. Also, she had not been to the nursery since the Flower Show. Even in her thoughts she avoided the look she wished she had never seen in Eric's eyes. She could not bear to remember the way his pride had been, even for a moment, broken.

She had no need to remember. Mark held her thoughts and her hours.

She sighed and stood back to view the recalcitrant coxcomb. The heavy-headed velvet blooms folded upon themselves and sank gracelessly over the edge of the bowl.

"I can't make them stand up," she wailed to Vivian and all else who might be listening, not caring how amused they were that Tosca, who had been, as it were, born among flowers, should not be able to exert her will over the coxcomb. And she clutched at the bowl as it toppled with its unwieldly bloom.

Then, holding it, she looked up and saw the dapper Matraia making his way between the tables, walking with grace despite the immense box he carried. Without smiling, he murmured words of praise or suggestions for improvement to the girls. The professional florists always took interest in the efforts of the amateurs, and besides, were not the Leaguers among Matraia's very good customers?

"Matraia, I couldn't be happier to see anyone! This thing falls over if I just look at it."

"Eric thought you might need help," murmured Matraia.

"Eric? Do you mean Eric asked you——"

"And why not? Are you and Eric such enemies that he cannot ask help from a friend?"

But his look was shrewd in conjecture.

Matraia put his box on the table and opened it, displaying a scarlet splash of carnations. He took pliers and a small coil of

206

wire from his pocket. Then, with a flourish, he became again the magnificent Venetian.

"One twist and it stands at attention like a soldier," he promised. His slender hands flashed between the cumbersome stalks, and the dusky red shape rose like an imperial crown. He grasped handfuls of the bright carnations and stabbed them, apparently willy-nilly, into the dark mass of coxcomb. Under his hands a painting became alive.

"Now your table will be noticed. *Che bella,* Tosca!"

She let her tired hands dangle.

"Why can't I do that, Matraia? Giacomo handles flowers so easily, and Eric touches them and they fall into place, and Mother——"

"You have not had to." Suddenly, in a gesture of revealed curiosity, he lifted her hands in his own and studied the graceful slender fingers belied by the square, efficient palms. "Maybe you are not by nature an arranger of flowers, Tosca. But the green thumb, yes, you could have that, and if the wish ever comes you can grow flowers because you love flowers."

"Stop helping Tosca, Matraia! Help us," came the musical voices of the O'Brien twins, and from all the other tables, even the completed ones, came demands for Matraia's opinion and skill. Matraia waved magnificently, and his pointed features were benign. "Immediately, my friends!" Then in the same low murmur as before he spoke to Tosca.

"Tosca, what is this about Eric?"

"What about Eric?" she demanded quickly. She knew how rapidly news traveled among the flower people. Matraia's dark clever features wore a look of concern.

"That I do not know. Giacomo is not one to talk. Only I am being told everywhere that Giacomo feels very badly about Eric. Everyone in the trade knows. Eric is seen here and there; he has been over at Ferrante's, who grows the orchids in San Rafael, and he has visited the other orchid growers around the bay region, and none of them will say why he has gone to them. Tell me, is he hunting a new place, this man who has been like a son to Giacomo?"

His eyes were black diamond points driving the truth from her. But she did not know.

"I haven't even heard," she said, and the words were painful, for she knew if this thing were true she, in some way, had helped make it so.

"Could it be Stoob, Matraia? Stoob is always making trouble."

"No." Matraia half smiled. "We hear of Stoob, and we hear he has been behaving himself."

"Well, it's very strange——"

"Here are your friends," said Matraia in the same soft voice. "I will help the other girls."

He moved swiftly over to the Heron girl's table.

How had he known, she wondered, seeing Mark and half a dozen of his friends making their riotous way along the mezzanine, that they were her friends and that they had come for her? She did not wonder how they had come through the unopened store's guarded door, for Mark could talk his way in anywhere. She felt the sinking of the heart that always presaged the arrival of Mark or any word from him. And she stood motionless, lost in her love for him, waiting.

He stood taller than the others, a laughing leader that made them shrink and seem mean by comparison. Roscoe was a snuffling courtier running between the tables, greeting the girls he knew and exclaiming comically over the displays. Only Kelly Green stood out, black and white and curiously beguiling, against Mark's arresting beauty.

He came straight to her and took her hands. Eyes met and she knew again he was her own.

"Tosca darling." The words were like lips brushed against lips. "Pick up your coat and come along. We're invited down to Del Monte."

"Getting away from the strike." Roscoe elbowed between them, his eyes protruding with excitement. "No fun in the city, so we're all going down to Del Monte. Hurry up, Tosca."

"I can't go." Her eyes clung to Mark's. "The store will open in a few minutes and I'll be stuck here all day."

"But that's unreasonable." Mark tossed her objection aside with a wave of his hand. "Nobody is staying in town who doesn't have to. There won't be any food or anything, and all the shows are closing—there won't even be enough to eat! And Del Monte is wonderful."

"Don't you think I want to go?" She saw Kelly Green, the debonair, the dreaded Kelly, talking with animation to the O'Brien twins. A twist of fear went through her as she looked at the girl. Fearing her, longing to follow Mark, she was willing in that moment to toss away all dignity and honor, for she knew now—Mark's look told her—what acceptance would mean. The insolent crest of coxcomb enraged her, for it was the table that held her, and her duty to the table.

"I can't go," she said dully. "I'm pledged to stand by all day."

"But nobody will come to see the tables," Mark argued gently. "You know what the town's like today; everybody's staying in their homes or getting away, and gasoline is getting scarce, and it's all impossible. There may be real trouble, you know. So it's really the wisest thing to come with us, isn't it?"

His look begged, secret and knowing, and his mouth tempted.

She felt the black diamond probe of Matraia's watchfulness. He was pretending to rearrange a crescent of camellias. His curiosity did not seem to matter. What did anyone matter save Mark? She stood racked with jealousy, longing, the passionate need to go with Mark anywhere. Under any terms. And because she was half mad with longing she spoke coldly.

"I can't run away, Mark. I'm staying."

She rearranged the silver on the table, with her back to them, not to see the group as they left the floor. She had glimpsed Roscoe's leer of victory. And she felt the presence of Matraia by her side.

"Can I help?"

She shook her head unhappily.

"They're going to Del Monte. Because of the strike."

"Very wise." He did not look at her. "It is very ugly, the strike trouble. If an all-out is called, well, no one knows what will happen to San Francisco. And certainly not to the flower business."

"You were speaking of Eric," she said dully.

Matraia never spoke of anything until he had a definite purpose in mind.

"I thought you might find out what is wrong. If anything is wrong."

She was silent. But like Matraia, she could not bear the thought that hurt should come to Giacomo. Especially that hurt should come through her. And she thought, I must see Eric without Giacomo's knowledge.

"What is today?"

"July the fifteenth."

"No, the day of the week—never mind. Eric will be at market tomorrow. Matraia, will you stop by for me on your way to market?"

"I do not like to." Matraia looked uneasy. "You know what is going on. The strike leaders are stationing goons on the water front, and tomorrow is the day the strike will be called—we think. No, I do not like——"

"I'm going to the flower market tomorrow." Her lips were set, but she tried to smile. "I can't help it if the strike is called for tomorrow. I'll go alone."

He shook his seal-sleek head.

"Very well. But remember, it will be early."

"Don't I know! I've been many times with Giacomo."

She watched him leave, suave, well groomed, flattering to all he met on his progress out of the store. She did not know that in his strange intuitive mind Matraia, the all-observing, saluted her.

It was a dull and anxious day. Mark had been right, and the people who came to see the summer tables, nearly all women, were fewer in number than they had been in any previous year. The impending strike was on everyone's mind, and while the visitors exclaimed over the tables, their thoughts were plainly elsewhere, and many of them left hastily with the explanation that they wanted to buy food for their households if any could still be found.

The store closed early. The club members had planned to dine together in the Palace's Palm Court to celebrate the success of the table show. But there seemed little success to be celebrated, and the store's manager, speaking to them privately in the emptying store, advised them to go to their homes. They came out into a foggy and strangely emptied city. Cabs and streetcars had apparently vanished, and Tosca, crowding four of the girls who had no cars into her roadster, delivered them to their homes in a silence unusual to what was ordinarily a talkative and merry group. Then, driving toward her own home, she noticed the gas was low and turned the car down the hill toward her favorite gasoline station. It was closed. The shortage had begun. There was an eerie, angry feeling to the streets as she raced the car up the fog-blanketed Presidio hill.

"Oh, but we are glad that you are home!" Marie welcomed her—Marie in checked gingham with a dish towel in her hand—in the white marble hallway.

She burst into a torrent of details. The afternoon maid had telephoned she could not come because of the strike. Marie had been to the butcher shops, and there had been no meat. Finally, owing to her many friendships along the shopping section, she had been able to come home with a small leg of lamb and a few cans of corned beef. As a last precaution she had bought and carried up the hill to her porticoed mansion a twenty-pound sack of corn meal.

"Nothing is better than yellow meal," she explained excitedly. "It is very nourishing, and we can live on it for weeks if we have to."

It was plain that Marie had rallied her pioneer faculties and was preparing, along with the rest of the city, for a state of siege. Vincent was barricaded behind his newspaper in the kitchen, relapsed in gloom. But he too looked up long enough to show his relief that Tosca was home.

"Tomorrow," he said, shaking his fine gray head over the newspaper, "tomorrow will tell the story. And it will be a black one. No doubt about it."

"Tomorrow——" And although both parents looked at her, Tosca did not finish what she started to say. Vincent was not a pliable man.

But she told Marie later, in her own room.

The blue French clock declared it was only nine, but Tosca was preparing for sleep. At this hour, of late, she had nearly always been on her way to meet Mark. She was tired and a little confused because she had lived for so long in the nighttimes, for with Mark reality existed only after dark and left the days drugged with sleep. Every night had been Mark's, and still, since that sad ending to the dinner at Fisherman's Wharf, not once had they been alone together. He sought her out, wanted her with him and close to him always, but there were also others. Roscoe, Kelly Green, others of the changing merry crowd were always there. And often, after he left her in the early hours of morning, the telephone on the landing would ring wildly and Mark's voice would be hers again, soothing and adoring, breaking her again with their longing. As today, when he had begged her, without words, to go with him.

Her breasts lifted with pride under the crepe chiffon. He loved her. With every gesture, every look, he assured her of his love.

Lately their fun had been curtailed by the impending strike. The difficulty in getting gas and the gradual eclipse of San Francisco's after-dark amusements had dulled the nights for the crowd. The evening before they had driven to Bird's Nest, only to find it closed, and the few places left open were forlorn as only gay spots can be when deserted. And Tosca, in a burst of conviviality she found difficult to explain eighteen hours later, had brought the entire party home. How many had made merry until dawn in the shell-pink-and-white drawing room below she had had, even then, no idea, and where they came from and who they were she did not know. Roscoe seemed to know them or pretended to, and it was he who seemed to have done most of the inviting; she had heard him at intervals on the telephone calling others and asking them over, all night long. She thought guiltily of Vincent's scant wine shelves depleted, but never mind, Giacomo's cache in the cellar of the cottage at the nursery could always be relied upon. And she and Mark had been a joyous pair, host and hostess together. It had been intimate and beautiful. And how long since this great house had echoed with laughter and music!

Not since Paul, she thought. This house died with Paul. Last night it was young and alive again because Mark was here.

She went to a window and opened it. The fog came through, chilling the warm flesh under the thin pajamas. Somewhere beyond the fog-frosted light-blazing city Mark had found escape from the doom that seemed to be threatening San Francisco. As long as brilliant doorways opened, promising amusement and music, Mark would find his way through.

In this moment, feeling lonely and forsaken, longing for him as never before, she sickened with regret that she had refused to follow along his bright and cheerful way. Mark had the rarest of all gifts, that of joyousness. She had refused her chance to share it with him.

Mark is alive, she thought. With every fiber of himself, in every moment, he knows he is alive. That was the way Paul lived. The gift he had.

Marie's tap sounded and the door opened, bringing a path of rosy light into the dark blue room. "Goodness, you are gloomy in here," she exclaimed, and her hand sought the light switch by the door. Sprays of crystal light sprang to life along the azure walls.

Marie was prepared for the night, but she seemed surprised and pleased to find Tosca was also. She had changed to a robe, and her hands were in pink cotton gloves which were lined with cream. Father has been scolding her again about her hands, Tosca thought. She dived into the wide bed and, piling the pillows at her back, smiled radiantly at her mother. Marie's well-tinted hair was carefully set under a net and her face was heavily creamed, but the structure of it remained Madonna-like and beautiful. Her answering smile was heavenly.

"To bed so early?" Marie looked pleased, settling on the chaise for conversation. She carried a book under her arm. *Anthony Adverse,* thought Tosca, won't she ever finish it? Marie repeated happily, "My, but it is good to have you home. Everything is so depressing—I can't listen to the radio. Home is best in times like these."

"I'm always home."

"Not at night."

"Last night I was," said Tosca, and regretted it. For Marie's face changed as if a veil had fallen there.

"Well, I did not want to speak of it, Tosca. But so much damage was done last night! There are burns on the furniture, and someone left the print of a hand in wine on the brocade sofa. And two of the Della Robbia plaques are missing."

Tosca turned her head restively against the pillows. "How often do I give a party!"

"We want you to give parties. Only, who were these people?"

"People. People we picked up. I can't remember their names."

Marie bit her soft lips, her eyes darkening with the familiar anxiety. To Marie, the walls of home were built to bar unpleasantness from those one loved. She had never learned to break those barriers down and let the hordes pour in. Paul had done that, and the house had been turbulent with his friendships, but then as now, Marie had condoned without understanding. Like so many women of Italian strain, Marie was at the supremacy of charm within her clan. For her father, who was her most frequent visitor, she dressed her table as if for royal guests. The silver service shone for Giacomo, the part-time maid wore her best uniform for him, and Marie cooked in her kitchen the day through when Giacomo came. Tenderly demonstrative, pouring forth the largess of her home, she was the perfect hostess.

But she had never been able to learn the devious art of general entertaining. With Vincent's business acquaintances and their wives Marie was stiff and insecure and without grace. In turn, many of them thought her arrogant and cold; the two attributes farthest removed from Marie.

She would have been happiest with a family deep-rooted and many-branched, given to endless visiting, much argument, and undying devotion. The thin lost branch of Daneri in California had never been satisfying to the deep-bosomed, maternal Marie.

And the love and anxiety that should have been distributed over so many she poured now over Tosca, sitting ruffled and defiant against the pillows and preparing for sleep.

"Mama, will you do something for me?"

"Anything, darling."

"Will you call me early tomorrow? I wouldn't ask, but I know you are always awake."

"The sun wakens me." Marie spoke apologetically, as if to Vincent. The sun, which had wakened her so early through her girlhood at Colma, could summon her through the heaviest curtains. "But why, Tosca?"

Tosca decided to be frank. "I'm going to the Flower Market with Matraia."

Her mother made a nervous movement.

"But tomorrow—with the strike—— Tosca, will you be safe?"

"Would Matraia ask me if it wasn't all right?" parried Tosca, bending the truth a little to avoid frightening her mother. "Of course I'll be safe. It's not a war, you know."

"Your father will not——"

"Please, Mama, I wouldn't have asked you if I thought—— Why should he know? It's a private matter, something about Eric and Giacomo."

"Giacomo wants you?"

"Yes," said Tosca without too much hesitation.

She saw the gentle features clear. Under the coating of cream Marie's face took on the longing expression of a child.

"I should like to see the Flower Market again," she said softly. "Some morning, Tosca, we will go. But it will not be the same as it used to be when I went to it years ago with Giacomo.

"When I was a little girl and Giacomo had his booths in the market—sometimes I rode into town with him."

Her soft voice stopped, as if she saw Vincent frown down such memories. Still, there had been a time when he had been touched by her accounts of a bare-legged little girl riding to market beside a giant father in a truck drawn by horses and filled with sweet-smelling flowers. Marie could still feel the sun's warmth on her small back as it rose over the wet black fields and tawny hills of Colma. Giacomo, towering over her, snapping the reins over the broad backs of the friendly horses, was surely the strongest person in the world! They left behind them the nursery with her mother, Maria, on guard in their fragrant kingdom, and she could remember the way the city came forward to greet them, stirring from sleep, and the clatter of the metal shoes of the horses on the stone streets, for San Francisco streets had been cobbled then. And her face shone, remembering.

How wide that child's eyes had opened to the early excitement of the old Flower Market—it had been moved to Bush Street by that time—as Giacomo pulled the wagon up to its gaping doors with the gusto of a charioteer. How gentle, how capable of holding his own anywhere, against anyone, had been the Giacomo Daneri of those years. Marie thought of him now with the broad shoulders sloping and the flash of eyes dimming with years, and her eyes were suddenly wet.

Tosca, watching, decided that her mother was developing hysterical tendencies and she must try to be kinder. And when her mother, leaving, stooped to kiss her, Tosca startled her by the fervor of her embrace.

"You'll call me? You won't forget?"

"Before six," her mother promised.

She was alone then, to indulge in loneliness, regrets, or any misery she chose. But she was thinking, as her mother had, of Giacomo. If there was some way she could find out what was wrong at the nursery, provided Matraia was right and there was disturbance there, she might find some way to help. The tormenting suspicion that she might be in some way responsible persisted in her thoughts.

She burrowed into the pillows. It was strange the way everyone around Giacomo wanted to protect him from all unpleasantness, when it was actually Giacomo who protected them all. For a moment, fighting away loneliness for Mark, she seemed to feel about her the healing warmth of the greenhouses and the all-enveloping and kindly peace that was Giacomo.

SIXTEEN

*S*HE stood with Matraia behind the entrance rope the next morning long before the Flower Market opened.

To all appearances, it was like any other morning in the low shedlike building that covered an entire block at Fifth and Market streets. There was always a certain amount of tension before the rope dropped. But this morning the retail florists representing the city's flower shops and stalls, lined up like horses at the post before the rope, the watchful police guarding the entrance, and the wholesalers who could be seen rushing about inside the whitewashed building, arranging the gay contents of their bundles and baskets on the ranked tables, all were laboring under added tension, as if a word dropped casually might start the city in flames.

And still the scene within was glorious. The flowers ran in glowing streams through the cavernous place—the finest wares from one hundred and fifty nurseries around the bay. From the entrance the flowers resembled vegetable displays. The yellow Pernet roses were like bunched carrots and the red rosebuds like radishes and beets.

It seemed incredible that this glowing scene lay in the heart of a city at war.

For it was war. The general strike was on.

Tosca and Matraia had driven to the market through a paralyzed San Francisco. There were no streetcars running, no taxicabs, and only a minimum of civilian cars. Gasoline was being hoarded; some people, it was reported, were burying cans of it in their gardens. Only a few restaurants had opened, and before these long lines of hungry women and children and men waited their turns at the dwindling food supply. Tempers flared, there were fist fights and police calls, and extra police were on duty everywhere.

Along the paralyzed water front the huskiest representatives of the maritime workers and longshoremen stood guard in the open street before bonfires that helped dispel the cool summer air. Along the water front baby-faced National Guardsmen made their appearance, shouldering rifles that seemed in some cases almost as tall as themselves. The bay region was on wartime basis, and fear lay heavy as the fogs of midsummer over the city.

And still business went on. Office workers rode down the city's hills and through the business streets on bicycles commandeered from their children. That morning Tosca had seen a dignified neighbor, an attorney, coasting down the hill on a pair of his son's roller skates, with his brief case clutched under his arm. San Franciscans had always been a little readier to laughter, it seemed, than people of other cities, and even now, with no one able to say what might happen in the next moment, there was a great deal of good-natured joshing in the city under siege.

The florists waiting before the rope talked of the situation in anxious voices. Strikers were bottling up the highways and railways to prevent food supplies from being brought into the city. There were reports of ugly riotings, but no one seemed to know where they had started. There were ominous sighs and headshakings, and all the time they were watching the flower banks rising inside the market place like colored tides, and no one thought to remark the miracle that so much beauty had been permitted to flow into a city threatened with hunger and—for who knew?—even death. The Flower Market burst into bloom each morning like a magic show, as it had farther back than the oldest florist or grower could remember. Each weekday morning, for a single hour, one of the most magnificent flower shows on earth was arranged solely for commercial eyes, for only "the trade" was permitted to pass the restraining rope.

"The trade" was fond of saying that more flowers were grown in the bay region than in any other place on earth, that no other city was capable of such floral displays, and that this was due to San Francisco's fog. In other regions the sun fell directly on a flower and warmed it quickly into bloom, but the bay fog diffused the sun and kept a bud unopened many days.

"The flower garden of the nation," San Francisco called itself, and this market, filling before their eyes with a thousand color shades, was the third largest flower market in the world.

For blocks around, the streets hummed with the industry. Every parking space was taken by the trucks and cars of those who had reached the market at dawn with their floral harvests and those who were there to buy. Across the street from the market wholesale flower shops were crammed with the fragrant wares grown by their grower-proprietors. Other shops were filled with ferns and other greenery by "green-grower" owners. And many stores displayed the paraphernalia of floristry—the wire shapes, holders, ribbons, figurines, vases, and papers and boxes and strings. In nearby streets larger shops were the headquarters of the cut-flower shippers, and in these men were already hard at work packing flowers in ice both wet and dry for shipment by express or air mail—wet ice to keep the flowers damp and dry ice to keep the wet ice from melting.

There was a great deal to be seen and heard while waiting for the rope to fall.

Matraia's black eyes searched the inner cavern, anxious to see that no one was missing on this ominous morning and that all the nurseries were sending their fragrant tribute into the city.

The Daneri stalls were still empty.

"Yes, this has changed since your grandfather began coming to market," he said, apropos of nothing, but remembering always, where flowers were concerned, to give credit to Giacomo. "Your Nonno and men like your Nonno are responsible."

And he said this to Tosca and to the other men and women waiting in the cold entrance, because he wanted everyone to remember always what Giacomo Daneri had done for California's flowers.

"Matraia, is it true about the fish?" asked Tosca, and everyone at the rope had an opinion to offer, for while it could not be verified by documentary proof, there was a legend "the trade" believed, that the first flowers shipped out of San Francisco had been a handful of violets laid over a shipment of iced fish.

"And see what has happened since that day!" said Matraia, and the waiting retailers nodded in respect and agreement, for the industry that Giacomo Daneri and a few others had begun so humbly less than a half century before was now sending twenty million dollars' worth of flowers and plants to market every year.

"When your grandfather began growing flowers," said Matraia, standing on his dapper toes to peer into the market cavern, "they were a luxury. Now they have become a necessity to the hearts of men.

"There is Eric," he added in a tone of relief.

Eric was entering from the rear of the market, bearing a pile of boxes in his arms, and followed by Ernesto and three men of the Daneri driving crew carrying similar boxes. They stacked them on the tables in the Daneri stalls, and Tosca saw Eric arrange his boxes and remove their covers, laying bare the cold frosted whiteness that was the magnificent giant gardenias—one of the Daneri specialties.

And now it was seven o'clock and the policeman at the entrance dropped the rope. The retailers surged into the market place. The policemen eyed each as they passed, looking not at the identifying badges they wore but at their faces, for they knew every flower person in the bay region.

The shed was so cold and wind-swept that no odor came from the flowers.

Tosca, swept into the flower-filled cavern with the eager buyers, felt the familiar bursting of the senses into an explosion of color and delight. The ugly low whitewashed cavern had turned before their eyes into a floral paradise.

Under its beamed roof, the unflagging magic efforts of the warmly dressed growers, with their hands stained with labor and their faces bitten with morning cold, had brought together all the California seasons. It would have been impossible for a non-professional flower lover, set down without warning in this paradise, to study the flowers massed there and name with assurance the month or even the season of the year. The Californian growers had usurped the floral calendar. Because of their perseverance, the summer flowers no longer gave up when winter came, but continued to bloom, and many of the spring flowers had been coerced into continuing to bloom throughout the entire year, immortalizing April. And all through the winter months, while in other states the seeds were still locked underground by ice and snow, forty firms would continue to ship their daily carloads and planeloads of iced flowers out of San Francisco to every state in the Union.

"Don't wait for me, Matraia, I'll find Eric," urged Tosca, for she knew how fast a buyer had to move in this rushing place if he was to secure the finest flowers for his store. He was off with a pleased glance from his jewel-like eyes and a murmured *"Buena fortuna!"*

He knows so much, she thought gratefully, watching him slip with the grace of a panther in and ahead of the other florists before the rose tables without seeming to jostle anyone and, hurrying on, stopping at stalls and tables to bargain with the assurance of a merchant prince, pointing out his selected choice blooms by the tens of dozens. For the representatives of the finest shops such as Matraia's had the best choice at the Flower Market, and the smaller shops and flower stands, whose bright displays charmed the busy street corners of San Francisco, must be content with the remainder. She saw him pause briefly in a group standing admiringly before a bright mass of the new salmon gladioli in the stall that bore the sign: "Brock Nurseries, Santa Cruz." A boy she did not know was in charge, but his square blondness marked him for a Brock. Some cousin of Eric's, she decided, and saw the blond head nod in brief agreement as Matraia, with a magnificent gesture, ordered all of the display of the new gladioli for his store.

Only where a new or finer flower, such as the salmon break, or an out-of-season flower was being shown did the buyers linger, and then only briefly. Otherwise the retailers hurried about, trying not to slip on the water-sluiced floor, and raising their voices as they bargained, protested, and complained. A great deal of protest came back from the growers, on the other side of the bunched, boxed, or potted flowers they had worked so hard to produce, at the steady stream of criticism from the florists. Little praise of the flowers was heard this early or in this place, for a few kind words might cost the admiring one a few pennies, and a few pennies, balanced this morning against a dozen roses, could mount up considerably for profit or loss in a buyer's or seller's year.

Tosca tried to keep out of the way of the florists as she picked her way over the wet cement. She spoke briefly to the surprised Eric, who was disposing of his gardenias as rapidly as if the snowy heaps were drifts of melting snow.

"Don't leave without me," she warned him gaily in passing. "I want to see everything."

Then she gave herself over to the deep and passionate draining of the wine of loveliness.

She walked in deepest summer, for this was mid-July, but all about her was springtime, and the glowing notes of fall, and the deep happy colors of winter.

Before her were tables of cut Easter lilies, an entire houseful of late-comers crowded together, and she thought, for Easter had come early this year: We might be back in April! She hurried to a stall filled with one of her favorites, the tiny pink Cecile Brunner rose that also normally hails April, but here it was now, and here it would be still, she knew, in all its Dresden sweetness, for Thanksgiving tables. And she paused by a rose and pink display of cyclamen that once had been solely for the winter trade and had been advanced by grower's magic to early spring, and here it was blooming like small rosy birds in flight through the timeless heart of summer. All about her in this most esoteric of flower shows, seen by the busy few and for so brief a time, were lavishly heaped tables of hardy perennials, as well as the choicest hothouse flowers, and "green" tables that were miniature forests of fern and branches of pine and oak and eucalyptus. The hothouse flowers were treated with even greater care than were the others, and most of the gardenias, lilies of the valley, and orchids were wrapped in waxed paper, but there were comparatively few orchids, as most of them had been sent directly to the flower shops or to the packing lofts nearby, where they were being packed for shipment.

Tosca walked between tables radiant with butter-colored calla lilies, pointed globes of hyacinth in the tints of fine porcelain, brilliant tulips and ranunculi and anchusa, and purple pools of larkspur; and all these, she knew, had been coaxed into forgoing their original times of blooming and were blooming according to the needs of the trade and a nation's demand.

Only in chrysanthemum season, when this low-ceilinged place was washed by a spiky sea of bronze and gold, would the ordinary person, looking about at the flowers, be able to say positively: "This is fall!"

She idled through the building. She did not love flowers as Giacomo and so many who grew flowers loved them, as extensions of self. She loved them with a proprietary love, as if they were her birthright. She had never looked at any flower and not been able to say, I want that for my own! It would be hers, at a wish, through the magic of Giacomo. In this place every face seemed that of a friend, every flower hers because she was the granddaughter of the best known and best beloved of all the California growers.

The market had changed but little since she had last seen it with Giacomo. There had been certain small changes and disturbances, she knew. She had heard the talk at Giacomo's table. The flower industry was not completely idyllic. Even in as friendly a group as Giacomo had gathered around him there would be backbiting and jealousy and a certain amount of disagreement. Flower people were people, after all. So, in the Flower Market, there had been of late certain labor disturbances—and no wonder, with the city at bay now, hungry and frightened all around! Then there had been the Eastern boycott, which had brought so much grief to growers like Giacomo who sent carloads of flowers East every day. But the East had capitulated and opened its arms to the Western flowers again. Then the marketing plan had presented difficulties, but now the co-operative marketing plan had been made workable.

Then, saddest of all in a cosmopolitan and friendly city, racial differences had sprung up like ugly patches of blight in the Flower Market. In these gardens of paradise hatred had slithered like snakes from other lands where, the newspapers were hinting ever more pointedly, there might soon be war. There had been a few feuds which seemed the uglier because they were staged in settings of exquisite beauty. As a result, this great main floor was now known as the "white market," and its stalls were given over to the displays of the "white growers," who were principally of Italian extraction. Tosca, having seen everything on this floor, wandered into the adjoining oriental market in the same building to visit the stalls of the Japanese and Chinese growers.

There were special beauties to be seen in this section. Tosca went from stall to stall, admiring and exchanging greetings with the growers. Many of them had been her friends since childhood. They were good friends, Giacomo always said, and good citizens. On Chinese New Year, he exchanged gifts and visits with many, and Tosca had been reared to regard as a special honor an invitation to a family dinner in San Francisco's Chinatown. The Japanese, too, were charming hosts, sparing no pains to spread their traditional best before the guests they honored.

The oriental growers showed Giacomo the respect due a patriarch. But a sense of fun came to the surface as they chatted animatedly with Giacomo's granddaughter as she moved about admiring their flowers.

The finest display in this section was the gigantic gardenia which had been brought to perfection by the hard-working and systematic Japanese. A few more months and they would be showing their fall specialty—the great-headed chrysanthemums. Also, the Japanese had brought to California the oriental art of dwarfing potted trees, partly, it was said, by amputating the tap-root.

The Chinese were fond of the sweet-smelling narcissi which they had been the first to popularize back in gold-rush days, so that to all "old-time" San Franciscans the white and gold blossoms were known as Chinese lilies.

Every group has its divisions, Tosca was thinking, walking with care back toward the main section over the wet floor that was made more slippery now with scraps of water-soaked greenery. Stoob, in the days when he had brought the Daneri lilies to market and watched the stalls in person, had fought bitterly with the Chinese lily growers. But Giacomo seemed to tower like a gentle giant over all divisional lines. As a "glass grower," especially as a grower of orchids, he ranked among the highest of the industry's leaders, but he met all living things—almost, one might say, all things that grew—with the same reserved and kindly interest.

The flower displays were dwindling now in the main room, and the flower folk were revealed, displaying, in their sum total, the whole human story of the trade. Each booth and table represented a different chapter of the industry, for each was presided over by the grower in person, or by his son or assistant and, in some cases, by a daughter or wife. Every division of the flower industry—the "glass growers" like Giacomo, or the "outside growers" like the Brocks, or the purveyors of greenery or potted plants or whatever branch it might be—had room in which to welcome large families, for work could be found for all.

"Hi, there!" said Tosca to Thelma Valli, whose father grew the famous camellias at San Rafael.

Thelma stood in the Valli stall behind a shrinking pile of boxes filled with red and white and variegated carnations. She smiled but did not pause in her work of selling, scribbling sales in a notebook, and hurrying her assistants off with the sold flowers to the trucks of the purchasers waiting outside in the streets. "I never get a chance to see you," Thelma complained, thrusting out four fingers to designate the price to a bargaining florist.

She was soft-spoken, and her distinguished manner was apparent through her brisk business air.

Thelma's eyes were sleepy—she had been at work since five—and her slim figure was huddled in a boyish reefer against the cold of the market, yet still she managed to retain a romantically lovely appearance over the heaped carnations.

"We must meet for tea," the two girls promised, and Thelma added, as San Franciscans do, "The St. Francis on Monday, under the clock!" Then they groaned together in dismay, for who knew what the strike might bring to Monday in San Francisco! But we'll meet if it's possible, they agreed, Tosca knowing that if Thelma was there she would be beautifully dressed and one of the loveliest in a room crowded with beautiful young women. Thelma was not an unusual type among the flower growers' daughters, many of whom had been given the advantages of private schools and European studies and tours, and still they returned, many of them, with renewed assurance and affection to the family greenhouses or fields. As a rule they became in time shrewd businesswomen, wise in the ways of flowers and their aesthetic and practical values.

Thelma was too busy to talk, and Tosca, feeling suddenly useless and in the way, strolled on between tables rapidly being stripped of bloom. She saw a small honey-colored snail pulling its anxious way over the wet cement. With a feeling of guilt— for was he not the ancient enemy of Giacomo?—she pushed him at toe's point to temporary safety under a table.

She looked at the clock. It was almost eight. Her feet were wet and cold and she felt the physical and emotional exhaustion that comes with too overpowering an influx of beauty. She found her way back to the Daneri stalls.

Within an hour after the rope had dropped from the entrance, the tables were barren. The empty trucks that had brought the flowers were gone from the street outside; gone, too, were the full trucks of the retailers with their tons of beauty that would brighten the shops and stalls and street corners of a hungry city for at least one more day. The lights began going out overhead, and only an ugly empty barn remained, with wet littered floor and dripping tables and a few figures clearing away the last of their paraphernalia here and there, like gnomes in the dimness. The show was over until another dawn—if, as all had said, departing, conditions permitted. The strike had lain heavily on the hearts of all who had taken part in the apparently joyous pageantry and had gone with them their separate ways.

"For an hour there was beauty," pronounced Tosca in a sleepy voice.

She was perched on a packing case in one of the empty stalls with her feet tucked up, well out of the way of the water. Ernesto and the other Daneri men had left to drive the emptied green trucks back to the nursery, and in the dimming light Eric was summing up the day's accountings in his cashbooks. So many buyers paid cash, others quarterly or semiannually, that the keeping of Giacomo's books was a complicated task. At last he shoved the books into the outer pocket of his heavy reefer and turned to Tosca with a relieved air that said plainly at last he was free.

"Now I can pay you a little attention," he said briskly, but there was no warmth in his voice, and he might have been speaking to a business acquaintance who had waited this long while for him. "I gather you're in need of some special attention, or you wouldn't be here."

He took a clean handkerchief from his breast pocket and wiped his wet forehead.

"We've been going like beavers all morning. Okay, so what brings you out on a day like this?"

The frontal attack startled her, and she made no answer as they walked together out of the deserted main section and into the oriental part of the market. She had not noticed the green Daneri truck in a corner of the shed. Eric changed his reefer for the coat he had left on the seat, and with it his appearance changed. He became more certain of himself, more urban.

"Well?" he asked impatiently, his foot on the running board. "I'll see you around, since you aren't telling me if it's important."

"You can't leave me!" she cried, startled.

"I can't?" He jerked his thumb, pointing into the truck, and she saw it was stacked to the roof with Daneri boxes. "I've got to get these gards off to Redwood City, and it will be a race getting them there. I'm late now."

He swung up into the seat of the truck.

"But, Eric!" She wrenched the door from his hand. "Matraia brought me and he's gone. I planned to go back with you."

"Good God!" He was staring at her as if she had lost her mind. "Today, of all days—the whole West Coast out of its mind—and I have to get you in my lap. What possessed you, Tosca? Matraia must be bats, bringing you here."

"It was Mother." She cast about wildly for an explanation, because it all seemed crazy now, as Eric said. And she remembered the stern faces they had seen coming through the downtown streets that morning. Panic went over her in quick, shameful waves. But she stumbled on: "Mother was talking about the market and seeing the flowers and Giacomo, and I——"

"You're crazy." He was still looking at her, but without anger. "Well, I'm not surprised. Listen, I have to get these gards off; I'm losing time jabbering to you. But I can't send you home alone." He groaned. "Lord, what I don't get stuck with. Crawl in. I'll have to take you along."

"That's wonderful." She bounced in beside him, her anxiety gone.

"Sure, it's just wonderful! And it's going to be the damnedest rat race you ever got yourself into."

He shot the truck out of the building and into the thin lines of traffic dribbling along Mission Street. Several of the oriental growers bowed and waved amused good-bys from their entrance.

"Let's hope we don't meet any of your League friends," Eric remarked caustically. "It might give them a shock to see you riding around in a truck."

"We met one of Father's friends this morning on roller skates." Tosca giggled. "And he had his brief case with him and looked perfectly dignified."

"Well, try and look dignified."

"How can I? I'm hungry."

He looked at her in exasperation.

"Didn't you have breakfast?"

"But I left so early." She was looking at either side of the street as they dashed by, driving faster than Eric usually drove in the city.

"You needn't look for a coffee shop. Not only are they closed— or have you forgotten about the strike?—but if we did find one open, I wouldn't stop. Planes don't wait, sweetness."

She did not like Eric in this sarcastic mood. Nor had she known before how very hungry she was; food was not terribly important if it was always at hand. They drove past a cafeteria, one of a chain that covered the city, where at any other time delicious cups of coffee or tea were served, with "refills" if desired, along with the crispest of toasted English muffins with melted butter and orange marmalade, and all for the price of ten cents! Her mouth watered, remembering the crunch of buttery muffins brushed with marmalade.

But there were no open coffee shops along the way, and anyway, Eric had said, and in so mean a voice, he would not stop if there were.

Dozens of sacks of spilled rice lay in the street. She wondered about them.

Eric was scowling, staring ahead over the wheel. He looked, she thought unkindly, as if he had been scowling like that since the day of the Flower Show. She wished that had never happened. She wished he would not look like that, as if it were her fault. And she remembered that this morning's excursion to market had been undertaken in his behalf, in her attempt to atone for a wrong she had done him without knowing.

Eric did not look wronged. He looked disturbed and very angry.

"Why do we have to go to the airport? Why didn't Ernesto take the gardenias to the plane?"

He decided to let her know.

"The highways are picketed."

"I know that. We heard it at the entrance."

"Don't you know what that means?"

After a moment's thought, she knew. She felt the skin tighten on her cheekbones. Driving past groups of watchful pickets on San Francisco streets in Matraia's light, high-powered car became quite a different matter in contrast to this vehicle and its destination.

"Are they waiting for trucks?" she asked in a small voice.

"Food trucks," he explained a little remorsefully, but she realized any trucks would be suspect.

And she thought bitterly, I could be safe with Mark at Del Monte.

"We'd better turn back." Eric looked worried.

They had reached the southern rim of the city, where fields opened and ran up hills blue with lupin, as if reflecting the bay on their other side. But Tosca caught his arm as he swung the wheel.

"No, the gardenias! I know why Giacomo wanted you to take them down, Eric."

His grin was not calculated to put her at ease.

"Yes, the old boy thought I could do a slicker job of talking my way through—if the truck is stopped."

Ernesto and his quick temper, she thought, and his musical speech that becomes incoherent when he is angry! No wonder the calmer Eric had been chosen for this dangerous errand. And she had hung herself about his neck at a time when a man needed to be free. She looked about in despair, but there were no busses, and they were too far out of the city for streetcars, had any been running. A few—a very few—automobiles were on the highway. People were gathered in small groups at corners. Even here there was a sense of hushed and agonizing waiting.

And she said brazenly, "Oh, let's go on. I think this is fun——"

In her heart was Mark, who knew how to keep the moment light, and she longed for him as never before. To have gone with him, to be with him now—yes, it would have been worth any cost to the future! She bit down the hot swollen ache in her throat and felt the pain subside. She was not with Mark, the tender, the fun-loving, but with Eric, and this was the more unjust, since Eric was unpleasantly angry, first because she had forced herself along on an errand that might prove dangerous, and second, for reasons of his own.

"Fun!" he snorted, no more than that, but he could have devised no uglier-sounding word.

He jammed his foot down on the accelerator. The good motor roared protest and shot the truck down the highway. The miles were flying; they were beyond the city and following the bay's blue curves toward the peninsula, and Eric's look was blue ice over the wheel.

Then he spoke.

"I know you well enough not to think your mother's sentimental reminiscences brought you to market," he said. "So what is it this time? Anything gone wrong with the glamorous Cantrell?"

"Nothing—of course not."

A cold glance raked her.

"My advice, you remember, was marry or sleep with him. Obviously you haven't married him——"

His hand jerked from the wheel in time to catch hers. "Try that, and I'll swing back."

"I'll bet you would," she raged. "You're that kind."

"Not a gentleman. No elegance. Just a guy that pays his own way."

The pointless tumult stopped as suddenly as it had begun.

She wanted to bring the conversation to the matter that had sent her on this strange pilgrimage.

"How is everything at the nursery?"

"You'll see for yourself, since you're going back with me."

"I wanted your expert opinion, Mr. Brock."

"Well, everything's as usual, I guess. Giacomo's always Giacomo. He doesn't change. Stoob is Stoob." His voice warmed with amusement. "And Ludmilla's off to a new start. She's a changed girl. Stoob isn't nagging her the way he used to and she's—well, sort of blooming."

Tosca decided not to go on with the subject of Ludmilla. She noticed another curious sight, a ton or more of potatoes heaped by the roadside and apparently belonging to no one.

"And yourself, Eric?"

"Me? I'm always okay."

It was a nonchalant reply. She thought the matter over and spoke bluntly.

"I've heard you were thinking of making a change."

"How do you like riding in a truck?" asked Eric. "Pretty smooth going, isn't it? Almost like a limousine——"

"Eric!"

"Ma'am?"

"Tell me."

"There's not a damn thing to tell. And may I inquire why I should confide in you if there were?"

"Because of Giacomo." The truck was racing too swiftly along the highway that was as empty as a race track, and she clung to the seat, suddenly experiencing the delayed shock of the unusual early rising plus no breakfast.

"You're not exactly the right person to speak for Giacomo." The deliberate cruelty of his words shocked her. "Besides," he added, "I hold to your theory—what each person does is his own business."

She clutched the seat again, feeling ill and with no way of answering.

"Then it's true," she said hopelessly. "You are leaving Giacomo."

"Whatever gave you that idea!"

"Matraia said——"

"Matraia talks too much."

"Matraia never talks!" She hunted for words to bring this torrent of difference into gentler terms. We have known one another too long, Eric and I, she thought hopelessly. Each knows what the other tries to say, and dodges the issue. "Eric, if only we could talk—— Eric!"

"My God, what's that!" He let the wheel go wild and the tires screamed and swung the truck about like the lash of a whip, and then they were streaking backward insanely across the highway. Eric looked back and saw through the glass slots of the doors the trunks of eucalyptus driving toward them like battering-rams. He took his chance with the wheel, and she saw his jaw strain as he swung the wheel and the skidding truck slowed and shivered to a stop between two giant white-fleshed tree trunks.

Eric, wiping his forehead on his coat sleeve, stared at the highway they had skidded over and exclaimed: "Lettuce! A half mile of it!"

The pale green globes were scattered by thousands along the highway. Not another car was on the road.

"Strikers?" Tosca asked in a small voice.

He nodded. "I heard they were overturning the trucks. Well, if we're going to make that plane——"

The motor was still running. Eric eased the truck onto the highway and drove it gingerly over the lettuce heads, not to skid again. They left the lettuce behind, and without a word Eric shot the truck around an open truck lying on its side across the highway. Tons of carrots spilled from it; not a human being was in sight.

"We'll meet them," said Eric. "Any minute now."

He spoke so coolly that Tosca, not to be outdone, took out her compact and powdered her nose with elaborate unconcern; and Eric, giving her a slight but not ungallant grin, looked to the highway again and said in a conversational way, "Well, here we are."

She saw the wooden barricade across the highway and the men clotted in dark groups on either side. Beyond the barricade, on both sides of the highway, trucks were lined up with the immobility of stopped clocks, some at strange angles, others overturned, and all burdened with, or spilling over, tons of vegetables and fruits from the inland valleys that had been intended for the strike-bound city.

"Shall we turn back? We can take the side road into Colma."

She thought of the gardenias, Giacomo's precious blooms, grown with such backbreaking labor, and waited for in Eastern cities. And she knew Eric's thoughts were her own.

"Softie!" she scoffed, and he grinned and shot the truck to a stop before the roughly built barricade.

The strikers were all large men, and their faces were bleak as stone. Tosca sat motionless, counting twenty-two on guard at the barricade. They held heavy clubs but no guns. Eric looked as stern as the strikers as he left the truck and walked to meet the half dozen men, evidently leaders, who came forward to surround the truck.

"What do you have in there?" Tosca, leaning forward in the truck to hear, noted the quiet force of the spokesman's voice; the crisp, sure voice of a trained leader.

"Gardenias," said Eric, and added quickly, "Flowers."

"Let's see." They moved around to the back of the car, and Eric swung open the doors. The cartons covered the floor, and Eric, pulling the nearest to him, opened his knife and released the metal clasps. The unbearably sweet fragrance of the giant gardenias filled the air. The men moved closer to the doors, sniffing, and their looks of ugliness and threat were ironed away.

"Gosh, they're pretty," the leader said. A look of hunger was on his face, and he leaned over to breathe deeply of the carton of flowers.

"How about a sample?" Eric dragged the box into the open. Work-scarred hands reached out as each man selected one of the flowers, and the men by the barricade came over and each made his choice. Faces that had been unfriendly were open now, showing the inner anxiety, and the moment of forgetfulness that can come with beauty's easement and the cool, sweet touch of a gardenia in a giant palm. Some of the men stuck their flowers in their jacket fronts, nearly all of which had collars turned up against the cold, and others in the bands of their hats or caps.

"Sure they won't miss these?" the leader asked.

"I'll mark the deficit on the box," Eric promised, marveling inwardly that men could weigh the loss of several dozen flowers when all around them were strewn tons of despoiled fruits and vegetables. And the strikers, wearing their snowy blooms and putting back their scowls as if they were weapons worn for defense, went back to the barricade and swung the heavy planks aside. Then, forgetting for another moment the heartbreak, the hatreds and unforgivable suspicions that were being born of this morning, the strikers pulled off their flower-trimmed hats and cheered the gardenias on their way.

"Get those gardenias to New York!" the leader called like a battle cry, and Eric, waving back, said huskily: "It could all be settled, no matter what the issues are, if only they could get together."

Tosca, deeply moved, added her own thought: "Giacomo could find the way."

Twenty minutes later they stood with upturned faces on the airfield, watching the silver plane wheel and turn in the skies toward the Sierra Nevadas, toward the Eastern cities, with Giacomo's gardenias. Where would they go, who would be wearing them, who would weep, and who would know ecstasy while their California fragrance lay upon their hearts?

Tosca and Eric wondered, watching the truckload of gardenias flying magically toward the East.

"We made it!" Tosca cried above the roar of the plane.

"Yep, we made it." And Eric, quieter but no less jubilant, also felt they had shared high victory in bringing the gardenias through.

Then, whether in the spell of victory or loneliness, she would never know, there on the wind-blowing field under the plane-thundering skies she lifted her face to his. For a long moment they clung together, the wind buffeting their bodies, the sound of wind and planes in their ears—for a moment the lonely flesh touched and met in understanding.

They drew apart and their hands dropped and they went back in silence to the waiting truck. Eric drove toward Colma over the hill roads, avoiding the highway. The hills fell under them, tawny with summer, tumbling down to the bay and, beyond, to the city. The road raced under trees in green dappled shadow. Eric stopped the car by the roadside and turned to Tosca. He studied her mouth, her eyes, and his look was cold with suspicion.

"Why?" he demanded.

"I don't know." She put her face for a moment in her hands, but he pulled them down.

"I don't like playing substitute, you know."

"It wasn't that." She tried to be indignant but succeeded only in sounding unhappy. "I meant it—when I did it, that is."

"Not now?"

She shook her head in a lost way.

"I can't help any of it, Eric." His look was sealed against her and she felt she could not bear his coldness. Mark would be loving, warm, evasively tender. "Eric," she whispered, "hold me!" And almost, Take me, make me forget!

But he shook his head angrily.

"That won't work. I've tried it."

"Ludmilla?" she asked in a spiteful flash that surprised her, but he only shook his head again, his eyes still on her face, probing, questioning, and said, "There's nothing sadder than trying.

"Cantrell can drink you out of his system," he added, still speaking impersonally, as if they were strangers. "Maybe it's as smart a way as any."

"He's not a drunk," she began, but his look stopped her.

"It doesn't matter what he is, or if he's anything. I've got it figured out, I think. You dropped a hint one day about him—sure, he's fun, he slides out from under, he knows when to duck! Tosca, think that over; doesn't it remind you of anyone?"

He was desperately in earnest, but she had no idea what he meant.

"Paul! That's what I think about all this, Tosca. It's Paul. You were always crazy about Paul. He used to tease you and pet you and dance with you, and you've built him up as a hero. He wasn't. He was a sniveling bellyacher and he broke poor old Giacomo's heart. What was he worth? What did he ever do?"

She had drawn away from him in revulsion.

"You're wicked!" she whispered.

"I look at the facts. Paul danced on the fringe of reality all his life. Sure, he was good-looking and good-mannered and everyone loved him, just as they do Cantrell. Paul took everything that was handed him, and when the source of supply shut down for a while he stopped living—why? To spite Giacomo—to get even with those who had no more left to give! He was a boy who might have been wonderful, but he never stopped being a boy. He wasn't real. He was an illusion of yours—a myth—just as Cantrell is a myth."

"Isn't it something," she asked in agony, "to make everyone around you happy? To be adored, admired, loved by everyone? Wherever Mark goes, people smile——"

"They smiled at Paul, too, while he lasted. But what happiness has he left behind him? And how much actual happiness are you getting from Cantrell——"

"I can't help it. I can't help loving him." She was sobbing, clenching her hands together in hysteria, until he caught and held them.

"Tosca, sweet, you don't have to live for a ghost. Paul's gone —don't you understand?—and this man——"

The words rang a familiar knell in her brain. Paul is dead, she remembered, as she had heard it that morning through Marie's cries tearing through the great empty rooms to a frightened girl-child shut away and alone, listening to the weeping, the emptiness, and, worst of all, the ending of joyousness and childhood. And after that the long dim watch in the funeral rooms and the heavy sweetness of flowers and the terrible lost sound of Giacomo sobbing. It was then ruin fell over a girl's bright blond head—over an adolescent sitting stiff with fear and good manners in a pretty ermine coat on a hard folding chair. The smell of grief went into her nostrils and struck down into the jerking stomach, and there was the sudden humiliation of creeping out to the corridor to the room marked "Ladies" and throwing up there alone and returning because she was afraid not to return, prim and terrified again in the stiff chair. And no one had missed her—that was the terrifying part—not even Giacomo, sitting with his gray head heavy between his hands, the broad broken-looking body shuddering with his tears—as if a mountain wept.

"Cry it out, darling," Eric was saying gently. His arms held her in the safety she had needed when Giacomo had not known she was there, staring wide-eyed with terror at the orchid-draped casket where Paul was beautiful and tall and asleep forever. Now for the first time when this terror came she was held and comforted, and the strangest part was that the arms were Eric's. And in that moment, in a crazy burst of inner music against her ears, she remembered the song Paul had been humming when they danced together in her dream—the song that she had never been able to remember upon waking! Paul, rhythmic and beautiful, shuffling on the rose carpet in happy fashion as he half sang and half hummed the melody of "Making Whoopee."

She remembered, and the sharp outburst of her own keening startled her.

"I'm all right." She pushed Eric away and gave him a wavering grin. "Thanks for helping me find out."

"I understand more than you suspect," said Eric.

He was surprisingly gentle, helping her mop away tears. He

started the car again and headed in a businesslike way for the nursery.

"I have work to do," he reminded her cheerfully. "And you'll be ready for breakfast and a jabber with Giacomo. Why don't you stay here for a couple of days? It's safer than in the city."

"I may do that."

She tossed him a radiant smile. She felt strangely light of heart and clear of mind, the way, she thought, one must feel after a ghost has been exorcised. Why had she not known before that this devouring passion she had felt for Mark was repayment of the loss suffered years before by an idolizing child turning wistfully toward womanhood? Eric in his hardheaded way had guessed how like Mark was to the lost Paul—also the pleasure hunter who had refused to be forced into what he termed poverty.

And her heart clenched as if a hand closed over it, remembering.

"Feeling better?" Eric asked as they drove up the Daneri lane.

"I feel swell." And suddenly, remembering the primary purpose of this strange day, and seeing, far up the hill under the row of eucalypti, the beloved gray figure of Giacomo, she put her hand on his arm.

"Eric, you aren't really thinking of leaving?"

He eyed her in a speculative way.

"Not now."

They went hand in hand to tell Giacomo the gardenias had gone through the barricade.

SEVENTEEN

*S*HE stayed three days at the nursery. It was best to follow Eric's advice and not go back to the city. The green trucks left at their appointed hours with their burdens of flowers and returned empty; the drivers and radio had strange reports to make of the strike-bound city, but it seemed impossible to believe, in the nursery's quiet, that only a few miles away a great city was under martial law.

During these days she rarely thought of Mark, and the aching loneliness that had possessed her vanished, as his image vanished from her mind.

The days were too active to hold memory.

She was wakened early by the foggy sun peering between the lace-draped window in the room that had been Marie's. She woke feeling clean and expectant, like a waking child. There had been no dreams—happiest of all was the knowledge that there had been no dream of Paul, and she was strangely certain that after the talk with Eric she would not again dream of Paul. She dawdled through breakfast with the second crew, sometimes with the first, learning from Cesare, who served as news vendor for the nursery, what had taken place or was about to take place that day. She followed Giacomo on his morning rounds through the glasshouses and hung over his shoulders, fascinated, in the laboratory. She tagged after Eric and the orchid-cutting crew. She went with Ernesto when it was time to water the gardenias and with Pietro for the cutting of the roses. She peered into the bulb houses, knowing Stoob did not want her there, and tried to avoid Ludmilla, who had developed a new persistence and was not easily avoided.

Ludmilla, as Eric had hinted, had changed.

Tosca was quick to decide that the change had to do with Eric.

When Eric returned from market or airport, Ludmilla was in wait at the shipping-shed entrance, watching the lane for the first sight of the green truck. When Eric called for a cutting assistant or needed a length of string or aid of any kind, Ludmilla was there.

And Stoob, who before had kept an uncomfortable watch on his daughter and had been known to pounce unexpectedly around corners on any member of the crew who was brave enough to start conversation with the lonely girl, Stoob, Tosca noticed, now looked the other way.

Stoob, who had never liked Eric!

Well, it was none of her affair.

As she had said to Eric, the nursery was a different world. It seemed easier to forget differences here than in the city.

"It's so peaceful!" Tosca exclaimed, stretching in imitation of the kitten in the warm, watery sunlight falling over the glass expanse, and Giacomo, summer-deep in flowers, basking in the joy of having her there and in the inexplicable but wonderful peace that permeated his small kingdom, said happily to Eric, "Now we are as we used to be."

But Eric knew better.

Tosca told Eric she had never enjoyed a vacation so much, but he replied that a person who never worked couldn't possibly have a vacation, and what was she talking about anyway? The words were gruff but affectionately spoken; the tenderness had held since they had raced the gardenias to the airport and he had spoken to her of Paul.

Each day she talked with Marie. Her mother had a hundred wistful questions to ask: had the hyacinth bulbs been stored for the winter; had Giacomo planted the row of asters he had promised, because she loved them, beside the compost? And in every word was her longing to be with them at Colma, but she would not leave Vincent in the hungry city. As for the food shortage, she was managing. Did she not have her friends in the shopping district?

"Tell your mama," Giacomo called cheerfully from the kitchen, where they were at dinner, "we are planning another festa for my birthday," and the men's voices rose in a hum of anticipation, for it was not every day that the Padrone would be seventy-five.

When she came back to the kitchen the demijohn of heavy red wine was being pushed over the oilcloth from hand to hand; she let it go by. There had been one bad hour that first afternoon at the nursery. For three months she had spent nearly every afternoon with Mark, for the day began for them at cocktail time, and the whiling away of three or four hours before dinner with drinking had become habitual. The bite of gin against her palate was detestable, still she found herself loitering in the kitchen, joking with Cesare, and all the time plotting a way to bring up from Giacomo's locked cellar a bottle of the stronger liquor that was found on Giacomo's table only on special occasions. That night when the wine was passed she pushed her glass forward with the rest, and Eric, leaning forward with a knowing grin, pushed it back. And she minded only the way Ludmilla lifted her silver-pale head to stare at them both, and Stoob, his spoon at his lips, eyed her furtively through puffy lids.

Now they both hate me, but why? Tosca wondered.

Now she did not miss even the wine. She had worked in the seedling house that afternoon with Eric and Giacomo, planting mossy swarms of baby orchids. "No matter how small the plant

237

is, you have to put your back into it if you want it to grow," Eric had warned. And as a result her back and thigh muscles ached, her fingernails were broken, and the stain under them, she was certain, would never come out. And she felt tired and carefree and very happy. "Good girl," Eric said under his breath as she let the wine go by, and she accepted the praise happily. The men were rising and stretching because they were already ready for their beds, as men are who rise at four. Giacomo rose. "Shall we look at the houses?" he asked, and Eric said he would go with him, adding in an offhand way to Tosca: "Want to come along?"

Was she the only one who noticed the long contemptuous look Stoob gave his daughter then? The girl turned paler and with her former sullen manner she left the kitchen without a word. Stoob gave a snort that might have meant anything; then, filling his thermos jug from the coffeepot on the stove and selecting one of the less crumpled of the newspapers Giacomo kept in the kitchen for the men, he followed his daughter out.

Tosca looked after them wonderingly, but Eric's hand fell on her shoulder. They marched in absurd lock step out of the kitchen and down the steps into the fog-frosted evening, with Giacomo and the kitten following more sedately. Only at intervals now did the long, ridiculous legs prance wildly as before. The kitten was growing up.

The three rambled amiably through the orchid houses. How much longer, Giacomo wondered, watching Tosca as in his mind he always saw her, against a background drenched with beauty, have we in which to look at the orchids together? The moments seemed more precious than ever before, with this monstrosity of a birthday looming only a couple of weeks away. And to enrich the beauty of this evening Giacomo played one of his transparent tricks on the children—as he thought of them—recalling a task that required his immediate presence in the seedling shed. Eric, he explained elaborately, could check the remainder of the orchid houses and Tosca might be of assistance to Eric.

"The old matchmaker," Tosca said fondly as Eric unlocked the door of the new orchid house, completed the week before and filled with the Laeliocattleya purchased from De Paoli. The plants had already taken on new vigor and some were in bloom. Eric sought out one plant showing sheathed promise. "Look at this one, Tosca. De Paoli had it twelve years and it didn't bloom, and now—three buds!"

She walked about, admiring the few but exquisite blooms, while Eric made the nightly tour of the long glass shed, peering under shelves, glancing through the potted rows, lifting leaves, and even examining the inner creases of the orchids in search of any stray pest that might have survived the insecticides. He checked heat and moisture, ran his eye along the glass panes to see that none was left open or had been broken, or if by chance a fly or moth or spider was lurking in the corners. At last, satisfied that all was well, he turned out the lights. The faces of the orchids seemed to spring forward, curiously luminous and human in the shadowed dark, and through the frosted panes they could see into the luminous core of the adjoining seedling shed where Giacomo was poking about among the nursery plants; they saw him stoop and say something which was obviously a gentle reproof to the kitten at his feet.

They stood watching him, and Tosca said impulsively, "I wish I were good like Giacomo. The way he lives, Eric, and the look he has, so contented and at peace."

"I know." Eric's voice was unusually gentle. "Sometimes I think working in dirt does it, Tosca. Things grow and you know they keep on growing and it gives you that forever and ever feeling. That's what peace is, I guess."

As he spoke they saw Giacomo go to the door and turn off the bluish lights, and for a moment the seedling house was dark, then the lights went on again. "He has forgotten the kitten," said Tosca, giggling, and again it was dark. They saw the heavy figure climb the cottage steps slowly with the feline silhouette bounding ahead, then both were swallowed up by the dark kitchen. Cesare and the others had left for their rooms.

But the two lingered in the tropical warmth, reluctant to leave.

"Are you going tomorrow?" Eric asked. "The strike will probably be over tomorrow."

"Don't you think I should? Besides, I've run out of frocks. You know I only keep this extra one down here for emergencies."

He put his hand out and smoothed the cotton skirt. "I like you in dresses like this. Those Paris things you go for—I'm afraid to touch them."

The fragrant dark made her brave.

"Afraid to touch me, Eric?"

His hands went up then and trapped her. The warm sweet darkness bred lethargy while it whipped the nerves, driving them together in a burst of mindless passion as if two insects drove together in the dark. He held her to press down the pounding of his heart under the thin cotton shirt, and she clung to him because she had been lost and this could be held to and remembered. And through the wild throbbing of the senses and the familiar tumult that was Eric a name was whimpered in the innermost secret remembering, and it was Mark's name.

"Eric," she cried wildly and loudly, as if to drive the other back and beyond reason, "we can go to Paul's house!"

She felt the shudder of longing through his body. But he spoke in a steady voice. "No, what do you take me for? That wouldn't prove anything."

"Don't you see, it would prove everything." Under the tumult and heartbreak was the need to end this uncertainty, the loneliness, and the terrible hunger. "Eric, talking of Paul made me see so much, and if we——"

"And you think I can complete the cure?"

He drew his hands back from her, and she saw them clench at his sides. "It's a chance I won't take, Tosca."

"But I'm sure!" Then, ravaged with doubt and longing, she wept. "Eric, can't you see that I have to know? And if we—Eric, if we go to your room, then we'll be sure."

Now he knew, decided Eric, what was meant by the phrase to be sorely tempted. And he also knew he would never again want any woman as he wanted her now.

But "No!" he said. "Not until you're sure." His voice sounded weary in the warm jungle dark.

"You could help," she said bitterly. "You know you could. You won't, damn you. You don't know what this has done to me—this waiting——"

"I'm not interested in why you got into this state over Cantrell, but why you stay that way. You know what he is."

"That's the terrible part. I know."

"Drink or drugs I could understand. This—well, it's beyond me. I love you, Tosca, but I wouldn't break up over you."

"No, you wouldn't." She spoke bitterly. "You don't want me enough."

"More than any other woman. And that's why. I want all or nothing, you see, that's how I care. But you can't see——"

240

She pushed blindly past him to the door. "I don't want to see. If you loved me, you would."

"If I didn't love you, I would." Eric spoke with finality, ushering her through the door with an air of dismissal, as if a naughty child were being sent home. But there was no lightness in his heart as he watched her climb the steps of Giacomo's cottage. Giacomo had left a light in the hall, and as Eric watched he saw her arm lift a moment against the light, the long clean line of it touchingly delicate, then darkness. His body ached as if muscles and bones had been racked, and his steps, as he nudged past the shipping shed and into Paul's house, were as heavy as Giacomo's. His room was dark, and a cleanliness was in it, like unscented soap and hair new-washed, and he was fumbling for the light switch when he was stopped by Ludmilla's shaking voice.

"Don't turn that on."

As logically as could be in that spinning moment, Eric reflected that this couldn't happen to a young man, not twice in the same evening! His vision adjusted and he saw her on the couch, folded into herself as if terrified, and when he went to her she reached up and pulled him down, and her body structure, nervously alive, folded to him and clung there, stirring him, by some unholy alchemy, more than Tosca, whose body he could feel even now warm in his arms. His balked hunger for Tosca was appeased by this melting, and his first thought was: Why not, indeed why the hell not? And then, in an orgiastic flight of fancy, Why not both of them and to hell with them both! Still Ludmilla did not speak; breasts and arms spoke in untested, intuitive sorcery, and the suddenness and shock of her offering drove its way into his manhood and his reserve. ("Now you see," Stoob had whistled at his daughter in hateful triumph, not twenty minutes before in the cottage across the lane, "how I am waiting my time and worming my way into Daneri's, and you—poor excuse that you are—cannot help me, or help yourself for that matter, because you see how she holds him and waves a hand and he runs! And you, know-nothing and good-for-nothing hung about my neck—helpless!")

She had run from that sneering, insistent whine, like the swarming of murderous wasps, and to escape, achieve immolation, she flung herself without words upon Eric.

For minutes he held her, surcharged with the demands of manhood and the paralyzing frustration that had gone heavily up the cottage steps with Tosca and turned out the light. Then holding back for one moment from clinging arms and stabbing bones, he was able to construct the lowering features of Stoob over the white pleading face under his own.

The imagined image was as sobering as an icy shower.

"Let's try a little logic, kid," he was able to say, for the second time, and in so short a space, pushing back the tearing need of a woman wanted—of want for a woman. He wiped his forehead on his rolled sleeve with a gesture of finality. "Things like this have to be thought over, you know."

He spoke to an open door. She had slipped from the room, and her bare feet were a whispering along the barren hall floor and a scurry in the gravel outside.

"Whee!" said Eric loudly. Weak and unmanned, he dropped on the edge of his couch and tried to cool his thoughts by remembering all he could about the surmounting of temptations by St. Anthony.

Life was so peaceful in a nursery, visitors to Daneri's were fond of saying.

Little did they know!

Eric left with the first delivery the next morning and did not return at noon. Giacomo noticed that both girls looked strained and unhappy, that Tosca was less talkative than usual, and *Dio mio,* what now? he wondered. Ludmilla carried a heavy grub hoe to the compost heap, which had been moved farther back against the hill by the encroachment of the new orchid house, and fell to a violent hoeing of the silver-green rows of chrysanthemums. But Tosca, who had seemed to be avoiding even Giacomo, greeted Matraia with inexplicable fervor when he stopped at the nursery on his way back from Burlingame, where he had been overseeing decorations for a country-club dance. He had heard on the radio in his car, he said with pride—for not every car had a radio—the news that the strike was really over.

Matraia drove Tosca back to the city, together with a large box of flowers for Marie. She marveled in the change in herself since she had last seen Matraia, and did he notice, this sharp-eyed friend of Giacomo's, how great the change in her since the day at the Flower Market? She felt calmer and renewed, as if the wild outburst of hysteria that had followed Eric's shocking attack on the memory of Paul had in some way relieved her of a burden long carried. She could not wholly believe it—no one so merry and affectionate as Paul could have been what Giacomo termed a "space taker," but she saw now that she had permitted herself indulgence in too long and too destructive an idolatry.

As for the scene with Eric in the orchid house, she closed her thoughts to that along with further puzzlings about Paul.

The sense of freedom lasted while Matraia drove her to the flower shop and left her there with a somber but friendly *"Arrivaderce!"* She hailed a taxicab and drove through the busy streets—busy and wonderful again, with taxicabs and streetcars running and the shadow of hunger and panic driven from the city. The happiness of returning and the freedom lasted until the heavy door of the white house swung back while she hunted her key. Marie had been waiting in the hall.

Marie, suppressing her usual demonstrativeness and her pleasure at seeing the box that promised flowers, had her finger to her lips. In louder tones than usual she said, turning her head toward the drawing-room arch: "Mr. Cantrell is here. He has been waiting for some time."

Then in a formal manner she carried the box down the hall and into the comforting anonymity of the kitchen region. The stiffness of her back betrayed her disapproval of Mark and of his presence in the house.

Call her back, caution whispered to a Tosca who for three days had tasted a strange freedom. She can say she made a mistake, I'm not here, I didn't come back, I'll never come home again. Never see Mark again—and at this thought the agonizing emptiness that was longing flowed over her; it clung to her breasts, her knees; it dragged her down to weakness, to uncontrollable longing. Oh, Eric, she thought brokenly, and oh, Giacomo, and all that is sane and kind and everyday, take me past that archway and up those white stairs to sanctity, or drive me out of this door again and let me go. But the hunger was stronger than reason; it dragged her, a slow-footed captive, through the white arch and into the rose-pink shell of the drawing room that assaulted the senses with its beauty, where in the setting of ivory furnishings and rose brocades Mark was slumped on a sofa, his head fine as a statue's against the dark blue rectangles of bay showing through the wide windows. The air was heavy with tobacco fumes, and a marble ash tray brimmed with stubs. He had been sitting there and smoking for hours, she could see.

Annoyance and distaste smote her at the sight of the stubs, and she made a quick movement and he heard—he turned his head and she could not bear the washed pallor and the look of defeat and the fact that he had grown thinner and older, like an ill person. For one moment she could not bear to look at Mark; she closed her eyes against his look of illness and capitulation, then she was in his arms and blind to all things.

The power to observe and to reason had no place in this fusion of selves that rose in devouring flames, so that only later would she remember that her mind sickened briefly with the thought of Eric and how could she ever explain to him now? Eric was right because he was always right, and he had said this was like drunkenness, or a disease, or a slow poison that devoured the will, but it was the highest peak of human desire. Nothing was said between them. It was enough to have the faunlike head fall like an infant's between consoling breasts, to hold Mark, to be held by him, to fall with him once more into that terrifying marvelous world of lostness and to be held there—spellbound, mindless, immortal.

In the fever of days that followed, one event stood out—tea down the peninsula with Mark's mother. The official inspection, Mark termed it, which Tosca felt was needlessly caustic. Mrs. Cantrell proved to be of large and firm construction—she had Mark's structure, surprisingly welded and made firmer by the years—and she wore large rimmed glasses and laid her knitting down only to pour tea. Tosca gathered that Mark's mother was never for a moment idle and that this was a source of great satisfaction to her. The contrast between her stiffly corseted figure and Mark's graceful lounging in a needle-point upholstered chair was indicative of their opposing points of view.

Mrs. Cantrell explained rather formally that Mark's father, a mining engineer, was away in Arizona inspecting a mine. Mark enlarged on the theme.

"We never see him, Tosca. He's a little gnome three feet high and he only comes out of the ground once a year to breathe."

Tosca smiled timidly at Mrs. Cantrell, but the framed eyes were blank. The room seemed bleak, although it was overly filled with lovely old Victorian woods upholstered in gros-point of Mrs. Cantrell's making. The heavy drapes opened on a yellowing lawn and neglected gardens. Only a sunken rose garden showed care. Tosca was not disturbed by the genteel parings to fit straitened circumstances, such as managing without a gardener and the absence of a maid to bring in the tea, which she could not help observing on every hand. She was accustomed to these. But Mark was obviously resentful of many things in his home.

He hovered over a silver tray of bite-size cream puffs.

"You didn't have to make these in my honor. You know I hate whipped cream."

His mother observed him dispassionately.

"I thought Miss Levenridge might like them. Most people seem to."

"Most women, you mean." He pressed his thumb into a puff, and a loop of filling shot out like tooth paste. Tosca suppressed a nervous laugh.

"Your rose garden is lovely," she said hurriedly.

The rimmed glasses focused her way. The unfemininity of Mrs. Cantrell's attention was oddly flattering.

"I take care of it myself. We haven't had help since '29, and these old houses take so much."

"Large houses do," agreed Tosca, for on this point she could be positive indeed, and she thought: This woman has no coquetry and no weaknesses; she loves roses; we could be friends.

Mark was looking restively around the handsome high-ceilinged room. "I don't see why you hang onto this place. It gives me the creeps. There's something indecent about the way a house like this struts all the old virtues. Tosca, you won't believe this, but we used to hold family prayers in this room. Grandmother insisted."

"You mean, all kneeling around?"

"Every one of us." His grin became seraphic. "Once Grandmother's coachman had the bad luck to kneel in front of me."

Mrs. Cantrell did not look up from her knitting.

"I think that was sweet," said Tosca, adding hastily, "Prayers, I mean. The family together."

It occurred to her that Giacomo was the last of the devout ones in her family. Marie had hunted newer and more elastic creeds, and for Vincent Levenridge Sunday was the day for contacts, with golf in the morning and dinner at the country club. She remembered Sundays had been lonely for her in childhood unless she had been left at Giacomo's to spend the day.

Mark was behaving badly, she decided, not at all like the charming Mark she was accustomed to, and they were both relieved when they had escaped the house and were riding toward San Francisco again.

"Isn't she terrible?" Mark exclaimed. "But I do adore her, and you'll love her when you know her. It's like having General Pershing for a mother."

I shall never love her, thought Tosca, but I respect her. Then she was overwhelmed with pity for Mrs. Cantrell and could not have told why.

But the visit had left Mark moody.

"That house gets me down. Well, it's over and we can be ourselves."

"I want you to meet my grandfather."

"I knew it! Uncles and aunts and cousins—God, what fun we're going to have! We can keep this up for years!"

"But, Mark, you love meeting people." And then she said, and it was the first carefully thought out statement of her life, "Maybe you don't like people as much as you think you do."

She was bewildered by his sudden anger.

"I can't stand them when they're bossy. Why should I? Or when they think they have hold of you and hang on—— God, that blasted tea has made me sick. Let's stop in here for a drink."

He shot the car into the driveway before a pillared mansion surrounded by well-tended gardens. Dozens of cars stood in the circular drive. It was, she knew, a private gambling club. The gaming rooms were open, although it was still afternoon, and men and women were already around the tables, deep in play. A furtive man with the complexion of a greenish-tinged water lily, made greener by the eyeshield he wore, brought drinks to a dimly velveted alcove from which they could look over spinning wheels and cages and green baize thudding with dice.

But Mark stared into his glass, and his face was white with strain. She had never seen him in a mood like this. The meeting with his mother had roused some curious resentment he now extended to Tosca, and he avoided her pleading eyes and ordered again by gesturing, without looking up, in the direction of the waiter with the eyeshade.

"I knew this would happen," he said finally.

She longed to understand, to comfort him.

"Mark dear, what has happened?"

"Oh, don't try being sympathetic. That's even worse. I just don't like it, that's all. And you like it! You fell right into it. Tosca, let's be sane! You don't push modern people to their knees! It's not dignified. It's for peasants!"

The anger his words roused in her was beyond reason. Giacomo prayed, as simply and often as one might converse with a close relative interested in one's most trifling affairs. Giacomo, who had built beauty such as no one could look upon without reverence! And she said between her teeth, dropping each word into place as if hurling a stone: "My grandfather is no peasant!"

What did she remember, what could she find to say, to annihilate Mark's smugness? For nearly a thousand years the Daneri had tended their own Italian earth, and was that peasantry, or was it being the rulers of that earth? But she had Mark's attention at last, and it was far from affectionate.

"Now what hit you? I wasn't even thinking about your grandfather. That's just an expression. Besides, I don't even know the man."

"You don't want to meet him. You've never wanted to."

"Touchy! What's the matter with you lately, Tosca?"

She was angry with him now for many reasons—her nerves whipped raw with fruitless love-making, for having learned at last that Mark loved the excitement of exciting women and was content for his own part to let that excitement be enough, and because she had not been able to understand his mocking-loving belittlement of his mother, and because he had squashed the little cake his mother had made! The drink Tosca had tossed down in her anger shaped itself into words that contained all her resentment against the long frustrating months of Mark's wooing that had left her again and again ravaged and bewildered, not knowing what to make of Mark or of herself.

"What do you know of men like Giacomo and Eric—men who work and create and live——" Anger bubbled like lava in her throat and she could scarcely make herself understood. "Who are your friends—tramps like Kelly, half-men like Roscoe—Roscoe with his nasty, jealous little mind—jealous of me!

"And you," she cried wildly, "in another way—you're jealous, too, of me!"

He sat frozen with rage, glass in hand.

"You've read that somewhere. Love and jealousy are synonymous. You read it in a book."

247

"I never read books. I don't want to read books. I want to live. And you're afraid to." She pulled the words out slowly because she knew they could never be forgiven. She had never loved Mark more than in this moment, while she was tearing his pride out, leaving him empty. "You're not jealous because you want me, Mark, but because you want to be me! Because I've been cared for and loved and always will be—because I'm a woman!"

He could hardly speak. "What do you think—that I'm a stinking pansy?"

"Oh, Mark, no." Now she was wretched and afraid. "It's only that I don't understand you. You won't let me understand you."

"Why should I!" For a moment, clear-cut, white with contempt, he was magnificent. "You've had everything—you're right about that part. He didn't hold back a thing you wanted. Now I'm the first person you've met who wants to hold back—and it's that you can't stand, because you're going to take everything or die—all you can take—your little hands full."

The eyeshaded waiter coughed warningly beside them, tray in hand, and they did not care. Their breath was released and held again, lungs swelled in anguish, and still they stared at each other in a miasma of resentment that divided and yet held.

"You have set your will against me," Mark panted. "You are determined to make me sit up and speak—like a spaniel."

And she knew it was true. Her will seemed terrible and without reason, and it swelled and burst within her, hammering against the wall of Mark's tantalizing evasiveness, which was as misty as fog and as impenetrable as the hardest metal.

His face was clammy white and his red-shot eyes those of an animal evading the trap.

"Don't say it, Tosca. I know what you want to say. Why not be manly! That's the woman-weapon. That's what you throw at us when we don't kneel on our capes in the mud and promise to love, honor, and pay your goddamn bills the rest of our lives. When we don't want that, we're not manly! But that doesn't work with me, either, because it's all part of the propaganda and I don't fall for it; I don't want to take care of anyone and cherish them—I don't even want to take care of myself!—and I don't want to be with anybody until death parts us. So save your words, Tosca, because I won't crawl."

The insanity of trying to understand, of trying to make him understand, made her stammer and lose all sense of what she was saying. "I love you," she repeated hysterically over and over, not noticing—neither had noticed—the waiter had left them again. "Mark, I love you."

"Love!" It was a four-letter word as he mouthed it. "Your idea of love is eating your male alive."

He's crazy, she thought, but she knew he wasn't. "You hate me," she wept, and he answered, "No! Only for making me like this."

She crouched against the velvet corner of the alcove, longing to hold him and comfort him because she knew he needed help to quiet this raving, but not daring to touch him. Her body slumped and she felt hated and old, and in that moment she looked as Mark's mother had when Mark ridiculed the little cakes.

"Oh, we must go." She tried to control her weeping. "Someone will see us here—this is dreadful—quarreling."

"I'm not going!" The twisted face was a gargoyle's. Not a trace of Mark's good looks remained.

"Then I'm going. Oh, Mark, how will you get home?"

"There you go, worrying about me." She shuddered before his smile. "I'll get along all right. I managed before I met you, God help me."

The contempt and hatred he had turned on her were re-doubled in her violence, blown up into monstrous shape. She leaned forward, her white face driving toward his like a blade.

"You'll be back!" Wild with hurt, the words were like words in a play, or something she had been taught sometime, some-where. "You tried to leave before, didn't you? When you went to Del Monte! And other times. And you couldn't. You can't get away from me any more than I——" She faltered a moment and then, willing it to be with the will of demons, she hurled the final challenge: "You'll be back!"

Within the hour, as she lay weak with nausea in her room, desolate and lost on the wide bed and staring through swollen lids at the azure walls, Marie knocked at her door. Tosca had been trying to reconstruct the nightmare scene, but she could not recall what had been said and what had been implied, any more than she could reconstruct the dangerous ride home alone—once a telegraph pole whisked dangerously close to the wind-shield while a woman screamed from the curb: "Why don't you look where you're driving, you drunken fool?" She was not

249

intoxicated, although she must have looked so with her hair wind-blown and eyes wild with tears, so that Marie had been terrified when she opened the door. And now Marie still sounded heartbrokenly anxious, and from the other side of the hall a steady rumble of disapproval showed that Vincent had been apprised of his daughter's desperate home-coming.

But when Marie said timidly, "Tosca, he is here and wants to speak to you," the words might have been foreordained and echoed from long ago. Tosca drew on the long woolen robe and pulled the zipper to her chin as mechanically as a condemned woman might before going to her execution. The sufferings of the past hour had left her emotionally benumbed, so that she went without tremor down the turning stairs, counting the steps and tapping each third step twice with her toe—it was a sort of game she sometimes played, and she played it now. She went into the drawing room as if it were empty, and stood frozen with amazement to see him standing there waiting, because it seemed impossible that Mark could be there. And still she had known—even to the way he would come to her, contrite and broken of pride. She sank to the lounge, and he knelt before her and put his head in her lap.

"I caught a cab up," he said tiredly. "You said——"

But he did not go on. He turned his face against her hands. His skin was clammy white and cold—she was afraid. This was capitulation, and she knew then what heartbreak was.

"You've won." His eyes begged for mercy. "I'll be what you want me to be."

And she knew this was as it was doomed to be. She who did not want to use and who feared her own indomitable will would break herself to mold the too malleable stuff of which Mark was made. Tenuous, evasive as mist, he might escape from her. But in the end he would be with her because she was the stronger and because he had need of that dark sweet splendid power.

"Hush!" she whispered dully. "I'll take care of you, darling."

She sat motionless, holding him. Where had the wild, wonderful fun they had shared been lost along the way? Mark's shaking bulk filled her arms. His tears pressed all else from her reason except horror and pity. She held him closely, murmuring wordless sounds that welled from the dark senseless depths of her horror and pity, and felt love settle like a dead and dreadful weight upon the heart.

250

*I*N the dream Giacomo was powerful, and his thick legs thrashed the waters running through the low arch into the Blue Grotto at Capri.

There were men with boats willing to row him through the entrance, but he must swim into the wonderful grotto because he was so strong and so young and because he remembered the darkling blue of it, having been taken there once when he was six years old. "Remember it always, Giacomo," his father had warned him. "You may never see it again." So he remembered the glittering overhead like that of many lamps and the water, which was warm and blue, like a field of delphinium. It laved him pleasantly, and he awoke to feel the stubble broken out on his chin and his knees aching from the summer fog that overwhelms the bay region in August. And without being greatly surprised he knew it was as his father had said—Giacomo Daneri would not again see the grotto of Capri, and on this morning he was seventy-five.

"*Ohime mi*," he mused in astonishment, regarding the crocheted spread fashioned half a century before by Maria. "Who would think it! When only yesterday a man is six!"

The sense of astonishment accompanied him to the breakfast table.

"Today I do not work," he told the others roguishly. "Today is my *natale*. Maybe I am too old to work, no?"

The men laughed at his cheerful jest. Some praised the fine suit bought for this day. Only Stoob did not laugh, and Eric after a moment lowered his eyes to his place.

It troubled Giacomo to see Eric in this mood—almost morose, and so unlike Eric. Since Tosca's visit he had noticed it. Ludmilla had not appeared, and there was no way to account for this new tension between Eric and Stoob. The gaiety of the table floundered, and even Cesare could not save it, although he was wearing a clean apron for the occasion and had been up since three to bake the fresh panetone Giacomo liked for holidays and which

251

they were having for breakfast. For tonight Giacomo would not dine at his own table, but with Marie and Vincent and Tosca and Mark Cantrell in the house on the Presidio hill.

"How long since I have taken a day off," Stoob remarked, with his mouth full, to no one in particular.

Cesare turned with polite attention from his stove.

"Indeed, it would be better if you took a vacation. Shall we say ten years? And who knows, in that time you may contract some mild disease, such as the smallpox."

"It is ever the point of the capital-eest," said Stoob, ignoring the fact, as everyone on the place knew except Giacomo, that Cesare's wages were being squandered in support of an intermittently blond creature in South San Francisco, "the capital-eestic point of view, to ridicule the indefensible——" Stoob floundered, and choked on his panetone.

"I would rather not go to the city this day," resumed Giacomo, determined to be good-humored.

It was true that he seldom enjoyed festivities away from his own land. He would have preferred to hold his *natale* festa in the Drive, as he had planned, or even in this comfortable kitchen with family and crew. He did not even enjoy the great Sunday dinner he gave each year after Christmas, when, the strain of the shipping over, he marched at the head of his small army of nurserymen into the best Italian restaurant in San Francisco and shared with them, from Stoob to the youngest apprentice, a tremendous holiday meal.

The men were disappointed, too, in the omission of a festa. But Tosca had made her plans. She had chosen Giacomo's birthday to introduce him to Mark.

He gave many messages to Eric. Eric listened, avoiding his eyes. Stoob listened, weighing every request with jealous suspicion. Then, while Cesare protested violently, meaning not a word of his objections, Giacomo drained wine into demijohns from the wide casks in the dark sour-smelling cellar under the kitchen.

"*Addio! Addio!*" he called at last to them all, having painstakingly backed his cheap seven-year-old car from the shipping shed. Not another man on the place had so cheap nor so old a car. The boys packing roses at the tables, the men bringing in baskets of carnations from the greenhouses cheered him soundly and from their hearts.

252

Ludmilla, looking listlessly out of the window of Stoob's cottage, gave a halfhearted wave as he drove by.

Gigantic in appearance in the small car, Giacomo drove contentedly along the curves of the Colma hills. So much empty land, even here, he was thinking, and so much space in America, and now there was talk of a wonder plan—a great housing plan—by the government, so that many who wanted homes would have them. It was a privilege to live in a country where such plans were made. The sun felt good on his face, and the scents of morning rose sharp and sweet on the August fields. The car ran well, too, and after all these years. What more did a man need in a car? Let Vincent Levenridge keep his two imported magnificences, which he could not afford to run and so far had not been able to sell. Giacomo's car was old like himself, and he was attuned to every sound and movement it made.

He glanced back at the rear seat to see that all was well with the boxes of flowers for Tosca and Marie.

The car carried him swiftly enough from the southerly tip of San Francisco to its northerly section, which was North Beach, the Italian colony that had been home to him before his purchase of the Colma land.

The narrow streets racing up Telegraph Hill spoke of homecoming. Reminiscent of early friends and early loves—so that at times a man looked twice while riding past—were the faces of the men and women and children who lounged on the steps of the homes and cheap apartments, or on benches in the willow-hung park before St. Peter's and Paul's. Through the spraying green branches the gray spires with their many gold crosses gave the church an old-world appearance.

There were many garages giving notice: "Fifteen cents for three hours' parking." But Giacomo drove through the slanting streets until he came to an empty space before a salami factory.

"Fifteen cents," he explained to the sausage maker, who was briskly hanging bargain signs outside his windows, "is still *quindici centissimis!*" The salami manufacturer agreeing upon this fact, Giacomo beamed. "Put aside for me," he said grandly, "two of your best salami, hard and with very little beef, and a plentiful slicing of prosciutto."

"Madonna," said the other, "it must be a christening!"

"In truth," agreed Giacomo, twinkling. "I am seventy-five today and it is time I was properly christened."

But no trace of levity accompanied him into the gray church.

Tiptoeing heavily, clutching his hat under his arm, he came with lighted candles before the understanding saints. He lighted them for the souls of Maria and Vittorio, and for the doomed soul of Paul, who had taken the life that was not his own but God's. Tears lay hot against his closed lids as he prayed for Paul. In the Italian cemetery they were waiting, and it was like Giacomo that the space he had reserved there for himself lay to the west, as if even in that last sanctuary he would shield them against the winds rushing in from the sea.

To the Virgin he spoke earnestly of Tosca.

"*Pazienza*, Blessed One," he urged in the dialect that was the speech of his heart. "Remember, please, she is very young."

He was kneeling before the tallest altar when he realized he was not alone. The scent of incense reached his nostrils, and over him a robed priest spoke in Latin, and around him, like ghosts manifesting in the dimness, he became aware of many familiar faces. Genoese and Neapolitan fishermen knelt and made murmured requests for the blessing of their patroness, Santa Maria del Lume. Giacomo responded in Latin to the appeal of these *paesani* who asked once more that the saint would send her star to guide them out of the Golden Gate and into the fulsome Pacific, and fill their nets with leaping silver, and bring them safely home.

Subdued, yet comforted, Giacomo spoke to many of the worshipers, who fell into Italian-speaking groups outside the church when Mass was over. And to many of the men who gathered about Giacomo Daneri he himself was not unlike a saint, for they had known him lifelong and heard much of his goodness. Not another man was more beloved in Little Italy.

But by eleven that morning he was in the Badaroccos' fine wine-smelling cellar, and he was a happy man because his oldest friends were about him.

"Now, this is like old days," said Giacomo.

He sat on a wine barrel, his friends on other barrels, and their festa was spread before them on a large cask. Not only were his salami and peppery ham and demijohns set out bravely, but Vincenzo, who sculptored the beautiful angels for the tombstones, had brought a cheese perfectly whole, and Lorenzo, who had been a fisherman, had donated the round loaves of bread baked by his wife for this occasion, and Luigi, now retired after developing the most efficient of scavenger services, and whose sons were doctors and lawyers, had with him his accordion. His fingers were almost as nimble as ever and skipped cleverly over the keys, and the old wine-warmed voices lifted together in songs remembered from Italy.

"Yes, this is indeed like the old days," said Vincenzo as the wine went around between songs. "Before the Italianos heard of the stocks—presto! presto! everyone get rich!—and bought the fine cars and moved away from the Beach. Then for a time everybody was too stylish to hold parties in the cellars and roll the cheese playing *boccie* as we used to in Italy. But now many are poor again, and we who are not so young sing in the cellars on Sunday afternoons and the young men are again rolling the cheese on the Marina."

"It can never again be the same," grumbled Lorenzo.

Giacomo, munching salami with the teeth he was frequently made to realize with humiliation were not his own, considered the cheese rolling. He had once been champion of North Beach, surrendering the title at length to Luigi. He remembered a young Giacomo in the stance of the antique discus thrower, snatching back the wound tape to send the round cheese spinning down the court, and he wondered, where was that young giant, and where his strong friends of that day, and who were these old men huddled together in the Badarocco cellar, warming their bones over long-extinguished fires! He looked with wonder at their faces, so changed, but bearing more strongly than in youth the stamp of their ancestry: Vincenzo with his hooked nose, Roman as an antique coin; Lorenzo, the fairer Tuscan; and Luigi, who so plainly portrayed the dark-featured southerner, the Neapolitan. The Nordic strain was strong in his own heavily hewn features; it had come out more clearly, refined and clarified, in the features and coloring of Tosca. But no matter from what part of Italy they came, and no matter how poor Giacomo's friends might be, behind them was spread the rich tapestry of antiquity, and over the most ignorant was the light of an ancient wisdom. With lighted faces they could speak of Dante Alighieri, Michelangelo, Verdi. They knew the street songs of their provinces and the scores of great operas. They loved color and passion and history and the sound of words. Old they might be, and poor, but each had contributed in his way to San Francisco. There were at this time some seventy thousand people of Italian descent in the city. They had donated to San Francisco their music, their foods to the restaurants that helped make it famous; they had made wines and planted fruits and vegetables and, beyond all, flowers. And in payment they had wrested every possible advantage from their new world.

"We will drink a toast," pronounced Giacomo. His lined face glowed with kindliness under the shock of gray hair. "To San Francisco, our mother city, so beautiful and so good to us all."

They drank to it, but Lorenzo was ever the malcontent. "We drink also to Firenze," he argued. "And Venezia is a very fine place, and have you forgotten Genova?"

Giacomo waved his arms in magnificent agreement. "We will drink to every city in Italy, but first and last, to San Francisco. I am not one of those *paesani* whose hearts and bank notes are in Italia and whose money is earned here. Not I. For I remember the crowded house of my father and the knowledge of too little bread for too many mouths, and because a man must be grateful for what has been given him, I am American! *Salute!*"

They drank, but Lorenzo persisted, "Then are you not untrue to our mother Italia?"

"Every man has both father and mother." Giacomo spoke a little sternly. "America has been one to me and Italia the other. Is it wrong that I revere the memory of one and serve the other that has fostered me?"

"Every man has children too," put in Luigi, pulling the accordion out to its sobbing length as he spoke. His sons were successful and had married well, and it was said that he could not get along with their wives. "That is, provided he is a man. But is he happier for that always? I ask you with honesty. Do they bring him happiness or sorrow? Can he understand them?"

Every man in the dark cellar, with the exception of Romeo, who had been a vegetable grower, waited the opinion of Giacomo.

"We are happier!" Giacomo spoke soundly. "No matter what grief they may bring to us"—suddenly Paul was with him, so handsome and gifted by God!—"we are happier to have had them."

Now for some time Romeo had been telling a story, but nobody had paid any attention because his mind ran on one subject at a time, and it was always the same subject. Once begun, there was never any stopping him, but fortunately it was not impolite not to listen because he did not notice.

"There were the eels, millions of eels, and all of them long as my arm," Romeo was saying, curled about his bottle on the barrel top as he droned through the many-times-told story. "Now who would have thought such things could live in San Francisco Bay? That was the time the dynamiting began under the place where the old fort stands because they were blasting under water so they could start building the bridge across the Golden Gate, and who can believe a bridge will be built across the Gate that will be longer than any other such bridge in all the world! Then the dynamite boomed under the water and the eels died and came to the top—longer than my two arms, some of them——"

"A child can be a knife within the heart," Lorenzo was saying tragically, and Luigi knew the conversation was growing too serious and he pulled the accordion out in a raucous cry. "We are not here to argue politics or the peculiar disadvantages of paternity," he shouted. "This is the birthday of Giacomo Daneri, and all the world knows there is no better citizen and no finer man of the *famiglia*, and we sing this song for you, our *buono compagno* Giacomo, *amico mio!*"

He burst into the opening words of "L'Espanola." The others joined in the rowdy ditty. " 'Oh, L'Espanola knows how to love,' " they sang, and if their voices were not so strong as formerly, at least gusto was not lacking. Only Romeo droned on with his account of the dynamited eels, and between verses they heard his voice in steady monotone. Giacomo sang loudly, and no longer was the gray of the morning in his heart, nor did he remember the aching places where his bones joined together.

They had been young together, these *paesani*, and friendship was an essence that contained the past and insured the future. Another glass, and they were reviewing the friendly years. "Do you remember," they said, and *"Ohime mi,* to think that he is dead! As for that slant-eyed girl Vittoria, surely she was sent to Telegraph Hill by the devil to tempt the soul of a man! Ah yes! She sat in the window, remember, in her house under the Observatory—and how long since that tower has fallen! Thirty years? Impossible, but we will not quarrel about it." And in their secret recollections there was a childish innocence.

"So we gathered them." Romeo's story had uncurled at last to the thin end that was its climax. "Some of them large as sharks and too big to fit into our baskets. Sharks there were, too, and bass of a largeness never seen from these waters before——"

"And you planted the eels with the vegetables!" chimed in the others, willing now to permit Romeo his moment of attention. For Romeo was one of whom they were frank to say, "He is getting on in years."

"Ah yes," Romeo droned in dull triumph. "And never were such gardens as grew that summer in North Beach."

And he relapsed into silence.

Giacomo was still a little lightheaded with wine and goodfellowship when at five that afternoon he crowded his big body into a cushioned booth in the hotel cocktail lounge chosen by Tosca. It had been her idea that he meet Mark for the first time over cocktails before the special birthday dinner Marie was preparing. She had asked him to choose a place.

"Take me to the place you like best," Giacomo had parried, and after a moment's hesitation she had named Mark's favorite lounge.

Giacomo tried not to stare too rudely. The music was good, but only a few couples were dancing on a floor as small as a mirror; the majority of the young people were crowded about the bar, and Giacomo had never before seen young women, some younger than Tosca, seated on stools before a bar.

And he did not like places where there were no windows to look through so one could make certain the world was outside.

But Tosca seemed gaily at ease. "I'm ordering," she said. "This is my party." Mike, their waiter, was an old friend, it developed, and Mike was charged to tell Sam, the bartender, another intimate crony, to prepare two special pink ladies as this was a special birthday—her grandfather's. Giacomo found himself being introduced to a great many people who turned out to be "old friends" of Mark or Tosca, and since it apparently did not trouble Tosca that she had either forgotten or had never known the last names of many, Giacomo made up his mind not to let it bother him.

"And where is Mr. Cantrell?" Sam beamed, delivering the pale drinks in person, which was a signal honor. "Oh, he'll be along," said Tosca carelessly, and pushed back Giacomo's proffered coins. "Oh no, you don't, handsome, not today! It's your birthday, remember!"

He noted the bill she left on the tray for the amused waiter, and the small amount of change returned, and the largeness of the tips left there for Mike and Sam. Never had he heard of such a price for a glass of liquor, and, making a wry face over it, such poor liquor at that. It was the leanness of his own beginnings, he decided in his determination to be fair, that made him want to see every penny accounted for in value. The sum Tosca had left on the tray was the profit on an orchid—the profit on seven years of work and watchfulness in exchange for two detestable drinks brought them by two able-bodied men.

"Salute!" cried Tosca gaily, and he had to pretend to taste the drink again.

In the dim light he saw her clearly, more so, perhaps, than ever before. She wore mink, which seemed too old for her, and that was another weakness of Marie's. They denied her nothing, did Tosca's parents, but neither, he reflected, had he. And did she not deserve all they could give? Against the warm brown of the fur her skin seemed touched with gold, like her hair, and her eyes were dark as sepia pansies. She put her hand to his lips in a quick caress, and it was incredibly soft and fragrant, like a flower, he thought, put forth from the loveliness that was Tosca. The day spent in North Beach with the old friends made her youth and her beauty seem more noticeable, and he realized then, so clearly that he marveled not to have known before, that the breed she— and he—sprang from was fiercely strong and that work was needful to their kind or their very strength would destroy them. Then he knew—Paul would have been happier and in fact alive if the Daneri orchid-built fortune had never been. Men like Paul—the children of the strong—were not decadent. They were wasted. They weakened under the burden of luxury; they tried with fast cars and planes to outrace their own desires; they perished. His look clung to her brightness, the flowerlike face, the fine-boned body in the loose-falling fur.

He wanted to weep for her, because she was beautiful and strong, and this beauty, this perfection he had developed and cherished, was tragically at home in this poor music-shaken place. She was beautiful and strong as one of his orchids, as the Aurea he had named for love of her, and, like them, she was fixed in helplessness. He looked around him at the other young women at the tables or the bar, and it seemed to him that they too were not unlike the hybrids. Was all beauty, he wondered, parasitical? Only it seemed to him Tosca was doubly victimized—caught between the clashing tempos of two racial strains and of two ways of life.

We have all helped weaken her, he thought. Vincent, ambitious and without understanding, and Marie, helpless in her unworldliness, and he most of all, because he loved her most.

Then, torn from the depths of Giacomo, the *mea culpa* rode like thorns, and the accusation: My children, what have I done to them! To love beyond reason, to share too deeply the life of another, that is a Calvary that does not end until one falls under the burden for the last time. So many times he had fought his way up and onward, and always for them. But all his love could not make him strong enough to help one who would not be helped.

Dumbly he searched his heart for the answer. Must we always fail our children?

Tosca had fallen silent before his silence, and she turned her head to signal Sam he was to bring another drink, one only, for her. And her eyes went anxiously to the door, and the first bright happiness was gone.

I have done this to her, he thought, and to Paul and Marie. But marriage will mean work for her hands. This man, perhaps, will give her purpose.

And he said kindly, "Tosca, you have told me so little of your young man."

"Oh!" She stirred the pink liquor, and a softness he had never heard was in her voice. "I can't tell you that, but he's darling and sweet and sort of crazy. Get him to tell you about the time he bought the forty burros in Acapulco."

"What did he want with forty donkeys?"

"Why, that's the point." Tosca rocked with merriment. "He'd been drinking, and he woke up with an awful headache and the hotel manager came and asked what he should feed Mark's burros, and Mark looked out of the window and there they were —forty of them—tied in a line in the patio of the hotel."

"But why——"

"He couldn't remember. He never has been able to remember."

"*Ohime mi!*"

"Mark never does anything like other people." For a moment he thought he caught a signal of fleeting doubt in her eyes. "But he's wonderful—he's—well——"

He was thinking back to having been Mark's age and remembering what life had been to him then. *"Bella bambina,* did I ever tell you how I first came to America?"

She shook her head, and her mouth was still curved with tender laughter. And in stumbling words he told of how he had been detained as a young lad with his father at Ellis Island. Each morning for breakfast he was given a splendid doughnut, but only one. The taste was new to his foreign palate and epitomized for him the luxuriousness of America. "Someday," the hungry young Giacomo had promised himself, "I will be rich, and I will buy a dozen doughnuts, and I will eat them all."

"And did you?" demanded Tosca, moved. But he shook his head and smiled. "After I had money enough, I did not want doughnuts any more."

But she did not hear him. And Giacomo, looking where her glance led, knew that the tall figure lounging through the doorway could only be Mark Cantrell. No one else could so galvanize the young beloved figure at his side.

Mark waved his hand and headed their way. His smile was for Tosca, but it was also for the waiter who hurried to meet him, for the man behind the bar, and a girl on the dance floor smiling over her partner's shoulder. He neared them, graceful and familiar and at ease with himself and this world, and Giacomo, his great paw clenched over the thin glass, found the music too savagely loud, the air too heavy with alcohol and perfume, and the friendly, nearing face—like this room—terrifyingly alien.

What stirrings of innocence could survive, he wondered, in such a place, with such a man? What sort of love survive?

Love! Giacomo Daneri had learned of it first through the old stories. He had known of Juliet and Romeo, who had lived long ago in Italia. As a young man he had stood in the arched doorway in Verona that had framed their romance.

That love was a good thing, he knew. It was a grace that warmed the veins of the young and the bones of the old. But what did this stranger coming toward them with the easy grace and ready smile know of such values? Instantly, as surely as he knew himself to be Giacomo Daneri, he knew this man Cantrell to be both sensitive and exquisitely selfish and, perhaps, thoughtlessly cruel.

Tosca turned her lovely head to tell him Mark had come, and his look of pain drove the words from her lips.

"Nonno, what is it?"

But Giacomo, lifting his suddenly weary body from the cushioned seat, was cringing, as he never had to any man, before that amused and expectant smile. But he could not explain to Tosca.

He was remembering a doorway in Verona.

NINETEEN

*T*HE kitten could no longer truthfully be called a kitten.

Lengthier, rangier, and more obviously masculine, it sat with new dignity on its curled tail in the doorway of the boiler plant and blinked in the thin sunlight of early fall. Giacomo was inside the shed, wearing his overalls although it was Sunday. He was trying to adjust the heating system.

Of late the steam pressure was almost impossible to control. Garibaldi was complaining of trouble with the boiler. Eric had a way with it, but Eric had gone to Santa Cruz for the day.

A whole new plant might be cheaper, thought Giacomo. He gave up attempting to set the gauges accurately and wiped his oily hands on a bit of moss. And he determined to drive over to Valli, the camellia grower, this very week and see how he was getting along with his new oil-burning plant. "In thirty years," Giacomo thought, "I have changed the patterns of thousands of orchids, but I still have the same old steam-heating system."

But he had donned his overalls and left the house to shake off gloomy thoughts. He had been reading the death notices in the Sunday newspaper, which showed how rapidly pieces of the world one knew could drop away. Now it was Luigi, who had brought his accordion to Giacomo's birthday festa in the Badarocco cellar. A home built, a family founded, a modest fortune put away, and now an old body shrunken in a coffin. I will send roses, thought Giacomo, but he was remembering Luigi, the champion of the *boccie* courts, and a broad chest lifting to the old songs, and where was that voice now?

I will cut the roses today, thought Giacomo, and since when one is touched with sorrow it is best to do something, he determined while gathering roses for Luigi to cut flowers for his own graves and visit the cemetery to see how matters went there. It was well kept, but there were always a few weeds to be pulled, and for Maria and Vittorio he would take outdoor flowers—Maria had loved heather—but the gardenias and bud roses would be for Paul. It was a matter of concern to Giacomo to see that flowers stayed fresh on the graves of those who in life had come to depend upon flowers.

Then he was pleased to see Marie and Vincent strolling up the path before the shipping shed.

"I know! You forgot it is Sunday," Marie scolded good-naturedly, but he knew she was embarrassed at finding him in his work clothes.

"I did not expect you." Giacomo was not abashed by her scolding, but by the blank expression worn by Vincent. And he was puzzled by their formal attire because Vincent often remarked tweeds were the only proper attire for Sunday. "You will excuse me, please, while I find better clothes? In a nursery, you know, only the bosses work on Sunday."

"Don't trouble, Father." Marie was already headed for the greenhouses. The pale sun flashed on her black satin dress as she opened the door to the Drive. "Let's go through the houses first. We need new plants for our conservatory."

"You do not need more plants," Vincent said impatiently. "The house is stuffed with them, and what do you want with more?"

"Never enough, never enough," said Giacomo soothingly.

The adolescent kitten led with long-legged dignity through the Drive and into the other houses. Marie hovered over the potted plants and cried out as door after door opened on the new glorious colors of fall.

"Oh, which are the most beautiful," she cried, turning to her father in ecstasy, "the fall colors or spring?"

But Giacomo smiled and shook his head, for whether spring or fall was loveliest in California, he, for one, had never been able to say.

Stoob, in meager Sunday best, was lurking about the tuberous begonia houses. If only he would go away, Giacomo found himself thinking, abashed by his own lack of hospitality; if only for a day he would leave the place, like the other men. But Marie and Vincent were impressed by Stoob's loyalty to his tubers and bulbs. "There is a worker for you," Vincent said with emphasis. And in the begonia houses Giacomo, defiant of Stoob's puffed face glowering through the frosted panes, heaped Marie's satin-bound arms with the waxen foliage and the flaming heads colored apricot and crimson, terra cotta and gold. Gold was the aura of summer's end and fall's beginning, it was the color of dominant September, and in the orchid houses the Aurea were now in their fullest glory, in the rare colors of yellow and gold. There were also many of the darker crosses of Cattleya and not a few of the dependable Odontoglossum and Odontioda.

The carnations were at their finest, and Giacomo was able to display with pride a house of new African daisies running the color scale of strange exquisite shadings. "I must say," he was forced to admit, "I have never seen better." Even the outdoor plants were flaunting defiance of a winter that would never come to Giacomo's land, and beside the compost heap rows of asters ripened to mauve and rose.

Marie hovered over every potted plant. Her fingers in their white gloves ached to be at the roots. She trudged happily between the tables, selecting a potted specimen or pinching a slip off some plant she wanted to try raising "on her own."

"I'll never have enough African violets. Do you mind if I take one more little one, Giacomo?"

"Take plenty! Take plenty!" urged Giacomo, blandly ignoring the disapproval of his son-in-law, as he had Stoob's. What a gardener she would have made, he was thinking, and when at last Marie was satiated with floral looting: "Come, let us see if Cesare has left out some little cakes."

Only two meals were served on Sundays in Giacomo's kitchen. The tremendous breakfast lasted through many hours, for some of the men took advantage of the free day to sleep late, and between its serving and the cooking of the Sunday dinner that was the only heavy meal served at evening during the week, Cesare withdrew to the house known as Vittorio's with a bottle of wine and the *Voce del Popolo* and, having set his alarm for five, snored musically through the afternoon. But there was no hour of the day when those living on Giacomo's place could not enter the kitchen for bread and cheese and the hard cookies to be dipped

264

in wine which Cesare left on platters under a clean cloth on the big table, and on the sink stood demijohns of claret, and pots of coffee to be warmed over were on the range.

In the kitchen Giacomo folded back the cloth and set cakes and thick glasses of wine before Vincent and Marie and excused himself. When he returned he had on his new suit and looked, Marie told him decidedly, very handsome.

"For an old man, yes," agreed Giacomo roguishly. He dipped an anise-flavored cake in his glass, and his forehead wrinkled with content. "*Mio,* it is good to see you. A fine birthday dinner we had, Marie. Oh, a splendid dinner."

Then he knew he had guessed rightly and they were there to discuss his birthday, when he had met Mark Cantrell.

"I am glad you enjoyed it," said Marie, and looked at her husband.

"A fine birthday dinner," repeated Giacomo with emphasis. "A fine time." And he spoke with the satisfaction of one who speaks only the truth.

To his surprise it had proved a happy evening. His first shocked impression of Mark had not changed, but it had been healed over, as it were, by Mark's wholehearted pleasure in being permitted to share the birthday celebration. Giacomo, with Tosca and Mark, had arrived in the Levenridge house after the cocktail meeting to find the seldom-used dining room magnificent with candles and Marie's finest dishes and silver. The red roses from the nursery added their luster to the green and white simplicity of the dignified room, and as for the dinner—Marie had worked for two days preparing the dishes her mother before her had prepared for Giacomo.

And the dread awkwardness vanished, for no one could be ill at ease with Mark. He won Marie with his praise, he wooed Giacomo with his tenderness toward Tosca, and toward Levenridge he showed flattering deference. "Mark has a genius for making friends," Tosca had once told her grandfather in passionate admiration, and Giacomo saw this now for himself, basking in that rare sweet warmth that is human gaiety, and not blotting pleasure with the wondering thought: did Mark, in his turn, have a genius for friendship?

They laughed the dinner through and would never remember why they laughed so; even Vincent unbent, and Tosca, hovering over Mark, was like a mother urging upon a rapt audience

265

the charms of a child. Not that Mark needed bringing out! Rather, he drew from them all a joy and a sense of being fascinating, and his attentive response was the most exquisite form of flattery. Giacomo felt himself expanding in spirit and telling long-forgotten anecdotes that had been funny half a century before and that seemed to hold humor still.

Marie brought in plates of ice cream; then, with an important air, she bustled out of the room again. The others stayed expectant and silent at the table, knowing that in the kitchen Marie was at the painstaking task of lighting seventy-five candles.

The phone shrilled in the hall. "I'll get it," called Tosca, but her mother came from the kitchen and picked up the receiver. "Yes," she said, her usually gentle voice revealing annoyance, and, "Yes, I will tell him. They are at dinner now."

She called to Mark: "Someone named Roscoe. He says you are expected at the Palace, at a party there."

Mark was contrite. "I forgot to tell you, Tosca. Well, we can skip it."

"You promised?" she asked.

It was plain to all that Mark had promised.

"Run along," said Giacomo kindly, because he was grateful for the reluctance Tosca showed, but it was clear that Cantrell wished to go. "Only first wait till we see what Marie has for us." And then Marie came in, smiling over the immense white and gold cake bursting all over with seventy-five budlike flames. And Tosca and Mark had waited for the wishing and the solemn blowing out of the candles. Then it seemed fair enough that the young couple should run along, and Tosca had kissed him. "This one's to grow on," she said, "I'll owe you the seventy-five." And Mark had shaken hands with manly sincerity and said warmly, "It's swell to have met you, sir, really swell," and how could one help but like such a friendly young man!

All this Giacomo remembered, dipping his cake in wine at his own kitchen table, and he remembered, too, that mere liking and Tosca's love could never be weighed on the same scales.

It was then he made up his mind not to discuss Mark Cantrell.

Vincent began the discussion after a prodding look from Marie. "Well, how did you like Tosca's young man, Giacomo?"

"Who? Oh yes. Very pleasant. And such nice manners."

Vincent looked at his wife as if for help.

"Would you say he's the right man for her?"

266

"Now what would I know about that? Isn't it for Tosca to say?"

Vincent's mouth settled in the line that in business hours had often warned some unfortunate that his loan could not be renewed. The old man could be crafty at times, he knew. But he did not want to hurt his father-in-law's feelings.

"We want her happiness, Giacomo," he said, softening, and saw the craglike visage crumple.

"Do we not all pray for that, Vincenzo? What else have we left to us but her happiness? Tell me, do you know anything that is not right against this man?"

Vincent shook his head quickly in denial.

"What then?"

"Well, for one thing," and Vincent spoke so slowly that it was clear he was as much in ignorance as Giacomo, "there's the matter of his not working."

"Many young men do not work these days, Vincent. It is not the disgrace it was when you were young, and certainly not when I was a young man and worked or went hungry."

"He has never worked."

"He is unwilling?" Giacomo was startled.

"Tosca says," put in Marie hurriedly, "that he has always felt before it was not necessary" (Not necessary? marveled Giacomo) "because he has a small income and of course when his mother——" Marie stopped as suddenly as she had begun.

"He has enough for himself, as he puts it," said Vincent, "but now the picture changes, and even in these days he cannot support two people and live as he does now. Now she tells me he is willing to work—willing!—and I am to find work for him!"

Giacomo saw that his hands were clenched on his knees like knotted clubs, and he loosened them quickly. He was not innocent of life. In his lifetime he had known many men. Most of those he had known had been hard workers, and some had drunk too much on their free days, and some had been brutal to their women. But this man, this Mark, he knew again he did not know.

The dog fights for his mate, he thought. In the forest the father deer defends his own, so that even in the jungle one finds —he groped for a word and found it, and how Mark would laugh if he knew—chivalry!

He laid his great fists on the oilcloth and faced them.

"It has been wrong. It has been wrong from the beginning. I knew then."

"She is like an entranced person." Marie's eyes darkened with bewilderment. "There is no reason in her, Giacomo. Why did it have to be this man? With your nice young Eric here with you, and I am certain she might have had him, Giacomo."

"Yes," said Giacomo wearily. "God knows, and this place has need of hands that are young."

"You have Eric," said Marie, but Giacomo sat silent, not knowing how much should be said, and not even certain how much he knew. But in some way the conversation was treachery to Tosca, and to temper the winds against her and, since she loved Mark, against Mark, he rallied his strength and spoke forcibly.

"Tosca has made her choice. You know she will abide by it. What can we do but help her now, as we have always? And if need comes, I am not so poor that I cannot carry a little more."

"That's outrageous!" Vincent had suppressed his feelings too long. He raised his voice. "You've given us all too much; you have given too much to Tosca always, and now if you start giving to Cantrell——"

"Not to him!" Giacomo's gray thatch shook emphatically. "Never to him, but to her! As you say, I have given always, so how can I withhold from her now? And especially in this matter that has all her happiness in it?"

"Happiness? The man's a bad risk. I give them two years."

"Vincent," said Giacomo gently, "how many people in this life are given two happy years?"

Vincent turned with a hopeless gesture to Marie. "We've all spoiled her. She's always been allowed to go her own way. Now we have ourselves to blame."

Never before had Giacomo realized the dominance of Marie. She put her hands out to Vincent with a brooding gesture. The bitter, austere lines relaxed, as if the weary face of Vincent were pressed to her heart. In that moment Giacomo looked as through a window into their lives and saw that the deep reassuring gentleness of Marie was as needful to Vincent Levenridge as his own blood.

He had never understood this son-in-law. Now he saw that Vincent was critical of Marie because he was critical of himself; she was part of him. He had not married Daneri's daughter for her money, as so many believed. It was this he had wanted—this deep power of kindliness as strong and imperishable as antiquity. Behind the shield of that gentleness Vincent Levenridge could face his own weaknesses and admit to himself that he was a failure. He was seemingly cold and critical toward her, harping incessantly upon her faults, but she was nevertheless his reason for living.

And to Marie this stern and lonely man was another child that helped take the place of the teeming fields and family she had desired.

Giacomo thought then, Why do we grieve over those we love when we are never certain what it is they have wanted?

"Vincent," he began with new firmness, "and Marie, now we are together, and it is so seldom we three are together, there is another matter I should like to take up with you. That of Stoob."

"Your lily man? What of him?"

"What do you think of him, Vincent?"

"H'm." The banker spread his well-cared-for hands on the oilcloth. "A thrifty man. Indefatigable. Not one to set the world afire, I'd say."

"Yes, a worker." Giacomo studied Vincent's face. Marie had gone back to the cookies and was not interested. "A poor man who has been willing to work. And there is no better bulb man, that is true."

There was an inner film of caution over the cold eyes across the table.

"I know all this, Giacomo. Why tell me?"

Giacomo dropped his head under that basilisk stare and pretended to look under the sink for the kitten. Then he looked up and with effort spoke the words he had hoped never to speak.

"Stoob is asking to buy the lily houses."

Marie dropped the cookie she had taken. She had never liked Stoob. And Vincent was drumming the oilcloth with his long fingers, as he always did when money decisions were to be made. The Vincent at the kitchen table became the Vincent of banking hours, secure in the atmosphere of wealth, banded in chromium and glass and shining vistas of mahogany.

"That is plainly nonsense," he said coldly. "Even if Stoob has saved enough to buy an interest in the nursery, why should you sell to a man you do not like?"

"He is a lover of lilies," said Giacomo simply.

269

Vincent looked his disgust. But Marie could control herself no longer. Her soft face had grown white and her eyes shown darkly against the camellia-white skin.

"He is their master, you mean, Father. Why should a grower like lilies and not all flowers? And you know what he is—he would have to be boss, and you would be living here and have nothing to say because he is that kind of man."

But Vincent had had time to look at both sides of the matter, and the opaque film was gone from his eyes.

"Could you run the nursery without Stoob?"

"Why not?" Giacomo's hesitation would not have been observed by one less trained in human weaknesses. "I am strong, and I have always worked."

"You are seventy-five," Vincent started to say, but the fierce pride on Giacomo's face stopped him. "It would be hard on you," he added gently. "Now, Giacomo, forgive me, but a banker learns that behind every need there is another. What reason have you for even considering this offer from a man I know you do not like?"

Giacomo waved his gnarled hands to drive away doubt.

"There may be other reasons," he said evasively, "which I cannot explain and perhaps do not fully understand."

Then he saw the comprehending look of the long-married pass between Vincent and Marie, and Marie put her hand over his. "Giacomo, is it Eric?"

"*Pazienza!*" Giacomo would not look at her. "We will discuss Eric when we know what there is to discuss about Eric. Sometimes patience settles our problems for us."

Again Vincent looked at Marie, and when he spoke his voice was icy with anger.

"Giacomo, you don't have to put up with Stoob or anyone else. That house of ours—you built it, and we think of it as yours. Let Stoob have what he wants, or let Eric do what he likes, since there is evidently dissension going on here we don't know about. And take it easy with us for the rest of your—— I mean, you have enough to live on in comfort, Giacomo."

And to his credit Vincent was thinking only of the comfort of Giacomo and not considering his own needs, nor those of the great house, nor even Tosca. Of the income reduced by the nursery's sale and the increased responsibility to himself, Vincent gave no thought. Nothing mattered now but Giacomo's happiness, and Vincent resolved to achieve this as he did all things, fairly, and a little ruthlessly.

Marie's eyes were wet with happiness. "Oh, Giacomo, I've prayed for this! Paul's—all that upper floor we've always thought of as yours. You can bring your furniture from the cottage so it will be like home, and"—her cheeks flamed into roses—"there is that long upper balcony, and we can put it under glass and you can raise begonias there, and even orchids." In her love for him she was ready to sacrifice the nursery that had been their mainstay through her lifetime.

"Yes, that might work out very well," agreed Vincent, with only a moment's hesitation at the mention of the orchids. And he added stiffly, "The house will be very empty when Tosca marries, unless you live with us, Giacomo."

Then, taking his pen from his pocket, he traced numerals on the oilcloth. "Now let us see, Stoob's offer." He jotted down a figure that made Giacomo remember that his son-in-law was also Stoob's banker. "Lease to him or sell outright, and it is still practical, and you are getting out while you are still able to enjoy life."

"Yes!" cried Marie, clasping her hands.

And Giacomo, deserted between them, knew that in this matter he stood alone and at the very end of his world. He was enjoying life—this they could not understand—as well as any man of his years might, for the nursery held a half century of that lifetime, and every hour of it had been well lived. His wine had spilled, and with the tip of a horny forefinger he traced a design in the oilcloth, and the pink outline became the petals of an Aurea, and protest rose in his throat and choked him. Because he could not hope to make them understand he smashed his fist down on the table so that the wine splashed and the orchid design was gone.

"No, I will not! Stoob would get rid of the orchids!"

"But that will not matter to you, once you are away from here," Vincent argued in his firm and reasonable way. "You've worked long enough to have a little peace."

"Cau Segnu!" Marie might understand, but Vincent never. Giacomo gave up trying. "Not yet, Vincent and Marie. Give me a little more time. Patience! Until we know what Eric has in mind."

And Giacomo even tried to make a joke of the matter in

271

Stoob's mincing manner. "We must consider the lilies," he said. But in his heart the cry went on loudly and sternly, "But first we must care for the orchids!"

TWENTY

𝓜ATTERS, when they came to a head, did so over so small a matter.

A bird was trapped in the Number Six lily of the valley house, where they were collecting lily pips for the winter drying. "A wild finch," one man said. "No, a tame bird," said another, and "Wait," Stoob said, "it may be valuable." But it was only a finch after all, smashing its fragile weight against the panes in its panic to escape; and the cat, which was nearly grown, showed for the first time stirrings of a predatory nature.

Ludmilla was there, and Eric.

"Scat!" said Eric, but Stoob put up his hand. "This is interesting," said Stoob. "It is a natural thing. Let the cat alone."

But Giacomo strode between the bins and picked up the cat and held it until the bird had found the open panes. Then, because he could not bear Stoob's expression, he carried the cat outside.

There he gave way to reproaches, privately expressed.

"What is in you that with all you are given you must try to eat one littler than yourself? There is room enough on this place for you and ten thousand birds."

The cat sang and turned against his arms, and its eyes were heavy with love.

"Of course Stoob is right," Giacomo told the cat thoughtfully. "You have a life of your own to live now, and what takes place on dark nights when you are away from me I have no right and no wish to know. But I will not have you set upon a little frightened thing, and for shame that you were so willing. Well, *Dio mio*. Perhaps I had no right to interfere. But the bird—had it not claimed sanctuary? In my lily houses, as long as they remain my lily houses, you will not crunch birds, my little friend."

Then, impatiently, because the incident had been unpleasant, he put the cat down. "Why do you not go to the loft with the other cats? It is time you were useful. Catch mice. Make kittens. Go!"

But the kitten wound about his legs and sang its love and would not leave—not yet.

"Look at him!" Stoob was watching through the glass. "Talking to the cat. He should be put away before he does some harm to himself." Then he saw Eric's expression. "My God, what have I said? Eric, why look at me——"

In the tumult that exploded in the lily house only Ludmilla stayed silent and without movement, pressed back against the glass wall, her mouth open, her eyes on Eric.

Eric jerked Stoob up by his shoulders and slammed the puffy body down on a lily bin like a man slapping a sack on a table. Stoob screamed, beating his head against the flowerless yellowing plants. The other men rushed forward but held their hands, for none of them liked Stoob. Eric's fist hovered over the open screaming face. Then, contemptuously, he dropped his hand.

"I can't even slug you. You're too weak." He pushed Stoob down in the pallid leaves until his face looked up, pointed and pale, like some hideous flower.

After Eric had slammed his way out of the lily house Stoob clambered awkwardly out of the bin. No one offered to help him. He stood rubbing his arms where Eric's fingers had lifted the shrinking flesh from the bones.

"Never mind," he said ominously. "Do not think that I will not get even."

Eric walked through the shipping shed without speaking to any of the men working at the tables. He picked up a carton from a stack in passing and carried it to his room in Paul's house. Methodically he adjusted the cardboard sides and began packing his books. He did not look up when Giacomo loomed in the doorway.

"Eric." Giacomo spoke sadly. "Lilies or no lilies, we can let him go."

But Eric was busy with the books.

"It doesn't matter about Stoob," he muttered. "I've been making up my mind along other lines."

Giacomo settled heavily on the foot of the couch. His shoulders sagged and the lines of his face ran down like water lanes on a weathered cliff. He had anticipated and dreaded this moment, but it was no less easier to bear. He wanted to speak, but he could not speak against this defeat that was pain and the years and repeated loss.

"You are going to another orchid house?" he said finally, and then Eric did look at him, quick with remorse.

"You've thought that, Giacomo? You know I could never work with another grower! Not after Giacomo Daneri. I guess you've heard I've talked to them all in this section. I've been feeling my way. Giacomo——"

He flung himself down beside Giacomo.

"Do you remember the day Ludmilla and you and I were in the seedling house and we talked of the orchid hunters? It started then. I was blue, and you know how something hits you when you're blue." (My talk, thought Giacomo sadly. My big and foolish mouth telling orchid stories because Ludmilla asked.)

"But here," Giacomo remembered to argue feebly, "you have a good living before you and you know the plans I have had for you."

"I'm grateful. Don't think I'm not. But, Giacomo—you know the crack flier that goes to Los Angeles? I've been like that train, tearing along, headed where I wanted to go, and then—what happened to me? Crash. Derailed."

This business of love, thought Giacomo. His great shoulders sagged in tentlike lines. Why had not all procreation been put on a practical basis? Then, as Giacomo only kept shaking his head, Eric pleaded, "Don't you remember, Giacomo? Can't you remember what it's like?"

"It did not happen to me," said Giacomo softly. "I was a man of good fortune even then."

There were, to be sure, the old legends, of love madnesses and women and men who had died for love. Some had put aside kingdoms, sunk to the depths. Giacomo had heard of these things, but while his own life had been simple and hard-working it had nevertheless been auraed with romance. He had loved his Maria, and love had been both simple and profound, like prayer or one's daily bread.

"Yes, you were lucky," Eric was saying. "You had the woman you wanted. At my age, a man has either found the woman he wants or a substitute, ambition, or adventure, and I don't want to be left without anything. I have a chance to join up with an expedition."

274

"South America?" Giacomo asked quietly.

"I'm not supposed to tell, but of course South America. You know how tough they are now on the fellows that go out after orchids. And the regulations are getting stricter all the time. But an expedition is forming next month in Bogotá, and I'm going to join them there."

He spoke with the force of a man who has only then made up his mind.

"You have been getting orders from the other orchid men?"

"Of course not. Do you think I'd go behind your back? But I have been hinting around and I have a pretty good idea who will give me orders, and of course, Giacomo, I hoped——"

"Certainly, Eric. Your judgment will be my judgment in such matters. Any orchids you may want to send me—— But, Eric, we have so many orchids! Thousands in our houses now, as you say, common as weeds, and it is so dangerous to hunt them!"

"Don't try holding me back, Giacomo." Eric's voice was pitying. "This is the first thing I've wanted since—well, now that Tosca is getting married it's the only thing for me to do. And you're the one who is always saying we can't have too many orchids! And I don't want the common-as-weed kinds, but the rare ones, the ones we've heard about and don't know whether to believe in or not. Finding out—that will be the adventure, and I've heard you say that as a man gets older he regrets not having adventured."

"But not at the cost of one's lifetime, Eric."

"It won't be a lifetime. I'll be back."

But Giacomo knew there was little chance of turning back, for he had known many orchid hunters, and many he had known had perished of hardship and tropical disease, and others had been killed by savage animals and savage men. Since the days of Darwin this had been happening, and tremendous sagas could be told of the hunt for a single flower. But still men hunted and could not stop hunting. Beyond the danger was the gleam that led men on—fired by the wild improbable tales of the once sighted and lost again, which kept men hunting as other men had hunted buried treasure and lost mines, until strength or reason failed. Like will-o'-the-wisp followers, they hunted in the wake of the fabulous tales of the lost white orchid of India, the vanished golden orchid of Borneo, and, most marvelous of all, the lost blue orchid of the Andes.

275

"Eric, there is no changing you?"

"If you needed me——" Eric began. Then he added lamely, "You don't really need me, Giacomo."

No, thought Giacomo, plodding back to his own house, in the ultimate wasteland of the years it was true that one could rise above the need of any other, no matter how beloved. One could live without Daneri's, too, and be cramped under the roof of the marble palace on the Presidio hill that could never be spacious enough for a man accustomed to walking out mornings onto his own patch of earth between skies and sea. And one could raise in that house a handful of orchids, and the memory of that Sunday morning when Vincent and Marie had come upon him in his working clothes added to his sense of desolation. It had not been so much a question of the overalls, but his shirt, for he had been made aware under Vincent's impassive survey that by some oversight it had not been changed that morning as it should have been for the Sabbath.

It was a pity that when there was no one about any longer to say, Giacomo, it is time to buy more shirts, or to change this shirt, and so on, there were always those ready to say, The old man is getting untidy. And it seemed regrettable that in the years one would most value attention and care one is oftenest left without either, while a great deal of both is wasted upon young people who have no way of valuing such things.

Beyond question, Vincent and Marie had been right that Sunday. He was too old to carry on Daneri's without Eric. Better to go to Marie, like an old baby in need of care, and be tended by her great motherly arms that were willing to encompass the world. He resolved to telephone Vincent that very evening, after Cesare and the others left the kitchen, and tell him Stoob could have his way and the papers could be drawn up as soon as Eric left. There, that was settled and as good as over, and from lungs and heart came the broken sigh that spoke of failure and foreboding, for Tosca gone and now Eric, and because even Giacomo's love had not been strong enough to save those who would not be saved.

He reviewed the wisdom of this decision later in the herb garden. There were roasts of lamb for the midday dinner, and Cesare needed sprigs of rosemary.

276

No hands but Giacomo's were permitted to touch the herbs in his savory garden.

Since where gardens are concerned no errand can ever be carried out without revealing the need for other tasks, Giacomo first watered the garden, since the morning was cool, washing down the clumps of basil, sorrel, fennel, sage, tarragon, rosemary, and marjoram. The cat fled before the spurting hose, to roll in ecstasy in its own catnip bed under the whitewashed fence. The dampened herbs flung their odors back at Giacomo, and he drank them in with a zest not unlike that being shown by the kitten. And for a moment, by the privileged alchemy of age, he was the solemn-faced boy leaving Italy, sniffing from the steamer's deck at dawn the aromatic coasts of the Mediterranean. "Behold, Giacomo," his father had said, pointing, "on our left is Africa." But of Africa, Giacomo remembered nothing, only the fresh wind blowing from the receding Italian shore spiced with basil and other herbs he did not know.

How could memory, or even the present, seem sad in an herb garden! The thyme was blooming and gray-blue as desert sage, and as he savored its healing pungency he remembered how he had once planned to build a garden of sweet-smelling flowers in which to grow old; a small garden with a wall. (So the beautifully groomed Marie, wandering through her splendid rooms, had grown wistful for a small place in which to pray.)

Small wonder, he thought, that the study of plants had begun as a science of healing. The earth healed. The fragrance of it! Giacomo's wrinkled lids drew down and his shaggy head lifted like a charioteer's against the salty wind. The watery sunlight reflected from the sea warmed his great shoulders, and in the wet pungency of the garden his weariness turned to peace.

And in nature, everywhere, one found certain signs indisputably left by God. Giacomo recalled with reverence the Holy Ghost orchid that wears the dove in its heart and its feathered replica, the South American dove, that wears the bleeding heart on its breast; and the shamrock's trinity, and the story of the crucifixion revealed by the passionflower—oh, the signs were everywhere! Through the open kitchen windows came the sound and savor of parsley and sweet basil and garlic being pounded in Cesare's marble mortar for the tagliarini, and Cesare's voice in thunderous Lombardian recounting to Laddie, who was helping with the vegetables, a strange and comical dream he had dreamed the night before.

A plane flashed far overhead, banked, and shot eastward toward hills the color of wild lilacs. It was the morning plane, Giacomo knew, carrying a consignment of orchids delivered at the airport earlier that morning by Eric, who was packing for departure now in the house that had been built for Paul. The hum of the motors was like the swarming of bees in the skies, and if a plane should crash into the glass houses someday, what a noise that would make! A good thing he was heavily insured against such accidents.

The plane vanished over the range, but Giacomo continued to look into the violet of the hills. In his mind vistas grew. He had these places, where no one could follow. He remembered a gold garden planned for his own pleasure, knowing it would never exist, but his thoughts formed banks of golden calendula, yellow African daisies, saffron pansies, orange tulips, golden viola, and narcissi, poppies, alyssum, and roses in all their shades of gold. These he planted in his mind against a wall of Italian cypress, and when it was pictured, not even thoughts of Stoob could hunt him there. There were other vistas he had actually seen and could call to mind at will, and he reviewed in turn a border walk blended of seven shades of blue pansies, a mile-long flame of Transvaal daisies, and a wall of Hawaiian hibiscus burning beside a blue lagoon.

Peacefully he began gathering the firlike tips of rosemary, planing the sprigs between thumb and palm and showing even in so simple an act the precision of a sculptor. In this fenced-in place was the sum of all activity, he was thinking, stripping the green from the stalk, the stalk from the root, the root from the earth. Here was the summation of the planting and reaping, with the final end of everything the compost. Here was the final truth of all things, from Giacomo Daneri to the rosemary, birth and the beginning, death and the implantation, and his story would soon be over and the earth would swallow all the words he had intended to speak.

Against the picket fence stood clumps of Queen Anne's lace and greasewood and wild yarrow, which he had left to mark the wild frontier of his land. The yarrow's blossom was grayish-white and its scent was acrid, as it had been when Indians had claimed this hillside. In Giacomo's cutting gardens the culti-

278

vated yarrow grew golden, renamed Achilles. The changing of even so simple a plant had required the patient attention of unremembered generations, through long years of selection and interbreeding, and of "roguing out" and failing and starting again. And after every failure, the compost.

And still the wild yarrow survived, fragrant and strong and as complete in its way as Giacomo's latest magnificent hybrid.

That is the trouble, he thought. I want everything beautiful and strong and I want it to last forever. But nothing lasts, except the law of inexorable change. This land he stood upon had been an Indian cemetery. They had found signs of Indian burial when they dug the gardens. Into this earth had been folded other flesh, and Giacomo considered this without qualms, for he had lived long and given much, and whatever might wait ahead now, he was not afraid.

Only meanness or weakness in others broke his courage.

He tried to figure it out, like a puzzle. It was easier to think in the herb garden, while one continued to gather the rosemary. Eric would leave, and Tosca would marry Cantrell, and this put an end to all planning. And Giacomo would live in the city and have no worries and no work.

But he did not like the city! It wearied him, for there was in it the strain of needing to be better than one's neighbor, and it was always good to come home to the nursery, where no matter how hard a man worked, or how long, there was no sense of nervous tearing apart, because the peace of work left only a healthy weariness, which was good for a man. And as long as plants grew, there was work for a man.

Even in this herb garden there was so much to be done.

And in the orchid houses, he remembered, there were dozens of tasks that he alone could attend to properly.

He drew himself to his full height, his feet planted apart firmly on the damp healing earth. No, he thought stubbornly, he would not telephone Vincent tonight about the papers for Stroob—let the matter wait!

"*Dio mio!*" shrieked the stentorian voice of Cesare.

His bullet head, encased in a paper sack that served as cap, was thrust through the kitchen window. "The *rosmarino*, Padrone! Or do you prefer we observe a day of fasting?"

A splutter of burning oil drew the chef's attention back to his range. Giacomo smiled with understanding. Cesare talked like a volcano and had the temper of a devil, but he was the sort of man one could understand. People like Stoob and his daughter —who ever knew what they were thinking?

Cesare was like Eric, bursting with life and as honest as life. What Eric said he meant, and what he planned to do was done. Nothing could stop Eric now.

Ah, Tosca, *bella figlia,* Giacomo thought as he plodded toward the kitchen with the rosemary clutched in his giant hand, truly you have been like a little death to him.

TWENTY-ONE

A bon voyage party should be gay because it is the starting point for the adventurous and unknown. But Tosca, walking up the gangplank ahead of her father and, like him, burdened with baskets of fruit and packages and magazines and books, could read little pleasure on the faces of those who had come to see Eric sail.

The fruit steamer lay in the estuary near the water front, which was beginning to show signs of activity now that the strike was over. It was a dreary setting of warehouses and lumber-yards, and the party was a dreary affair. Several tables had been set on the cramped forward deck with plates of canapés and bottles of champagne, and before these stood Eric, surrounded by swarms of the blond Brocks, all so alike that, seeing one in any part of the world, one would say at once, "There goes a Brock!" There were other people with them, all flower people from San Francisco or the peninsula or across the bay, and upon them, as upon the Brocks, was an air of bewilderment.

The news that Eric Brock was leaving Daneri's and, worse still, going to South America had come as a shock to the flower people.

As a group they found it difficult to approve of change that apparently held no advantage for the changer. They were as a rule contented and happy people. Their daughters and sons in the main took up the good life on their small rich sections of land. It was not often a young life shot off at a tangent from the growing world, as Eric's was now.

"I just don't get it." Thelma Valli had crossed the deck to meet Tosca. "Eric Brock, of all people, going out to hunt orchids."

"Oh, hush." Tosca looked around as if spies might be listening. "You know we aren't supposed to talk about it."

"Oh, sure, one of those secrets everyone knows. But Eric Brock —a born grower if ever one was born. Honestly, Tosca, if I'd dreamed Eric was on the open market! I thought you had him all wrapped up for Christmas."

Her friendly curiosity annoyed Tosca.

"Eric and I? Heavens no!" But Tosca's hoot of laughter sounded shrill in her own ears. She added more courteously, "I've other plans."

"Tosca! Not Mark Cantrell? He's too good to be true!"

"Well, thank you, Thelma!" Praise for Mark was becoming a rarity in Tosca's life, and she tried not to sound surprised or too grateful. So she said warmly, "He's precious, and I want you to meet him," and followed her father across the deck.

The lustrous Brocks made way, holding paper cups of champagne and studying her with the same blue-eyed impersonal gaze. As one person, curious, not unkindly, they watched her, and the message in their eyes was clear: She is the one! But no regret was openly shown, no one was in tears, and even the sturdy Adolph and his sensitive girlish wife were apparently unmoved by the fact that their son was leaving them and, with them, a life that until a few weeks ago had seemed the finest of all ways of living to Eric and to them all.

"You're just in time," said Eric, coming forward. He shook hands with Vincent with more warmth than he showed Tosca. "Unless you want to come along with me to Colombia."

"That is for younger blood, Eric." Vincent smiled without changing the firm line of his lips. "Isn't it so, Adolph? Adventure is for young people, like Eric and Tosca."

"I am not so sure," said Adolph, bringing forward champagne. "Sometimes I think it is more practical to adventure after one reaches a sensible age, so we can appreciate what we are doing."

He winked to his wife, then looked at his son severely. But Vincent, lifting the paper cup in a toast to Eric, replied with unexpected vehemence, "No, then it's too late. And few of us ever do what we want to do."

The conversation surprised Tosca, revealing as it did a side of her father's nature he had never shown before, at least to his family. She looked at Eric's mother, who was standing beside Eric, holding one of the newest Brock grandchildren, but she was cooing to the child and not paying attention. But one knew she was grieving, and Tosca felt her grief with inner guilt, and still this was not her fault and why should she feel guilty because Eric had behaved as no one would ever have dreamed a Brock would behave! So many times she had envied Eric's practical, calm nature. But these calm and certain ones, she decided, who are apparently so sure of themselves and where they are going, are capable of behavior as unexpected and even erratic as the more volatile kind.

With all Mark's nonsensical moods, she was quite certain he would never have tossed aside his world, or even a fraction of it, for her!

"I took the safe road," Vincent Levenridge was saying. It was strange the way he was appealing to Eric, as if there were something he wanted the younger man to understand. "That is, I thought it was safe. Twenty-nine showed us there was no such thing. Well"—he drew up formally—"make success of it, Eric."

"And all the talk again of trouble," Eric's mother said, looking up from the baby with the anxious air any mention of '29 could bring. "I just don't understand any of it, Vincent. Now we hear talk of war and inflation and all sorts of other things we never heard of before."

"We will hear more," said Vincent, very much the banker again.

Then Leni Brock turned to Tosca. How formally all the Brocks are behaving, Tosca was thinking, and how different they always seem in public from the lighthearted, playful people they are on the Brock farms. But Eric's mother, searching Tosca's eyes in pain, only asked simply: "Giacomo could not come, Tosca?"

"He didn't want to. He was afraid he'd cry. You know how Giacomo is, and Mother too. They both feel so badly." Then she realized she was speaking to Eric's mother, and the stabbing sense of guilt and pity stopped her voice.

Brock had been listening. He went over to Pietro, who was eating canapés and talking with Thelma Valli.

"How's the old fellow?" he asked.

"Giacomo? Oh, he's fine." Then, as Thelma drifted away, Pietro made a grimace of distaste. "Confidentially, my friend, already Daneri's is changing. That Stoob! Always after the old man. Picking on him, the way I have seen chickens picking on another at feeding time. Whatever Giacomo says is foolish, what he buys is too high, what he plants is wrong. How he stands it—but you know Giacomo, putting up his shoulders and pulling his head in"—Pietro illustrated, like a turtle pulling into its shell—"and sometimes he groans a little, but he has nothing to say. Eric kept Stoob at arm's length—he and his lilies—but now that Eric is gone——"

Pietro spat over the side into the sluggish water. "All day—every day—we have to listen to him, following Giacomo about, pestering like a bee. Giacomo, who has been like a king and who has no way to answer that *malcontento!* Oh, it cannot go on. And all the rest of us are wrong, whatever we say to Stoob—and Stoob is *superbo—superbo* Stoob!"

Pietro drank the last of his champagne in a splutter of wrath.

"Did Eric know?" Brock asked, but Pietro became suddenly secretive, and he muttered, "How do we know at Daneri's what Eric knows or what has happened? Giacomo has been like a father to us all, and now——"

"And now!" Brock's cold blue gaze went without expression to Eric, who was leaning with his back against the rail, talking to Tosca.

"Thanks for all the gifts," Eric was saying. "Did your conscience hurt?"

Instantly she was in a rage. She had bought lavishly, more than she had been able to afford, because she had seen so much she wanted to give Eric.

"Can't I do anything without your misinterpreting my motives? I wanted you to have a few little things to remember me by."

"Now that," exclaimed Eric, "is at cross-purposes with the reasons for my going. How's the joy-boy?"

There was no use being angry with Eric.

"Mark is fine. And he never makes snide remarks about anybody."

"He sounds like an ideal pet."

"Oh, shut up," she said wearily. She wished she had not come to the ship. Everyone was unhappy and unpleasant, and

283

the feeling of resentment against her was plain. No matter how serene they seemed to be and how politely they behaved, it was plainly readable on the aggregate Brock countenance that Tosca, and Tosca only, was to blame. She looked about for her father, but he had joined a circle of Brocks and was deep in conversation.

She did not want the parting to be in anger.

"Giacomo's going to miss you, Eric. We all will."

The sunburned brows lifted quizzically. But she would not be baited.

"Does this boat take you to Colombia?"

"No. I'm stopping over in Los Angeles for a few days with the Bannings. Maybe I can pick up a few orders there. And I'll look in on some of the other houses."

"Remember me to them." The Bannings were old friends and their orchid houses among the finest in Southern California.

Still he watched her, with the same steady attentiveness that met her everywhere on the deck, the Brock look, so that the friendly small talk she was attempting seemed without meaning. She put out her hand.

"Well," she said helplessly, "bring back lots of orchids."

"I don't want lots of orchids. Where I'm going, they hang from the trees, common as weeds, but those aren't the ones I'm after. I want the rare ones, the ones we hear about and are never sure if they really exist or not. I believe they do. So we'll be going inland, into the real jungle."

As he spoke she felt his excitement and knew that Daneri's had become as a book closed and this adventure was to take the place of all Eric Brock had once desired. She too, reared on the tragedies and conquests, knowing the stories of the orchid hunters as other children know fairy tales, caught his excitement like a flame whipped between them.

"Oh, Eric," she cried. "Not the blue!"

"Ssh!" He looked about as she had when speaking to Thelma. "That's not to be talked about, girl."

But the blue! The fabulously lost and desired, the once-found and never-glimpsed-again orchid that many orchidists claimed did not and never could exist, but which Giacomo believed in because orchid hunters had told him of natives who with their own eyes, they said, had glimpsed such a flower.

And forgetting everything else between them, she caught

Eric's hands. "Oh, Eric, if you could find it for Giacomo! Has he ordered you?"

"Well, in a way he gave me orders."

"In a way! What do you mean by that?"

"Well, you know how Stoob is," said Eric.

"Why should Stoob have anything to say about the orchids?" she said fiercely, but he stared at her for a long moment before he answered. "Do you mean to say you don't know what's going on at Daneri's?"

"Of course I don't—what do you mean, Eric—what's going on?"

At that moment the first warning bell sounded.

"There it is." Eric seemed relieved.

But she would not let him go. "Eric, tell me. I want to know."

"You want! That answers everything. It always does, doesn't it? Well, not in this case, baby. Not any more." Then, to her amazement, he softened. "Oh, ask your father. Or ask Giacomo. I'm out of it—and Giacomo will be better off without me."

"That isn't true. Giacomo needs you." She was almost crying. She would have made any sacrifice to hold Eric then. The image of Giacomo, the great body slanted in defeat, was in both their thoughts. It was sad, the way they both knew that, and the way they both wanted to protect Giacomo. But Eric said, "If I could help, I'd stick around. But I can't help."

"But if you could, Eric?"

"I'd be around." His hard young mouth touched her own. "So long," he said briefly. Then he turned to his family with a smile he tried to make fatuous. "Now don't crowd," he said. "And for Pete's sake don't stand on the pier waving handkerchiefs."

The second bell rang and the cry went around the deck: "All ashore going ashore."

The Brocks began streaming down the gangplank in orderly rows. The others followed, Tosca and her father among them. Eric's father and mother were the last to leave the ship.

Once ashore, those who had come to see Eric off apparently took him at his word and prepared to leave the pier. They went to their cars and some started the engines, then they sat in the cars, pretending not to watch the little steamer and Eric standing on its deck, equally unconcerned, talking to another passenger and pointing to the empty bay as if some matter of interest were taking place out there.

"I want to wait too," she told her father. "Please, Father, until the ship goes out?"

The car was parked over the estuary. It looked too splendid in that setting. It was one of the two foreign cars Vincent had imported in the boom years and seldom drove. Once in the car, they pretended not to watch, just as in the other cars along the water front other friends of Eric's, and his family, were also pretending.

And Eric, talking with animation to his new friend, far above them on the deck, seemed most unconcerned of them all.

"Father, what is going on down at the nursery?"

A studied air of caution covered Vincent's first start of surprise.

"What do you mean, Tosca?"

"About Giacomo."

Vincent lit a cigar. The air of the neighborhood was sour-smelling, alleviated by the fragrance of the piles of newly cut lumber fringing the estuary. Thoughtfully he estimated the value of a clean stack of Washington pine.

"We didn't see any reason why you should know," he said carefully. "There may be certain changes. Now that Giacomo is without an assistant—well, there's no reason to hide it from you. Stoob wants to buy in."

"Stoob!" It was astonishing, the way Stoob's name was always pronounced in a certain key. "Why, Giacomo doesn't even like Stoob! How can he get along with Stoob, if Stoob has the right to say more than he does now?"

Vincent studied the fine long ash.

"Giacomo may not be there. We want him to live with us. You see, Tosca, you will not be with us much longer and——"

"And as usual"—she was striking out, she knew, like the unruly child she felt herself to be—"I'm to know nothing about it until it's all over. You ask me to be responsible, and what responsibility have you ever given me? I'm the village idiot, the sheltered baby, who mustn't be bothered about anything until it's all settled and done for, and still you expect me to grow up!"

She had not taken her eyes from the ship and from Eric, as if Eric and the ship moving slowly down the sluggish estuary helped feed her unreasonable anger.

Vincent was equally angry. But he made an effort to control his temper and succeeded.

"You are behaving rudely and, may I say, ungratefully. Of course we've tried to keep you happy, and when things are—pain-

286

ful—we keep them from you. None of us want to see Giacomo leave the nursery. But we have talked it over from every angle, and your mother and I think he should stop working so hard and take life easy with us. We want him, and we think we can keep him content. And after all, Tosca"—resentment crept in despite his care—"you will be married, and you say you plan to travel, so why should you be concerned over what happens to the nursery?"

This is the way it always is, Tosca thought hatefully. They shut me away, out of their love for me and their passion for protecting me. But I don't want to be protected. I want to know—to be hurt, perhaps—to feel that I'm part of it, whatever it is, and not living in a dream.

Even Eric, she thought, and suddenly her rage against Eric blinded her so that she could scarcely see the blond Viking-like figure standing forward in the small ship now scraping the rough wharf and moving toward the open water of the bay. They had all kept reality from her—even Eric, running away now after refusing to discuss with her what was happening at Daneri's—all of them—yes, even her mother, even Giacomo, keeping their hurt from her, holding their kind hands over her eyes so that she could not see, holding her safe so that she knew not how to live.

"Oh, Father, I'm sorry," she said wretchedly, but her loneliness and her rage against them all turned her wholly in that moment to Mark—for only Mark, of all she knew, succeeded in living supremely in himself and refused to be hurt or to accept responsibility beyond his own personal desires. He had made this clear to Tosca. And Mark was solace, now that she saw things his way.

"People let themselves tie up with all sorts of troubles," Mark had explained in his amused but serious way. "They like them. They even like other people's troubles! But we don't have to do that, and if we promise each other that we won't, no one can ever get us down."

"You mean—no responsibilities?" she had asked.

"None. We don't have to have them, you know. We'll get along. We'll always get along."

"But isn't there anything, Mark, you'd like to do?"

"I can think of a million things. Right now I'd like to put you in a speedboat at Tahoe and ride around the lake with you forever and ever."

"The gasoline would give out."

"What if it does? We'd swim ashore and wire home."

287

"Stocks?" she had suggested. "You like stocks."

"Imagine me in a broker's office! I could never convince any-one they should buy anything, because I wouldn't give a damn if they did or not."

"Maybe Father can help." It was then, diffidently, she had made that suggestion. "He knows so many people. Maybe he will know something you can do."

"Swell." He spoke carelessly, and his eyes danced as he kissed her. "Okay, Missus Boss. Whatever you say, Missus Boss."

And then he had forgotten the conversation, and so, apparently, had she. Mark was not driven by panic, or conscience, or the longing to be independent, as most people are. He had enough to maintain him in modest living, and quite frankly he counted on his wealthier friends for the luxuries. For these he paid lavishly with his talent to amuse and to be amused.

Mark is the only person I have ever known, thought Tosca, who is truly free! And the lost empty longing for him broke through the loneliness and gripped her with an almost physical agony, for she felt terribly alone, with her father not looking at her, but with his gray profile cold and estranged, and all around them in the other cars the Brocks apparently not watching, but straining every nerve and muscle now as the little steamer turned against the stream and stood for a moment limned against the bay waters, streaked with copper and rose from the late sun, before it vanished behind the pier. In that moment she saw Eric's mother lean from the door of the Brock car and wave in one last gesture of good-by toward the ship, and on the deck Eric put his hands out and wriggled his fingers in a boyish gesture that broke the heart because it was a boy's signal to his mother that he was still her son. And then others, from the cars or points of vantage, began waving, and all over the wharf and from the ship a rhythm was given in gestures that was the heartbeat of a clan. Only Tosca did not wave; she had put her face in her hands, shutting out and holding in the image of Eric in that last moment, with his hand wriggling in boyish salute and his head red-gold against the sun.

She wept for them all, but most of all for Eric and the placidity that had been Daneri's and the lost safe strength that was Eric's, vanishing now behind the dingy pier. She had known, seeing Eric in that final moment, that an entire way of life was vanishing for them all, and one that Eric was fitted for, as was Giacomo, and now Giacomo was yielding up the nursery and never again could she escape to it when life became too wildly fast to be borne.

Vincent sat helpless, wishing he knew of a way to solace her, but not even knowing why she wept.

Now, she thought, I must build my own pattern to live by, and I do not know how to begin.

Mark would know. Or, better still, he would say no pattern was required. We can't count on anything, Mark said so often.

One simply lived.

TWENTY-TWO

"THERE will be many things," Marie had warned her father, "that it will be hard for you to do without. But we'll try to make up to you for everything you'll miss when you leave the nursery."

Giacomo was realizing this more surely hour by hour. The life of a grower teemed with pleasures others could never know. The cool smooth power of the planting stick in a man's hand, and the satisfaction of setting out baby plants in orderly rows. The hot drowsy atmosphere of the orchid houses, perfumed at times with their perfume, and the thrill of discovering each morning, in one form or another, the newest and most perfect bloom. The hours spent in the laboratory, locked in, with all reverence, with God. And the pleasure of being with the flower people, the only people who really understood Giacomo Daneri, and to whom he could speak in their own tongue, which was that of growth and change.

The Orchid Society was made up of these.

There was always something to which a grower of flowers could look forward, and for Giacomo this was the Orchid Society banquet, and this year he was guest of honor. He would be awarded something, probably a bit of bronze. Giacomo was fond of bronze. It seemed akin to him, as were cypress trees, for such things lie deeply rooted in time and survive more than one country and many centuries. Yes, Giacomo had respect for bronze and for cypress trees.

He thought this, permitting his thoughts to roam as they willed, because even though he was seated beside the president of the society, at the head of the rectangle of tables in the club's dining room, Giacomo felt relaxed and at ease.

He sat well forward in his chair, his wide shoulders bursting in a broadcloth coat of ancient pattern. How calm he was, and strong, thought Tosca, like a gray wall shielding them all. The shock of hair he had tried to tame for this important evening rose like a lion's mane, but his face shone with happiness.

As a grower Giacomo exhibited under many banners, but his most cherished trophies had been won at the large exhibitions held under the auspices of the Orchid Society. There were, of course, other groups, and for these, too, he had his honors to show, such as the Rose, Begonia, Horticultural, and Garden Clubs, and all the annual exhibits, culminating in the two outstanding spring events in Boston and Philadelphia.

But in all the growing world, Giacomo considered, it was among the orchid growers that he felt most at home. In the banquet hall this evening were three hundred men from differing cultural, economic, and racial backgrounds, bound together by the passion for orchidry, their brotherhood sealed by the society's pledge "to advance the cultivation, the importing and improving and hybridizing of the exotic orchid in America."

Many were hobbyists—devoted amateurs who had learned that money alone could not help a man grow orchids and who were also willing to devote their time to the development of choice seedlings. One was a famed West Coast millionaire who had spent eighty thousand dollars on orchidry before he had been able to develop one master house. Some were professional men— dentists, attorneys, a few physicians. Giacomo's old friend Dr. McFee, whose rare hours away from his patients were spent in the growing of every type of yellow orchid, was sitting at the opposite table with Tosca. And many of the members, like Giacomo, were professional orchidists.

Since all the members shared a common ideal, which was a vision of the perfect, Giacomo, looking about him in content, knew that each man there, no matter what his creed or origin or status in the outer world, could also say, looking around him: These are my people!

His happiness was the greater because Tosca was there and because she seemed eager these days to be with him. As if she guessed what he was going through at the nursery! But there, she could not dream of such a thing, nor could anyone who knew Giacomo. Behold the respect with which these men of the orchid group regarded him!

The talk at the president's table was all about orchid culture, and the means of preserving pollen, and of crosses and compact growth and free-flowering qualities, and much of the subject matter was turned back to Giacomo for verification, for was there anything known about orchids, the others asked, that he did not know? He basked in their attention and in the privilege of being guest of honor, for how often can a man be that in an orchid group—even a man who has survived for seventy-five years! And in that time so many changes—and Giacomo's gentle look went from Tosca, where it rested with the pleasure one who lives by beauty takes in the living appearance of beauty, and went to the display table against the wall, which was set with glass tubes that held orchids.

Each member was showing here in competition a single seedling of his own rearing. Giacomo let his gaze wander like a bee from flower to flower, recognizing each bloom and its story, as if they were the children of old friends. His intelligent eyes went to a Laeliocattleya Melahoe out of a Laeliocattleya Lustre. He recognized characteristics of the magnificent bloom and remembered with pride that he had owned one of its grandparents. What pleasure to see a familiar family line holding its own! From another tube a dozen splendid lavender Cattleyas rose on a single stem, and from still another a Cymbidium in full bloom sent forth sixteen yellow motes—like butterflies in flight.

Giacomo studied with special pleasure his own contribution, which was not in competition. It was a violet-tinted Cattleya Amabilis, an aristocrat among orchids. For Tosca's sake he wished the Daneri display might have been one of the Aurea hybrids he had named for her. The plants had ceased flowering but were growing vigorously. He might have selected another type that would have bloomed in another season, but he had chosen the springtime for Tosca.

"Look at him!" Tosca remarked to her dinner partner, Dr. McFee. "Even if we couldn't see the table, I could tell by Giacomo's expression that he is looking at orchids. He has that special look some women have when they look at babies."

"Aye, he's a grand old lad," said the doctor, and they both sat smiling at Giacomo, whose attention was lost among the orchids, and Dr. McFee said admiringly, "I never can make up my mind if he's a wizard or a saint."

But Giacomo, who in his dreaming survey of the flowers had lost track of the conversation around him, had become aware of a buzzing in his thoughts that was heard only too often in these days. "Clear out the white Cattleyas! It makes too much work for you now Eric's gone. Get rid of the Traina." And it seemed to Giacomo that Stoob was always following, no matter where one went in the nursery, and Stoob's voice was always in his ears.

The gentle green kingdom of Giacomo had become a sorrowful place.

Stubbornly Giacomo defended his seedlings. But it is not easy to close the doors of orchid houses against the sound of a human voice.

That voice had grown in volume since Eric sailed. Stoob had at once broached a plan for cutting down the orchid houses. Times were uncertain, despite the New Deal, and people would buy ranunculus, Stoob claimed, but certainly not orchids. And Giacomo, repeating wearily that this had been told him many times before, reiterated his faith that people would still marry and make love and die, and for all these they would need orchids.

But where could Giacomo find another assistant, Stoob argued, for everyone knew that orchidists, like lily masters, were born and not made! Of rose specialists and carnation growers and outside men, Giacomo had plenty to choose from, but where could another Eric Brock be found?

"Eric is important—now that he has left us?" Giacomo once found himself saying, for he could not help reproaching himself with the suspicion that if he had sent Stoob away in time Eric would not have left Daneri's. Then he would think of Tosca and know there was nothing left to argue over, not even with Stoob.

Why waste my words? he thought more than once. *Bella Santa,* for whom am I saving Daneri's? Who wants the nursery now—except Stoob and that girl of his with the hungry mouth!

But the president was beginning his speech, singling out each individual orchid on the table to be adjudged and praised, and speaking briefly of the man who had achieved it. The president's voice drove the thin high voice of Stoob from Giacomo's ears. Giacomo listened, again content, and not forgetting to clap his hands as each grower rose in turn and was applauded.

And then the president was speaking of Giacomo. He brought the regal violet Cattleya to the edge of the table and showed it to all, and beside it, as Giacomo had suspected, was the little velvet box with the lid up and the bronze medal showing. The president, explaining that he would call on Giacomo Daneri in a few moments, went on to praise him as "the peer of hybridists, who is in every way upholding the ideal of the orchid growers to make ever more beautiful that which is already perfect."

Ever more beautiful, Giacomo thought in agreement, his eyes fastened to the violet Cattleya. Yes, even this flower! If one could superimpose upon those royal lips a flange of gold, and why could that not be done, and why should it not be! An almost unbearable excitement filled him. Surely it was a duty one owed to such a flower to see how far one could carry it along the already perfect way. Yes, next year, one might begin!

Then he found himself remembering. "Perhaps next year I shall not be growing orchids. Perhaps next year I shall not be here at all!"

His dreams stopped in consternation. Without Daneri's, what would become of Giacomo Daneri, who was known around the world as the Orchid King? And what would the orchids be without Giacomo?

Brooding over this point, Giacomo did not hear when the president called his name.

TWENTY-THREE

 I T was a wonderful meeting and the medal is wonderful and you're wonderful." Tosca was yawning frankly as they drove past the moon-silvered water hazards of the golf courses and up the twisting road to Colma. "Now the whole world's asleep, and that's where I plan to be in exactly ten minutes!"

For a moment the alluring vision rose of the bird's-eye-maple bed in the little white cottage; the mattress of lamb's wool brought over from Italy by the first Maria—and one sank far down into it, so deeply that before one stopped sinking, almost, one was asleep.

"You spin around too much," said Giacomo kindly. "You and Mark—like tops. Always in motion."

"I have a giddy grandfather. Always having affairs given in his honor. He wears me out."

She had not let him know that the attention she paid him, spending all the time with him she could bear to spend away from Mark, was the result of the conversation she had had with her father the day Eric sailed.

Should she let Giacomo know she knew of his problems? she wondered, swinging the car into the familiar lane. The glass-houses lay like frosted planks against the hill, bluishly lighted by blue lights in the Drive. Stoob's house lay in darkness, and all the other houses were dark except Giacomo's, where the light burned in the hall against their home-coming.

As they left the roadster in the open shipping shed with the trucks the cat moved out of the shadows and greeted them loudly.

"Always he greets me, the *gatto!*" said Giacomo proudly. He stooped, awkward in his formal attire, to stroke the Maltese from its nose to its spike of tail. Then, regardless of the broadcloth, he picked it up. "Such a good friend, this little one."

"Come along. He should be asleep, and so should we," she scolded him affectionately.

But Giacomo hesitated by the boiler house. In the befogged moonlight he was an incongruous but splendid figure, like a ship's figurehead in modern dress. "It would be better to look at the houses," he said almost wistfully.

"Oh, very well." Laughing, she took his arm, determined to keep his evening perfect to its end. She knew Giacomo could not sleep without a final glance through the orchid houses.

They walked through the blue-lighted Drive and out where the houses stood moon-pale under the moon. Giacomo opened door after door to survey sharply the potted jungles within, and it seemed to Tosca that he was giving thanks to the plants for the fine showing they and their orchid relations had made that night at the testimonial dinner.

How many times, as a child, had she made the final rounds of the houses with Giacomo! She could remember him, casting a gigantic shadow as he moved through the darkened glass buildings, swinging his flashlight and pouncing at times upon a slow-moving slug that was nibbling the delicate lips of a ten- or fifteen-dollar flower. In those days he had sprinkled lettuce shreds under plants about to bloom, to lure the brigand gastropod.

The red spider, green fly, and pellucid snail had been their dragons then.

The modern insecticides had done away with the night hunting of the snails. Daneri's held other dragons now, and Giacomo did not speak of them.

The orchids were in magnificent bloom. The plants were preparing for the season of theaters and operas and the gaiety that would mount up toward Christmas and the year's end. Seeing the orchids like phosphorescent faces in the gloom, Tosca remembered something she wanted to tell Giacomo.

But he said uneasily before she spoke, "I do not like the houses. They are too warm."

"Can't you turn down the heat?"

"Something is wrong with the pressure. I do not know why, but I keep turning it low, and she turns up again."

In the boiler plant beside the seedling house he studied the gauge.

"Wouldn't it be safer to build a new plant?" Tosca asked, but he parried the question, as he parried it in his own mind. How foolish it would be to plan ahead; so he tightened the valves, as he had many times, to lower the pressure, and his features knotted with worry. They came up the steps of the cottage, and he turned at the door and looked out anxiously over the long silvery-blue fingers of the glasshouses clasping the hillside, and the dark squares that were the houses built for Vittorio and Paul, and the other houses, including the darkened cottage of the Stoobs' that lay between the lane and the hills running down to the sea.

Then he shook his head, thinking of the behavior of the boiler, and said slowly, "I do not like it at all."

"Well, I have news to cheer you up," said Tosca briskly. She was wide awake now after the walk through the houses, and in the kitchen she warmed milk for herself, for the kitten, and for Giacomo, who made a face over his but drank it to please her.

They sat at the oilcloth-covered table drinking their milk, and she told him her news.

"Guess who is coming in November. Bori!"

"Lucrezia Bori?"

And before such splendid news Giacomo forgot the troubles with the boiler, and the buzzing persistences of Stoob, and the sorrow that was the emptiness of Paul's house now that Eric slept there no longer but was at the moment staying in Los Angeles with the Bannings, consulting with them and other orchid people in Southern California as to orders for orchids if any were found. But there was no trouble in the world that could not be washed away by the very name of Lucrezia Bori, of divinest voice in all the world's history—so Giacomo rated her—and how could a man have dreamed of ever hearing her voice again!

"Yes, she's really coming—to the Opera House—in November!" Tosca was making a happy chant of her news. "And guess who's taking you to hear her sing?"

"Who but you, Tosca *mia!*" Because he could not bear to hear Bori with anyone but Tosca, and only for a moment the thought came, "Your Mark?" and she brushed it aside gaily. "Mark loathes opera, and besides, I've never heard her, and she's your favorite, and I want to hear her with you!"

They sat drinking the milk neither wanted, with the medal propped before them on the table, and because imagination was powerful in them both, the evening to come was with them, as if already they were there! And on opening night Giacomo would wear his old but dignified black and Tosca a skirt widespread and a jacket of silver—fortunately one can charge these things, she was thinking, as Vincent Levenridge was behaving oddly in the matter of money. There would be certain changes, he had hinted, when she married.

She would dress, for opening night and for Giacomo, she decided, as carefully as she would for Mark and his most worldly friends. The white-and-silver dress she planned would dazzle the dimming eyes of Giacomo and fill them with an appreciation no other man's—not even Mark's—could ever hold.

There would be many women in the Opera House that night, but none so beautiful, Giacomo dreamed over his glass of milk, as Tosca, wearing the snowy Cattleya Daneri bred in his houses— no, the Aurea named for her—it would be blooming then! He would look about the brilliant tiers and recognize with pride the familiar faces of his orchids nestled on ermine or velvet or satin or sequin shoulders. And he would not say, as other opera goers might, "See, Tosca, there is a lady I know!" but, "Look, there is a Laeliocattleya Daneri," or, "There is one of yours—an Aurea Tosca."

How wonderful it seemed, although he and others had planned it so, that the festive season that held the opera arrived at the peak of the orchid-growing year! Men and women would plan excitedly for gay opening nights, and in his orchid houses the plants were forcing their buds into magnificent blooming, as if they knew! Had he not shown Tosca, this hour in the houses, how the Traina were coming into bloom, and many of the hybrid Cattleyas, and the Aurea, and Phalenopsis, and so many more? And all beautiful, and all Giacomo's, for he had seen them grow under his guiding hands since he had planted them—the invisible seeds falling into agar—so many years before. This was the stuff of his dreams, and it was beautiful, and he went to the opera as Cesare and Ernesto and all the others went, because they loved opera, and also to see the flowers they had grown, and the women who wore them, and the new magic the florists such as Matraia made of their dreams. In his mind he could hear Cesare bellowing "Bravo!" from the gallery, as he had so often, and his mind went back through the years, back to that first time in La Scala when the opening notes of *Otello* had captured the hearing and soul of a child Giacomo hunched in a topmost seat in the darkened gallery.

"Tosca," he said, and his dim eyes were gleaming, "do you remember last year?"

"I remember!" she said as softly, and their eyes met over the cooling milk; a touch not human but of angels.

They had been looking over the gilded balconies and commenting, not only on the changing style in flowers, but in the ways they were worn. They had noted a bracelet made of small green orchids, a necklace of yellow butterfly orchids, sprays of white and lavender orchids pinned to furs and jeweled bags, and great white orchids built high to form coronets. Until it seemed to Giacomo that the women around them, even Tosca, were not real women at all but creatures of air like the orchids they wore. It was a curious illusion that made him feel lightheaded and insecure, and he shook his head with annoyance and looked down at his hands. They were gnarled like roots, and why not, for they

297

had built fifty-four glasshouses and filled them with flowers of every species and color and fragrance known to California, and they had built the marble mansion on the Presidio hill, and the flowers nodding about them on the shoulders of the beautiful women. But they had no place here, and because of Tosca he was suddenly ashamed of his hands and their ugliness and the stain of earth that would never come off, no matter how one tried. They were like hands a sculptor had started to carve from some ancient wood and then abandoned.

Giacomo folded his hands together to hide them.

And Tosca saw, and the golden head went high and the smooth planes of her cheeks grew scarlet. She put her petal-soft hand over Giacomo's clasped hands and held them, proudly and tenderly, and the first notes of the overture floated over the great hall and the darkness began and tears were torn from Giacomo, who always wept to music.

Music drew the soul out of Giacomo. It pushed back the harsh decades that had nevertheless been stippled with beauty. It put into his hand the hand of the first Maria and held before him the glorious young faces of his sons. It gave back the golden dreamy-eyed child that was Tosca. At times, when the violins were muted and the long-familiar and ever-new arias rang out, Tosca saw him sink his chin on his breast and close his eyes tightly to prevent the sound of his tears. But Tosca would not have eased a moment of this sublime sorrow, because she knew it was part of Giacomo and his capacity for grief and for happiness. Instead she let herself follow him in this world of sound and light and tenderness that held no others, only an imperishable, incomprehensible love and, weeping in it in an orgy of abandon, Tosca and Giacomo.

"I remember," she said softly, and thought of Mark, knowing that she could never expect him to understand why she could not go to the opera with anyone but Giacomo.

And Giacomo was remembering their weeping and their divine happiness, and how he had known then more than ever before that in spite of the French gown and the orchids she was a Daneri, strong and magnificent and humble and easily hurt and impossible to break—and he had felt in her then the black flame of race and antiquity and the eagerness and the faith and the heartbreak and the knowledge that one could never perish—for what other reasons had one for weeping to music? So Giacomo

298

had reasoned, with his great hands clasped in Tosca's, and he had wept shamelessly and happily. All this, in Giacomo's kitchen, they remembered.

"Madonna, it is late and you must get some sleep," said Giacomo, coming back to reality. "And tomorrow, first thing, we hang our medal in the seedling house with the others."

His happiness was beautiful, and Tosca, preparing for bed in the upstairs room, remembered that she had planned to discuss Stoob and the nursery's future with Giacomo, and other matters such as Mark and Eric's leaving, but she had found no place in which such matters could be intruded into the magic evening. So she thought: Tomorrow, when we are in the laboratory with the trophies, I will make him confide in me.

Giacomo heard her steps overhead as he put the cat outside. He stood a moment in the open doorway, looking over the glasshouses and Stoob's dark cottage to the sea. Peace was in his eyes and a great happiness in his heart, because Tosca shared with him the gift of vision, and he knew how rare that gift could be, and because she had also the gifts of feeling and of happiness and tears. And he was happy because the great Bori he had never expected to hear again was coming to San Francisco and he would hear her voice again—and with Tosca—and because he had learned once more that life still held surprises, even for one who is seventy-five.

TWENTY-FOUR

But although Stoob's house was in darkness no one slept under its roof.

In the boxlike living room the dregs of a fire sent short shafts of lights from the iron stove. It did not light the room where Stoob and Ludmilla were sitting. Ludmilla sat by the window, and her pointed features were outlined to her father, who was huddled over the stove. There she had sat, without moving, for many hours. She had watched Giacomo and Tosca leave for the orchid dinner in Tosca's car. She had watched their return and their tour of the glasshouses.

Stoob had slept and returned to the room, muffled like a gnome in his woolly robe, and found her still sitting there.

Hunched in the low rocker, he watched her. She was behaving like an imbecile, he thought. It was the letter she had from Eric in Los Angeles. Stoob had read the letter, although she did not know this, and what was there in it to madden her so? Something about blue orchids for Tosca, plainly a poor attempt at a joke. Brock humor. They were always laughing at nothing—those people from Santa Cruz.

Stoob's mouth curled.

"Orchids," he grunted. "They do things to men's brains. I have trimmed Eric's orchids for him."

"They are to blame for everything," came in a queer voice from the window.

He was startled, and then angered because she had agreed with him. He did not want agreement. He knew what he knew. Once he had shown her his ambitions. She had not shared them. She had only wanted that pigheaded son of Brock's. And now what had she? Nothing. That happened to people without ambition. He knew! Ambition had kept Stoob aflame for years, so that nothing else, no one else, mattered.

And now he had won and there was no one to share his victory except this girl staring into the dark like an imbecile.

He liked that word. It expressed what he wanted to say, which was his opinion of her, and one to set her thinking.

"You are behaving like an imbecile," he said. "That is all I need, at my years, to be saddled around my neck with someone who has no mind."

But she might have been deaf.

He sat watching her, and his throat swelled and his eyes became tormented slits, and still she did not turn, and it might have been that she forgot he was there. And in him the malignancy of his frustration, because he had no one to speak to and boast of his triumph, swelled slowly, poisonously, until it burst into a spatter of evil words, incredibly cruel because of the half-guessed truth.

"You would not help me! No, but I worked without you, and without you I have done what I wanted to do. I have wormed my way in, as I told you I would, and now you will see 'Stoob and Daneri' on the shipping-shed door, and after that it will be my name only and what have you done to help put it there? What were you doing?—throwing yourself at him like a strumpet until

300

I was sick for shame. I drove him away and he will stay away. Eric Brock will never come back; I will see to that. Because now I will have the lily houses, and after that I will have Daneri's!"

And as suddenly as the outburst of rage began it quieted, and Stoob settled back in his chair like a spent gnome and seemed to forget it all.

"Is there coffee?" he asked in a normal tone.

He saw the silhouetted head shake in denial, and behind it, far up the hill, the last light went out in Giacomo's house.

"The old man's room," he said. "Up late, so he will be good for nothing tomorrow." He stood up and pulled the robe about his puffy frame. He spoke peevishly. "Well, will you go out to look at the lilies, or must I? Helplessness! A dependency to be hung around a man's neck all his life."

She interrupted his disjointed mutterings. "I'll look at the lilies."

As she crossed the damp lane hatred, trapped in her stomach, twisted and caught her up panting against the fence. She clung to it for support. After a few minutes she straightened and walked on, clammy cold and panting for breath. She did not use the flashlight she carried. She went past the Drive and the first glasshouses with aversion, hating her father, this place, the carnations, the gardenias, loathing them and, most of all, the orchids. In the entrance to the shipping shed she stood a long time, shivering as if with cold, thinking as coldly of the loft and the vats stored there marked with the word "Poison"; hating the flesh that had sired her, longing to see it cringe and shrivel and die. But she was afraid of him; his malignancy reached up the hill in the night and drove her on toward the lily houses, and on her way— she was running by this time, afraid of him, fearing many things, hating many more—a blast of heat struck at her through the cool night air. She was near the entrance to the boiler plant, and from force of habit she stepped inside and turned her lighted flash on the gauge. It was low, very low, and still the pressure was high.

She stood a long time before the controls. Her thin body throbbed to the beat of the machines that fed the life stream of Daneri's. This was the heartbeat of the orchids—the orchids that had always stood between Ludmilla and all she had been brave enough to long for. They were Tosca's flower; they meant Tosca to her, and Tosca, she knew, and not her father, had driven Eric from Daneri's. Her hatred of the orchids sent shudders of nausea through her thin body, the way her father's voice did when he jeered at her. Under the tricklings and torrents of abuse a life had been turned in upon itself to feed in loneliness. She hated her father, but she feared him too much to attempt revenge on him.

But even more, she hated the orchids that had taken Eric.

Eric had made her feel like a woman for a little while. But Eric would not come back.

She had been brave once, in Eric's arms.

Now she was afraid of the dark, of her father, of many things. All her life she had been afraid. Still a terrible courage enabled her to reach up, stretching the thin frame painfully, to grasp the valves. With eyes starting and fists clenched she whirled the valves as far as they would go, until they were left wide open and uncontrolled. Then, dropping to her heels again, she fled from the building and through the yawning shipping shed and down the lane.

She ran as if someone ran after in the dark, with her breath tearing from her lungs in sobbing gasps and with her work-hardened hands clenched over her ears.

TWENTY-FIVE

*I*t is a satisfying fact that, as a man has fewer hours in his life left for sleeping, the nights demand less sleep from him. Giacomo considered this philosophically toward three o'clock that morning as he put aside the thick crocheted cover and stepped carefully into his bedroom slippers.

Beyond doubt there was unease in the night air. *Ma perchè!*

So it had been in those early-morning hours before the great earthquake and fire in 1906. Again, as on that April morning that had left his then half dozen glasshouses without one unbroken pane, he sensed suffocation in the night, as if somewhere lava was flowing, and a sound, as yet unheard, that sent out primary vibrations of warning.

Moving a little faster, he pulled on his thick robe.

On the porch the cat joined him sedately, surprised to see him but pleased to join in so late a stroll. Apparently not another living thing was awake on the hill. Against the fog-misted night the greenhouses still spread like transparent fingers, illumined by the dim bluish lights in the Drive.

In the small room over the porch Tosca was wakened by his soft greeting to the cat. Now her sleep was broken. The interruption was familiar, for he had often wakened her, during her visits to the nursery, as he prowled around the grounds by night, driven by the not unpleasant sleeplessness that besets the aging. From the nearby fields she could hear the voices of the truck gardeners as they gathered the carrots and artichokes and cabbage for market; earlier risers, these gardeners, than the growers of flowers.

No use trying to sleep! Soon the first of the vegetable trucks would be rattling down the highway. She lay with her hands behind her head, looking dreamily into the square of moving slate that was the window-bound sky.

How remote seemed Colma in this hour! So far from the great house on the hill and Mark's tempestuous way of living and even from Mark Cantrell! She thought of him as another person, in another world. In this room, cold and fragrant with the night air sweeping up from the sea, and the scents of loam and flowers and pungent herbs and growth domesticated and wild, Mark seemed as strange to remember as a strain of song heard once in the dark street of an unknown city in some far-off land.

She put the thought of Mark to her heart and held it there, looking into the dreamlike dark.

Outdoors the heavy steps of Giacomo shuffled over the gravel toward the orchid houses.

This room, thought Tosca. It made her a child again. The room held not only her own girlhood, but those of her mother and of the first Maria. For Maria Daneri had been little more than a girl when she came to the nursery with Giacomo. Tosca, lying under the clean white spread crocheted by the first Maria, thought of the grandmother who had been younger than Tosca was now when, shawled and with gold hoops in her ears, she had stepped shyly, bravely, down a gangplank and into a strange new world as the bride of Giacomo. So far away, so long ago!

How far, since then, had come the children of Maria and Giacomo!

That Maria had been led by her trust in Giacomo. Ah, to believe like that in one's love! To know that only death, and perhaps not even that, could dissolve fidelity!

In the dark an image that was the heavily framed Madonna on the wall resolved slowly. Tosca, watching, saw the limpid painted image appear, with the look strangely gentle like Marie's and humble like Giacomo's.

She remembered then she had promised to meet Mark at the Cliff House at noon.

I must try to sleep, thought Tosca, and, turning in the deep bed, thought she heard someone cry out loudly.

In his flannel robe, his gray hair shocklike, Giacomo was an impressive though invisible figure approaching the seedling house in the dark. The instant he opened the door he knew what was happening to the orchids. A hoarse cry tore from his throat, and he ran to the locked inner door that guarded his seedlings and with his fists broke the glass through to give life and air to the plants within that he knew were dying.

His cry was heard by the men sleeping in Vittorio's house and by the families who lived across the lane. This was the cry Tosca thought she heard in the room that had been Marie's.

Then it was lost in an explosion that seemed to lift the hillside and all the houses and thousands of square feet of bursting glass, and the heat lifted and sucked into an anguished spiral the sounds of breakage settling and the open and terrible moaning.

Tosca caught up her robe and stepped into slippers without knowing what she was doing, and as she ran over the carpet of her room in the dark her soles crackled on splintered glass. She ran outdoors to find the dim blue light was gone from the Drive and the Drive itself was gone, and of the fifty-five houses that had sealed in glass the Daneri flowers, only acres of skeleton steel and shattered glass and crumbling potted plants remained under a white mushroom of steam. She was the first to reach the orchid houses, as they were nearest Giacomo's cottage. The house that held Giacomo's seedling orchids, which had been nearest the boilerhouse and most heavily charged with steam, was the most completely in ruins.

Cesare ran trumpeting down the path. "*Dio*, the boiler has burst!" He was the first inside the boilerhouse, which was hidden in wreaths of writhing steam. The others came running, Pietro and Ernesto and Stoob and many others who slept on the place or nearby. Nobody was fully dressed, and everybody crowded and shouted around the boiler plant because they did not know what to do and were not certain what had happened. "Turn on the emergency lights," someone shouted, and someone else ran into the metal shipping shed, which had not been damaged, and the lights sprang out over the paths, revealing the nightmare destruction of Daneri's. "My roses, the so beautiful roses," Pietro was lamenting, but Garibaldi had gone inside the boiler plant and now he backed his way out again with his arm over his eyes to protect them from the steam, and in his hand he carried a flashlight.

"*Jesu Maria,* what is left of the controls!" he shouted, turning to face them. "Someone left her wide open." He waved the flash like an insane person. "This was under the gauge."

Laddie's mouth dropped open, and Stoob leaned forward, staring.

But Laddie spoke first. "That's Stoob's flash!"

"Madonna?" breathed Cesare, so gently it was like a prayer. A pronged weeder lay by the path where someone had dropped it. He picked it up and began to drive it with all the power of his massive arms down upon Stoob. "Murderer!" he thundered. "You might have killed us all!" But Pietro swung the flashlight up as the heavy blade came down, and the blow was broken over the shoulders of the screaming lily master. The men shouted; they were like wolves turning, and they had Stoob backed into the boiler plant and against the hot and ruptured iron belly of the boiler, before they were willing to listen to the sense made by his cries.

"I did not—it was the girl!" he kept screaming over and over. "She is crazy, I tell you; let me get to her. I will fix her! I will put her away."

Cesare lowered the pointed tool.

"God pity me, he is right," he said in horror. "I saw her running down the lane when I came from my house—she is gone by this time. Calamity—such as I have never seen, and who will tell him, poor Giacomo! The Padrone—where is he?"

Cesare's bellow rose to panic. Then he stood gripping the weeder, his eyes fixed and staring, and the others turned, and many crossed themselves with horror. And no one noticed when Stoob slipped out of the boiler plant and ran through the ruins down the lane to his house, a comical and terrible little figure in the flapping robe.

For the steam clouds had broken and settled over the ruins of the seedling house, and coming toward them over the broken glass and the slaughtered orchids was Tosca, blind-eyed and tall in her white robe in the rolling steam, and in her arms—how, none of them ever knew—she carried the heavy broken body of Giacomo. They ran to her then, and as if she had heard what they had said she answered, not looking at anyone, with her eyes still blind and her voice dead, "Let him go. Let them both go. Only see that he doesn't hurt Ludmilla."

"I will telephone the police," promised Cesare. "Telephone Dr. McFee first," said Tosca, and he ran, choking with great sobs, up the cottage steps, while behind him a dozen pairs of arms went out to carry Giacomo with tenderness up the narrow stairs and into his own room.

The pre-dawn air came gray with fog through the broken panes. Tosca pulled the white spread to the relaxed and stubbled chin; he was lying very still. She removed the pillow from under the thatch of gray hair, settled his head gently, and lifted his great hand and saw it fall back nervelessly. There was no breakage, no wounds, but his stillness was terrifying. "There is nothing we can do until Dr. McFee comes," she told those who had crowded into the small room with her, and not wishing to choose among these who loved Giacomo, she begged, "Leave me alone with him now and I'll call if there is a change."

Then she sat alone with Giacomo in the quiet room, and the eternities began. If only he would move, she thought. If only a finger lifted. The stifled breathing was torment, but when it paused she put her head on the great chest to know that he still breathed. When she lifted her head his eyes were open.

"Listen! That is the sirocco wind," said Giacomo, perhaps because the sea wind was stirring the gray hair over the lined forehead. "It blows across our decks from Africa."

And she knew a boy stood on a steamer deck looking back at Italy.

Through the window the sound of hushed voices grew in volume as the families from farther across the lane came to the scene of disaster, and with them neighbors and gardeners from the nearby vegetable fields. She heard the long steady scream of motorcycle police wending from the highway up the lane and after it the answering wail of an ambulance. The gray face of Giacomo looked troubled, as if the sounds reached a far-off place where he had entered into hiding against disaster and pain, and she was crouching over him as if to protect him when the police came through the door.

"Please," she begged, "can't you leave us alone? He is sleeping."

A young intern brushed by the uniformed men. "That's not sleep," he said. He took out his stethoscope and bent over the bed for a few moments. "Shall we take him now?" he asked.

Tosca shook her head. "Wait!" she whispered. "Wait for Dr. McFee."

"Okay." He went to the police, who had taken stations on either side of the door. She heard him say, "Just as well," and something else, so low that she could not hear. But she knew.

"Did you notice the glass?" one of the policemen asked. "I never saw such a mess. Looks like a bomb hit the place."

"How did it happen?"

"Some crazy girl blew up the joint. Wonderful houses—Daneri's," said the other.

But Tosca was alone with Giacomo, and the voices by the door and outside did not matter to either of them any more.

To hold him to life—to hold him! She put her arms around him and held the gray head close and felt it move against her arm. She waited. She could not breathe.

"Mind if I use the phone?" asked the intern.

She moved her head impatiently, signifying yes, that it was in the hall below, and she heard him talking in the hall but did not listen because Giacomo spoke.

"Now I will tell you of Paul," Giacomo said, firmly and quite distinctly. "My thoughts have been long with Paul, and only with you, Maria, can I speak of our son."

She held him, shocked and still. This was trespass! But she knew that it was important to her and for the rest of her lifetime that she learn of Paul.

"Tell me, Giacomo. Tell me of Paul."

"There was the flaw." The kind unseeing eyes were open. "I do not think it was so much what was done to Paul as what Paul was to others. He did not know others lived and wanted too. It was always his wanting—and the wanting of the too fast and the too much—and we, when we love, we give too much, and what had Paul left then? He had nothing!"

The despair in his voice drifted into silence, but she had glimpsed at last what he had kept hidden, the flaw that had never been permitted to show through the love and the laughter that clothed the memory of Paul. In that moment of realization she knew, too, it was not life the gay Paul had been hunting—it was death—and that she had found Paul and her first love again in Mark, and Mark too was rushing halfway to meet the end of all things, demanding greater speed and heavier drinking and wilder excitements with which to race against the last adventure.

She put her head to the rough gray head; and gold and silver melded before the watchful police in the thin light of approaching dawn.

"That is why you have been afraid for me. Oh, Giacomo, you were afraid I was like Paul!" And she held him, knowing his love and his dread that had cast the shadow of loneliness over her adolescent years, and under that shadow she had been hunting always the sweet wild joyousness she adored in Mark because it was her memory of Paul.

In that moment, seeing Mark for the first time, she pushed him back and away and held Giacomo closer to drive back the living presence of death in the room.

"Now, lass, take it easy," said the voice of Dr. McFee.

At the sound of that kind rough voice she burst into tears. "Oh, Dr. McFee, send them away!" she begged, and he said as firmly as before, "Aye, lass, they're going, and stop your nonsense now or the old lad will hear you."

His stethoscope was out and his hand was on Giacomo's wrist, and she saw the nod he gave to the others at the door, and then they were really gone. She heard the police in the hall below talking to the men on the porch, and the young intern evidently left with the ambulance, which backed away from the porch and went screaming its way cautiously down the glass-scattered lane and into the highway. The doctor stripped the covers down, and his hands went swiftly over the long body in the flannelette gown, then he pulled the covers again over Giacomo.

"Doctor?" she whispered as the long scream of the ambulance ended.

"It's well to have him here. Giacomo was a man who loved his home, and it's best to have him in it now."

He is going, she thought, Giacomo, who is all our lives.

"No breaks. No pain. Paralysis. The old heart is very strong." He added, "I have sent word to your father and mother."

He put the stethoscope over his ears again and sat, waiting.

"Strong as an ox," he muttered.

And again she watched with Giacomo in the passing eternities, but they were no longer alone.

"It's a wonder," the doctor said, not taking his eyes from Giacomo, "you made your way out in all that steam."

"I followed the cat." She watched the gray and sagging face, prayed to it, willed it to show life again.

The doctor looked across at her with a puzzled expression, but she was too weary to tell him that when she found Giacomo— had she not known where to find Giacomo, among his beloved seedlings!—the cat had been lying stunned beside him, and when it darted away through the thickest of the rolling wet clouds she had trusted its instinct and followed.

She saw the doctor move forward a little and saw his fingers search along the veins of the gnarled wrist unhurriedly, hopelessly.

"Giacomo!" she flung herself down beside the long settling body, clinging to it. "Don't leave me!"

There is a pinprick of space between death and living, and in this pin point in time Giacomo knew all was well. On that last dim flickering edge of the subconscious, with the last transport of the numbing brain, the shades of dreams, or memory, or whatever they might be, were more real to him than they had been in life. And the wonder was that he could not remember doubt, for he had been certain they would be with him when the moment came. Science might claim this cannot be, but the millions of years and the millions of flowers that live in one invisible seed, and the universal forces that struggle for power in the atom, and the millions of years that compress in a pin point of time, are these more or less a miracle than Giacomo's, who in this last moment in which it could be said, "He is living!" knew the oneness complete and the miracle perfected? Maria was there with her warm sweet eyes, and the clear young faces of his sons, and his mother as he remembered her, glorious and young, and his father with the look of peace and, beyond him, the sunny hillsides and the ripening grapes, and all the others, known or unremembered, before he was born, and after and around and over and beyond them all the bright immortal avalanche of the orchids.

Now they were there and at last together, and, knowing this, he opened his eyes and saw Tosca clearly with the beauty and goodness limning her as he knew her to be, and with this divine conviction upon him he spoke, and his voice held all the old tenderness.

"Tosca. Tosca *mia*." And then, with growing strength: "It is all right, my loved one. Everything is all right."

She clung to him, kissing the lined cheeks, feeling the great tired body settle heavily in her arms.

"Yes, everything is all right, Giacomo. Everything will be all right. Eric will come back. He will take care of the orchids."

Did he hear, or was he past caring? Either way, she could be at peace, for he had set his seal of faith on her in that last moment. Then his eyes dimmed, for he could look no longer and he had gone back.

Now Giacomo lay ageless, the strong features quieted, the great hands lying like knotted branches on the crocheted spread. The doctor's fingers were still about his wrist. She watched the doctor's face, trying to tear the answer from his professional façade, and she saw that he looked many years older than he had at the Orchid Society dinner—centuries ago, a few short hours ago. He looked older than Giacomo now.

"No more." Dr. McFee did not take his eyes from Giacomo's face. He laid the great hand he held over Giacomo's heart. "I had no better friend." He did not look at her.

"Oh no!" The words dragged from her. She caught the great quiet hands in her own and held them over her heart as if to quicken them to life. The long still shape had settled in craglike lines. "Dr. McFee—dear God—help him."

"There, lass, I'll give you a sedative. And I'll talk to your father and mother when they get here. Don't think of anything. Take this, and a glass of water, and go to your room."

She pushed her way past him, ignoring the pellet in his hand. "I've work to do."

In the hall below she put in an emergency call to Eric at the Banning orchid houses near Los Angeles. One of the policemen, hearing her, came in and helped hurry the call through.

There was no need of long words with Eric once the first shock was over.

"I'll be good to you, Tosca."

"I'll be good—oh, Eric, hurry!"

"You'll be happy. You think you can't be now, but you will be."

"I'll try to be."

Happiness! she thought, hanging up on the familiar voice that had brought her back to reality, to all the pain of reality and the need for action. ("Get busy," Eric had urged her over three hundred miles away, "do everything you can until I get there.") Not as she had dreamed it, the wild ecstasy, but the sobering processes of fulfillment. Giacomo's had been stronger than any other love. The strength of that promise streamed through her as she realized that Giacomo, in that last moment, had known this was to be.

She heard the first of the vegetable trucks rattling like chariots down the hilly highway and knew that at last it was morning.

She walked out onto the porch of Giacomo's cottage. The policemen were standing by their motorcycles before the steps. The ranks of the crew had swollen, and the wives and older children were there, so that a hundred faces, all known to her and all gray with concern and the long waiting, looked up at her. Seeing them, the realization came of all that these people had meant to Giacomo, and he to them, and she flung her loose-sleeved arms over her face and bowed her head in an age-old gesture of loss she could not control. Then they knew, and a wail of grieving broke out, and the men wept as loudly as the women because they had lost a father and been left roofless in a single blow, and the older men seemed to feel this most of all.

Cesare came up the steps. His face was a sponge of grief.

"Our poor Padrone," he blubbered. "Wherever they go, those two should devour each other."

"Poor things," she said, recalling the sick fear of Ludmilla, the malignant greed of Stoob, and several of the people around looked at her with surprise and respect, for that was the way Giacomo had of forgiving.

"Fifty years," grieved Pietro. He looked about at the faces that had taken on a family similarity despite the difference in physical cast or origin. "An organization it has taken fifty years to build, and it is wiped out and our Giacomo taken from us in one single night."

They were good and talented men, thought Tosca, and no finer crew had ever worked together. She went down the steps and made her way along the shattered length of the Drive. In the farther houses comparatively few panes had been broken, for the pressure there had been lighter.

Some of the men followed, watching her in a hopeless way.

"Where is Garibaldi?" she asked Pietro.

"He is in the boiler room. He thinks perhaps he can make some repairs."

She bit her lip. She was tired, too tired and weary to begin what Giacomo would want her to do and as Eric had ordered. Then she pulled herself erect.

"Pietro, if we work fast, can't a lot of these roses and carnations be cut in time for the morning market?"

"But certainly!" He seemed to take fire. "Only many of our men are not here. The ones that live away."

"Then take Giacomo's old car and round them up. Let's see what we can get done before the plants die."

Pietro was off to the shipping shed, running with new life. His eagerness and the renewed vigor of the others made her feel wide awake and vibrant. Laddie rushed up to her. There were streaks of ashy tears on his young cheeks, but his eyes shone.

"Which crew shall I work with, Tosca?"

She nearly broke then, for Giacomo had loved this boy.

"Laddie, his cat! Could you find it for me? I'm afraid it's hurt."

The others had caught the fever of action and had found tools, and some were commencing to rake the glass from the scattered plants, and others, with baskets and shears, were hurrying through the shattered areas clipping undamaged roses and carnations. She watched them a moment and then with a resolute air turned back to the orchid houses.

In the dawning light, shivering in her thick robe, Tosca surveyed desolation. Giacomo's laboratory had burst open, and its secrets were no longer secrets and were without meaning. Books and shattered tubes crusted the floor, and over the broken walls where Giacomo's medals and trophies hung askew, long green lines were trickling that were tubefuls of agar threaded with his last breeding of orchids. His dreams trickled down a dusty wall he no longer remembered, and for the first time, for a moment only, she pressed back the terribly hopeless tears.

All the orchid houses seemed irreparably wrecked, because they had been nearest the boiler. Their shattered plants lay shriveling on the twisted tables. But this, the seedling house, holding in its wreckage a fortune in Giacomo's newest and most glorious orchids, was the most tragic loss of all.

"I found him, Tosca." Laddie had picked his way through the wreckage, carrying the Maltese. "He was hiding out in the loft. He's acting terribly scared."

She took the cat in her arms. She had never held it before; it had been Giacomo's. It pushed its soft small head against her throat and sang in a troubled way that showed it was still frightened.

"Don't be afraid," she told the kitten. "I will take care of you."

And she handed it gently back to Laddie.

"Put it in the kitchen, won't you? There's milk; Giacomo and I didn't drink it all"—her voice trembled—"last night."

She went on alone over broken glass and shard and plants left limp by the scalding steam. At her feet something shone like new gold.

An Aurea Tosca hybrid! It was the first of her orchids she had seen in its second blooming. She stopped and lifted the plant, and the broken shard fell away, leaving the tenuous roots and moss in her hands. The petals of the flower were limp but beautiful and the roots strangely cool.

The orchid was still alive.

The strong survive. Giacomo had said that. What was it he had called the flawed second-rate orchids he consigned to the compost? Ah yes, the space takers, wasters of room and warmth and air. Like Mark, she thought, like Mark Cantrell.

In that moment she knew he must be put out of her life. It would be like tearing out her own veins, but she knew at last this must be. Eric was returning. She had asked him to come back. And when Eric returned to tend Giacomo's bit of earth, he must not be alone.

This was the way she willed it. She would not change.

Calmly, as that day at the Flower Show when Eric had slashed through the Aurea, exposing the delicate organs, the quivering inner folds, so she turned the blade of her will against Mark and cut her way free.

Mark! she thought in the agony of severance, as if a cry escaped of birth and renewal, and a burden she had not known existed dropped from her in that moment of agonizing severance and exquisite freedom; a burden that had been made up of many things, including the exposure and dependency of another soul.

And to Mark she knew it would not matter, because to him nothing mattered. He had his friends and his nights, and to him Tosca would become in time someone with whom in a foolish mood he once had risked reality. Roscoe would convince him of that—Roscoe and Kelly Green and all the others.

She breathed deeply and pulled herself up, commandingly tall in the white robe. She held the Aurea in her hands. Laddie had come back, and he and several of the others who were not on cutting crews were standing near the ruins watching her.

Suddenly the blood rushed through her body, charging it with life. Her hands closed over the cooling leaves of the Aurea.

"All right, let's not just stand here. Get baskets and collect all the plants you can and get them back into the farthest houses where there's still some heat, or will be, if Garibaldi gets the boiler going. And some of you, go up into the loft; I think there are some spare panes up there, and if there are, put them where they'll do the most good. Lizzie!" she called to Pietro's wife, who was standing with a forlorn group of other wives and their children before Giacomo's house. "All of you can help here, even the youngsters. Gather up all the moss you can find scattered about, and help cover the baby orchids."

Those who had worked so long with Giacomo heard her in wonder, and then with energy in their bodies and love in their hearts they scattered about the work of saving the orchids, for they knew now for a certainty there was no death; Giacomo was speaking!

Laddie was working swiftly, stooping for the plants and storing them in his basket with delicate precision. Laddie was looked upon by all as a child, because he had been so young when he started to work with Giacomo. But he was not a child; he was twenty, as old as Giacomo had been when he began Daneri's. And he had the touch—yes, a little more time and he might be one of the foremost of lily masters. I must ask Eric what he thinks of this, Tosca thought, watching Laddie, and was certain Eric would approve.

She felt calm and certain, as if Eric were already there to be depended upon. For the work ahead, for the long life ahead, only

Eric could serve. Giacomo had been a man among men, and only a man could take his place and continue his work on the earth.

"Laddie, please," she called, "a basket?" And when he tossed a basket her way she caught it and began filling it with the limp plants of the Aurea. She worked swiftly, tirelessly, feeling that every plant that was saved was restoration of part of the life that had been Giacomo's. Eric would understand that. He would help with the continuation. Being strong, being sure of his love, she willed it. It was true, as Eric had told her, that she belonged with him. He was part of herself and of Giacomo. That he was not the love of her heart no longer mattered. But life was more than the swift ecstasy. Life was the work and the building. It was the ancient wall erected against eternity. Her own had been shaped in lost centuries and furthered by the goodness of Giacomo Daneri. The race went on, families survived, and the individual built as best he could to the strength of that ancient wall.

This Giacomo had believed.

He had taught her this, and his life had gone into the teaching. Scattered at her feet were his orchids. They had been, they would be, salvaged, and long after he was forgotten, long after the passing of this humble dynasty of the Daneri, other centuries and lands would be blessed with the beauty of the Daneri orchids. Like songs, she thought, sent into timelessness. Like the high glorious notes of Bori that Giacomo would not hear again.

Dante had sent his words ahead like the smiting of iron on stone. Michelangelo had left his paintings. Others had handed down their songs or a poem or a high act of courage. Giacomo, the inarticulate, had given orchids.

She straightened, and the basket of Aurea hung heavy on her arm.

The sun had come to the peak of the hill and looked down over a Daneri's bustling with strange activity. Men, women, and children, more than a hundred in all, were crowding the still-standing glasshouses with the tons of plants they had rescued, among them the thousands upon thousands of priceless orchids. The seedlings that had littered the wreckage with their tenderer green had nearly all been saved. Tosca relaxed a moment, and her tired body drank in the humid warmth of the new sun. Her thin gown under the thick robe was wrapped like wet leaves about her thighs. But she stood valiant, with her feet apart and braced, with her face lifted to the sun.

So Giacomo had been wont to stand, but stalwart, the sire, rooted in earth.

We are runners in darkness, she thought, running through the unlighted centuries, carrying the seed and the torch, and it does not matter how far we run or how our hearts break, if only the flame and the seed go on.

In that moment of quiet knowledge her face, lifted to the sun and wearing the look of courage and of the peace that is so closely akin to joy, was strangely similar to the darker, craggier features in the upstairs room under the white counterpane that had been crocheted so long ago by the patient fingers of the first Maria.

She looked down at the orchids on her arm. The purple and garnet blooms stared back impassively as stars. Of all the orchids of Giacomo's breeding, these were among the last and most beautiful, and truthfully, they were his children.

And someday, she thought fiercely, there would be other children, among them sons who would become men like Giacomo Daneri, whose feet had been rooted in the earth.